TWO SKIPS OF A STONE

Book One of Operation: Eleanor

MATT BRAUNLIN

FriesenPress

Suite 300 - 990 Fort St
Victoria, BC, V8V 3K2
Canada

www.friesenpress.com

First Edition — 2021

ISBN
978-1-5255-9923-1 (Hardcover)
978-1-5255-9922-4 (Paperback)
978-1-5255-9924-8 (eBook)

1. FICTION, SCIENCE FICTION, TIME TRAVEL

Distributed to the trade by The Ingram Book Company

Dedicated to Jasmine Flagg, Ginger Meyer,
Sue O'Halloran, and Sandy Passmore, without whose praise
and support I could never have found the
courage to finish this book.

Part One

Chapter One

Jason smiled at the familiar deafening din. Gales of obnoxious laughter filled the room as the spectacle unfolded. Four fifteen-year-olds were pouring their hearts into an improvised skit involving Albert Einstein, a lumberjack, and a stolen bike. Jason was good at inventing the kind of lunacy that teenagers ate up like popcorn.

It was sloppy, but superb. As usual, Chelsey was stealing the show. All of Jason's grade nines were at least competent, but Chelsey was a wonder. In eight months, she had never once failed to come up with the perfect line, the perfect delivery. She loved drama with a passion. She was easily Jason's favourite student this year, and he hoped he was good at hiding it.

'Ten seconds!' he shouted at last. The quartet ran the skit out in their primitive way, involving Albert Einstein murdering his hapless offenders with a shotgun and peddling away on his newly recovered property.

The other students applauded as the performers took their seats.

'Pretty good, I guess,' Jason muttered with mock-indifference. 'Three quarters of you, anyway.' Chelsey, of course, didn't miss a beat, turning dramatically, hands on hips and ponytail swinging, to glare at Jason before sitting down. Without standing, he addressed the performers.

'As ever, you all impress me, even though you never fail to use as much profanity as you know I will let you get away with. You have PASSION.' He spoke the last word with ridiculous melodrama. 'You have PRESENCE. You have SERIOUS PROBLEMS!' The room broke out in fits of giggles. The grade nines always loved this kind of nonsense. He had made a first-class fool of himself the first time he tried it with the Grade twelves.

'Just remember,' Jason advised, 'that chaos needs a focal point. You need an eye for the hurricane. When everyone is going over the top at once, the scene gets overwhelming. Remember the *Trailer Park Boys* Principle: Ricky and Bubbles get all the laughs, but Julian holds everything together.' The class laughed with nervous delight, less at Jason's wit than at the simple fact that he should make a reference to such an evil show. Jason didn't give a damn about such taboos. He treated his students like people, not porcelain figurines, and they loved him for it.

He stood up, grabbed a small stack of papers, and addressed the class.

'Now. We are warmed up, so straight to business. Your next assignment is very simple. A flash soliloquy.' Blank stares. Jason passed out the small sheets at random. 'You are being handed short dramatic speeches from various movies, and you will have five minutes to prepare. After that, you will act them out for the class.'

This was met with several groans and more than a few looks of horror. This was unprecedented. Goofy comedy was one thing; they had never done serious drama before. Out of the corner of his eye, Jason saw Chelsey's eyes light up, despite her otherwise straight face. Girls like her were the reason he loved his job so much.

'I can't do that, Mr. Roberts,' squeaked a curly-haired boy at the far table.

'Oh yes you can, Mr. Davies,' Jason replied. 'If I thought anyone in this room was incapable of a dramatic reading... well, for starters, I would wonder why they took a class called Drama–'

As he spoke this last word, the class intercom buzzed, and the nasal voice of Principal Recketauer blared through the room.

'Jason, can you come to my office immediately please?'

Annoyed, Jason answered, 'Kind of a bad moment, Ms. Recketauer. Can it wait five minutes?'

'No it can't, Jason. Immediately, please. Tim is on his way to cover you.' Silence.

Jason stood for a moment. The room had gone very quiet. None of them had ever heard a page like that before.

'Well,' Jason muttered, 'better go and face the music.' Only scattered laughter as he left.

He moved quickly down the stairs, paying no one any attention. Recketauer didn't like him much more than she liked anyone, but even she usually showed more manners than that. And she had sounded less angry than... nervous. Like she was keeping fear in check. And she never, *ever* used first names in front of students. He knew he had done nothing wrong, but that didn't often deter her from making trouble, and he didn't feel like dealing with her crap today.

His pudgy boss was standing in the main foyer waiting for him, her face ashen.

'What is it, Linda?'

She didn't say a word. An all-time first. She pointed a shaky hand into her office. He obediently walked through the door. She did not follow. He crept inside, marvelling even at such an odd moment at its unearthly neatness and order. He almost had a heart attack as the door slammed shut behind him, but this was quickly forgotten.

Two men stood behind old Recketauer's desk. Enormous bruisers with identical pinstripe suits were eyeing him sourly. Archetypal muscle, straight out of a Bond movie.

'Hello, Mr. Roberts.'

So completely had these two chumps grabbed his attention that he had failed to notice the figure sitting between them. A balding, plainly dressed man, about fifty, with a heavy five o'clock shadow, was sitting in Recketauer's chair, his hands folded neatly on the desk. He was looking straight at Jason, a warm smile on his face. Nothing from his appearance suggested in the slightest that he should have such expensive-looking bodyguards.

'Don't mind Chester and Steve,' he said with a chuckle, gesturing with his eyes at the two goons behind him. 'I've said all along they weren't necessary for this little visit, but so little is up to me these days. As a teacher, I'm sure you understand.'

The smile never left his face. He spoke as if he were in a chance meeting with a friend at a supermarket. He paused and adjusted his glasses. Jason, utterly nonplussed, said nothing.

'Ah, where are my manners?' He stood up and offered his hand. 'My name is Dr. Horace Wagner.' Jason hesitated for a moment, then reached out his own. The man's grip was like iron. Dr. Wagner sat down again, and was silent. He continued to study Jason. There was a hint of affection in the grin he continued to give him. Jason's confusion gave way to frustration.

'What is this?' he demanded. 'What's going on?'

The situation was so bizarre that he didn't know what else to say. Chester (or Steve) turned and glared at him for a moment, then continued to look out the office window.

Dr. Wagner's smile broadened, and Jason could see satisfaction wash over his face.

'A perfect opening statement, Mr. Roberts. Simple, strong, no ruder than necessary. And a resonant, confident baritone as well!'

'What–'

'And your presence! Self-control, cool countenance, visibly wary, but clearly not intimidated. Very promising, Mr. Roberts.'

Another long moment of increasingly irritating silence.

'You are a drama teacher,' Dr. Wagner stated.

'Yes,' Jason replied.

'But Ms. Recketauer tells me that you are also a history buff.'

'Yes.'

'Then why did you not become a history teacher?'

'I like drama better.'

'And you are recently divorced, yes?'

That was enough.

'Will you *please* tell me why the hell you're wasting my time like this? What do you want? Why am I having this conversation?'

Dr. Wagner's face grew reflective, his eyes dropping from Jason's for the first time. After a moment, he said, more to himself than Jason, 'Yes. You are what we need.'

Jason turned to leave.

'Mr. Roberts, *please.*'

Jason paused, his hand on the doorknob. Only the stark change in Wagner's tone of voice could have kept him in the room any longer. It was urgency. For the first time, Jason felt like he should hear a little more. He turned around. The doctor was still smiling, but something in his body language was different.

'It is a known truth amongst business-owners that, when they conduct interviews, they usually know whether they will hire an applicant within ten seconds of seeing them walk through the door.'

'Fascinating,' replied Jason. Dr. Wagner breathed an appreciative chuckle.

'Mr. Roberts, a great deal of time and money has been spent to bring me here, but ten seconds was all it took for me to see that I have come to the right place.'

'So this is a job interview.'

'Yes.'

'For a job as a history teacher.'

A look of dawning delight came over Dr. Wagner's face.

'How lovely! We never once thought of putting it that way. But yes, I suppose that's exactly what it's for.'

'I like my job,' Jason stated.

'And you are very good at it, Mr. Roberts. That is a crucial part of why I am here.'

Jason stood silently for a moment. He couldn't decide how he felt about Dr. Wagner. Half of him wanted to end this insane conversation on the spot, with a few choice words for 'Chester and Steve' on the way out. And yet he was fascinated by this infuriating man. He wanted to see where this was going.

'Why don't you sit down?' asked the doctor, gesturing to the chair on the other side of the desk.

'Are you done with the stupid riddles?'

'Indeed I am, Jason. You have more than passed this phase of the interview.'

'That's another riddle, you jackass,' Jason muttered, as he finally sat down across from Dr. Wagner. The doctor smiled openly for the first time, revealing flawless teeth.

'Mr. Roberts, I like you more by the moment. Now. Shall we begin?'

'Who are you?'

'As I have already stated my name, I assume you mean: *What* are you? A good place to start. I am many things, Jason, but for our purposes, I am a professional people-person. I *read* people. Tone of voice, choice of words, facial expression, body-language, all of it. The closest word to it I know of is *empath,* if that helps.'

Jason raised an eyebrow. 'You *read* people for a living?'

Dr. Wagner smiled. 'Possibly better than anyone else on Earth. But it goes further. I specialize as what you might call an *occupational empath.*'

'Meaning?'

'Meaning I can tell almost instantly what a man should be doing with his life. Sit me down with a sixty-year-old carpenter, for a chat about the weather, and within two minutes at most I can tell you whether he has wasted his life or not. Your lovely Ms. Recketauer shouldn't be allowed within a hundred miles of children, or anyone else. She has the social skills of a drunk baboon.'

Jason brushed off this remark, which would otherwise have made his day. The doctor continued.

'And, for our purposes, I am equally adept at finding the right man for the job. Any job.'

'How about we get to the point?'

'Indeed,' said Dr. Wagner, and for the first time, he grew very close to serious. 'Mr Roberts, my current assignment is of utmost importance. My superiors are looking for a very certain type of person with a very specific skill set and a very particular type of personal history.'

'And I meet those requirements?' asked Jason.

'To a *staggering* degree,' said the doctor, shaking his head. 'On paper you were ideal. In person, you are *perfect.* I think the closest I have ever come to a moment like this was with a gardener back in 1997. Annoying woman.'

'I'm just a teacher.'

'You are cool-headed. You have confidence. Not for one moment during this conversation have you stammered, or been at a loss for words, or betrayed even a moment's intimidation. You grew angry at precisely the right moments and to precisely the degree I wanted. You hesitated to within likely a millisecond of the space of time I had hoped, before you shook my hand. You haven't even glanced at my escorts here in several minutes. Every attempt I have made to bait you into asking the questions most people would have been asking all along has bounced off of you as if you were made of iron. You like a good fight. You are quick with a comeback. You are *exactly* what I am looking for.'

Jason scowled. 'As I have said, I like my job.'

'You won't like this one.'

'What does it pay?'

'Nothing.'

'You're starting to piss me off.'

'Jason, at this point, there is very little I am authorized to say that *won't* piss you off. All I can say is that we need you. There is a job that desperately needs to be done, and I doubt there is a man alive who has better hope of completing it.'

Jason gaped. That inexhaustible smile had vanished from Dr. Wagner's face; he was dead serious. Out of the corner of his eye, Jason saw one of the doctor's bruisers turn his head slightly to look at him. For the first time since entering the room, he felt a chill go up his spine. He took a breath and spoke.

'You said the job was for a history teacher.'

Dr. Wagner nodded.

'Since when did anyone *desperately need* a history teacher?'

'Throughout history, I'm afraid. But never more so than now.'

'Then why are you coming to me? History is a hobby for me. I read bits and pieces when I have time.'

'That will be explained later.'

Aggravated, Jason continued.

'And who would I be teaching?'

'Some very important people.'

'WHO?!'

'I cannot tell you.'

Jason stood up, pounding his fists against the desk, shaking with fury.

'This is a goddamned joke, you know that? You're lucky Chester and Steve are here right now. Now either tell me what the hell this is about, right now, or I walk out that door and call the cops.'

Dr. Wagner did not flinch. Neither, it dawned on Jason, had his bodyguards. The doctor gazed up at Jason, with an expression that was hard to read. Finally, he shook his head, his eyes shining in triumph.

'*Flawless,* Mr. Roberts,' he whispered. 'Absolutely flawless.'

Jason's fury did not diminish. He continued to snarl at Dr. Wagner. A sidelong glance at his bodyguards told Jason that they had not so much as glanced at him.

'So you've been trying to make me lose my temper.'

'In a manner of speaking,' replied Dr. Wagner.

'So you could measure my reaction.'

'Yes. This entire conversation has been a wonderful pleasure, of course, but it has also been a test of your emotional intelligence and control. You will need both, where you are going.'

Jason's lip curled. 'I'm not going anywhere.'

'But you are, Jason.' replied Dr Wagner. 'I can see it already. I don't even have to make the offer.'

'And why is that?'

'Because you want to go. It's written all over you. I have told you nothing, really, about why you were summoned to this infuriatingly clean office. I have led you around in circles, snubbed every attempt you have made to make progress. I have confused you, agitated you, and at last, enraged you. This entire conversation has been a complete waste of your time. And yet, one simple fact remains.'

'And what is that?'

Dr Wagner smiled.

'You are still here.'

Jason said nothing. His fury ebbed away, despite his best efforts. He knew the bastard was right. He was entranced by this entire situation. He glared as he sat down. Dr. Wagner nodded in satisfaction.

'No more games, *Doctor*,' Jason spat. 'I want answers. What exactly do you want me to *do?!*'

A new, businesslike expression appeared on Dr. Wagner's face. He clasped his hands on the table and continued.

'The precise nature of this job is highly classified, Jason. I can only explain the details one step at a time, as we reach them.'

'And the first step is?'

Dr. Wagner beamed with enthusiasm.

'An all-expenses-paid trip to Africa.'

'...WHAT?!'

'A trip to Africa, Mr. Roberts. To Kenya, more specifically. That is the first step. Step two will be explained when we get there.'

Jason was struck dumb.

'I feel I should explain further, as this is an odd sort of twist. Tomorrow morning, you and I will be flown on a private jet to Nairobi. We will then drive you, as comfortably as we are able, to a classified location outside the city. There, and only there, can your orientation begin. Everything has been arranged.'

Jason spoke slowly. 'I don't know anything about African history.'

'You are not required to, Jason.'

'Then why the hell am I *going* there?!'

'Jason, I respectfully ask you to put aside the history aspect of this scenario for now. It is irrelevant at this point. And I cannot tell you why you are going there. But you are needed there, more desperately than you know.'

'I don't *know* anything,' Jason shot back. 'For all I know, this whole thing could be one gigantic joke.'

'You know it isn't, Jason, or you would have already said so. You are nobody's fool. This is very serious indeed.'

Jason glared, measuring this latest absurdity.

'And if I say no?'

'Then your life will go on as it always has, Mr. Roberts. At no point will the right to back out be taken away from you.'

'And how am I supposed to derail my entire life at a moment's notice to go halfway around the world?'

'As I have said, everything has been arranged. A substitute has already been found for your classes. Your passport has been updated. You will receive preferential treatment at the airport and will be driven there by Chester here, as you know you can trust him. And,' he finished, ignoring the look on Jason's face, 'as an added incentive, right about now your mother, sisters, and best friend should be personally receiving cash payments of fifty thousand dollars each.'

Jason stared, open-mouthed. The same calm smile had returned to the doctor's face.

'Bullshit.'

'Well, I'm getting bored,' Dr. Wagner said, groaning as he stood. 'It has truly been a pleasure, Jason! You may call me Horace from now on. I will see you tomorrow morning. Please be ready at 7:45. Until then, enjoy yourself!'

Chester and Steve turned together and glared at Jason, who was so taken aback by this sudden finish that he was still sitting down. 'Horace' was still beaming at him. Jason jumped to his feet, knocking over his chair, and almost ran out the door, not looking back. He closed it and stood paralyzed for a moment. Recketauer was gone. A couple of girls chatted noisily as they walked by. Jason shook his head in stupification.

'What... the hell... was that?'

Chapter Two

Five minutes later, Jason was just getting into his car, still not even beginning to process all that had just happened, when the calls began. He spent a full hour sitting in the school parking lot feigning enthusiasm to his mother and three sisters in perfect succession as they screamed with joy at the massive chunk of cash that had been delivered to their respective doorsteps. He had to explain what was going on. Without much to give away, he told them he had gotten a job offer with incentives. The whole thing was agony. His nerves were shot to hell already and pretending to be happy with his bubbly family made him want to scream. Worst of all, the calls themselves confirmed the awful truth: whatever had just happened in his stupid boss' office was no joke.

At last he managed to escape his younger sister's trilling rants about her plans for her cash. He sat for half an hour in his idling car, fighting to gather himself, but it was no use. His mind was on fire. He picked up his phone again and dialed the only number he could at such a moment. He loved his mother and sisters dearly, but they were not who he needed. He needed Markie.

He put the phone on speaker and sat it in his lap. Even at this moment, he did not worry that she wouldn't pick up. She was *always* home.

After barely a ring, he heard the phone connect. A violent cough.

'Hello?'

'Hi Markie.'

'Hey Jason. You're calling earlier than usual.'

'I need to talk.'

'Sure.'

'Are you high?'

'Just weed.'

'Can I come by?'

'Yep.'

'See you soon.'

'Bye.'

A conversation so ordinary that he already felt better. Any semblance of formality was wasted on Markie.

Jason shoved his phone in his pocket and pulled out of the parking lot at last. He put on some Allman Brothers and quickly got on the highway.

Jason loved this twenty-minute drive, a winding country jaunt to the outskirts of Dunnville. As the piano solo on 'Jessica' swirled and the trees rolled by, he smiled in relief and relaxed. He would figure this out. Jason had spent most of his thirty-three years learning not to worry, and it was a skill he treasured now that he had it.

He pulled onto Markie's boring side road and ten seconds later was pulling into her driveway. She had a smallish place of white brick that shrank into insignificance behind the masses of shrubs, flowers, and apple trees that dominated the front lawn. There was no rhyme or reason to any of it: two andromedas here and another ten feet away, daffodils surrounding raspberry bushes, no colour co-ordination whatsoever. The whole thing was a baffling, chaotic barrage that Jason absolutely loved.

He made his way up the narrow stone pathway and onto the porch. Two oversized wicker chairs sat on either side of a small wooden barrel that functioned as a table, mostly for tea. Jason hoped they would be sitting there soon.

He went inside without knocking (she shook her head in exasperation every time he forgot that rule). As usual, the smell of marijuana and incense immediately overwhelmed him, and some obscure psychedelic blues band (probably with the word 'marshmallow' in their name), droned all around him.

'Leave the door open,' came a melodious voice from the kitchen. 'If I'd known you'd be coming so damned early I'd have aired the place out by now.'

'It smells exactly the way it always does, Markie,' Jason called back. No response. He rolled his eyes affectionately and sat down on the couch. She could be twenty minutes for all he knew, so he made himself comfortable.

He had sat in this room for countless hours, yet it was so busy with decoration that he still often noticed something new. Markie's own paintings and crafts hung on every wall and sat on every shelf. Small houseplants and herb gardens were everywhere. The ceiling (despite Jason's desperate protests) was in the process of becoming one gigantic mural, made up completely as she went along. A little hippie cathedral built entirely for herself.

'Hello Jimmy,' Jason said, as the black and white cat jumped on his lap. He nuzzled Jason for ten seconds, then went about his business. The corner of the couch was torn almost to shreds by Jimmy's handiwork. Markie didn't care in the slightest.

Finally, the beads in the kitchen doorway parted and Markie appeared. A freshly-rolled joint was in her hand, and she wore the same look of serenity and contentment that Jason almost never saw her without. She sat down in the ancient armchair to Jason's left and put her feet up on the coffee table.

'Hey.'

'Hey.'

Nothing unusual there. They saw each other so often that nothing even so polite as a glance in each other's direction was a necessary part of a greeting anymore.

Seven years his junior, they had met at a friend's bonfire eight years ago. Within two months, he couldn't imagine life without her. Some frowned on their age gap, many frowned on her huge drug intake, and pretty much everyone shook their heads at the idea that two people as different as Jason and Markie could become such powerful soulmates. Jason understood it least of all. They just clicked.

Considering how unbelievably busy her home was, she dressed rather simply: usually cropped cotton t-shirts and denim cutoffs, and the same faded red, woolen slouch hat that she wore day and night. Her intensely wavy, dirty-blonde hair hung over the tops of her shoulders; a couple of plain brown beads hung in it here and there. For all her apparent lack of effort, it was effective.

'How was your day?' she asked, as she carefully lit her joint.

Jason sighed. 'Messed up. Something weird happened.'

'They let you out early.'

'This guy... came and offered me a job. But he won't tell me what it is. All I know is he wants me to go to *Africa* tomorrow, and my family are all fifty grand richer.'

'So am I,' Markie croaked, her lungs filled with smoke.

Jason started. The doctor *had* mentioned his best friend! He stared open-mouthed at Markie, who was still savouring her first toke.

'Who brought it to you?!'

'Some dipshit named Wagner. He came by an hour ago. Insisted on talking to me for fifteen minutes; it drove me nuts.'

Jason was floored. He had delivered it to her personally. What was going on?

'And when were you going to bring this up?'

She shrugged and said nothing. When Markie shrugged like that, it meant that no explanation was possible or necessary. She more or less based her life on that shrug.

Jason slumped back into the couch, smiling in resignation.

'You're not gonna spend it on drugs, are you?' he asked.

'Not most of it,' she responded, again with a chest full of smoke.

'Markie, my job would be in danger if my principal even suspected I come here.'

'I think that's why you come here.'

Jason chuckled.

'So,' Markie said, suddenly attentive. 'Are you going to Africa?'

Jason considered the bizarre situation. 'I don't know.'

'Why wouldn't you?'

'It was sprung on me so suddenly. I don't even know what I'm supposed to expect.'

Markie looked at him as if he were an idiot. 'I said why WOULDN'T you.'

'Stop being a smartass,' Jason snapped. 'I just had a very weird day. This Wagner guy just rearranged my whole life for me, and now he wants to take me to another continent tomorrow for reasons he won't even tell me. Would you do it?'

She looked up from petting Jimmy and gawped at him. She was almost laughing. He was asking the wrong person.

'You know I'm not like that. I don't like these freakin' surprises. Least of all after a conversation with a nutjob like that.'

'Jason, you need this,' Marky said motherly. It got on his nerves when she used that tone. 'You gotta get out of that mindset and learn to have fun. I swear you weren't like this before Kyla.'

Jason glared. He did not like it when she brought up his ex. She held up her hands with mock remorse, cracked her neck, and pretended to mind her own business.

The grinding, overdriven guitar reached a fever pitch. 'Damn it, Markie, can't we put on Cream or something? Compromise.'

'Cream is mainstream,' she responded as she examined her nails. Argument over.

They sat in the grey haze. Jason fiddled on his phone and tried to settle himself. Then he heard a creepy *Poltergeist* voice.

'You'd see liiii-ons.'

Jason turned his head to glare yet again. Markie was still slouched out, staring at the wall, a small smile on her face. She was in her element today.

'You drive me batshit insane, you know that?'

She nodded and said nothing more.

'Can't you take just one little thing seriously?! I came to here to vent, not for you to take Horace's side.'

'Oh, so he's *Horace* now!' she said with delight. 'You two are moving awfully fast.'

'STOP IT! I don't need this crap right now. I'm a little on edge, and I don't know what I should– OW!!'

Markie had reached out with blinding speed and given him a massive, excruciating charlie-horse. Jason grabbed his thigh and rolled back on the couch, howling with pain. Jimmy bolted. Markie smirked mischievously, her crooked left canine the only flaw in her otherwise perfect smile.

'WHY did you do that?!' Jason managed at last. 'God, I hate it when you do shit like that!'

'You love it, and you know it,' Markie replied, as Jason rubbed his throbbing leg. 'You're in a rut, and I'm the only source of spontaneity you have. It's too much responsibility for one woman, Jason. I need some space.'

Jason straightened out, still putting pressure on his leg and cursing under his breath. Marky had backed off and sat with surprising grace on the edge of her chair, watching him with amusement. As usual, she had scored a total victory.

'I guess a vacation would be nice,' he muttered. Markie smiled with satisfaction.

'Yep.'

In spite of himself, Jason grinned.

'Go take a shower,' she ordered, 'and I'll pour you a glass of scotch. Then we'll go out, so I can send you off proper.'

Jason nodded and made his way to the bathroom. Though he would never admit it to her, he could not get enough of her endless lunacy, even if it meant a bruise.

Upon getting out of the shower, Jason set about the arduous task of informing his family that he was leaving in the morning. His mother was delighted (as Jason knew she would be) and asked about four hundred questions. His two older sisters were similarly ecstatic, but his younger sister was a bit problematic. She always got emotional at moments like this, and despite his protests, was a bit upset at the suddenness of the whole thing. He talked her down after half an hour or so and promised to call her as soon as he got home. Then it was over.

Jason shook his head as he hung up the phone. He had always been the odd one out in his family – a controlled, introverted bookworm among four excitable socialites. Since his dad died when he was twenty, his mother had never remarried, and Jason had become the unofficial patriarch, the one to whom his mother and sisters turned incessantly for comfort and strength. He accepted the role, but it was draining. Finding Markie had been the blessing of blessings.

The two of them sat on the porch all afternoon. Jason savoured his Glenlivet and darted a laser pen around for Jimmy. Markie fiddled with a Rubik's Cube and chatted him up endlessly. As usual, the conversation bounced around wherever it wanted, from Socrates to Looney Tunes. They managed to get into their normal philosophical arguments over blueberries versus raspberries and the importance of image in music. Soon the enormity of his looming adventure was gone from Jason's mind.

At dusk, they got in Jason's car and drove to Niagara Falls to see Clifton Hill, one of the few places they both enjoyed visiting. Markie ate a tab on the way. Jason hated her acid use, but had learned not to complain; it was one of the few subjects that she had no sense of humour about.

After the usual routine of slow traffic and dodging tourists, they parked a kilometre away from the Hill by the cereal factory (no one from the area would pay twenty dollars for parking) and strolled into the bustle of the beating heart of the honeymoon capital of the world. As usual, they had made no plans; they just dove in. Jason led the way, marvelling at the enthusiasm of first-timers who had probably come from half-way around the world to see this place he knew like the back of his hand. Once he said hello to a friend; otherwise he simply enjoyed himself, reflecting on what he had at last decided to embrace.

Markie, of course, was in her own world; she set an annoyingly slow pace and gazed around in LSD-inspired wonder at the spectacle around them, though she did avoid the haunted houses. She said a bright hello to every child she saw and almost melted with joy upon encountering a woman with a beagle on a leash. Every now and then she turned and smiled at Jason and cooed, 'You're going to *Africa!*' After about the fourteenth time, he told her to shut the hell up, but it *was* encouraging.

Jason let her stare at the Skywheel for ten minutes, and then she reluctantly agreed to walk down to the Parkway. They stood leaning against the railing in front of the American Falls, silent and thoughtful.

'Think it's like this in Egypt?' Markie asked.

'What do you mean?'

'We're standing in front of one of the Wonders of the World, and from your face you'd think we were watching reruns of the *Simpsons*. Think locals are the same with the pyramids? Or the Northern Lights?'

'Probably,' Jason replied. 'You could live on the Moon, and it would feel normal after a while.'

'How do you know we're *not* on the Moon?'

Jason rolled his eyes and pointed at the crescent almost directly in front of them.

'Maybe that's the MOON's moon,' Markie whispered, her eyes bright.

Jason turned to look at his friend. 'Peaking, are we?'

'Yep.'

He let her have this one. The conversation would make less and less sense if he didn't. Arguing with Markie was hard enough on a normal day; in her current state she was invincible.

For a while they stood in silence. Jason reflected on this massive blow to his routine. There was so much he didn't know about what was about to happen; the fact itself not being something Jason was used to. He rarely travelled. He never travelled alone. The most unusual trip he had ever taken was to Montreal with Kyla, and *that* had given him culture shock. And above all, he was not going to Kenya for fun; he was 'desperately needed' there. What the hell did it mean? A hundred riddles tattooed his mind.

He glanced at Markie and was startled to see her eyes scrunched up in emotion, her lip quivering as she gazed across the swirling river.

'Markie, what's wrong?' he whispered. She *never* cried.

'Nothing,' she whispered back weepily. 'This is just the stupid face you're making.'

At the same moment they both burst into uncontrollable laughter. Jason, furious and delighted, put her in a headlock, knocked off her hat, and knuckled her scalp as hard as he dared.

'HEY!' she shouted into his hip. 'Fuck off with the hair, you know better than that!'

Still laughing, he released her gently. She picked up her hat from the sidewalk and placed it back on her head with a murderous glare at Jason. He knew better than to take that deathstare seriously; he'd seen it more times than he could remember.

They pulled away from the falls and started the climb back up the Hill. Jason stole an affectionate glance at his friend as she continued her sightseeing. He had never met anyone like her. She was the only person in his life who could possibly have made him so happy in this moment.

They bought overpriced pizza for the walk back, and ate in silence. Jason avoided looking at her, lest she show him a mouthful of chewed mush, as she was prone to do.

The drive home was quiet. Markie was more or less back to normal and dozed off quickly. Jason turned the radio off and took the long, dull drive in silence. Markie stirred the moment they hit the gravel of her driveway. The car slowed to a stop, and they looked at each other for a moment. At long last, Jason asked the question.

'Wanna come?'

She shook her head. 'I can't, Jason. Whatever this is, it belongs to you. Embrace it. It's gonna set you free.'

'I feel free already.'

'Nah. You don't know free until you travel. See things. Do things. And from what happened today, you're gonna do things in Kenya.'

Jason smiled. 'Then why haven't you asked me to travel with you before?'

She shrugged. No explanation possible or necessary.

'Whatever happens, Jason,' she said quietly, 'remember one thing.'

'What's that?'

'Your fly's been down since the pizza shop.'

Jason's eyes closed in self-loathing as he adjusted himself. Markie gave a girly giggle and hugged him tight.

'Have fun, Jason.'

'Thank you for everything, Markie.'

With a sad sort of smile, she opened the door and disappeared into her garden.

Jason watched her go, and then, with a new fire in his belly, pulled out of the driveway.

Chapter Three

Jason woke up a full hour before his alarm. He had half-heartedly packed after getting home the previous night and then fell on his bed and passed out. Now he had two hours to kill.

He made sure everything was locked for the fourth time and then put on Netflix and made French toast. Even at a moment like this, Jason relished every second. Drama class notwithstanding, he enjoyed being alone.

At seven he showered, shaved, and tied his hair back. He put on a simple navy t-shirt, blue jeans, and his watch. Socks. Casual shoes. And on impulse, he pulled out a simple silver chain and fastened it around his neck. Ready at last, he brought his bag out to the porch, sat down, and waited.

At 7:45, almost to the second, a black Lincoln cruised up the road and pulled to a stop in front of him. Its windows were as dark as the paint job, and its exterior was so polished that even in the dim morning light it twinkled like a star.

How original, Jason thought. He grabbed his bag and marched to the trunk. It popped open on cue. Jason got rid of his luggage, opened the passenger door, and looked inside. Sure enough, there was the monstrous, square-jawed form of Chester, looking far too big for his job as driver. He turned his head and glanced at Jason, which Jason took as a sign to get in. He stepped inside without hesitation and slammed the door. A fantastic rush overcame him as the car accelerated away from his home.

The twenty-five-minute drive to the airport was dull and quiet. When Jason asked feebly when the flight would be taking off, Chester grunted and replied that it was 'classified.' Jason laughed to himself. It was the only thing the gigantic man said the entire way.

When they reached the massive airport, Steve was waiting. He took Jason's bag and walked away without once looking at Jason. At another glance from Chester, Jason followed him to the food court. Jason's head was on a swivel; he hadn't been in an airport in a long time. Looking at last in the direction he was going, he saw Horace Wagner standing in the middle of the walkway, in deep conversation with someone Jason had never seen before. He was a sturdy, stocky black man, dressed very casually, with a strong goatee and a short, scraggly Afro that was shot with grey.

Horace glanced in Jason's direction, noticed him, and turned to face him with a smile so genuine that Jason couldn't help but feel a little disarmed.

'Welcome, Jason!' He held out his hand. Jason, in spite of himself, took it immediately. 'Very happy indeed to see you!

I am glad to see you didn't dress up. There is no dress code in our circle, as you can see.'

'I wouldn't have if there was,' Jason replied with a small smile. Horace laughed, a strong, free, relaxed laugh that he had not used in Recketauer's office. His companion remained silent, studying Jason with powerful dark eyes.

'Ah yes, of course.' Horace gestured to the man at last. 'Jason Roberts, this is Omondi Mutua, a colleague of mine from Kenya.'

'Please, call me Omondi. It is a pleasure.' He shook Jason's hand firmly, only a hint of a smile on his face, his unnerving eyes continuing to search Jason's own. He spoke with a strong Swahili accent, and his voice was raspy and resonant.

'Please join us, Jason!' Horace continued, gesturing to the nearest table. 'We may leave for Kenya at any time, but first we were hoping we could have a chat with you.'

Jason hesitated. Horace laughed again.

'It will not be like our encounter yesterday. I assure you. Omondi and I simply wish to have a conversation with you about history.'

'So we're back to history.'

'Yes, Jason, the time has come to explore the Great and Tragic Past. Please join us.'

Horace and Omondi sat together on one side of the nearest table, ignoring the coffee stains, and waited for Jason to join them. Jason considered for a moment, then rolled his eyes and sat across from Horace. 'You're used to getting your own way, aren't you?' Jason shot at him.

Horace shrugged with a smile. 'I would deny it if I could, Jason. Now. To business. What areas of history do you study?'

A bit taken aback, Jason responded. 'Twentieth century, mostly. A little of the Middle Ages.'

'Those of Europe.'

'Yes.'

'What draws you to the twentieth century?'

Jason shrugged. 'It's more spontaneous, I guess. There's a lot more that's interesting.'

Horace frowned. 'What is it about the distant past that bores you?'

Jason thought for a moment. 'Well, when they weren't having wars, life was pretty humdrum back then, wasn't it? Chores and church and conformity.'

'And what makes the twentieth century different?'

'A million things,' Jason replied. 'Technology, culture, music, politics – they all skyrocketed in the last hundred years.'

'Have you ever thought that perhaps it is merely the exponentially larger body of records and data that makes the twentieth century *seem* more interesting?'

Jason shrugged skeptically. 'Not from what I've read. Every book on the Middle Ages spends about two thirds of its time on Church life and growing food and making clothes. There was no time to make life interesting.'

Horace looked thoughtfully at him, then altered the conversation.

'What would you call the defining event of the twentieth century?'

Jason raised an eyebrow. He was not an idiot.

'World War Two, obviously.'

'And I assume you have studied the War?'

'Extensively. It's my favourite subject.'

Horace shot a quick glance at Omondi, and then leaned closer to Jason, a certain solemnity touching his eyes.

'There is something almost biblical about the Second War, is there not? Something divinely inspired. The greatest storyteller who ever lived could not create something half so compelling if he lived a thousand years.'

Unnerved, Jason nodded. Was he actually beginning to like this guy?

Horace continued. 'What would you consider the defining battle of World War Two?'

'That's a foolish question,' Jason replied.

Horace's eyebrows raised, and his head moved back an inch. For the first time, Jason had surprised him. 'And why is that?'

'You can't ask a question like that. Not with World War Two. Every event was defining in and of itself. Who are we to compare the importance of North Africa and Normandy? They were all massive triumphs of good over evil, paid for in blood.'

Horace looked at him for what felt like an eternity, his head cocked slightly. Then he turned to Omondi, who had not said a word through the entire conversation.

'You see, my friend? *Perfect.*'

Omondi measured Jason yet again and said, 'You know much, Mr. Roberts. Or at least, you think you do.'

Jason frowned. 'And you think you know more?'

'Yes.'

Horace smiled. 'Omondi here may well be the world's foremost authority on the Second World War.'

'That's great,' Jason replied impatiently, 'but why have we gotten so focused on it?'

'That will be explained,' Omondi snapped.

Jason turned his head sharply and glared. 'You're kinda picking the wrong day, pal.'

'Gentlemen, please!' Horace said with a laugh. 'Let's not start that way. We will all be seeing a lot of each other from now on; we'd best start things off on the right foot.' He smiled reassuringly at Jason. 'Let us simply say for now that the War and your knowledge and passion for it are important aspects of why we have come to you, Jason. All will be explained when we get to Kenya. Shall we go?'

'What, just like that?' Jason asked. 'No customs, no security?'

Horace smiled. 'As I said, we have preferential treatment. If we leave now, we will be in the air in twenty-five minutes.'

Jason didn't bother to ask why they had such privileges. He knew he would not get an answer. He stood up and followed Horace and Omondi.

Ten minutes later, he was sitting comfortably in the comfortable interior of a beautiful private jet, buckling himself in and beyond the beginnings of belief that this was happening. He had taken the window seat without bothering to ask, and Horace had parked himself next to him with similar disregard. Omondi sat across the aisle, wearing an expression akin to someone doing the laundry. He made himself comfortable and closed his eyes.

Horace smiled with excitement. 'You have a great adventure ahead of you, Jason! This is indeed an honour!'

Jason turned his head. 'An honour?'

'Careful, Horace,' Omondi droned, without opening his eyes.

At that moment, the plane roared into motion, picked up astonishing speed, and took off into the sunny sky.

The moment he was able, Jason unbuckled his safety belt and stomped into the next room to the plush, cream-coloured couch. He sat down grumpily and grabbed a Coke from the nearby mini-fridge. He switched on the thirty-two-inch flatscreen on the wall that was likely worth twice the value of the fifty-inch in his living room. Finding only daytime variety, he turned it off again and pulled out his phone. He fiddled on youtube for a minute or so, then slammed it down in frustration onto the cushion beside him. He could not relax.

'Penny for your thoughts?'

Horace had appeared in the doorway of the cramped but luxurious lounge, a cup of tea in hand.

'Shut up.'

'Come now, Jason. I understand completely. This is a massive step out of the ordinary for you. It is perfectly normal to feel restless.'

'You're not helping.'

Horace was silent for a moment. He sat down on the chair farthest from Jason and sipped his tea.

'Even now, in this offhand moment, you impress me, Jason.'

'And how is that?' Jason asked.

'You are rude, but not for the sake of it. You are restless and agitated, but not afraid. You are stoic. Even your body language is superb. Not for a moment during our strange time together have you forgotten to carry yourself with grace and dignity. You are going to do very well indeed.'

'Enough with the goddamned riddles, already,' Jason snapped without looking up.

Another moment of silence went by. Jason downed his Coke and continued to stare morosely at his phone. Horace (whom Jason suspected was rather enjoying himself) made himself yet more comfortable. Finally, he spoke again.

'There is something to be said about the word *goddamn,* is there not?'

Jason looked up slowly. 'Why?'

'That is the second time you have used that word against me. Both were well chosen. As a Christian, I don't use it myself, but I understand why people do. It has punch. It has aesthetic power. Its meaning is inherently rotten to its core, but there is no denying its effectiveness as a sound.'

'Why are you saying this stuff?'

Horace shrugged. 'Making conversation.'

Jason shook his head and looked back down at his phone. 'You are *crazy.*'

'Stay with me here, Jason. You have a remarkable way with words. I would not deny that I have done most of the talking in the...' he glanced at his watch. '...nearly twenty-two hours we have known each other, but you, sir, have a remarkable gift of brevity and minimalism. The mark of a genius, as they say. I could go on for hours and hours and have less of an effect on people that you can with a single word.'

'Agreed.'

Horace howled with laughter at this. He beat a fist on the nearby endtable in delight.

'WONDERFUL, Jason! I haven't been drubbed like that in years.'

Jason couldn't help himself: He grinned.

Suddenly a voice came from behind them. 'I think it is time to be serious for a moment.'

Omondi had emerged from his solitude in the dining room. There was no trace of a smile on his face. He was holding a chrome clipboard. He came and sat down next to Horace so that the two of them were yet again staring Jason down. Horace's smile grew strained. Omondi handed him the clipboard and sat straight as an arrow in the reclining chair.

Jason sighed. 'I'm about to get really pissed off again, aren't I?'

'We must confirm a few things with you,' Omondi said. 'To avoid any complications in the future.'

'Yes, Jason,' Horace said with a patronizing smile. 'Simple questions, a few things for us to remember in Kenya. First of all, you were born in McMaster Hospital, Hamilton, October 6, 1987?'

'Yes.'

'Married March 31, 2016 to Kyla Sandford, divorced on relatively peaceful terms on January 6, 2020.'

Jason frowned. 'Yes.'

'Mother Ruth Roberts nee Anderson; Father Charles Roberts, deceased March 15, 2008 of bone cancer.'

Jason made no reply.

'Clean criminal record, no major health problems, two-inch scar on left shoulder from minor incident in high school woodworking class–'

'How the hell do you know all this?!'

'Background checks, Jason, simple background checks. You must have realized by now that you are involved in something very big. We could not bring you aboard without making sure of your personal history, which, as I mentioned in our first meeting, is superb.'

'Let's see if I have this lined up,' Jason hissed. 'You explode my life, invade my privacy, screw with my head over and over, and expect me to just follow you around Africa feeding me nothing but *bullshit?!*'

'This is a necessary part of the process, Jason,' Omondi consoled. 'All will be explained in Kenya. We ask that you be patient and answer our questions.'

Jason stared at Omondi, caught off guard by his sudden fit of manners.

'What exactly about my personal history is *superb*?'

Horace beamed with enthusiasm.

'Emotionally bullied as a child, now a favourite teacher of nearly all your students. Runner-up for valedictorian at grade eight graduation. Kicked out of your first high school for shoving your English teacher into a wall, but a model student at your second. A well-known drinker through grade twelve; now only a moderate partaker of Glenlivet and Budweiser. Introverted, but not a hermit. Lovely home, a wonderful relationship with your mother and sisters. You are effortlessly popular and generally humble. I could go on. You are a success story, Jason. A success story of precisely the kind we need.'

Jason stared in shock. He had never been spoken to like this in his life.

'Also,' Omondi added, 'you have what you Canadians call *star-quality*.'

'No, I don't.'

'Yes, you do, Jason,' Horace insisted. 'Strong jaw, piercing hazel eyes, broad shoulders, a boyish smile that instantly disarms. You have a presence about you. Charisma. It is necessary, I would imagine, as a drama teacher, but you have something about you that is exceptionally rare and crucial to this little jaunt of ours.'

'Star quality isn't necessary for anything,' Jason protested. 'Churchill didn't have it.'

'Oh yes, he did,' Omondi countered. 'He had mountains of it. He may not have been dashingly handsome, but he had a force of character unrivalled in modern history. No one could have led the Free World to victory against Hitler without looking the part.'

Jason was impressed.

'But we have gotten off topic,' Horace said. 'There are a few details our background checks were not able to decipher, which we would like to confirm.'

'Okay. Awesome. I'm bored.'

'Your religious beliefs?'

'Whatever.'

'No astrology, no churchgoing, no Buddhist philosophical attachments?'

'No. Nothing.'

'But also no militant anti-theistic attitudes.'

'Believe whatever the hell you want. I don't care. Next topic.'

Horace scribbled some notes, then looked up suddenly. 'You're not a pacifist, are you?'

Jason stared. 'No...'

'Good,' Horace replied and returned to his notes.

'Why does *that* matter?'

Omondi answered before Horace could. 'A pacifist would not have the right kind of mind for the job that you have been hired for.'

'This is getting weirder by the second, Omondi,' Jason replied.

Horace looked up again. 'You don't use wikipedia in your research, do you?'

'Give me some credit, please.'

'Good,' Horace replied and returned to his notes.

Omondi spoke again. 'One question further, and then we will let you relax.'

Jason scoffed. 'Oh, this is gonna be good; I can feel it.'

'Are you happy in Canada?'

'What do you mean?'

'Do you enjoy your life there? Are you content? Or do you wish for something more?'

Jason was so used to bizarre questions by this point that he took this one without resisting. He pondered. He had always thought he was exactly where he wanted to be. But since yesterday, even up to this conversation with these two lunatics, something had arisen inside of him. He did wish for something more. In fact, he longed for it.

'Thank you, Jason,' Horace said with a smile. 'That will be all.' He scribbled a few more quick notes and handed the clipboard to Omondi, who returned to the dining room without another glance at either of them.

'I didn't answer the question,' Jason said.

'You did, Jason, and as impeccably as ever. As an empath, I picked up exactly what I was hoping for.'

Jason sighed. He had had enough.

'Just leave me alone, and get me to Kenya.'

'Fair enough, Jason. I will let you be. Please do your best to relax. There is food two compartments that way. Enjoy. Indulge. You are our guest and will be treated as such.'

'You mean from now on?' Jason asked, but Horace had already joined Omondi in the dining room.

'Son of a *bitch!*' Jason whispered, and stalked off to get some lunch.

Horace and Omondi sat together at the dining room table. The lights were dimmed, and Bach played elegantly in the background.

'This is too risky, Horace,' Omondi growled, barely above a whisper. 'Duni never implied that we should invest all our training in one man. What if this is too much for him? What if he gets hurt? What if he says no? We won't have time to start over at zero.'

'He won't say no, Omondi,' Horace replied. 'I saw it in him the moment he walked through the door yesterday. There is no one else. No other man we have investigated even comes close. It *must* be Jason.'

'You know what is at stake! There are too many variables, too much that can go wrong–'

'You have seen him!' Horace spat. 'You have spoken to him. To be honest with you, Omondi, I had serious doubts about this whole operation until we found him. You hired me to do a job, and I have done it. That should be enough.'

Omondi shook his head, stood up, walked to his room, and shut the door. Horace, unfazed, leaned back in his chair, closed his eyes, and enjoyed his music.

Chapter Four

They had made one effortless stop in Nigeria, refueling at a remote airstrip not likely worth half as much as the jet. Four hours later, they touched down in Jomo Kenyatta Airport, skidded to a stop, and were still at last. The passenger door opened, and Jason stepped out into another world. He was terrified. He was exhilarated. The fact that he had not slept in twenty hours was forgotten as he beheld the beautiful city of Nairobi to the north of the bustling airport. The sound of roaring airplanes and unintelligible shouts of Swahili were all around him. Jason smiled, as he beheld his new surroundings. At long last the foreplay was over. He had made it!

It was sunny and blindingly hot, but Jason took it in stride as the beautiful hustle and bustle of Kenya's main nerve washed over him. Horace and Omondi appeared on either side of him. Horace put a hand on Jason's shoulder and beamed. For reasons he could not understand, Jason welcomed the gesture.

Omondi viewed his home through trendy sunglasses, a small smile touching his lips.

'*Nairobi,* Jason!' Horace gushed as they took in the city skyline. 'It has been my home for years and is still my favourite place on Earth.'

Jason smiled and said nothing. For the first time since this fiasco began, he was genuinely happy. Suddenly he felt a tap on his other shoulder. Omondi got his attention and pointed west of the city. Jason looked out into the nearby plains and could make out three giraffes grazing in the distant trees. He was floored.

Suddenly, a red SUV came cruising across the runway and stopped three feet in front of them. Jason deflated. They couldn't give him two minutes!

'I know, Jason,' Horace soothed. 'But there is much that needs to be done. You will have time to enjoy yourself, but surely you are ready to know why you are here?'

This was, Jason admitted to himself, a compelling argument. Omondi was already closing the front passenger door behind him. Jason immediately followed, taking the seat behind the driver, with Horace beside him. For a moment, the vehicle continued to idle.

'Now, Horace,' Omondi said, again without looking at them. Horace opened a small folder in a slot in the front seat. A single, cream-coloured business card was fastened to it with a paper clip. He pulled it loose carefully.

'Do not lose this, Jason,' he said and handed it to him. Jason took it and examined it closely. On one side, in a stark black font, it read:

Kenyan Restoration Agency

Jason glanced up at Horace, who for once said nothing. He turned the card over. A thin black line framed this side, and in italicized blue writing were the words:

two skips of a stone

'What does that mean?' Jason asked.

'You will find out very soon, Jason, but for now, remember that phrase. It is very useful in this city.'

Omondi checked his phone and cursed loudly in Swahili. 'The Southern Bypass is blocked off, Horace. We'll have to take the 104.'

Horace smiled at Jason. 'Looks like you'll be seeing the city proper sooner than we thought.'

Omondi made a soundless gesture to the indifferent driver, and they motored across the hazy tarmac and out of the airport gates. They cruised steadily down Jogoo Road, and before long, they were into the heart of the city of Nairobi.

Jason stared out the car window in amazement. He had always associated Africa with endless plains and quaint villages; never had he imagined that such a powerful metropolis as this would be his very first impression of it. Advertising, from tremendous smartphone billboards to simple Coca-Cola posters, dominated the cityscape. Throngs of people bustled along narrow sidewalks – well-dressed businessmen dodging their way through rough-looking men and women in plain garments, stopping at endless rows of brightly coloured shops to barter with the keepers. Jason had never seen anything like it.

Suddenly he was jarred out of his wonder when the driver slammed on his brakes, stopping inches from a stylishly dressed woman who had run, without looking, into his path. They exchanged brief, heated Swahili, and then the trip resumed, everyone but Jason unfazed. Horace smiled and patted his leg. 'Driving in Nairobi can be intense, my friend. You can expect at least another sudden stop or two before we reach the far side of the city.'

'Thanks for telling me after the fact, you asshole,' Jason muttered, shaking from head to toe.

After about an hour and a half of city driving (giving Jason continuous, alternating fits of boredom and terror), they pulled out at last onto the open highway. They drove westward for forty-five minutes until at last, they turned onto a dusty, unnamed sideroad. After a bumpy, anticlimactic ten minutes, during which Jason grew more agitated by the second, Horace turned and said, 'Here we are, Jason.'

Jason rolled his eyes and continued to look out the window. And his jaw dropped.

The dense brush cleared to reveal an enormous complex of gorgeous modern buildings, all of matching beige brick, lining two simple streets. A wide strip of carefully kept grass lay between them, with short, black lamp posts standing neatly every sixty feet. Ordinary Kenyans dotted the landscape, some looking half-heartedly at them as they passed. Straight ahead, two hundred yards away, sat a sprawling complex, the size of a large mall, with an iron gate opening to a barely visible stone courtyard. The whole place would have seemed like a high-end retirement plaza were it not for the ferocious fences topped with barbed wire and the fearsome towers, complete with armed guards, lining it every one hundred feet.

Jason couldn't believe his eyes. 'What is this place?'

Horace glanced at him and smiled. 'This is the main headquarters of the Kenyan Restoration Agency.'

'And for the time being,' Omondi said without turning around, 'it is your home.'

A sense of foreboding filled Jason's mind. Whatever he was here to do, it was not to teach history.

They pulled to a stop at last in front of a small office building.

'Come with us, Jason,' Horace said without a second look as he opened his door. 'Important registration and security matters. Shouldn't take more than half an hour, and then we can get started.'

'No.'

Horace and Omondi stopped and looked around at Jason together.

'We're getting started now,' Jason spat in quiet fury. 'I am not answering one more question, signing one more form, taking one more order from you two dickwads until I find out what's going on. I've had it up to *here* with this horseshit, you know that? So either show me why you've brought me here NOW or get me back to Ontario and never contact me again.'

Horace and Omondi stared at Jason, their mouths hanging open. Finally, Omondi looked at Horace and asked, 'What is a *dickwad*?'

Horace ignored this and nodded once. 'You are right, Jason. Our apologies. It is time for the riddles to end. Now that you are here, you are our equal, not our guest, and will be treated as such. The final, vital step begins with a very brief meeting with the head of the Agency. He is already waiting and is looking forward to meeting you.'

'Has he been informed that my tolerance for bullshit is extremely low at the moment?'

'You will receive none from this man,' Omondi stated. 'And from a friend, he had better not receive any from you.'

They closed their doors, and the SUV drove toward the gates of the huge structure at the end of the complex. They opened inward, and they passed through the threshold. Jason's jaw dropped yet again.

A stunningly beautiful scene met his eyes. The street shrunk to one lane, to be surrounded by an exquisite courtyard of bricks and stones of at least ten colours, far larger than he had imagined. Small fountains, streams, and bridges integrated themselves seamlessly into the design, surrounded by trees and small gardens. There were people here as well, some reading on benches, some in intense discussion. But here, everyone who recognized the vehicle stopped what they were doing and strained their necks to catch a glimpse of them and continued to stare long after the SUV had passed. Jason noticed a powerful racial diversity here: Faces of every shape and colour stared into him as they drove by.

'Ninety-six countries are represented in this facility, Jason,' Horace told him.

'You say that like it's on purpose,' Jason replied.

'It is,' Omondi chimed in from the front.

At the very centre of the courtyard, surrounded by a perfect circle of sparkling white stones, was a strange statue, about five feet high. A featureless female figure of simple grey stone lay upon a V-shaped iron pedestal, her hands across her stomach. A brass plaque stood prominently before it, its engraving in enigmatic Swahili.

Omondi's voice came from the front seat.

'This is where our people come to think.'

'What about the people outside?' Jason asked.

'Those were our employees, Jason,' Horace said softly. 'These are our *people.*'

'What's the difference?'

'You, my dear friend, already know far more about this operation than our employees will ever know. Our *people,* on the other hand, have been preparing for this moment for a very long time.'

They finally passed through the courtyard, and after travelling through a simple corridor, Jason found himself in a small, ordinary parking lot at what could only be the back of the complex. They parked a few feet from a dull firedoor.

Horace and Omondi unbuckled and stepped briskly out of the vehicle. Jason followed quickly. Once he had a chance to look around, he was amazed at the sudden ordinariness of his surroundings; other than the barbed-wire fences sixty feet away, the back of this bizarre facility could have passed for the rear end of a crumby strip mall.

'Come with us Jason,' Horace said. 'Our boss – and yours, if you like – is waiting.'

Still refusing to take this seriously, Jason muttered, 'It isn't Morpheus, is it?'

'Who says he is black?' asked Omondi, as he opened the door. Jason just caught view of a small jackal loping carelessly along the outside of the fence as he followed Omondi inside.

They climbed two large flights of stairs, opened another door, and found themselves in a warm, luxurious corridor reminiscent of a classy hotel. To their right was a short enclave with a single door, and at this door the three men came to a stop.

'This will not be painful, Jason,' Horace said kindly. 'Our Head of Operations is, in fact, a very personable man. But he knows much. And he must be the one to approve of you. I know you are agitated, but please be patient for just a little longer.'

Omondi opened the door.

Jason got an instant view of a huge window with a panoramic view of the nearby plains, the skyline of Nairobi distantly visible. Other than that, there was nothing. The creamy walls were devoid of decoration of any kind. The floor was a dull brown hardwood, and there was no furniture to be seen other than a small black office desk.

In a simple grey computer chair sat a thin man with short hair in an ill-fitting white, short-sleeved dress shirt (he was indeed black, Jason saw with a stab of annoyance at Omondi), hunched in concentration at a small laptop. Jason was surprised to see that he didn't look much older than himself.

'Come in, boys,' he said in a carefree tenor voice. He did not look up.

The three of them stepped inside and walked to his desk, Horace and Omondi manoeuvring not so subtly so that Jason was forced to the centre. They stood before the strange man for almost a full minute. Then without warning he closed his laptop with startling speed and looked straight into Jason's eyes.

'You are Jason Simon Roberts.' He had only a faint accent.

'Yes.'

'You are a drama teacher from Central Canada.'

'Yes.'

'And you have a sincere, if not extensive, knowledge of the Second World War.'

'If you must put it that way, yes.'

A sly, playful look flashed across the man's face. 'What do you think of Kenya, good sir?'

'Everyone I've met so far spends too much time asking me questions.'

The man's black eyes widened. A sincere grin appeared on his face.

'A refreshingly brave response! Though of course, you do not yet know anything about me. My name is Mugo. I, along with your friend Omondi here, watched Duni Kimani die.'

Mugo allowed a lengthy pause, apparently expecting this to mean something to Jason. When he got no response, he frowned and looked at the two men standing beside him.

'He doesn't know?'

Horace responded, 'No sir, he doesn't. We were ordered to use discretion until he was approved.'

Mugo grinned in warm satisfaction. 'Discretion *and* common sense, Horace! He is the one! He is the man! I can see it clear as day! Surely you of all people could see it?'

'Yes sir, but–'

'Go, go!' Mugo said with a wave of his hand. 'Begin! You will both be decorated handsomely. Grab the box, tell him everything and begin!'

Horace and Omondi made for the door, Jason close behind. Mugo gave a small chuckle as they left. Jason shook his head in bewilderment. He hadn't even had *time* to get angry...

They made their way down the elegant hallway, which was more than wide enough for the three of them to walk side by side.

'Even by Mugo's standard,' Omondi muttered quietly, 'that was a short meeting.'

Jason glanced at Omondi. For the first time since he had known him, he looked unnerved.

'I've never seen him smile like that.'

Jason turned to Horace and saw him wiping his forehead with a handkerchief.

'All of a sudden,' he said, 'it is time to begin.'

They stopped at an unremarkable door marked *Employees Only*. Omondi unlocked it with shaky hands. He opened the door to reveal a small, very ordinary storage closet. Cardboard boxes lined cheap white shelves. Omondi stepped inside and grabbed a small, unlabelled package, barely a foot square. He stepped out, locked the door again, and they resumed their march. Just as Jason was about to lose his temper yet again, they stopped in front of another door, marked *Room 209*.

'These are your quarters, Jason,' Horace said calmly. 'You will live here for the duration of your stay at the Agency.' He handed Jason a simple key. 'I am in possession of the only other key to this room, and I will use it only in emergencies. Your privacy will be respected.'

Jason sneered. The generally calm ambiance of these new surroundings had reminded him of just how exhausted he was. He fumbled with the key and unlocked the door. 'This had better be damned good.'

And even in his current state, Jason had to admit that it was. A stunning white marble floor greeted him, trimmed with ebony. Tastefully decorated, it was connected to a spacious kitchen on the right, with expensive appliances covering his every need. On the left sat a cozy living room; comfortable white armchairs and couch set up aesthetically around a glass coffee table, two standing lamps already illuminating the painted green walls.

A stunning stereo system stood in the corner, with surround-speakers dotting the corners of every room. Straight ahead jutted a short hallway, presumably to the bed and bath.

Without hesitation, Jason walked to the kitchen and looked in the fridge. A heavenly vision of fruit, chocolate milk, and cheeses met his eyes. He was starving. He grabbed what he wanted, and without looking at his companions, crossed to the living room and made himself comfortable on one of the armchairs.

'Please enjoy,' Omondi growled, 'but understand that the moment has arrived. You have not slept in a day, and we would like to give you the opportunity to do so.'

'Nope,' Jason retorted, his mouth full of grapes. 'This is a nice pad, but it doesn't change anything. Sit your asses down, and tell me why I'm here.'

Horace and Omondi looked at each other in anticipation, as Jason obliviously spread Brie on a cracker. Horace sat next to him on the other armchair; Omondi remained standing.

'To this moment, Jason,' Horace said quietly, 'you astound me. After all you have endured, you are still more concerned about your empty stomach than what we may be about to tell you. You are what we need.'

Jason spared Horace a dismissive glance. 'Heard this shit about fifty times. How about you stop patronizing me and just show me what's inside that scary cardboard box?'

Horace's eyes closed for a moment. Omondi opened the box. A pale green light emanated from it. Omondi took a breath and held it out to him. Horace reached inside and pulled out something small and blue. His palm glowed a bright green. He held his hand out over the table between them, and opened it.

Jason stared, first in incomprehension, then in alarm, and at last, in full-blown horror at the small object which had been placed in front of him. He reached out a shaking hand and touched it. He tried to scream. Nothing came. It was too much. Two days of insanity and twenty-five hours of sleeplessness overtook him, and he lost consciousness.

Horace and Omondi looked down together at Jason's unconscious form.

'I can't believe he lasted this long,' Horace said quietly.

'He is strong,' Omondi concurred. 'How strong remains to be seen. How would you gauge his reaction?'

'Encouragingly natural. At the very least, it will get him some rest.'

'He looked about the same as you when you first saw it.'

'Are you ever going to tell me *your* reaction?'

Omondi did not respond. As one, they moved Jason as carefully as they could to the couch. Horace stretched out his hand to the green glow.

'Leave it,' Omondi said. 'It will make a good first impression when he awakes.'

'What if he destroys it?'

'Even I know that he won't.'

Horace took a small notepad out of his pocket, scribbled a quick note, and left it on the table. With that, the two men left Jason to sleep at last, closing and locking the door behind them.

Chapter Five

Jason's eyes fluttered open in the glare of the morning sun. He started awake as the unfamiliarity of his surroundings attacked him. He took a deep breath, stood up, and walked to the large window in front of him. A lovely view of the stone courtyard lay below him. Mugo's *people* were going about their business, whatever the hell that might be. The enigmatic statue sat in the centre, no one paying it much attention.

Suddenly, a red-hot jab of memory pierced his mind. He turned to the coffee table.

And there it was.

A small, blue disc, about three inches in diameter and shaped like a hockey puck with rounded edges, was hovering unsupported about ten inches from the glass surface. It was motionless; it might as well have been buried in concrete for its complete inertia. It was covered in small, simple, silhouetted drawings of dinosaurs. At the centre of the object was a protruding dome of glass about a centimetre wide, from which a green light, faint in the sun, was emanating unceasingly.

Jason stared down at it in frightened wonder for ten seconds; then, like a caveman entranced by his first sight of fire, drew close to investigate. He examined it from every angle, putting his hands above it, below it, and confirmed that it was not a trick. Finally, he reached out and attempted to move it, and cried out in shock.

The object moved with his lightest touch, with a resistance almost too faint to be detected. But the moment his finger drew away, it stopped dead, and resumed its perfect stillness. Jason doubted it had taken even a millimetre to shed the momentum he had given it.

He moved it more forcefully, and again it stopped on less than a dime. With rising panic, he smacked it, with the same results. Snarling, he reached out, and threw it with all his might across the living room. It seemed to vanish. He looked up, and there it was, hovering ominously, perfectly level with the ground, at the exact point it had left his grasp.

Breathing his panic, he wiped the sweat from his eyes and tried to collect himself. His eyes darted around his apartment, but saw nothing out of the ordinary. Except the small disc, which seemed close to driving him mad. His eyes found a small piece of paper on the coffee table. He snatched it like a snake and read the neat blue cursive:

Good morning Jason.

I imagine you have questions. Please stay calm and come to Room 103, directly beneath you on the first floor. Omondi and I are waiting for you. Bring the disc, if you remember.

H.

Jason closed his fist around the note, grabbed the disc with a snarl, and flew out his door without closing it. He flew down the hallway at top speed and kicked open the firedoor. He took the stairs three at a time and blasted open the door at the bottom, feet away from the dusty frame of the back entrance he had used what seemed like minutes before.

There were people there, some plainly dressed, some in lab-coats, some in business attire. At a shout from someone he had just passed, all of them, in unison, pressed themselves against the walls, avoiding the painful crashes Jason would otherwise have surely caused. He bolted up his newly cleared path, and by pure luck found Room 103. He turned the handle with such force that he winced with pain when it seized, swung it open, and barged inside.

He was in a large lecture hall, six-foot whiteboards hanging throughout, but that was all the detail he took in at that moment. He had eyes only for the four men standing at the opposite end of the room. Horace and Omondi looked up in unison at his loud entrance, a complete lack of surprise in their faces, but they were quickly obscured from view by the gigantic bodies of – he couldn't believe it – Chester and Steve. There was no doubting their intentions this time; they stopped directly in Jason's path, balled their fists, and stuck out their massive chests like territorial apes.

Jason skidded to a stop ten feet away from them, gasping for breath but never looking away. Horace and Omondi strolled to Steve's right and stood facing their hysterical companion, Horace moving closer than Omondi.

'Relax, boys,' he said. 'He means us no harm. Take your time, Jason.'

Jason tried to speak, but could only heave his lungs as he dropped his hands to his knees in a fit of dizziness. Horace stepped forward, but Omondi grabbed his arm. 'Let him,' he said.

Jason stared at the floor, steadied his breathing, and got himself under control. He straightened up, stared with burning eyes at Horace and Omondi, and held out the glowing disc.

'What... in God's name... IS this?'

'It is a novelty hover device,' Omondi replied in his normal rasp.

'What does it do? How did you BUILD it? What... WHAT'S GOING ON??'

'It is a toy, Jason,' Horace said. 'A simple trinket meant to amuse small children. And we didn't build it.'

As if on some invisible cue, Chester took a nearby computer chair and rolled it to Jason, who deflated even as it approached him. He sat down, blasted to exhaustion, and put his face in his trembling hands.

Horace walked up to him and handed him a pill bottle and a glass of water. 'Take these, Jason. Clonazepam. They will calm your nerves.'

Jason opened the bottle, dumped the two orange pills into his hand, and gulped them down.

'After speaking with Mugo last night,' Horace continued, 'we have decided to give you the bulk of our secrets in one blow.'

'Who built it?' Jason whispered.

'We do not know who built it. But we do know that true hover technology was invented in the year 2051 and perfected to the level you have seen by 2060. It is one of several powerful pieces of technology given to us by Duni Kimani.'

Jason's face grew more intense by the second, and he spoke not a word.

'Duni Kimani was a very ordinary Kenyan woman, born in 2080. In 2102, she left her time and travelled to us on February 19, 2017.'

'Bullshit!'

Omondi stepped forward and tossed something to Jason. Jason fumbled it in a panic, but managed to grab hold of it. It was a perfect, purple orb, the size of an orange, and had the same small, glass dome at the top with green light emanating boldly. A small button sat ninety degrees from the glow. Jason pressed it.

The orb sprang open in twenty thousand places. Thin, spindly branches sprouted far thinner ones, and those did the same. In four seconds at most, a small, robotic peacock of countless microscopic gears and ligaments sat on Jason's hand, metallic feathers ruffling, head turning randomly with almost perfect fluidity. It looked Jason in the eye and settled its legs on his hand.

'Robotic technology of this capacity,' Omondi said as he took the terrifying contraption back from Jason, 'is relatively new in Ms. Kimani's time. 2074.'

Jason, mellowed by the chemicals he had ingested, finally found voice. 'How do they work?'

'We do not know, Jason,' Horace said sincerely, 'And we have never bothered to try to find out.'

'Why the hell not?'

'How they work is irrelevant,' Omondi responded. 'What matters is that they exist.'

'A hired hand named Adamu was working in a barley field thirty-eight kilometres south of us,' Horace continued. 'He felt a brief, faint tremor of wind, but didn't think much of it. A few seconds later, however, he heard a terrifying scream, followed by anguished sobs, about one hundred feet behind him. He rushed to investigate and found Duni, collapsed in a heap and in utter hysterics. Any attempt the frightened man made to console her was useless. It wasn't until he turned to rush for the police that she managed one word: 'Stop.'

'After another short time, she managed to compose herself. She refused to answer any questions and insisted that she was not injured. She was plainly dressed and carried an unusually designed, trapezoidal knapsack and a bundle of metal poles. She asked to be taken to Nairobi's city hall. Adamu, who proved to be an immeasurably useful bystander, did so himself. He brought her directly to the front steps of the building and escorted her inside. There, she gained an audience with Omondi here...' Jason's eyes jerked quickly to Omondi, whose face remained passive. '...who until that moment was one of President Kenyatta's upper-level advisors and had been visiting the local government on dull business. She clandestinely handed him the very device you continue to hold, Jason.' He paused, evidently expecting a reaction from Jason. Jason did not bat an eye, merely continued to grip the arms of his chair, waiting like his very breath depended on what Horace might say next. Horace cleared his throat and continued.

'Omondi immediately dropped what he was doing, escorted her out of the building, accosted and enlisted

Adamu, and the three of them were immediately driven to the Parliament House. Adamu, after finally being shown the device, became her unofficial bodyguard and refused to be removed from her sight. President Kenyatta and Deputy President Ruto were summoned; Duni refused point-blank any offers of food, sleep, or medication, although she did accept two shots of vodka. She refused to speak to anyone but Omondi, Adamu, Kenyatta, and Ruto.'

'What does this have to do with me?!' Jason hissed; his face as white as snow.

'Please be patient, Jason. The five of them met privately in a quiet narthex. As Duni relaxed in an armchair, she took on an air of stoicism and revealed the awful truths with which she had been charged.'

Horace turned to Omondi. A meaningful look was exchanged between them. Omondi nodded. Horace turned to Jason and continued.

'Duni revealed that she had been charged with a prototypical time-travel device, one never having been intended for use. She was chosen out of necessity, the strongest of a small group of ordinary minds who had happened to be available on the extremely short notice her people had been given.'

Jason's face grew ever more intense. At a small glance, Chester moved from his comfortable leaning against the wall and stood next to Horace, never looking at Jason.

'Duni was chosen to come to our time, abandoning a crumbling world, to give us, now, a chance for change.'

'A crumbling world?'

'Yes, Jason. A world that was spiralling rapidly and irreversibly into destruction. A race that had lived to see its curtain call.'

'HOW?'

'We do not know,' Omondi murmured. 'Ms. Kimani told us not one detail about her world, other than the fact that it was ending.'

Horace stopped for a moment. He and Omondi stared into Jason's eyes. Jason's fingernails pierced the fabric of his chair.

'A fortuitous set of circumstances and advanced technology,' Horace continued, 'allowed for a powerful makeshift plan to be developed. Several men and women of powerful knowledge and influence were available to give Duni the understanding she needed to bring the necessary tools and information to our time.'

At this point, Omondi passed Jason a small, beautiful object. It was a large jewel of deep red, surrounded by a simple metal frame.

'What is this?' Jason whispered.

'A simple ruby of considerable value,' Omondi replied. With care he handed Jason another glowing object, a bizarre metallic horror with twenty or so pincers, reminding Jason simultaneously of a daddy longlegs and the type bars on a typewriter. A coarse body, about the size of a lemon, lay at their base. Jason held the two objects in his hands. He brought them together... and screaming, dropped them both.

The device sprang to life and snatched hold of the ruby even as it was falling. Unaffected by the impact, its pincers fell upon the jewel and began cutting it into tiny flakes and slivers, each one drawn ruthlessly into the machine's small core. It was the most grotesque thing Jason had ever seen, reminiscent of some slimy sea creature drawing particles of food into its mouth.

In less than a minute, the ruby was consumed, the dull metallic frame completely untouched. After another ninety seconds or so, Jason gaped in wonder as a tiny, shining, crystalline figurine of a dog emerged from the machine with a comical dinging sound, constructed from the tiny pieces of the jewel. A priceless Monopoly piece had been constructed before his eyes from one of the hardest substances on Earth.

'2099.' Horace stated. 'Not yet developed enough to be brought to an aesthetically pleasing appearance. Anything short of a diamond will be brought to the appearance of that figurine.'

Jason was on the verge of tears. 'Why are you showing me this shit?'

'For the same reason Ms. Kimani showed them to me,' Omondi replied with growing intensity. 'So that you will believe what comes next.'

'Why I'm here.' Jason replied.

'Yes, Jason,' Horace droned. 'Please forgive us. There was no way to make this moment both easy and believable.'

'Why am I here?!'

'The objects you have seen were enough for us to decide to take Duni's apocalyptic claims seriously. As an old-fashioned ribbon on the package, she brought flawless replicas of sixteen prominent world newspapers from February 21, two days ahead of schedule. When we asked why she had come, she told us that the means of preventing the world's end had been discovered. But doing so would be up to us.'

There was a moment of shrieking silence. Jason, his head between his knees, spoke again.

'Why do you have to make me hate *every single conversation* we have?'

'You have been shown every piece of technology Duni brought with her, Jason, save one. The most crucial of all.'

Jason's eyes darted to Omondi. He was unlocking a small safe. He opened the door and pulled out an object wrapped in thick burgundy cloth. This time he made no motion toward Jason, and Chester and Steve moved to his sides, glaring at Jason in a wordless warning to keep his distance. Omondi unwrapped the cloth.

An ergonomic, slightly phallic object of grey metal sat in Omondi's open hand. A sturdy black rubber grip went around its middle. Yet again, the green light glowed at the top, but otherwise it could have passed for the handle of an expensive bicycle.

'What is it?' Jason asked. Horace looked distressed for a moment, but spoke quickly.

'It's a time machine, Jason. Or rather, the trigger of it. A prototypical device that will allow a single person to travel up to eighty-five years, three months, and twenty-three days into the past or future, and to any point, anywhere on Earth.'

Jason stared into Horace's eyes with the force of a freight train. Horace met his gaze, all trace of comfort gone.

'You want me...' Jason whispered, 'to travel back in time?'

'Yes.'

'How do I know this isn't bullshit? How do I know you aren't trying to take over the world with all this stuff? How do

I know you're not planning to use me as a guinea pig for your next little toy?'

Horace ignored these accusations.

'Duni told us so painfully little about the end of the world, Jason, but she did tell us that they had identified its singular, irreversible source.'

'WHAT?!'

Horace's eyes hit an intensity Jason had not yet seen.

'World War Two.'

'What *about* World War Two?!'

'We do not know,' Omondi called out. 'Ms. Kimani told us absolutely nothing about the nature of the world's end, other than that its deepest root lay within the unfolding of events of the Second World War in Europe. Only the complete prevention of the European War as we know it could alter the course of history radically enough to prevent the end of life as we know it on this Earth.'

Only the calming effects of the pills he had ingested could have kept Jason from having a complete breakdown. He stood, knees rattling, and took on the alpha-male body language of Chester and Steve at his appearance in the lecture room. He stuck a darting finger at Horace and Omondi.

'Are you telling me... that you want me to go back in time... to...' his voice rose to a scream, 'TO PREVENT WORLD WAR TWO?!!'

Horace met his crazed eyes and nodded.

'Yes, Jason.'

'That is enough,' Omondi said firmly. 'There is no point in going further, Horace. The man is ready to explode. Surely you can see it. He could not absorb more even if you tried.'

Apparently seeing the wisdom in this, Horace stepped up to Jason and put his hand on his shoulder.

'Take time, Jason. As I stated in our first encounter, the choice is yours. You will be forced into nothing. Take a day to enjoy yourself. Our facility is well equipped. Play basketball in the gymnasium. Swim in the pool. Relax and read in the library. Or rest in your quarters and do as you will. But please understand: You are the reason this facility was built. Absolutely everything you do, every smiling face you encounter, has been assembled with the hope of finding a man with half the quality I saw the moment I laid eyes on you.'

Jason said nothing. His pale face turned from Horace's. 'You've ruined my life,' he said and made for the door. Then one question arose out of the haze. He turned.

'What happened to Adamu?'

'Adamu Mugo.'

The voice came from ten feet away and shocked Jason off his feet. He fell flat on his backside to stare up at the gangly form of Mugo, who had appeared in the doorway in the three seconds Jason had been distracted. He was smiling sadly as he looked down at the hapless Jason.

'We may have ruined your life, Jason, or perhaps not. But I do not need Horace's gifts to see your worth. I knew Duni better than anyone who encountered her during her short time here. She told me more than any other. She made her desperate needs more real to me than to Omondi, or even our honourable Prime Minister. You are the one. You have my trust.' His smile brightened, and he turned and left.

There was something in Mugo that neutralized Jason. His smile was warm and genuine; his voice was free and musical.

And, however unthinkable this situation was, to be spoken to with such respect was unexpected and refreshing.

Jason finally remembered himself and climbed to his feet. Horace and Omondi walked to either side of him, exchanging looks of quiet shock.

'You have brought something out in him that even we had no idea was there, Jason. Mugo is normally the most solemn man I have ever known.'

'Right,' Jason muttered. 'I'm honoured. Now leave me alone.'

'When you are ready to learn more,' Omondi said, 'ask one of our people to direct you to our shared office. We will continue at your discretion.'

Jason stepped out of the lecture room at last and found his way back to his room. Everyone he passed avoided his eyes.

Five minutes later, Jason was closing and locking the door of his quarters. He stood in his lovely foyer and for ten minutes attempted to come to grips with the absolute destruction that had been wrought on everything he knew.

He walked to his new living room, sat down in an armchair, deciphered the TV and put Monty Python on Netflix. Not really absorbing it, it was at least somewhat therapeutic to give his senses something familiar.

Too many questions. Time travel. The end of the world. Alone. Jason liked solitude, but the sense of desolate isolation that had swept over him was more terrifying than any stabbing revelation those bastards had just thrust upon him.

Suddenly, Jason was jolted out of his comfortable chair by a polite knock at the door. Jason considered for a moment, and then answered it. A young Asian woman, not possibly twenty and wearing a white chef's jacket, met him with a smile. She was holding a huge platter of steaming food, and the powerful aroma of chicken, shrimp, rice, and vegetables attacked him even as she beamed at him.

'Please enjoy, Mr. Roberts,' she said kindly. 'We are happy that you are here.'

Jason took the platter. He did not return her smile, but this did not faze the girl. She nodded once and stepped lightly away.

Jason moved quickly, but noticed that a simple room service sign had been placed on his doorknob. He turned it over to read ***Do Not Disturb***. Somehow, he knew that would be enough.

He closed the door and locked it. He drew the curtains on his large window and sat down at the table, the huge TV still yammering in the living room.

The sumptuous meal calmed him far more than those stupid orange pills. The monstrous tray was empty in ten minutes. Jason leaned and cracked his back, more relaxed, he reflected, than he had been since he left his home. He thought things over, examining the lunacy that had dominated the eternity of the last two days of his life.

He was in Kenya. He was in a top-secret government facility constructed for him. He had been assaulted with a 'mission' so unthinkable that he had not yet begun to try to wrap his mind around it. Yet a delicious meal and some quiet solitude in a luxury apartment (of sorts) had been enough to give him the quiet of mind to reflect on the whole damned thing. It was, for lack of a better word, *interesting*.

He stood up, strolled to his new living room, and relaxed on the couch. He even managed to chuckle a few times as the

Argument Clinic sketch played out. Even as he found comfort in this tiny touch of familiarity, he also found strength in the ultimate principle by which he had lived his life since his Dad had died: Don't take anything too seriously. Laugh at the things people take to the streets over. Enjoy yourself.

On a sudden impulse, Jason stood up, walked to the door of his quarters, and opened it. A greying, middle-aged man in a simple long-sleeved shirt approached to his right. He stopped in shock upon seeing Jason. The plain fact that everyone in this whole damned place clearly knew him by sight did not faze Jason.

'Can you tell me where I might find the library in this place?' he asked.

The man recovered himself. 'Other side of the facility. Room 134. Shortest way is across the Sanctuary. Green door, straight that way.'

Jason thanked the man and found his way out into the gorgeous stone plaza, which, he now realized, he was anxious to see.

Two croton trees rose twenty-five metres on either side of the white stone pathway before him, shading him from the intense heat of the sun. Simple shrubs dotted the pathway, which curved forty feet ahead before splitting into three, each one meandering where it pleased. A plump blonde woman sat reading on a shady bench. She looked up and smiled at Jason, then returned to her book.

Jason walked out of the shade and into the open courtyard. The path to the right turned to beige and climbed up a small hill near the corner of the building. Jason climbed it and surveyed the huge, Shire-like sanctuary. He had never seen anything so lovely.

The statue at the centre yet again caught his eye. The library now forgotten, he walked purposefully up to it.

The life-size female figure lying upon it could only represent Duni Kimani, but it was by far the most rudimentary feature of the courtyard – a rough, flawed, featureless form of a woman at lifeless peace. The pedestal upon which she lay was made of iron, angled to create a simple, inverted hexagonal pyramid. At last, his eyes fell to the plaque at his feet. Made of simple polished wood, a shining ebony plate was carefully fastened to it. In simple lettering were engraved the same six lines of mysterious Swahili.

'We call this place *Shwari Mawe.*'

Jason turned to his right, and there, ten feet away, was the same teenager who had brought him his lunch. Her long, lovely black hair shone in the sun, and her sparkling eyes looked affectionately up into Jason's.

'It means *Calm Stones,*' she added.

'Why was it built?' Jason asked.

'It was built for this moment.'

'What about this moment?'

'It was built for everyone who works here, when they need this moment. A moment to pause and find peace, away from the troubles of our duties.'

Jason reflected on this. 'I suppose you people need this place a lot.'

She nodded. 'You will, too.'

Jason liked the girl. He held out his hand and introduced himself. She smiled as she took it.

'I know who you are, Jason, and it is an honour. My name is Vickie Phan. A fellow Canadian, actually. I lived in Calgary until sixteen months ago.'

Jason smiled, scarcely believing he was doing so. They stood together for a moment, their backs to the statue, taking in the serenity around them.

'Horace thinks the world of you,' Vickie said. 'I overheard his conversation with my supervisor. He said there would be hell to pay if your meal wasn't cooked properly. Very out of character for Horace.'

Jason brushed this off with a shake of his head. 'Where in the hell is he from, anyway?'

'Flatbush, in New York City. He decided to lose the accent when he went to school.'

Jason turned to gape at Vickie. 'Horace is from *Flatbush?*'

Vickie nodded, biting her lip mischievously.

'Like *Bugs Bunny?!*'

'Like Bugs Bunny!'

They laughed uproariously together. More than the pills, more than the food, this good belly laugh brought Jason down to Earth at last.

'My break's over,' Vickie said. 'It was wonderful to speak to you, Jason.'

With that, she headed toward the door he had used. Jason called out his last question.

'What does the engraving mean?'

Vickie turned and smiled once more. 'That's a question for Omondi, Jason.' She opened the green door and disappeared.

Jason turned again to the simple statue. He reflected for a few minutes, when suddenly, inexplicably and like an explosion, the avalanche of the last two days aligned like music and made sense. A dam seemed to burst in his mind and ten thousand thoughts and emotions flowed through him.

Without looking back, Jason followed Vickie into the facility. He asked his way to the heart of the building, and kicked open an office door. Startled almost off their feet, Horace and Omondi turned from their discussion.

Jason stepped inside. Without any pretense or preamble, he met their eyes boldly.

'What do you want me to do?'

Horace read Jason's face for a moment. Then he shot a look of triumph at Omondi.

'Come with us, Jason.'

The three of them marched out the door and turned in a direction Jason had not yet explored.

His life as he knew it was over.

Part Two

Chapter Six

Jason sat in a firm but comfortable brown armchair. A strange mixture of leisure and academia surrounded him. The room was about thirty-foot square, painted in a simple royal blue. Three matching armchairs made a triangle in the far-left corner of the room. A huge screen dominated the wall on Jason's right, reminiscent of an Orwellian telescreen. The rest of the room was crowded with simple folding tables with papers, maps, food, and a single state-of-the-art computer. On a separate table against the far wall, sat the hover disc, the robotic peacock, and the gruesome gem-eater, the blue wall illuminated by the combined green light that emanated from the three of them.

The walls were the worst part. Posters of Pink Floyd, Benedict Cumberbatch, Denzel Washington, James Stewart, Rachel Weisz, Billie Holiday, Marlon Brando, Hunter S. Thompson, and several more of Jason's favourite cultural icons hung everywhere. How they had managed to impeccably discern Jason's heroes, Jason reflected, seemed a minor issue at this point. Horace and Omondi remained standing.

'This,' Horace announced melodramatically, 'is our study. This is where the bulk of your preparation will take place.'

'Alright,' Jason rumbled, 'that's enough. Preparation for *what?*'

'That is precisely the first thing you will learn, Jason.' Now that Horace had seen the new determination in Jason's face, he was speaking to him for the first time as an equal.

'Duni travelled the furthest back the prototypical technology at her disposal would allow, in order that you, Jason, could do the same and complete the great task that she brought with her.'

Jason shook his head as light dawned in his mind.

'Two skips of a stone.'

Horace nodded.

'You will be travelling to London, England in 1935 to complete the task Duni assigned to us.'

'What?'

Horace frowned. 'What do you mean *what?*'

'Why not Germany? Isn't this about killing Hitler? Because if that's what this is leading to, you can count me out. I'm no assassin.'

'A fair statement, Jason, but we are not looking for an assassin.'

'Why not? Seems like a simple fix, to me.'

'One man's death,' Omondi said, 'even that of Hitler, is not sufficient. Ms. Kimani made that quite clear.'

'Even Hitler was not as gigantic as the fearsome powder keg that was post-Versailles Europe, Jason,' Horace stated grimly. 'Could you travel far enough with the technology at our disposal, Versailles is where we would be sending you.'

Jason nodded. He knew it was true.

'Well then, for God's sake, what am I supposed to *do?*'

Horace looked at Omondi, and at last, they sat down; Horace at his left, Omondi at his right.

'One man's death,' Horace said, 'will not suffice. But you, my friend, have the unparalleled potential to fulfill Churchill's vision of a world at peace without a shot being fired.'

Jason stared laser beams into Horace's eyes. 'How?'

Horace gazed at Jason for a moment, and then responded.

'This brings us back to the *utter perfection*, Jason, which I have seen in you all along. As an expert in the dramatic, you will have the ability to read your audience – a vital skill for what we require – and a powerful taste for the theatrical. And as a self-appointed student of Second World War history, you already have a passion (hard to come by these days) for the battleground into which we wish to drop you. A head start beyond our wildest dreams. Finally, as dear Omondi has said, you have *star quality*. Never did we begin to hope that we would find a man with the presence, confidence, and charisma that you have, Jason.'

'Why do you need all this crap in a History teacher?'

'Because of the nature of your role and the jaded, indifferent audience you will be teaching.'

'And who would that be?'

Horace's mouth curled in a strange grin.

'The British House of Commons, Jason. You will be teaching history to the very men who helped make it.'

Jason, already a new man through and through, felt a fantastic rush.

'Cool.'

The closest thing to a smile Jason had yet seen flashed across Omondi's face.

'Your mission, in a nutshell, will be to present a dramatic description of the death and horror that lies at their doorstep; to rouse decisive, pre-emptive military action against the festering threat of fascism that will otherwise devastate the world, and ultimately, 167 years later, consume it entirely.'

'So you're telling me, in a nutshell, that preventing WORLD WAR TWO is a means to an *end?!'*

'It is many things, Jason. It is the beautiful beginning of a new path for humanity. It is the end of the imminent threat of our utter extinction. And in and of itself, there can be no greater good.'

'But why me? How did you end up in Canada? Why did you travel halfway around the world to happen to land in the Niagara Region?'

Horace's eyes twinkled.

'On Duni's orders, Jason. It was agreed that a foreigner would have the most compelling effect as a messenger from the future, and Canada was the first place she suggested we start.'

'Why not a Kenyan?'

Omondi spoke up. 'Duni herself insisted that it must be a white man.'

'Why?'

Omondi's eyebrows contracted. 'You will be speaking to British politicians in the nineteen-thirties. Even had Ms. Kimani not given the order, who else would we send?'

Jason let this pass him by. 'Why not the States?'

'Duni clearly had clear thinkers working with her,' Horace continued. 'Canada has close historical ties with Great Britain that the US does not have.'

'So?'

'Canada was an ideal place to look for a man with at least a rudimentary understanding of British history and culture. Your accent will add a touch of otherworldliness to the people you encounter, a powerful finishing touch to the perimeter of your mission. Finally, a bond of cultural affection was likely to be found in Canada that could not be found in other former regions of the British Empire. Tremendous friendship and understanding still exist between Britain and Canada, both today and in 1935, far more so than in the US. In short, Jason, all the pieces fit.'

Jason nodded.

'Your preparation will consist primarily of three classes.'

'Classes?'

'Yes, classes,' Omondi said. 'The first will be a simple course on the history of World War Two. You will cover much, but most especially the areas necessary to make the appropriate impact on your audience.'

'I have to study the subject you brought me here for?'

'History is no longer a hobby for you,' Omondi replied. 'It is your major. You will be studying the Second War as if the fate of the world depended on it. Because it does.'

'And who will be teaching me?'

Omondi looked down upon him, another faint smile touching his lips.

'I will.'

Jason could not prevent a visible deflation in his shoulders.

'Why you, Omondi?'

'As I said at the airport, Jason,' Horace chimed in, 'Omondi is an unparalleled expert in World War Two history.'

'How long have you been studying it?' Jason demanded.

Omondi looked down his nose at him.

'Three years, eleven months, and eighteen days.'

Seeing the bewildered look on Jason's face, Horace stepped in.

'Once our plan was set in stone, Omondi began an obsessive study of the Second World War. It very nearly consumed him.'

Jason shook his head. 'I still don't see how less than four years of study could make someone the world's foremost expert on *anything.'*

'Omondi possesses total recall. He does not forget anything he reads.'

'Does EVERYONE here have a superpower?'

Horace smiled. 'Everyone that matters, Jason. Anyway. Your second class will be titled Application of Dramatic Understanding. It will be taught by a woman from England whom you have not yet met. Her job will be to orient your considerable dramatic prowess to fit the culture and environment to which you are being sent.'

Jason scoffed. 'I already know to drink tea with my pinky out.'

'A good start, Jason. But we must be sure that you are capable of integrating yourself into a British culture so very different from your own. One wrong move could destroy your chances.'

Jason brushed this off. 'And the third?'

'The third is an unprecedented course, the construction of which was completed a mere eight months ago. It is titled Ethics of Time Travel, and will be taught by myself. It will outline what you must do, and what you must NOT do, as a man engulfed in the constant moral dilemma of existing in a world more than eighty years in the past, which you have invaded.'

Jason said nothing. Of all the craziness sent his way, this made the most sense. He raised no questions and instead altered the course of the conversation to the greatest of all subjects. 'How do I get back?'

Horace's head gave a small jerk. Jason did not miss the muffled turn in Omondi's direction. He stared at Jason stonily for a moment, and then finally spoke.

'We don't precisely know, Jason.'

The placid calm Jason had acquired took a stabbing blow at this one. *'What?'*

'The device you will be using has been pre-programmed for one jump into the past. It will then be useless scrap.'

'So I'm supposed to go back to 1935, change history, and then rot there for my trouble?'

'Although Duni assured us that your return would be possible, she refused to tell us anything about the nature of doing so. She merely said, 'When the task is completed, the way home will present itself.'

Jason's teeth grew steadily more visible. 'So if I fail, I'm stuck forever on the bad side of the Second World War?'

Horace nodded. 'According to Duni, the way home would not be made clear until the war was irrevocably prevented.'

'How on Earth would it be *possible* to get back?! If I prevent the war, then that would alter time so massively that there would be nothing I love to come back to! Right?!'

Horace shook his head. 'The technology, as Duni put it, *hovers* over Time. Wherever you go, whatever you do, when you return, you will return to the present as you know it, albeit a corresponding amount of time later.'

A sigh of relief was interrupted by a bad jolt. 'Wait... then how do we save the world in our time?'

'We don't.'

Jason's gut seemed to contract in slow motion. 'We don't?'

Horace's face remained calm. 'Our time, our world, is doomed, Jason. Nothing within our power can change that. Duni made that clear. The three of us will live long and fruitful lives and die peacefully, but there are millions of children alive right now who will live to see the end of mankind. It is as certain as the sunset.'

Jason closed his eyes and fought for breath. His mind was flooded with existential darkness. He thought of his sisters' children. He thought of his own life. He thought of the beautiful ambitions of billions of people. He thought of ten thousand years of human history that were headed straight off a cliff.

'In reality, I'm saving another world.'

Horace nodded. 'More or less.'

Jason began to snarl. 'Do you realize how much you're hitting me with? How much you're *asking* of me?!'

'It is impossible to overstate how much we are asking of you, Jason. If you accept this mission you will, for all intents and purposes, die twice.'

'And I assume there's some stupid security clause that prevents me from speaking to anyone I care about while I'm here?'

Horace nodded. 'That is the policy. The complications will be dealt with. However, we have decided to relax it in favour of your dear Miss Ellesworth, back in Canada.'

Jason started. *'Markie?!'*

Horace nodded with a small smile.

Jason stared open-mouthed at the two of them. 'But... she's an acidhead!'

'She has graciously agreed to curtail her... hallucinogenic activities in order to keep you company during your training.'

'No, no,' Jason snapped, 'I mean, you're going to trust the darkest secrets in the world to... to *Markie?!*'

'Miss Ellesworth is a remarkable young woman, Jason. I saw it in her as instantly as in you. She is powerful, courageous, and *exceptionally* difficult to read. Rarely has a fifteen-minute conversation taught me so little about anyone. She will be invaluable to you.'

'How will we be contacting each other?' Jason asked.

'State of the art video chat, Jason. A private room has been set up with the finest technology available, three doors down from your quarters. And,' he finished with a smile, 'unless I'm mistaken, she is connected there now, waiting for you. Room 212A.'

Jason stared for a moment and then bolted without another look at either of them. He found his way to Room

212A, opened the unlocked door, and there, on a large screen atop a hardwood desk, was Markie.

'So you're a time-traveller now,' she said with a sarcastic half-smile. 'Big man. I travel in time three nights a week.'

Jason deflated in joyous relief with the sound of a zooming balloon. He shut the door and collapsed in the expensive chair in front of him. Markie abandoned her smirk and smiled genuinely, her crooked left canine a more welcome familiarity than if they had airdropped his own home onto the roof.

'Jason, how the hell do you do these things to yourself? You were supposed to go on safari.'

'You convinced me to go, you dumbass,' Jason snapped, his joy suddenly forgotten. 'I've still got the bruise, remember?'

'Life is about more than humdrum routine, Jason, but less than travelling back in time to prevent a World War.'

Jason chuckled, then started in wonder. 'Wait... you didn't know all along?!'

Markie laughed, a dismissive 'no' on her lips. 'They told me everything last night. Some fruitcake showed up at my door with an open laptop, with Horace's face already glaring at me. Set me up with unlimited high-speed, and I guess this thing is mine now. Horace blabbed on and on; the guy's more dramatic than you are. End of the world, time travel, my best friend being the last great hope for mankind… pretty heavy shit.'

'Pretty heavy shit,' Jason repeated with a shake of his head.

'I saw those gadgets of theirs too… that gem-eater is a bad trip in and of itself.'

Jason snorted. 'Try holding the damn thing as it works…'

'Did you like the posters in your study? I had a hand in that.'

'There is ZERO surprise in me at that,' Jason said with a smile. 'Thank you, Markie.'

She nodded once, like the Queen of England. 'I told Horace you like Bo Grumpus, but he said they couldn't find the poster.'

'Who the hell is Bo Grumpus?'

Indignity flashed over Markie's face. 'I play them all the time, asshole.'

Jason sighed in exasperation, a familiar enough feeling when dealing with Markie that the fact itself brought a belly laugh out of him. Only her...

'I'm proud of you, Jason.'

Jason's eyebrows raised. She didn't say things like that often.

'I always saw something special in you, and not just when I was tripping. Nobody gets us. Who would expect a charismatic hippie chick and a square like you to work so well together?' Jason raised an eyebrow, but let her continue. 'But right from the start, I knew that I needed to stick with you. That you were meant for something and that you were going to need me. I saw it in the cards. I saw it in the ether, in your aura. And now I get to be your knight in shining armour whenever the vibes get bad. It's... pretty cool.'

The beads in her hair shone in the quiet light beside her. She looked into his face and leaned in close. 'You need a shower, Jason.'

Jason grasped at his greasy brown hair. She smiled again.

'Are you ever not going to fall for that?'

'I damned well do need a shower, more than ever in my life. But I thought I'd wait for your blessing. Pour me some

Glenlivet and mail it to me. I should be out by the time it gets here.'

Markie rolled her eyes. 'There are other whiskies, you know.'

'No, there aren't,' Jason replied. 'How's your mum?'

'I don't know. I never know, you know that. She asked about you yesterday, though. You're my only hope, as far as she's concerned.'

'She still thinks so, eh? Apart from getting you off the hook with the cops, I wouldn't change a thing about you if I could.'

Markie scowled. 'That happened *twice*, and I have made my eternal gratitude clear.'

Jason smiled. 'Yes, for about as many years as you would have gotten if I hadn't been there.'

In the rarest of moments, Jason had scored a point. Markie shook her head and said nothing. Jason smirked, but let the moment pass.

'Anyway,' he said, 'Sinatra beats Crosby.'

Markie bared her teeth. 'If I hear you say that *one more time...'*

The conversation sprouted wings, and within moments they were off, jabbing at each other over everything from the greatest meme of all time to the proper way to cook a steak. Jason poured his heart into the conversation, sparing a corner of his mind for the quiet gratitude he felt for Horace. Jason lost all track of time until, at last, a firm knock came at the door.

'Jason,' came Horace's voice, 'it's getting late, and there are a couple more things we must discuss.' Then silence.

Jason turned back to Markie, who shrugged with a sad smile. 'Get to it, soldier.'

Jason returned her smile. A powerful peace, which he knew sadly wouldn't last ten minutes, had settled upon him. He nodded to her. She cocked her head slightly, moved her arm, and vanished.

Jason stood and opened the door of his small comms room. Horace and Omondi were waiting. A small, hinged wooden box was in Horace's hand. Before they could speak, Jason laid out his new ultimatum.

'I'm in. I'll do it. But on one condition: Markie is mine. From here on out, she speaks only to me, and in private. If I find out that you are speaking to her at all, or that we're being monitored, or any other garbage like that, I'm done. I know how much you guys like to snoop into my life, and if I find out that you're invading my relationship with *her...'* Horace raised a hand gently.

'Calm down, Jason. You are absolutely right. Your privacy will be respected to the utmost.'

'However,' Omondi added, 'there are conditions on our side, as well.'

'Such as?'

'Many things will be asked of you here,' Omondi continued, 'and you must not refuse even one of them. Billions of dollars, hundreds of minds, and thousands of hours have been invested into preparing you properly for the task you are about to undertake, so that you do not suffer the same fate as Duni Kimani.'

A chill settled in Jason's stomach. 'How did she die?'

Omondi's eyes caught fire, but his voice remained calm. 'After giving us the information we needed, she sent Kenyatta and Ruto out of the room. Then, as Mugo and I watched, she pulled a pistol out of her pack, put it to her head, and shot herself.'

Even as Jason's jaw clenched in horror, Horace held the box out to Jason. He opened it, and there sat a very ordinary .38 caliber revolver. He picked it up, wordlessly asking why he was holding someone's suicide weapon. Horace gestured to it with a nod of his head, looking close to tears. Jason examined it, and found an engraving on the shaft. Its detail was impossibly intricate, decorated with detailed images of heartbreaking pain, each only a few millimetres in diameter. At their centre, in a deep, flowing script barely thicker than a human hair, Jason was frustrated to find the same six lines of Swahili staring at him again.

'What does it MEAN?!' he snarled.

'Poetically translated,' Omondi whispered, 'it reads:

Two skips of a stone
Do not dare make it three
After your sad goodbyes
The song goes on
To where it began
Where the green light dies.'

Jason looked up at Omondi. His eyes were glossy. Jason almost shrunk away under the intensity of the man's gaze.

'You must not fail. Not one minute goes by where I do not see Duni's body fall to the ground. My heart breaks for her, and for humanity, a hundred times a day. I see now what Horace has seen in you all along. You are what we need. But you *MUST NOT FAIL.*'

And with that, he stalked away.

Blasted to his core, Jason watched him go, then turned to Horace, who was still looking down the empty hallway.

'He's my hero,' he said.

Jason said nothing. Yet another level of enormity had been breached in his mind.

Horace turned to Jason and smiled. 'Take it easy, Jason. You'll have some fun yet. For now, relax and get some rest.'

He turned and picked up another package from the floor that Jason had not noticed, a long, plain paper bag, and handed it carefully to Jason.

'A gift. Ms. Ellesworth gave us the idea. We trust you'll use it responsibly. Goodnight, Jason.' He left without another word.

Jason stepped into his apartment, locking the door. He was finally coming to terms with the emotional roller coaster that he knew his life would henceforth be. He sat in his recliner and reflected. He thought of Chelsey. He thought of his family. He thought most of all of Markie. He shrugged and opened the bag.

Inside was a beautifully contoured bottle of golden liquid, the like of which Jason had never seen. He found the label.

Glenlivet 50. He was holding half his yearly salary in his hands.

His jaw dropped halfway to the ground, his eyes savouring the treasure they had given him. He found a glass, poured a small shot, and drank it eagerly.

Never, in all his life, had he tasted anything half so good.

He put the bottle in the back of the cupboard above the stove, a smile on his face. He laughed once at the strange life he had led, and at last, went down the short hallway to his new bedroom. It was predictably gorgeous, but he had eyes only for the queen-size bed in front of him. He stripped to his boxers, crawled into his newest luxury, and for reasons he didn't understand, said a short prayer to whatever might be listening. He closed his eyes and was asleep in three seconds.

Chapter Seven

Jason's eyes popped open and his body jerked into a ninety-degree angle like a catapult. A blaring low-frequency sound was reverberating through his quarters like a rising tide in the Bay of Fundy. His mind centred into focus just as the hideous sound ceased. With infuriating promptness, there was a firm knock at the door. Jason looked at the clock on the wall. It was 6:30 a.m.

Wanting to scream, Jason put his pants on and stomped to the door. He opened it and took a breath, ready to howl his fury at whoever might be on the other side. Then he deflated. It was Vickie. She was holding a platter of eggs, sausage, Canadian bacon, toast, and homefries, and smiling up at him.

'Hello, Jason!' she said brightly. 'Sorry to bother you. Horace and Omondi sent me.'

'What are you, Vickie? A sweet little spy?' Jason growled. Only her youth could have kept him from shouting at her. Her smile did not diminish.

'No, Jason, I promise. I volunteered. I didn't have much competition, actually. I was told to tell you that you should go to room 100 after you've finished your breakfast. It's a gym, actually.

'A gym?'

'Yep. It's KRA policy that everyone goes there. I go three times a week.'

Jason rolled his eyes and took his sumptuous breakfast. How, he wondered, had this girl managed to neutralize his outrage with only a few sentences?

'Well,' she finished, 'I'll see you later, Jason! Take it easy at first. I couldn't move for days after my first round.'

Vickie smiled once more and stepped lightly away. Jason glanced after her, smiling dismissively, then shut his door.

He turned on his radio and ate his breakfast quickly. He was done with any illusions: He liked this. He liked his luxury apartment; he liked the strange attention he was getting. He liked the craziness. Markie was right, goddamn it: He *had* been in a rut. This was the life. Whatever insanity awaited him in the future – in the past – seemed like peanuts right now.

He hadn't taken a shower! Jason stood as if pulled up by puppet strings and marched to the bathroom. He had taken an absent-minded leak last night, but this was his first real view of the thing. Walls of gentle peach; a gigantic tub stood to his left and a beautiful granite sink to his right. He looked straight ahead and jerked back in shock; a poster of a nude Frank Zappa playing guitar on a toilet overlooked his own high-tech throne. Jason bowed his head and smiled at the continued conspiracy Markie was involved in.

After the most magnificent shower he had ever taken, he found a comfortable t-shirt and gym-shorts in his dresser, grabbed a towel, and made his way to Room 100.

He was barely through the door when he was accosted by a truly gargantuan South Korean named Joonheong, who proceeded to plow Jason through an hour and a half of light weight-lifting, calisthenics, and cardio, the intensity of which Jason would not have believed himself capable. He hadn't worked out in years, and it felt good. He could have done without the not-so-subtle stares in his direction from his fellow fitness-freaks, though, and the omnipresent radio-station featuring the likes of Abba, Lionel Richie, and the Backstreet Boys was downright creepy.

After a second shower and a thick, repulsive protein shake, Joonheong directed Jason to the office building outside the complex. When asked why, the great ape simply told him it was, 'Register and security for you to do.'

Muttering to himself, he passed through a small portion of Shwari Mawe, and the gate at the front of the complex opened just wide enough for him to squeeze through. He was unsurprised at the clanging behind him.

A strange feeling settled over Jason as he sauntered down the pristine street, seeing it clearly for the first time. He had eyes only for the KRA *employees*, ordinary Kenyans without the slightest idea of what unthinkable truths lay at their doorstep. What these people did did not concern Jason; some of them were Vickie's age; many would live to see the green light gleaming out of the prophetic innovations he had been shown. Some of them might even live to 2102. And then they would die.

Doing his best to let these thoughts pass over him, Jason found his way to the same damned bureaucratic hub that had so infuriated him the day before last. He entered the reception room and was directed to a 300-pound Kenyan man with dull hair, his breathing rapid and heavy. Clearly the workout regime did not apply to the employees. The man led him through one final round of admittedly useful questions, including blood type, allergies, and all the other boring trivium Jason was fed up with. After an hour and a half, he was cleared to go, and he stalked through the door, vowing never to enter it again.

As he stepped out, a man about his own age chased him down and gave him a clearance card, which would allow him back into the KRA complex. Jason obliged without hesitation.

As the iron gate closed behind him, the still-unexplored complex was forgotten; he had eyes only for Shwari Mawe. The humble hill from which he had first surveyed it stood to his left. A simple but lovely stone fountain stood to his right. The moss-covered quartz walkway beneath his feet led him eastward, and he followed it, passing dark stone statues of beautiful melancholia and flowerbeds with blossoms he had never imagined. He found the door to the library, a far more elaborate door than any he had yet seen. It was trimmed with a faded brown wood which matched the decor of the perimeter of the sanctuary, which grew steadily more intricate as it extended into the centre, where a carefully carved flame like that of a candle dominated the lower half.

Jason admired the door for a moment, then made his way inside the library. Marvelling at its quaint beauty, Jason browsed the shelves in the English section and found a copy of Robert Frost's poems. Even Markie didn't know his love of poetry.

He found the nearest bench and sat down, cracking his back as he did so. The shade of the nearest tree completed his comfort, and he spent two hours reading the small volume from cover to cover, from 'Blueberries' to 'The Gift Outright', forgetting the immense worries of a world that was working with all its might to crush him like a Coke can.

He looked into the sunlight creeping through the leaves. What was he doing here? How was it possible that this surreal, sandblasted loony bin, half a world away from all he knew, was already starting to feel like home? His family, his friends, even shitty old Linda Recketauer had been shoved aside to allow this uppercut of the unfamiliar to knock him flat on his back, only to help him up as a new man, ready to stare the end of the world in the face.

Jason stood, surveying the beauty around him one more time, and then, like the introvert he was, found his way back to his quarters, smiling at everyone he encountered. He had no idea how long this lack of responsibility was going to last, but he meant to enjoy it. Feeling too lazy to cook, he grabbed what he liked from the fridge and a hunk of Italian bread, and feasted in silence.

Half an hour later, as his mind struggled under the heavy yoke of his digestive system, there was another knock at the door. With a lighthearted roll of his eyes, Jason answered it. To his pleasure, it was Vickie yet again.

'Hi Jason!' she said once more. All cares neutralized, Jason smiled at her.

'Hi Vickie. Horace sent you, I'm assuming?' She grinned.

'This time, yes, actually. He said to ask you to come to the office you kicked down the door of, whenever you feel like it. He said to tell you...' she pulled out a small piece of paper and read carefully, '...that your next assignment will be utterly devoid of any apocalyptic nonsense.'

Jason melted at Vickie's adorable sincerity.

'Well, Vickie,' he stated with mock diplomacy, 'you can tell the good doctor that I will join him at said office within the hour.'

Vickie returned his nod, clearly fighting back a smile. 'Thank you for your cooperation, O Hero of Time. This finishes our discussion.'

They exchanged one more affectionate grin, and she stepped away. Jason watched her go, and then shook his head.

'Hero of Time...'

Jason stood alone in his marble lobby (a fairly useless room, now that he thought of it) and thought things through. At last, he shrugged and decided there was no use in waiting. He left his quarters, turned back with a curse to close and lock the door, and found his way to Horace and Omondi's office. He thought a polite knock would be best at this point.

The door opened slowly, and Omondi appeared. Horace was not there. Omondi stepped aside, his face as neutral as ever, and Jason walked in. Closing the door, Omondi spoke in his normal deadpan rasp.

'Today you have a chance to blow off some steam, while at the same time learning what we trust will be a valuable lesson.'

'Great to see you too, old man.'

Omondi scowled and handed Jason a large wad of cash.

'Forty-five hundred Kenyan shillings,' he said flatly. 'Enough for a decent meal and some modest personal spending.'

'Spending where? Where am I going?'

'Nairobi.'

Jason stared, nonplussed.

'Where in Nairobi?'

'Anywhere you like,' Omondi replied, his voice losing some of its usual edge. 'You will be dropped off in the heart of the city's commercial district and spend the day there. Explore, and enjoy yourself.'

Jason, for once, liked what he was hearing. 'Who's coming with me?'

'No one. You are going alone. You are being thrust into a chaotic and unfamiliar world by yourself. That is part of the lesson you will learn. Sorely needed, according to our background checks.'

Ignoring Omondi's continuing bluntness, Jason pursued. 'And what is the other part?'

'The experience of being a minority,' Omondi replied. 'There are very few white people in Nairobi. It will open your eyes in a much-needed way.'

'I don't see how.'

The look Omondi gave him said many things.

'It is impossible to describe the experience of being different and unusual, but it will hit you like a bomb. And the moment you pull that trigger, you will be a minority of one.'

Without giving Jason time to reflect, Omondi opened the office door.

'Steve will meet you at the back exit in fifteen minutes. Stay away from the slums; you would not like them. Spend how you will, but we leave it to your good judgement not to return with anything stupid.'

Jason stood, and made for the door. As often as he wanted to punch Omondi, he was nonetheless fascinated by the man. Finally, a thought occurred to him, and he turned.

'*Where the green light dies.* What does that mean?'

'We will never know for sure,' Omondi replied. 'Perhaps the technology plays a part in the end of the world. Perhaps it is a metaphor for the past. Or it could simply refer to the single charge of your travel device. Perhaps all three or something else. In any case, do not be distracted by riddles.'

Steaming with the irony, Jason stormed out of the office without another word.

After another terrifying and silent jaunt (Steve was as unresponsive as Chester had been), Jason stepped out onto Tom Mboya Street, the blinding heat again forgotten. The small Hyundai sped off, earning several blaring horns. Jason adjusted his sunglasses and stared in wonder, as he at last got his first good glimpse of the City of the Sun.

He had seen New York at fifteen, and though this was smaller, it was an entirely different animal. Its design was ferocious, instinctive, with relatively small buildings that stood guard for the mighty skyscrapers towering a few blocks away.

Small groups of people moved past him, some giving him a second glance. An old radio, an unused cassette deck glaring at him, blared Kenyan hiphop in the hands of a passing man in a red tracksuit. Humble green gardens surrounded him, a quaint green Eden from which the mighty fortress beckoned. Jason walked.

Twenty-five minutes later, the fertility of his starting point was obliterated. Towering buildings seemed to reach for him, and throngs of people made an obstacle course the like of which he had never known.

African faces glanced at him continuously. More than one young child stopped and pointed, cooing primitive Swahili to their parents. Perhaps twice since his landing had he seen a white face. Jason attempted to brush it off, but it was useless. The first aspect of this soiree that really sunk in was that Omondi was right: Being a minority was a profound and powerful experience.

Vendors selling trinkets stood twenty feet from upper-class jewellers and craftsmen, a quick glance at which was enough for Jason to know that they were not within his budget. He shifted gears and stopped at a small shop to the side of a travel agency. A man, woman, and a boy of about thirteen greeted him with warm smiles. Beautiful beaded jewelry was on display. Jason spoke as simply as he could, but to no avail, so he simply browsed. The humility of this tiny family business overwhelmed him, and he knew he would buy something.

Finally, his eyes fell on a very simple, braided leather bracelet, plain and brown, with a braided black strap that coiled around it. He liked its simplicity, and after a few friendly gestures, was welcomed to try it on. He examined it and found it already meant something. After crude communication, he handed over what even he knew to be a terribly small amount of money. He smiled at the small family, and, overwhelmed with the moment, strolled into Nairobi's commercial district.

The Briton Tower blocked the sun, its stout underlings supporting it. Jason stopped to crane his neck at the construction site of the pit of the ruins of the Pinnacle Towers, advertised in beaten-up Swahili, English and several other languages as soon to be the tallest buildings in Africa. He walked away with a shake of his head; even here, the phallocentric competition continued.

It was noon, and he was getting hungry. He turned into a small, classy diner and ordered *pilau*, which turned out to be a sumptuous platter of spiced rice with chicken. Jason devoured every grain, paid his shillings, and returned to the street.

A greasy-looking fellow on a bicycle approached him and held out colourful t-shirts and a dirty scrap of paper with prices crudely scribbled. Feeling uneasy, Jason pulled out the wad of cash from his back pocket.

A mistake.

The man reached out with blinding speed and seized the money from Jason's hand.

'HEY! YOU ASSHOLE, WHAT–'

But the thief had already mounted his bike and prepared to speed off. Jason grabbed the back of the man's wife-beater in fury. He lost control and fell straight into the busy street. Horns blared. Two seconds later, the slam of a car door behind Jason sent him instinctively into a fighting stance. Another mistake.

It was a cop. His sky-blue uniform screamed at Jason as he pulled out a club. A quick glance showed that the thief – and his cash – were already gone. The officer's eyes were like iron as he stopped two feet from Jason, whose hands were already raised in a feeble peace-gesture. A couple of bystanders chuckled.

'English, yes?' snarled the cop.

'Yes,' Jason replied, trying to stay calm. 'I can explain–'

'Identification.'

Jason slowly took out his wallet and pulled out his driver's licence. The brutish cop looked at it dismissively and stuck his billy-bat under Jason's chin.

'Why are you here? Why are you in Nairobi?'

Jason's mind exploded in panic. What the hell should he say? That he was here to travel back in time to the 1930s?

His hesitation was yet another mistake. He was grabbed by the front of his shirt, turned a hundred and eighty degrees, and pushed hard against the nearby concrete wall.

'You are under arrest.'

'This is RIDICULOUS!'

The onlookers laughed again as Jason heard a jingle of handcuffs. Grotesque panic overtook him as his hands were forced together. What was going to happen to him?

A final, desperate thought pierced his mind. Without consciously trying, even as he felt the cold metal slide against his wrist, he shrieked out his final hope:

'Two skips of a stone!!'

The cuffs dropped to the sidewalk beside his right foot, and the calloused hand gripped his arm like a pitbull. Five seconds of forever went by. Then he was released, and not daring to move, heard the click of a pin and a roaring shout in Swahili. A loud, short commotion. Rapid receding footsteps and silence.

Any creeping relief was obliterated as the officer grabbed Jason by the shoulder and whipped him around to face him. He held his pistol close to Jason's face, pointed mercifully in the air, and pierced him with a burning glare.

'How do you know those words?!' he hissed in a deadly whisper.

Jason fought for breath. 'I... I work at the Agency.'

The man reached down, picked up Jason's wallet, and found the cream-coloured card. He looked at both sides, and then carefully examined its outer trim. His eyes widened, he looked up at Jason, and pointed his finger into his face.

'Stay there.'

The officer jogged back to his cruiser and closed the door, taking the card and Jason's licence with him, and spoke to his partner at the wheel, whom Jason could not see through the glare of the sun.

After forty-five seconds or so, the driver-door opened and another cop – tall, thin, and about forty – stepped out calmly. He wore an unconvincing smile as he strolled up and stopped five feet away.

'Jason Roberts.'

'Yes.'

'Our apologies, sir. We can only act on what we see.'

Jason said nothing, his heart still ready to burst.

'You work at the Kenyan Restoration Agency.'

'Yes.'

'What do you do there?'

'I'm a cook. Vickie Phan can confirm that.'

The officer smiled and chuckled. 'No need to lie to me, Mr. Roberts. You are the Time-Traveller.'

Jason felt a jolt. 'How do you know about that? And about me?!'

'Your card,' he said calmly, handing it back to Jason. 'Look at the trim.'

With shaking hands, Jason examined the black line surrounding the blue letters that had saved his ass. Finally, just above the bottom left corner, he found a tiny gap, less than a millimetre wide.

'Everyone at that complex has a card like yours. But only the Time-Traveller's card has that imperfection. I will remind you of what you must have been told already: Don't lose it.'

Almost ready to faint, Jason leaned back against the wall, shaking his head.

'I am Inspector Samuel Kipkeino. Please forgive Corporal Chege; it is his second day. We would be happy to escort you back to the KRA. I daresay you have seen enough of Nairobi for one day.'

Jason obliged without a word. The mellowed Corporal opened the back door and Jason stepped inside.

With sirens blaring to clear the way, the cruiser sped through the city and out into the open prairies. They crawled and bumped through the thick brush, stopping a hundred feet from the gate.

'Wait,' Samuel ordered as Jason grabbed the handle. Turning to look, the man's eyes were intense.

'I wish you luck, Jason, but I also wish you... wisdom.'

Jason stared. 'What do you mean?'

Samuel looked down for a moment, clearly choosing his words.

'You are involved in something very big and very serious. And such things always have very big secrets.'

'Such as?'

Clearly fighting to keep a neutral face, Samuel's voice was calm.

'Have you heard of the concept of a… how is it called… a *time-loop,* Jason?'

'... yes. Why?'

'Well then, ask your superiors about Duni Kimani's great-grandfather. Now go.'

Jason stared at Samuel, whom until that moment Jason had been starting to like. Then he opened the door and did not look back as he stepped through the gate.

He stalked his way into the complex and, with annoying familiarity, found the head office. He threw open the door without knocking and saw Horace sitting alone at his corner desk, hard at work at his laptop. Horace turned and smiled with an infuriating hint that he knew what was coming.

'Enjoy yourself?' he said brightly. Jason grimaced and pointed a finger.

'You are SUCH an asshole.'

'I know, Jason,' Horace consoled. Nairobi, like all major cities, is a bit of a trick to get used to.'

'So those shitheads have already told you everything?'

'You were being monitored the entire time, Jason. Only the enthusiastic corporal was unaware originally. Did you really think we would throw you into the lions' den like that without a safety net?'

'Oh, this place is just so insane sometimes,' Jason muttered. 'ALL the time.'

'It takes a little insanity to make sense of most anything, Jason.' Horace returned to his laptop.

A long moment of silence followed, and Jason did not move. Horace glanced, and then turned his head sharply.

'What is it Jason? You haven't looked at me like that before.'

Jason kept his voice calm, irritated as ever by Horace's superhuman empathy. 'Is there a possibility that some kind of time loop could be caused by what's happening here?'

'Such as Duni being born again and again, only to have to return here and start the whole thing over?'

'Yes. Such as that.'

Horace nodded with approval. 'Very astute Jason, and yes, that did enter our minds. Not to worry, though, my friend,' he finished with a smile. 'It has been taken care of.'

He returned yet again to his laptop, even as an icy chill filled Jason's stomach as he remembered Samuel's prophecy.

'You killed him.'

Horace froze. His head turned slowly, and his eyes pierced Jason's like daggers.

'Killed *who?*'

Jason did not desist.

'Duni's great-grandfather. You killed him to prevent the time-loop.'

Horace's eyes continued to burn into Jason's own. Finally, he shook his head and chuckled merrily.

'Jason, we didn't *kill* him, for God's sake, we just paid some idiot to kick him in the balls!'

A look of astronomical stupification stretched Jason's face like silly putty. He stared like an idiot as Horace continued.

'His sperm production was altered, he was good as new in two weeks, and we mailed him fifty grand for his trouble!'

The two men gaped at each other for a moment, and at last, a laugh spiralled out of Jason that sent all the furies of this God-forsaken day to the heavens. He rested his head against the door, his torso still heaving with giggles. Horace shook his head in amazement once more as he returned to his typing.

'Honestly, Jason, you're not in a Bond movie!' 'AGAIN with the Bond movie,' Jason muttered as he left the office.

Jason sat in room 212A, retelling his day's adventures as Markie listened with a smile. They guffawed together at Jason's confrontation with Horace.

'You sure had a more interesting day than I did,' Markie said. 'I worked in my garden and took a weed nap.'

'I'd have traded all of this for a nap, believe me.'

'That's bull-hickey, and you know it. You're loving every second of this.'

'Bull-hickey?' Jason repeated.

Markie shrugged. 'Just watched *Walk Hard*.'

Jason spread his hands in glad frustration. 'Do you realize how bizarre you make everything?'

Markie rolled her eyes. 'And do *you* realize you've been eating that up for eight years?'

Jason had no answer. She was too good, *always* too good.

'You should go to bed Jason,' she said, and for once Jason welcomed her motherly tone. 'I'll talk to you tomorrow.'

'Night, Markie.'

'Night, Jason. Don't dream about any weird sexual stuff.'

Jason shook his head, smiled at her once more, and disconnected.

Chapter Eight

The blazing chaos of yesterday's day trip still fresh in his mind, Jason now sat in the Blue Room, as he was indifferently calling it. Two of the leather chairs had been moved to the centre of the room, angled slightly to allow easy view of the telescreen. Omondi sat across from him as Jason gauged his situation. A teacher for seven years, he was now learning history like an over-privileged fifteen-year-old.

'What was the cause of the Second War?' Omondi asked without warning. Jason was unsurprised and determined to hold his own.

'Various causes, mostly leading back to the unfair treatment of Germany following their defeat after the First War.'

'Wrong,' Omondi replied. 'The cause of the Second War was *pride*. Pride by the Allies in their victory after the First War. Pride in the power they could exploit from it. Pride by aristocratic individuals as they revelled for a decade in the decadence of the twenties.'

'So Hitler was blameless?' Jason replied with a raised eyebrow.

'Watch your mouth!' Omondi snapped. 'Every man, every political party, every nation is guilty of pride, none more so than one whose pride is wounded. Hitler could have been a truly great leader; he could have changed the world profoundly for the better were it not for the megalomania he felt for himself, his hatred at those who humbled his country, and the insidious concept of racial superiority that infected and reinforced both.'

Jason shook his head. World War Two was not a hobby for Omondi.

'Okay, maybe you're right. But isn't pride the cause of any war?'

'We are talking about the Second World War. The bloodiest, most world-changing war of all time. Your first lesson can be summed up in one word: *humility.*'

'Humility?'

'All of human history is woven by the hellish concept of pride. If you hope to be the antidote to that, you must be *humble.*'

The two men glared at each other for a moment. Finally, Omondi blinked, took a breath, and continued.

'Now. To a simple review. If you wanted to make friends with the House of Commons, which would you imagine to be the primary battle that you would bring to their attention?'

'The Battle of Britain,' Jason replied without hesitation.

'Yes. This is crucial. What do you know of it?'

For once, Jason felt confident.

'It was the battle that stopped the Nazi advance in the West. The first entirely aerial battle ever. Faught by RAF Spitfires and

Luftwaffe Messerschmitts. Churchill's leadership was crucial. Had the RAF been defeated, Britain would have been invaded and overwhelmed. Hitler would have been free to overpower Russia, and all would have been lost.'

Omondi looked at him for a moment, then gave a jerk of his head, whatever that could mean.

'And do you know the total casualties of this battle?'

'How the hell could I know that?'

'People need numbers!' Omondi growled. 'Numbers make an impact! As with most any old battle, total casualties cannot be said for certain, but roughly 1500 Allied Forces died, taking down roughly 2500 German fighters and bombers. Meanwhile, over forty thousand British civilians died in the Luftwaffe bombings.'

'Listen, Omondi,' Jason snarled, 'I don't have your precious total recall. I don't have a perfect mind. How can you expect me to remember all of these stupid details?'

'BECAUSE YOU MUST!!' Omondi roared. 'Do you know how indifferent people are? To EVERYTHING? One detail, one single syllable of what I will teach you, could mean the difference between action and inaction against the darkest evil the world has ever known! You are a teacher! Surely you have encountered the little bastards who care nothing for what you try to bless them with! WINSTON CHURCHILL could not change the minds of those to whom you are being sent! If *you* hope to have a prayer of doing so, you damned well better have your facts straight!'

Humbled and stressed, Jason slumped in his chair. The unthinkable nature of his new life burning his mind, he conceded defeat.

'1500 Allied casualties, 2500 German, forty thousand civilians.'

Omondi nodded and changed the subject again.

'Are you familiar with the phrase *life unworthy of life*?'

Jason's stomach clenched. The topic he had been dreading had arrived.

'It was the general term given by the Nazis to those deemed racially dangerous and inferior.'

Omondi pointed to the computer to Jason's right. 'Your first assignment is to take fifteen minutes and reflect in writing on that term. We need to know precisely how much you feel for your fellow man.'

Jason shrugged, and migrated to the computer. He reflected for a moment, and wrote:

'Life unworthy of life' is the darkest phrase ever coined. Unlike any crude racial slur, it has a hideous eloquence to it. It poeticizes genocide. It is the beautiful mask that hid the face of the most barbaric, drooling insanity the world has ever known.

'Finished, Mr. Mutua,' Jason said cynically. Omondi stepped over to him and read what Jason had written. He frowned, but not in anger. He looked at Jason's blurb for what felt like minutes, and then turned to look at him.

'Impressive.'

Even as Jason almost fell off his chair at the shock of a compliment from Omondi, the old man took out his phone and made a call.

'Horace. Contact the speechwriters and relieve them. Yes. The situation just got much less complicated.' He hung up.

'Wait, wait, wait,' Jason said with rising alarm, 'What did THAT mean?'

'You know perfectly well what that meant,' Omondi quipped.

'Hold on! No one ever said anything about writing my own speeches!'

'No one knew you were capable of doing so.'

'I already have enough on my plate without *writing the speeches!'* Jason exclaimed. 'You're making me feel more alone by the minute!'

'Then I am doing my job,' Omondi responded.

'I CAN'T DO THIS ALONE!!' Jason shouted in shrill panic. 'There is no way ANYONE can accomplish something like this by himself! I'll end up in an asylum or murdered in my bed or–'

'You are quite right, Mr. Roberts,' Omondi interrupted. 'You cannot do this alone. But if you play your cards properly, you will have a powerful ally.'

'WHO?!'

Omondi leaned in until his face was a foot from Jason's. His eyes burned with a frightening intensity.

'Churchill,' he whispered. 'You must... find... *Churchill.* You must bring him out of exile and rally him to your side. It is *essential.* Ultimately, this is *his* mission, and you are simply its face, the ace up his sleeve. Only with his guidance could a poor fool like you have any hope of penetrating the apathy and cowardice that will come to doom us all.'

Jason slumped back in his chair, numb with horror. It was madness. It was obscene. It was beyond the beginnings of comprehension.

'I am a drama teacher,' he croaked.

'No, Jason,' Omondi replied. 'You are a *history* teacher.

Forty-five minutes later, Jason stepped out into the hall. Winston Churchill? He was supposed to RECRUIT Winston Churchill? Was such a thought even allowed to enter one's mind?

Omondi's last words to Jason as he stepped out were to 'have some fun.' He spoke the words with care, as if having never used them before. Jason had never more needed to have fun in his life. Yet what on Earth, let alone in this snake pit, could provide it?

He slowed to a stop and grew thoughtful. A small smile touched his face, and he turned around, asking his way to the kitchens.

At last, he pushed his way through the swinging grey doors, suddenly becoming aware that there was nowhere he could not go in this damned place, as he was the star of the show. Tantalizing aromas assaulted his nose, and clattering cutlery and urgent English in half a dozen accents overwhelmed his ears. But the din grew quieter and quieter (excepting a gasp or two) as one by one, the cooks recognized Jason and stopped what they were doing to gawk. Two waiters stopped mid-stride, nearly dropping mounds of food.

Rolling his eyes, Jason was about to ask for a supervisor, when Vickie came striding into the room, a spatula in one hand and a box of frozen jumbo shrimp in the other. The moment her eyes fell on him, the grim determination in her face evaporated, and she smiled in delight.

'Hi Jason!'

Jason returned her smile and addressed his rapt audience: 'Would you mind if I relieved Vickie of her duties for an hour?'

Vickie blew a raspberry. 'Who the hell is gonna tell *you* otherwise?'

Jason chucked, and the two of them left the kitchen together.

They took their time, strolling the corridors and getting to know each other a little. She was a fascinating girl, who spoke four languages fluently and was an avid fan of *Lord of the Rings*. She listened to his simple stories of home with rapt interest and almost exploded with wonder when, after careful consideration, he told her some details of his history lesson.

'You're going to meet *Winston Churchill!*' she whispered. She shook her head, staring into space.

'You know him that well?'

She looked at him slyly. 'Give a poor young Asian girl some credit. He was amazing.'

They walked a while longer, ignoring the stares they attracted from passersby. Jason looked at her and shrugged. 'I didn't really have any plans when I came to see you...'

'Would you like to go to Shwari Mawe and play catch?'

Jason started. 'Catch?'

'Sure!' Vickie said, smiling. 'There's an open space for such things at the northeast corner. I do it all the time, actually.'

Jason hadn't played catch in fifteen years. Something so simple and earthy was appealing. They got hold of a ball and a pair of gloves from the rec centre, and Jason soon found himself in a small stone courtyard surrounded by the sanctuary he had come to love. After over a dozen pitiful throws he got back in the groove of it, and the conversation continued.

'Do you prefer *Lord of the Rings* or *The Hobbit*?' Jason asked lightly.

'I've read everything Tolkien ever wrote,' Vickie replied. 'Narnia too. British writers are so amazing.'

'So, we're both Anglophiles.'

Vickie smiled. 'Apparently. My dad lived there for a short time before he moved to Canada. Guess it stuck.'

'What about your mum?'

'Second generation,' Vickie said, smiling. 'My mom was adopted by Canadians. My grandparents were killed in a napalm attack during the Vietnam War.'

Jason's heart broke. And then it turned to ice as his ever-conscious mind penetrated: the Vietnam War – one of the defining events of the century he had studied so devotedly. It would not exist as he knew it, if he succeeded in his mission. And the WORLD WAS ENDING.

His breathing accelerated. His arms fell limp to his sides as he ignored the baseball that flew over his head. All of a sudden, it was all too much.

'Jason,' Vickie said in alarm, 'are you alright?'

He was not. His mind seemed to collapse like a paper cup as the history of the world came back and forth to rest on his shoulders. He fell to his hands and knees and vomited.

'JASON!' Vickie screamed in horror. Already raised voices could be heard, but Jason had already fallen onto his side in a faded haze. The last thing he remembered was Vickie's hands gently cupping his jaw, her terrified eyes looking into his.

Even as he awoke, Jason was amazed at his surroundings. It was his own living room, in Room 209. The blinding light of the Kenyan sun was washed away in a single swoop of white blinds. A shadowy figure turned to him and sat in the white armchair, moved at an obtuse angle to the couch upon which he lay. A confused, fiery animal instinct arose within him as he began to find the strength to rise.

'How are you feeling, Jason?'

The annoying familiarity of Horace's voice sent Jason falling slack as a doll where he had awoken.

'You stupid, limp-dick, inbred son of a bitch.'

'Look at me, Jason.'

Jason shifted irritably and glared.

'Still think you found the man to save the world?'

'Indeed I do. More than ever, in fact. Even I never imagined it would take this long for you to come to this.'

Jason turned onto his back and glared at the ceiling. 'Will you people *please* stop placing bets on when I will act like a human being? It makes me sick.'

Horace chuckled. 'Touché, Jason. You are clearly in a very normal mindset. You haven't yet been conscious two minutes, and you have already seen right through my riddles.'

'If I hear that word ONE MORE TIME...'

Jason lay in silence a moment longer, then sat up, looking at the floor. Horace remained quiet as Jason got his thoughts together.

'How's Vickie?'

'She's fine, Jason. She sends her love. Your bond with her is an unexpected blessing, I must say.'

Jason glared. 'She's my *friend,* you robot.'

Horace fell silent again. Jason sat a moment longer, and found his strength.

'How, by the way,' Jason asked, 'am I supposed to do this? Why the hell would anyone take some Canadian yahoo seriously enough to take him to anyone relevant?'

Horace smiled with approval. 'An important question, Jason, which we hoped you would be wise enough to ask.' He stood up promptly. 'Come with me, my friend.'

Jason sneered. 'You honestly think I consider *you* a friend?'

Horace stopped and looked at Jason, his eyes narrowed in focus. After a moment or two, he beamed at him.

'Yes, Jason, I do.' He turned and left the room. Jason shook his head and followed with a small smile.

He was barely out the door, when he was knocked nearly off his feet by a running blur, which turned out to be Vickie, who hugged him tightly around his chest.

'Jason, are you alright?! I knew you would be, actually, but I wanted to be sure. Are you?'

'I'm fine, Vickie, really,' Jason groaned. He would not have imagined a hug like this.

She finally released him and smiled. 'I've been given permission to cook dinner for you tonight. But it's a surprise.'

'If you please, Ms Phan,' Horace said gently, 'Jason is needed at the moment. Please, Jason, come with me.' And he turned to leave.

'Sure Horace,' Jason said with a smile, 'but when this is over, will you take us on a tour of Flatbush?'

Vickie gasped. Horace stopped dead. He turned to look at the two of them, his face expressionless. Then, in an eerily alien, wascally-wabbit accent, he spoke. 'Sure thing, doc. Now go fuck yaself.'

And he stomped off, leaving Jason and Vickie bent over in screaming hysterics.

After parting with Vickie, Jason tracked down Horace (who said nothing) and followed him to a secure steel door, absurdly out of place against the classy wallpaper. A swipe of a card, a fingerprint check, and a 19-digit password later, Jason found himself in a huge chamber, the size of a respectable basketball court. Men and women in white coats went about their business in the first third of it, but the far end was decidedly barren. The lights there were dimmed, and from some unknown source the green light glared brighter than Jason had yet seen. No one looked at Jason.

Horace recovered himself and began, 'All of a sudden, you find yourself at the heart of the hope of humanity.'

Jason's mouth curled in amusement. 'How pretentious.'

'Indeed?' came a voice from his left.

Omondi stepped into Jason's view once again. His eyes were as fiery as ever.

'Here you will see the ultimate shape of what your future holds.'

A hundred lame puns were put out of Jason's mouth, and he stayed silent.

'To answer your first question,' Horace said, 'we would like to show you the device that will gain you the attention you will need.'

'But first of all,' Omondi interjected, 'are you alright?'

Jason looked at him in surprise.

Omondi's face remained flat. 'Breakdowns such as yours are not unheard of here. But you are the Time Traveller. Are you certain you are ready to continue?'

'Indeed he is, Omondi,' Horace answered for Jason. 'Our investment continues to pay off.'

Jason flipped Horace off without looking at him and nodded to Omondi.

'Then come.'

They walked briskly to a table at the west end of the chamber, bodies making way for the three VIP's.

'Who funds this operation, anyway?' Jason asked.

Omondi answered without looking at him. 'Generous and trustworthy Kenyan donors, a single American corporation, the Kenyan government, and those of three other African nations who prefer to remain anonymous.'

'Taxpayer's money, siphoned into a suicide mission,' Jason said silkily.

'The investment of the people will pay off shortly,' Omondi replied. Jason decided not to pursue this.

'What about the US government?'

Omondi looked at Jason.

'What about them?'

'Do they know about this?'

'Why would they?'

'Here we are, Jason,' Horace cut in.

On the table in front of them, on a burgundy cushion, sat the trigger – the mechanism that would perform the terrible act of time travel. Beside it, sat a simple smartphone in a thick protective case.

'So where's the device?' Jason asked.

'That's it,' Horace replied, pointing at the phone.

Jason raised an eyebrow. Horace smiled.

'Just as the hover disc was enough for us to take Duni seriously, a smartphone will be enough to do the same for you. You will reveal that phone to the right people and use it to convince them of your legitimacy as a man of the future. It is all the foot in the door you should need.'

'In addition,' Omondi said, 'it has been equipped with all the programs and information you will need to review, prepare, and deliver your warnings effectively.'

'And when the battery dies?' Jason asked smartly. 'Or if it breaks?'

'Several power chords have been modified to fit the power sockets of the day,' Horace replied promptly. 'And it will not break. Well over a million dollars went into the creation of that single device. The screen is bulletproof, and most of the metal within is titanium steel. Nothing short of the swing of a sledgehammer could do the job.'

Jason looked closely and raised an eyebrow.

'Is that an *Otter Box?*'

'Better to err on the side of caution.'

'And if I lose it?'

'Then it is lost,' Omondi replied darkly. 'To be found by a fool and to distract the world further from its doom.'

Jason refused to be pulled into this game. He took it in stride. 'Don't lose the phone. Got it.'

Horace nodded. 'Now. You have seen the trigger. Would you like to see the gun?'

Jason nodded. Omondi picked up the glowing trigger, and the three of them marched to the north end of the chamber.

It was completely empty, save for a strange chrome structure, a tripod stand about eight feet tall with an overreaching arm. A hula-hoop-like circle, about four feet in diameter, hung sturdily from it. A thin glass window ribboned around its underside, from which the green light fiercely stabbed the air beneath, giving Jason a chilling notion that he would not like what he was about to learn. The three men stopped ten feet from it.

Horace looked at Jason, took the trigger from Omondi and gestured to the light. 'Step inside.'

Jason looked at Horace, all trace of mockery gone. 'What are you going to do?'

Horace shook his head. 'Step One, Jason, is to walk under that light. Step Two will follow.'

Shaking at the knees, Jason balled his fists, spared a stab of hatred for this moment, and moved into the bathing glow. He turned his head in all directions. Nothing had happened. He breathed deeply, in spite of himself.

Then Horace stepped forward, trigger in hand, and joined him.

Jason's knees gave out, and he collapsed on the hard floor.

The moment the green light touched the trigger, it dimmed almost to nothing, and the chamber melted away. Omondi vanished, and the two men were standing on a snow-scattered hilltop; a towering grey sky appeared over their heads; a small, gnarled birch exploded into existence twenty feet to their left, its leafless branches tossed about by a strong breeze that Jason could neither feel nor hear.

'We did hope it would be a windy day.'

Jason looked up weakly at Horace even as the man rested a comforting hand on his shoulder. With his other hand, he pointed to the east. Jason turned his head and almost puked again.

A little over two kilometres away sat a great city, sprawled over the winter fields – huge yet humble, with not a skyscraper to be seen. Just beyond that sat the grey ocean, which stretched into eternity. His eyes returned to the city, and with the tiny mite of consciousness left to him, he identified a gigantic clock tower, which could be nothing other than Big Ben.

London.

'Are you alright, Jason?'

Nothing. Nothing had prepared Jason for this. He would have eaten the hover disc before exposing himself to the nightmare of which he was now a part.

'If it makes you feel better, Jason, we are not part of this image. Only when you pull the trigger will you be integrated, and the world you now see become real.'

With every ounce of strength he had, Jason got to his feet. A swallow landed on the nearby tree, its head bobbing with a song not heard for eighty-five years.

'This seems like a literal miracle,' was all Jason could manage.

Horace nodded. 'And like all great human innovations, straight back to the wheel, it *is*, Jason.'

With that, Horace gave him a gentle push out of the light. The dreamscape vanished, and Jason found himself in the chamber once again.

'I don't think I can do this, Markie.'

Markie's face had appeared at Jason's call, and her smile turned to shocked alarm when she saw the tears running down his face. He briefly explained what he had just witnessed and put his face in his shaking hands.

'This is too much, Markie,' Jason whimpered between sobs. 'No one is supposed to see the things I'm seeing here. Why did it have to be me? How did they find me? My life is over. I want to go home, I–'

'Jason.'

Jason gasped for breath and looked at Markie through his tears. She was gazing at him with the firm, steady look in her eyes that always seemed to calm him down.

'I don't know why it had to be you. I don't know why there have to be *why's*. I don't know much of anything, but I do know that if I had known that one man had to be chosen for this craziness, I would trust you more than anyone else in the world.'

Jason couldn't manage a smile.

'No one is making you do this. If you want to come home, then come home. This whole thing is insane; you're not wrong about that. But I like Horace. I get a good vibe from him. And I know you probably better than you know yourself, in some ways. I'd bet twenty bucks that, if you stick this out, the next time you see that view of pretty little London, you'll like it.'

Something close to a smile touched Jason's trembling mouth. In a far greater miracle than that which he had just witnessed, he was calming down. Markie had scored a total victory. She grinned at him, and winked.

There was a quiet knock at the door. Without thinking he rose in anger, ready to spit in the face of Horace or Omondi. But it was neither. The calm, smiling face of Mugo met his eyes.

'Hello, Jason,' he said kindly. 'I know very well that I am breaking the rules at the moment, but I was wondering if you and Markie might allow me to join you for a conversation.'

Something in Mugo's aura continued to disarm Jason. Not sure what to think, he turned to the screen behind him and wordlessly consulted Markie, who shrugged. Jason opened the door and allowed the enigmatic man inside. He smiled, set up a folding chair, and sat down, Jason joining him.

Jason measured Mugo as he made himself comfortable. Markie twirled her hair and mostly watched Jason. Mugo's smile never left his face.

'A troublesome day, I am sure,' he said at last. Jason ignored this.

'What exactly do you do here, Mugo?' he demanded.

Mugo shrugged. 'Nothing, really.'

Jason's head jerked in surprise. 'What??'

Mugo gave a sheepish gesture. 'I do nothing at all. The only reason my position is even possible is that I was raised bilingual. I am a farmhand who lucked out,' he finished with a small chuckle.

A quick glance at Markie told him she was as bewildered as he was. 'Then why are you in charge?'

'Because Duni put me in charge.'

'Why?'

'It is hard not to sound arrogant, but I am in charge because of my character. Because Duni saw my integrity. I took care of her. Kept her safe. I did everything in my power to make her terrible situation better, without thinking of personal gain. After our honourable Prime Minister saw what you have just seen, she made him swear that all important issues would go through me. You learned about humility today, and each day I pray for the humility required of a man in whose hands lies the fate of the world.'

Jason stared in wonder.

Markie's eyes were wide. 'That's badass,' she murmured.

Mugo chuckled. 'I like you, Markie.'

'You won't,' she warned, 'if anything happens to Jason.'

'Jason has nothing to worry about, Markie. His own character will see to that. I am aware of what awaits him, and he is capable. More than capable. I cannot wait to see him come back to us, after his final triumph.'

Mugo nodded respectfully, smiled at both of them, and left without another word.

Jason was calm. The atmosphere of Room 212A felt more like a sanctuary than ever. Markie shook her head with a smile.

'Damn, dude, you sure know how to pick your friends.'

'You don't know how right you are, Markie,' Jason murmured.

'Oh, shut up,' she replied, though a warm grin stretched across her face.

After saying goodbye to Markie, Jason stepped into the hall and shuffled the short way back to his room. He stopped dead, just before he would have stepped on a platter lying in front of his door. It was covered, but the aroma was enticing. After recovering himself, he picked up a note sitting near the edge:

From one Canadian to another
Love, Vickie

Jason uncovered the tray and burst out laughing at the massive poutine, the bowl of multi-coloured smarties, and the stack of still-steaming pancakes with a small bottle of maple syrup sitting humbly next to them.

Filled with joy at Vickie's devotion, he picked up his blessed dinner and, at long last, settled in for the night.

Chapter Nine

Jason ignored the loud droning of his morning alarm. He was deep in thought.

At four o'clock he had awoken from a bad dream and had not pretended he could sleep again. After collecting himself, he laboriously dragged the writing desk to the right of his bed into his marble lobby (which he had grown fond of), switched on the chrome reading lamp, and found a slick black pen and some creamy white paper. He had no idea what he was going to write, only that he needed to write. Something in the moment compelled him to put aside his phone and do whatever he was about to do the old-fashioned way. He tried to draw his mind away from this madness, but it gripped him so tightly that he knew it was all that could inspire him. And so he wrote.

Hitler and his underlings were PERFECT evil. No human being who ever lived better embodied the terrible depths to which a human being can sink. As the embodiment of hell on earth, they were flawless.

Churchill, the man who led the free world to victory against this perfect evil, was NOT perfect good. He had flaws. He had failures. Many of his words and actions before, during, and after the war, such as the firebombing of Dresden and his decision not to bomb Auschwitz remain fiercely controversial to this day. And that is why I trust him.

Churchill was a man. He was not an archangel. Perfect good is impossibly more difficult than perfect evil. Yet this man found it within himself to rise above the petty controversy of his imperfection and do what was within his incomparable power to lead Christian civilization to the most glorious victory over evil the world has ever known.

Even as that damnable sound reverberated through his quarters Jason finished his last few sentences in satisfaction. He knew they served no purpose, would not likely leave this room. It was one of those things that one writes to keep from going insane.

Not wanting Vickie or some jittery idiot to have to knock on his door, he quickly dressed in his goofy exercise clothes, grabbed a towel, and sauntered to the gym. Joonheong motored him through a grinding regime that seemed to specifically target every muscle that was already tender. Jason didn't fight it; the simple distraction of sweat and Joonheong's yammering broken English was therapeutic.

After another shower (never would he take one for granted again), he geared himself for another day of awful surprises and weird people. By some miracle he found an obscure

Viking movie on Netflix, which he had seen a million times, and watched it twice, losing himself in the familiarity that the modern world enabled him to enjoy at will even as the unprecedented had him by the throat.

At last, the bubble burst and there was a knock at the door. A short, weak-chinned man, clearly an *employee* rather than a *person,* held out a garment bag with an almost frightening lack of expression on his face. Jason took it, closed the door, and never once thought about the man again.

A note was crudely taped to his new gear. Jason opened it, and saw what he managed to recognize as Omondi's staggered penmanship:

> *Your first Application of Dramatic Understanding class begins in forty-five minutes. Blue Room. Miss Jaspers will be waiting. Wear this.*

Jason laughed with – he couldn't believe it – affection. Omondi certainly got top marks for consistency.

Jason unzipped the bag, pulled out his new wardrobe, and couldn't help giving a whistle. He almost ran back to the bedroom.

Twenty minutes later he stepped out into his lobby, knowing for a fact that he had never looked this good. A light grey casual suit, gleaming sterling-silver belt-buckle, white dress shirt, and – he had checked the label – Italian leather shoes. He had tossed aside the stupid bowtie, but was otherwise thoroughly satisfied. Even the invasive perfect fit – straight up to the top of his inseam – didn't faze him as a new sort of confidence filled his lungs. He could almost hear the slap-bass in his head. Luxury and misery were his ever-present companions in this damned place.

Jason reported for his Application of Dramatic Understanding class without much enthusiasm. He opened the door of the Blue Room, expecting to see some crotchety old lady glaring at him over her spectacles. What he did not expect to see was a stunningly beautiful black woman, about his own age and nearly as tall as himself. Her shining hair was tied back in a bun, flawless bangs framing her tastefully shaded eyes, and dark lipstick lined her curving mouth. She stood up, revealing a long, ravishing black dress. Her perfectly posh persona was thrown off only by a simple nose ring, which rocketed her appearance into a dimension Jason had never seen before. Her smile made that of his ex-wife seem like cold soup.

Thank God I didn't wear the bowtie.

'Good afternoon, Jason.' Her accent was as refined and debonair as the rest of her. 'My name is Megan, but *you* will refer to me as Ms. Jaspers.'

'... okay...'

Her face twisted like lightning into a scowl.

'Where the dickens have you been, anyway? You are four minutes late, you silly fool! Lollygagging, were we? We will set you straight yet. *Sit.*' She pointed at the leather chair beside her, her mouth pursed like a sixth-grade teacher.

Jason's eyebrows contracted, and his mouth opened wider and wider. He didn't know what to do. When she persisted, he moved to obey. Her overbearing first impression broke into pieces, and she laughed musically, her hands clasped in delight.

'Forgive me. Thought a playful pull would get things started properly.'

Jason glared, hating the flare of red that came to his face. 'No wonder you got this job.'

Megan's eyebrows raised and she smiled, clearly accepting a challenge. 'I *got this job* because I am damned good at it, sir. My parents are of lesser nobility. I am a leading writer at Debrett's. I am good friends with William Hanson, and before accepting this position, I had nearly got in at Hendon.'

'And what the hell is *any* of that supposed to mean to me?!' Jason shouted.

She burst again into beautiful and infuriating giggles. 'Forgive me,' she said again, wiping her eyes. 'You're just... rather an easy target, that's all.'

Jason turned to leave.

'Jason, please stop.'

He slowed and turned to face Megan with what dignity he had left. Her smile was now warm and genuine, or at least a professional reproduction of it.

'Gauging my reaction, were you?' Jason shot at her. 'Or are you just out of your mind?'

'I do apologize, Jason,' she said, her liquid accent already chipping away at Jason's resentment. 'When I see a well-dressed man, I instinctively think of him as sport. I am, in fact, a very relatable woman, and I look forward to educating you.'

'Cut the crap, and let's get to work.'

Megan nodded. 'Indeed.' She grew serious again. 'One thing must be made very clear: From this moment on, I am a *lady,* and will be treated as such.'

Jason waited for another fit of giggles, but it never came.

'I am quite serious, Jason. Where you are going, there are rules. There is protocol. Particularly among the aristocracy, with whom you will spend much of your time. And I assure you, the fact that you are a time traveller will be *insignificant* in the face of that protocol. If you come across as anything less than a gentleman, your mission will be in *lethal* danger.'

Damn.

'The cumbersome title of this class is pretentious nonsense. We shall call it for what it is: *Etiquette.* Nothing more and nothing less. It is my task to make you into a man who, despite your vulgar accent, can be accepted into the inner-circle of the last and greatest empire on Earth.'

Jason lingered in trepidation. 'I don't want to lose who I am.'

Megan closed her eyes and shook her head in dismay. 'We do have a lot of work to be getting on with, don't we?'

'What do you mean?'

'Etiquette is *bullshit!* Complete rot from beginning to end. It is the costume that everyone, everywhere puts on when they aren't fighting or fucking or sitting on the 'loo. It is the blinders that every society puts on its people when we need to pretend that we aren't fundamentally insane. As a teacher you have surely mastered Canadian etiquette, and this is merely another notch on that lovely leather belt you are wearing.'

'You *are* out of your mind.'

Megan's smile threw daggers. 'Working on it. Now. Bow to me.'

'We're there already, eh?'

Fire erupted in Megan's eyes. 'NO EH'S!' she shouted. 'EVER!!'

Jason almost fell over. Megan regained her composure with lightning speed and continued as if nothing had happened. 'Bow to me, Jason, as if you were meeting the Queen.'

Jason sighed and bowed as best as he knew how. As Jason knew she would, Megan gave him a look of purest disgust.

'Even for a colonial, that was embarrassing. You look like one of those stupid drinking birds that the whole world wants to take credit for.'

'Well, I'm sorry, but I've had better things to do in my life than practice bowing to the Queen.'

'For the next hour, Jason, I AM the Queen, as far as you are concerned. A proper bow was a crucial first impression to make to an honourable politician in 1935, and judging by what I just witnessed, we might as well begin there.'

She walked to his side with stunning grace, put her right hand on his chest, her left on his lower back, and adjusted him until he was as straight as a ramrod. She then sidestepped in front of him and looked him in the eye as she forced his shoulders back to a perfect horizontal line. She stepped back with a satisfied smile and admired her work.

'This is very uncomfortable, your Majesty,' Jason muttered.

Megan raised an eyebrow and smirked. 'You had best get used to discomfort, Jason,' she said. 'It is a way of life, where you are going. Now. Keep your waist still. Bend at the shoulders. Eyes to the floor. Make your movements slow and fluid. Bow to me.'

Infuriated by his own enthusiasm, Jason made another attempt, following Megan's direction.

She glowered for a moment, then nodded with a smile. 'Proper.'

Jason stepped out of the Blue Room and slouched with a groan. Megan's posture lessons had taken more out of him than Joonheong's workout regime.

Before parting with a perfect curtsey, Megan informed him that he had an hour to spend as he would and was then to return for his first Ethics of Time Travel course with Horace.

Jason felt like being around people. He got the attention of a passer-by (not difficult, as the young man was already gaping at him) and asked if there was a café or restaurant in the building. He made his way to the southeast end, not quite subconsciously deciding not to change. He opened a grey door marked *Coffee House*. He stepped inside, and his face sagged in disbelief.

'Seriously?!'

It was a Starbucks. Employees in green aprons bustled around behind the counter; a short line-up of KRA members chatting amongst themselves as they waited to be served. Jason joined the queue and was instantly greeted by a blond, formally dressed man of about twenty-five.

'Hello Mr. Roberts. Enjoying yourself?'

Jason gawked like a fool. 'How is there a *Starbucks?'*

The man chuckled. 'Vice President Ruto is friends with their South African CEO. The company donated a good deal of money to the Operation and set us up with a little taste of home along with it.'

Jason closed his eyes and shook his head. Starbucks, Saviour of the World. Now he knew the 'single American corporation' Omondi had mentioned...

The young man took his drink (probably with fourteen hyphens in its description), shook Jason's hand, and left. Jason got a Flat White and sat down at a small corner table. He sipped his drink and smiled… it tasted almost as good as the Glenlivet. He sighed, yet again wondering how he could feel so content at a moment like this.

'Care for some company?'

Startled, Jason looked up and behind, and there was Horace, smiling warmly, a tall cup of coffee in his hand. 'Looking sharp!' he said, with a twinkle in his eye. Jason spread his hands and glared.

'We're meeting in *half an hour!*'

But Horace was already sitting down.

'Surely a nice chat between friends is something different from an Ethics lesson, Jason.'

'With you, I'm not so sure,' Jason muttered, frowning at Horace as he sipped his coffee. 'And I wish you'd stop stalking me. What do you want?'

'I saw this as an opportunity for us to get to know each other.'

Jason snorted. 'Before you met me, you already knew my weight on the Moon in kilograms.'

'Alright,' Horace replied with a smile, 'for you to get to know me, then.'

Jason measured Horace, wondering how different this moment was from their first encounter. At last admitting to himself that he had come to like this strange man, Jason decided to play along.

'How did they find you?'

Horace smiled sadly. 'I had developed a name in the right circles. My talents had helped numerous businesses and corporations prosper beyond their wildest dreams, and I was essentially the power behind the throne in large portions of the New York economy. When Kenyatta and Mugo founded the KRA, they quickly got wind of me. Omondi himself stepped into my office less than five weeks after Duni's death. He brought the hover disc, of course.'

'So you gave up the life of a business kingpin for *this* crap?'

'After the situation was explained to me, yes.'

Jason drummed his fingers on the table. 'Why you, Horace? What did they need you for?'

'They needed the gifts that helped me find you, Jason: my unrivaled ability to find the right people. Every single man and woman who works in this complex, from chief scientist to the idiot from Finland in charge of the laundromat was personally interviewed and recommended to Mugo by me.'

Jason was impressed. 'Sounds like a pain in the ass.'

Horace nodded.

'Seems like you've reached beyond that, though,' Jason continued.

'I was kept on as a senior member because of my excellent social skills, an area where Omondi is a bit lacking.'

Jason chuckled at this understatement. 'How the hell did he ever get into *politics?*'

'Kenya is a strange country.'

Jason exchanged a wordless glance of renewed respect with Horace. The two men smiled genuinely at each other for the first time.

'Had *you* studied the War before they found you?'

A strange look of awkwardness came over Horace's face. 'Indeed I had.'

'I suppose that must have been an asset, then?'

'In a way.'

It was the first statement Horace had made to Jason without looking him in the eye. His face suddenly brightened as he stood.

'Anyway, we might as well get started, Jason. I'll meet you in the Blue Room.'

And with that he left the Coffee House, a perturbed Jason rising to follow.

'What is your mission?'

Horace was back in his element. The Blue Room, still smelling faintly of Megan's perfume, seemed to radiate as he stared Jason down. Jason gathered himself and spoke.

'To prevent the Second World War.'

'No, Jason! Your mission is to save the world. However great a good the prevention of the War may be, you cannot forget that, as you have said already, it is a means, not an end. It is for that reason that we were glad to learn that you are not a pacifist.'

'Why does the difference matter? How is one bigger than the other?' It's World War *Two,* for God's sake!'

'Eighty million people died in that war in order that the world could be saved. You are the point of that spear. The ultimate goal for which those people paid with their lives will be in your hands.'

With all his strength, Jason kept his voice level. 'I already knew that.'

'But you have not begun to consider the implications, Jason. You will be thrust into a world adamantly indifferent to the rise of the ultimate tyranny of history. The First Great War will be fresh in its mind. You will know that your surroundings will be bombed to rubble in a few short years. You will know that *Hitler is alive,* Jason! And in the meantime, you will be surrounded by the height of peace and prosperity. Even in the midst of the Depression, you will spend your time with the affluent. You will be surrounded by charming simplicity, beautiful women, and extravagant luxury. If any of this overcomes you, all will be lost. Your only hope will be the indivisible fact of the total Apocalypse you will have come to prevent.'

'Take a breath, Horace.'

Horace deflated, scowled, and chuckled. 'Thank you, Jason. Now. We have come at last to the very top of the mountain. Greater than any means or end. Greater than the future or the past. The absolute focal point of why you are here.'

Horace waited, perhaps a bit too long, and spoke just above a whisper. 'Stop the Holocaust. Above all else, stop the Holocaust. It is your number one priority.'

'Did Duni say that?'

'No. This is the one aspect of this operation that we have decided to take into our own hands.'

'Why is it my number one priority?'

'Because it is the Holocaust.'

'Even at the expense of saving the world?'

'The Holocaust was *worse* than the end of the world, Jason. Were you to see it, or Nanking, or Rwanda, or any other genocide happening, with your own eyes, I wonder very much whether you would consider the world worth saving.'

'To me this sounds very close to playing God,' Jason said doubtfully.

A look of intense frustration flashed over Horace's face. 'Why do we have to keep explaining these things to you?! You're smarter than this! Interfering with time is playing God by definition, Jason. It is the rape of history. Quite against our will, we were given two choices: Either save the world, or let it die. We chose the first, and if that involves playing God, we consider that an acceptable side-effect.'

Jason sat stone-faced, at a loss for words. Horace collected himself and took a breath.

'However, this does not mean playing God should be embraced. As a God-fearing man I deplore the necessity of the evil to begin with, and a large part of this particular course is meant to ensure you are prepared for the moral dilemmas that will inevitably come with the package.'

'Such as?'

'Use your imagination.'

Jason considered for a moment. For some reason, Markie came to mind, and a light dawned.

'Women.'

Horace nodded. 'An excellent example, Jason. Where you are going, men run the show. Women marry, submit, and obey. To even suggest a friendly game of soccer with a woman would be scandalous.'

Jason nodded. 'And I am not to fight that.'

'No, Jason. You are not to fight that. You are not to fight segregation. You are not to fight Imperialism. You are not to invent Velcro and make a million dollars. However morally right the issue may be, it is fundamentally immoral to change or suppress the natural course of history.'

'It's basically the Prime Directive from *Star Trek*.'

Horace grinned and nodded. 'Basically. Were the world not hanging in the balance, we would have smashed that Time Machine to pieces before attempting something so nefarious as preventing World War Two.'

'You said there could be *no greater good,*' Jason shot back.

Horace raised a condescending eyebrow. 'That, Jason, is what is known as a paradox.'

'Kiss my ass, I get it. What happens if I see a man *assaulting* a woman?'

Horace's shoulders sagged, and his jaw slackened. He looked as though he had never been asked a dumber question.

'Then you do what *any* decent man, at *any* point in history, would do, Jason. Put the sonofabitch in the hospital.'

Jason laughed his appreciation.

By God, I'm actually starting to enjoy this!

'Go chat with Markie, Jason. This has been an exemplary first lesson. I will be in touch this evening.'

Jason stood and left the Blue Room; for the first time, he realized, with a smile.

The moment the door closed behind Jason, Horace's smile faded, and he stood. He made his way to the crowded cafeteria. He waved wordlessly to a friend or two and headed to the far corner, where Omondi and Vickie were waiting.

Horace smiled warmly at the girl, who looked nervous, despite Omondi's assurances that the meeting was friendly.

The moment Horace sat down, Omondi spoke. 'We have asked you here, Vickie, because we need your help.'

'How?' she asked.

'In three days' time, we will be presenting Jason with a challenge. A challenge he will not like. We believe that you may be able to help.'

Vickie looked apprehensive, but her voice was steady. 'I'll do my best.'

Omondi leaned close to Vickie and whispered in her ear. Her eyes widened, and darted back and forth between the two men. They gazed steadily back at her.

'Well?'

Vickie recovered herself, and nodded. 'Yes. I will.'

'This is no small thing, Vickie,' Horace warned her. 'Jason needs you, but when the moment arrives, you will need him equally. Are you sure?'

'Yes. I'm sure. Positive, actually.'

Horace nodded in approval, and Omondi said, 'You are invaluable, Vickie. You may take the rest of the day to reflect.'

The two men stood together and left. Vickie sat alone at the table for a long time.

'... well of course Ringo was a brilliant drummer, Markie, but that doesn't mean you should *end your friendship* with someone who says otherwise.'

Markie shook her head bitterly. 'It's not just that. Kat's been pissing me off lately. She owes me three tabs, she's riding my ass about talking to her boyfriend for her, and she keeps forgetting to return my diggory doo. This is just the last straw.'

'Those aren't real problems, Charlie,' Jason said in a high, bitchy voice. Markie pointed a finger at him in fury.

'Don't you DARE quote Dee Reynolds against me!!'

'Okay, okay, Markie. I'm just saying, you should think it through. Kat's alright. Even I think so.'

She sighed and nodded. 'I know. Thank you. Kinda reminds me of when you talked me down from beating up Laura.'

'She was just bugging you, Markie.'

'Bullshit! I wrecked the plumbing at her place, *once,* and she wouldn't drop it for six months! If I hadn't been straight at the time, you wouldn't have stopped me!'

'Markie!' Jason said with a laugh. 'CHILL!'

She put a hand to her face and rubbed her temples. 'I need a joint.'

'That's your solution to everything,' Jason reprimanded her. 'When I'm stressed, I drink a cup of tea and read a book.'

She shrugged. 'Tomato-tomahto.'

Jason shuddered. 'According to my Etiquette teacher, it's tomahto.'

Markie giggled with glee. 'The key to preventing World War Two is the pronunciation of *tomahto?!'*

Jason rolled his eyes. 'If only that were the worst of it. The British are insane.'

'I know,' Markie agreed. She took on a bizarre, bug-eyed caricature. *'Oh yes, Mr. Bodkins, the kippers are off until Guy Fawkes Day!'*

'You're psychotic,' Jason chuckled.

'No, I'm not,' she replied. 'Everyone else is.'

'That's pretty much the exact mentality of someone who is psychotic.'

She giggled. 'Every now and then you can be pretty clever, Jason.'

'Oh, you are just too sweet.'

They looked at each other a moment longer before Jason decided to settle for the night.

'You're doing well, Jason,' Markie tendered.

'I hope so,' he replied. 'I get the feeling it's gonna get worse.'

'Well, duh. So what? Just keep doing what you're doing, and you'll be fine.'

Jason smiled. 'Thanks, Markie. See you tomorrow.'

'Word.'

The screen went dark.

Chapter Ten

Jason strolled the cobblestone pathways of Shwari Mawe at a bit of a loss. It was 9:30 in the morning, and he had awoken half an hour ago, quite naturally confused at the fact that that ridiculous drone had not sandpapered his eardrums. After tracking Omondi down, he had been informed that he had the day off, that Vickie was busy, and that he was free to do as he would.

The stillness of the idea hit Jason hard. He knew Markie would be sleeping, so he made his way to the stone Sanctuary. A day off in a place like this seemed more intimidating than anything he had yet encountered.

He shuffled along the outer path, the faux wooden panelling ten feet away. The mossy quartz stones gleamed in the dull morning light. An aged Middle-Eastern man smiled as he passed. Small saplings formed a humble gateway to two tall trees *(how the hell did they get them here?),* which provided superfluous shade under the cloudy sky.

A muffled fit of giggling shook Jason out of his reflection. Jason looked to his left and saw two young women sitting on a nearby bench, eyeing him without subtlety, whispering to each other. At a loss for how to act, he ignored them and quickened pace, drawing louder giggles. For all his dramatic bravado, Jason had always been hopeless against bold women.

He collected himself and turned right, the white stones turning grey. He made his way easily to a small brook, its probable artificiality not affecting its beauty. The scent of lilies and lavenders overwhelmed him as he stopped at the middle of a simple wooden bridge. He leaned on the railing, feeling okay.

A roll of thunder came ominously from the North. Not wanting to test the Kenyan weather, Jason turned and headed for the nearest door to the facility. Suddenly he heard a call.

'Mr. Roberts!'

He turned to his left, and in the nearby clearing against the wall was a small patio with a plexiglass roof. It was empty, save for a diminutive African man sitting in a wicker chair, whom even at a distance Jason could see was at least sixty years old. He beckoned Jason over with a single wave of his arm.

'This is a good place to watch the storm!' he called out. The rain was beginning to fall.

Jason had always enjoyed a good thunderstorm, so he strode and then sprinted to the patio as lightning lit up the sky and the rain turned to a downpour. The merry fellow laughed as Jason scrambled into his shelter.

'A fine run, Mr. Roberts. I would still be on the bridge.'

Jason chuckled and sat down in the wooden lounger next to the stranger. He was almost a head shorter than Jason, with short grey hair and a thin, bearded, memorable face.

His clothing was relaxed and simple – a wrinkled collared shirt with rolled-up sleeves and a pair of faded olive pants. A wooden cane leaned against the arm of his chair.

He held out a hand. 'Yaro Kapesa.'

Jason shook Yaro's hand and made himself comfortable, despite a wince at a mighty crack of thunder. He looked through the ceiling with a thrill at the spectacle above him, reflecting at how long it had been since he'd sat front-row-centre for a thunderstorm.

'You look like a child.'

Jason turned and saw Yaro smiling at him.

'Do they have storms like this in Canada?'

'Almost never where I come from. I've heard it's worse on the coast, but I've never been there.'

Yaro chuckled. 'I marvel at a single nation as large as Canada. It's hard for Africans to imagine.'

'Are you from Kenya?'

Yaro shook his head and with a note of pride, replied, 'I am from Tanzania, just to the south. I am a respectable tobacco farmer, and I was brought here to maintain the Smoking Room.'

Jason couldn't hide his shock. 'You have a *smoking room* here?'

Yaro stared. 'Why wouldn't we?'

'Never mind,' Jason said. 'Just lived in Canada too long, I guess.'

'Far worse things to lament,' Yaro said with a laugh, as they both winced at a crack of thunder. They sat peacefully, enjoying the show. Jason had always wondered at the feeling of serenity one felt in a small bubble of safety surrounded by the chaos of a storm. It felt vaguely spiritual.

'Do you believe you are ready for this, Jason?'

Jason looked at Yaro. There was sincere compassion in his eyes. Even Mugo had not given Jason such an instant air of warmth. Jason looked into the angry sky and shook his head.

'The answer to that question changes all the time.'

Yaro smiled approvingly and nodded. 'I would doubt that you were the man for the job if you had given any *other* answer, Jason.'

Jason tried to brush this off, but could only chuckle sheepishly at such a compliment. He gave Yaro a grateful grin. Yaro nodded again, looked around, and pulled a flask out of his pocket. 'Care for a drink?'

Jason considered for a moment and then took the flask. The liquid had barely touched his tongue when he pulled back in wonder at the extraordinary flavour.

'What the hell *is* this?'

Yaro smiled in delight. 'Mbege. Banana beer. It's popular back home. Alcohol is rationed in this place, not supposed to have that, but... to hell with them, I say.'

Jason smiled and drank again. It was almost as good as the Glenlivet. 'I didn't even know you could *make* alcohol from bananas.'

Yaro grinned. 'If the gods made it, men can discover how to drink it.'

Jason passed the flask back to Yaro with a thank you. The two men sat without a word for almost half an hour. A bizarre mixture of contentment and horror settled upon Jason; the lightning and torrential rain gave Shwari Mawe an amazing new kind of beauty. The storm itself brought forth a terrible reminder of the doom he had come to prevent, as well as the doom he could do nothing about.

An ear-splitting explosion rattled the complex. Jason's stomach clenched as the small lamp above them died instantly. It was far too much, too much drama even for Jason. He stood up and left the makeshift porch and sprinted like a child for the nearest door.

'Be careful!' was all he heard Yaro say.

Small emergency lights made creepy silhouettes out of the bustling men and women clamouring to lock down the KRA. Jason fought lonely panic as he entered his dark, deserted hallway, the thunder still tearing at his senses. He needed Markie. A desperate homesickness had overtaken him. He pushed open the door of Room 212A, hoping against hope… and found the small room lit up, the computer on, and Nick Drake playing gently from its speakers. A note sat on the keyboard. Jason picked it up and read.

> *We were prepared for this eventuality, Jason. This room and your quarters are being powered by generators, and your internet should work. Relax, and try to enjoy yourself. I have not contacted Markie.*
>
> *Horace*

Jason reread the note twice, heartened by the simple gesture. He was beginning to love that man. *And how,* he wondered, *did the bastard know I would come here first?*

A quick press of a couple of buttons sent his cry for help around the world. He still did not worry that she would not respond.

Markie appeared, her slouch hat on her head even at what was surely dawn back in Ontario. She yawned and gave Jason a corny smile.

'Hey.'

'Hey.'

'Everything okay? You're soaking wet.'

'Just homesick, I guess. There's a nasty storm going on, felt like chatting.'

A certain knowledge in her eyes, Markie pressed the conversation forward. 'There was a windstorm here yesterday, my garden's a freakin' mess. Gonna take all day to fix it up.'

A thought occurred to Jason. 'Did you ever name your garden?'

She shook her head. 'Nah. Never thought it needed one. My house is named Patrick, though.'

Jason stared. 'You named your house *Patrick?'*

'Just now, yes.'

Jason shook his head at her for what might have been the millionth time. Knowing Markie, this ludicrous impulse would stick forever and that asking why would only get him a shrug.

'Remember Bob Ross?' she asked.

Jason smiled. 'I always told you you don't need drugs when you have Bob Ross.'

'I love his afro!' she said affectionately. 'I want to live in it.'

'Have you ever painted along with him?' Jason asked.

'Only once. I got really pissed off because he thinks it's so damned easy. I ended up kicking my TV over.'

Jason smiled in delight. 'THAT'S why you got the new TV?!'

Markie nodded with a roll of her eyes. 'That stupid, softspoken know-it-all *bastard!!*'

'Markie, *take it easy!*' Jason said with a laugh. 'You're sketching out over *Bob Ross!*'

Markie took a breath and collected herself. 'I know, I know. I'm just stressed out. You should see my apple saplings. I think I actually heard them crying.'

Jason smiled.

'Anything cool happening today?' she asked.

'They sprung a day off on me. Kinda threw me for a loop.' He frowned. 'I wish they would give me some semblance of warning before… well, *everything.*'

Markie looked thoughtful and said, 'They're probably trying to get you used to surprises.'

Jason chuckled, and knew she was right. 'Probably a handy skill for preventing World Wars, eh?'

She smiled warmly and said, 'Now THAT'S Jason.'

The storm forgotten, they chatted for half an hour in their old meandering way before an emboldened Jason decided to let her tend to her ravaged garden.

Jason leaned back in his chair as the melancholy music played on. He pondered, as much as ever, his bond with Markie. How was it possible that this lunatic had become his best friend? Nothing about it made sense; neither of them was especially fond of the other's social circle, there was a great deal of mutual compromise in keeping each other happy, and, however much they pretended otherwise, there was a good deal of frowning upon each other's lifestyle that had to be kept carefully in check. And yet, here they were.

The storm was passing. Jason stood up and opened the door. The quiet glow of the emergency lights still struggled against the darkness, but now seemed not creepy but comforting. Jason walked back to his quarters, shut off the lights, and lit candles, smirking at the irony. He made a bowl of popcorn and put on *How to Train Your Dragon,* basking in introverted contentment at the incomparable pleasure of doing absolutely nothing. Yet, this new life was beginning to take root in his mind.

Before the movie was half-over, he shut it off, blew out the candles, and left his quarters, and again pushed his way through the green door.

A quick glance showed him Yaro was gone. Only a gentle drizzle remained of the terrible storm. The clouds were passing, and the sun was shining above the western wall of the Sanctuary. The sounds of dripping water and chattering birds mixed with the running of the brook. It was lovely beyond compare, but Jason took it in only for a moment. He had, at last, decided to take this seriously.

He made his way to the library and stepped through the decorated door. He found the history section quite easily and was unsurprised to find a disproportionately large selection on the Second World War.

A familiar act of browsing books was now discovered to be a terrible, pummeling task. *The Battle of France. Joseph Goebbels. Stalingrad.* Two weeks ago, these were vague, distant, tasteless ideas. Conversation starters, really, even to a thirty-three-year-old who cared about them as he did. And now here he was, gathering ammunition for a terrible showdown with their very existence.

Jason pushed this claptrap away and grabbed a paperback on the Battle of Britain, a short volume on Dieppe, and a not-so-short tome on the War in Africa, which Jason knew vaguely to have been referred to by Churchill as *Hitler's soft underbelly*. He avoided looking at the Holocaust shelf; he was not ready for that yet.

Back in his living room he sat reading for two and a half hours. The Anglophile in him was captivated as ever by the distinctly British heroism that had made that tiny island the centrepiece of human history for eleven hundred years, to climax as the great Bastion of Retribution during their terrible Finest Hour. When he, Jason Roberts, was sent back, he would wander into the city of London and find himself surrounded by thousands of glorious heroes, from sixteen-year-old boys who would one day fly Spitfires against the Luftwaffe, to four-year-old children who would be pulled sobbing from their parents to live with strangers across an ocean, to seventy-year-old women who would scramble with pounding hearts to shelter from thousand-pound bombs. If he failed.

It was, for lack of a better word, *exhilarating.*

He would meet Churchill. He would finally visit London, over fifty years before his birth. He would charm ladies, make friends with his heroes, and teach cowards and sophists the terrible consequences of the actions that anchored the most violent century in history.

... humility...

Omondi's voice tore a hole in his mind. A jolt went through Jason, and he deflated. He sat back in his recliner, frowning his surprise.

'What was *that?*' he whispered aloud.

His teacher's mind answered the question for him: He had just demonstrated applied knowledge.

Shaking this off, he continued to stay busy. He spent forty-five minutes in the gym (the delight in Joonheong's eyes when he saw Jason was heartwarming) and then went to Starbucks for a change of scenery and read some more. Though he got plenty of second glances, most everyone left him firmly alone. Jason wondered whether the *People* were given orders to do so when necessary.

He went back to his quarters and had a cup of tea. Deciding at last to abandon shame and indulge himself, he put on the *White Album* and grabbed a Budweiser from the fridge. He thought of the priceless bottle of liquor in his cupboard, but felt some sentimental need to save it. He ran a bath. He munched on cashews and soaked, looking at the textured ceiling in a haze of pleasure. Lounging in decadence the like of which few would ever know, his conscience demanded, *Do I deserve this?*

He promptly told his conscience to fuck off.

Just before ten, Jason had dried off and was in a comfortable maroon bathrobe. He was heading for the door to talk to Markie again, when a powerful knocking rattled it, scaring him out of his euphoria. Alarmed, he swung it open, only to cower behind it amidst a barrage of giggles.

It was the two young women who had eyed him with such interest in Shwari Mawe. The redhead on the left blushed crimson, put her hands over her mouth, and said nothing. Her companion, a shockingly beautiful blonde with an Icelandic flag painted on her cheek, was not so bashful.

'Hello Jason. I am Johanna, and this is Julie. Why aren't you at the dance?'

Jason raised an eyebrow, not quite knowing how to hide his fear at these two aggressive sirens.

'What dance?'

'Horace never told you?!' Johanna cried in patronizing dismay. 'Every other Saturday there is a dance and a party. Just for fun. Keeps us happy. It's in Shwari Mawe.'

There was a hellish silence as Jason struggled for something to say. Finally, the girls dissolved yet again into giggles. They reminded him of Megan, minus the wit.

'Well,' Johanna said at last as Julie continued her trilling laughter, 'see you there, Jason!' They scurried quickly off to who-knows-where. Jason wanted to scream. That kind of nonsense didn't happen to him often, and when it did…

His door was not yet closed when he began to get the urge to check out the dance. The two parts introvert in him had thoroughly enjoyed this relatively quiet day, but the one-part extrovert hadn't let loose in a while. And he hadn't been to a dance (at least, when not supervising horny seventeen-year-olds) in a very long time.

He had not done a *lot* of things, he now realized, in a *very* long time.

He quickly dressed in the collared suit and grey dress pants he had worn for his Etiquette lessons. He shrewdly left the jacket on his bed; he didn't need lessons to teach him the agony of overdressing. He brushed his teeth, tied his hair back, and even found a bottle of Old Spice in his bathroom cabinet to douse himself with. He felt like the nervous jackass he had been in grade eight.

A short walk later, Jason stepped out into Shwari Mawe, and his eyes widened.

A powerful half-moon was made insignificant by a dazzling array of lights, beaming from the rooftop, the bridges, and along the pathways, as large numbers of People walked to and fro, chatting and laughing carelessly. That stupid 'Fireball' song played prominently from the open courtyard, where a sizeable throng was dancing. He saw the two women who had so cordially invited him swaying like silk, rather against the mood of the music. Jason swallowed; he was not much of a dancer.

Luckily, that night he would not have to be as over twenty people, confident and disarmed by their biweekly festivities, stopped him for a chat. Some were clearly couples. Jason had wondered about dating in the KRA, but it was clearly not only permitted, but a lovely place to meet a mate; a woman from India held hands with a man from Brazil, brought together in Kenya almost three years prior by their KRA duties as counsellors. They informed him that KRA members referred to themselves as *Servidors,* a simple Spanish translation of *servants*. Jason felt a rush of relief; he felt stupid calling them *'People'* all the time.

The warmth of the Sanctuary and the genuine smiles Jason received allowed him for the first time to enjoy his celebrity status. He stood chatting with admirers, answering questions, and gratefully acknowledging compliments. There was no doubt that Horace had hired men and women of character; they were careful not to overwhelm Jason, waiting patiently for their turn to pay their respects to the man whom they had been gathered to support.

Several of them hugged him; one elderly American man was clearly biting back tears. He pulled Jason aside and told him that all Servidors over sixty had been allowed a glimpse of past London by Mugo and that his mother had nursed his wounded father to health at a military hospital north of the city in 1944.

Jason thanked the man who, he knew, was dealing with pains and emotions as complex as his own.

Another shock came at the sight of an Italian woman in her forties, who worked in the Research & Development department. She was wearing a simple chain, and hanging from it was a sparkling ruby dog identical to the one whose violent construction he had witnessed five days earlier. She smiled when he gaped at it and informed him that they functioned as medals, given as decorations for exceptional service and achievement. A million questions arose in his mind, but she was not concerned about it; she promptly got him on the subject of his mission, and it took her roughly thirty questions before she was satisfied.

Finally, Jason decided to call it an evening. He politely excused himself (politely to the point where the word 'Canadian' was murmured delightedly just loud enough for him to hear) and quickly made his way back to Room 209.

As a teacher Jason was used to busy days off, but even he raised his eyebrows as he exhaled his exhaustion. Nevertheless, he smiled as he stripped and crawled into bed, reflecting on the new shades and colours this powerful day had added to his vacation. His last thought as he passed out was: *'I wonder if the LC sells banana beer…'*

Chapter Eleven

Omondi once again stared Jason down. He stood next to the telescreen, which was now blasting a massive, detailed map of Europe into Jason's face. Omondi wore his usual academic expression, akin to a man about to enter a fight to the death. Jason sighed and wondered why the biggest hassles in life always came right after a day off.

'Today,' Omondi began, 'we will discuss Hitler's conquest of Europe. It will make a critical impact on your audience. As an aside, I must reiterate: *Do not lose your phone!!*'

Exasperated even more quickly than expected, Jason frowned and spread his hands.

'I *won't,* Omondi! God, why are you bringing *that* up now?'

'Because for this warning, above all others, you will need it to be taken seriously. Hitler's domination of mainland Europe was so rapid, so complete, and so humiliating that it could not possibly be believed beforehand without irrefutable, prophetic evidence.'

'So, I'm a prophet now,' Jason rumbled.

Omondi frowned. 'It was a figure of speech, you dickwad.'

Jason bellowed a laugh, shocked at this unlikeliest of roasts. 'Not bad, Omondi, not bad.'

Omondi's face remained in its perpetual scowl, but Jason saw a distinct softening in his eyes.

'Anyway,' Omondi continued in a tone that forbade further interruption, 'Hitler's army was outnumbered and outgunned. His dreams of ruling Europe were astronomically improbable. There were three keys that made it happen. Can you imagine what any of them might be?'

'One, at least,' Jason replied. 'The prep-time he was given by the Allies' refusal to act.'

'Indeed. The very nature of your mission is designed to cut out that leg of the tripod. Had the Allies… bitten the bullet, as I believe you would say, and taken decisive, preemptive action, or even had they charged into Germany with guns blazing instead of allowing the protracted phoney war, Nazi Germany would have fallen like a herd of sheep. Instead, Hitler was appeased, reasoned with, catered to. He built his army into a genuine threat. The helpless nations he was permitted to assimilate gave him rich pools of resources. Inaction, above all other things, gave birth to the Second World War as we know it.'

'Would you say we've learned our lesson since then?' Jason asked.

'Irrelevant,' Omondi said rather rudely. 'Do you know a second key?'

Jason racked his brains, but came up empty. He had a feeling he would kick himself at the obviousness of the answer.

'The second key came out of the mind of a German General by the name of Erich von Manstein. It was a powerful military innovation that utilized overwhelming speed and pinpoint land/air coordination, allowing German forces to cut through Allied defenses and capture huge expanses of territory with frightening efficiency.'

Jason nodded. 'Blitzkrieg.'

'While this may not seem a necessary point to discuss in London, we feel it to be crucial, because-'

'Because if I fail,' Jason cut in, 'at least they'll still see it coming.'

Omondi's head cocked to its side. It was the closest Jason had seen from him to an expression of surprise. 'Yes.'

Jason took a breath and asked a weighted question. 'Do you believe I'm likely to fail?'

Omondi's face grew harder still.

'Even with the most painstaking training we can give you, it is very possible. The determination to avoid war in 1935 is great. You may make terrible mistakes. AND,' he shouted over Jason's indignant rebuttal, '...and, something greater than ourselves may not want such a venture to succeed in the first place.'

Jason's jaw clenched. He could see as clearly as ever that Omondi was serious.

'So you're a *God-fearing man* too, eh?'

'I am agnostic,' Omondi droned. 'But if a God does exist, it is not taking this lightly. It may well be frowning deeply upon this very conversation. Or maybe it approves and is leading you to victory. Or maybe it is not there. But until you are certain, the possibility of a third presence in this room is not something I would take so lightly as you do, Jason.'

Jason stifled a chill. He didn't quite know what to say. Omondi didn't pursue the subject.

'But we digress. The third key to the unstoppable Axis onslaught was a German pharmaceutical company called Temmler.'

Jason stared blankly. He had never heard that name.

'Temmler manufactured and distributed a miracle drug called Pervatin which became standard issue to German military forces.'

'Pervatin?'

A dry look of amusement came over Omondi's face. 'It is known colloquially in the West as *crystal meth.*'

Jason's jaw dropped. 'That is *true?!*' He had long heard tales of drug use in Nazi Germany, but had dismissed them as conspiracy theories.

'Yes,' said Omondi. 'It is lethally true. The consequential effects of the narcotic were not well understood, and the euphoria, wakefulness, and focus it provided made the German army, particularly its infantry, appear superhuman to their foes.'

Jason smiled at the murky humour... an entire continent of military might, overrun by tweakers.

'What-*ever…*'

'Painting a dramatic picture with these three terrible facts will create a fearsome foe in the minds of your audience and, more importantly, a logical one. *Everything* you tell the House must be made to make sense. There can be no holes in the net you weave.'

'Where the hell did you learn English, Omondi?' Jason asked.

'There's an app for that,' Omondi snapped and continued. 'There is another ace up your sleeve, which will serve you well when you encounter the French leadership–'

'The FRENCH LEADERSHIP?! I'm meeting them too?!'

'Yes, you are. You must compel them to London through your initial English audience. And when you do, you will have the bait you need to gain their support.'

'And that would be?' Jason asked.

'The humiliation that has been a boil on their neck to this day, following the blithering incompetence that led to their total surrender to Germany in less than six weeks. You must appeal to their egos.'

Jason instantly thought of Groundskeeper Willie. 'Turn their pride against them,' he said.

'All evils can be turned upside down. Now go. Your next *Etiquette* lesson, as we must now apparently call it, begins in half an hour in the cafeteria. Wear your suit. You will need it.'

'Don't I get a second suit eventually?' Jason asked. Amusement again flashed over Omondi's face.

'You are getting too used to this.'

Dressed in style once again, Jason opened the door of the cafeteria. Knowing what awaited him, he reflected on his lack of trepidation. He entered the room and blinked in surprise.

The windows were darkened and decorated with rich burgundy curtains; candles burning between them from newly fastened sconces. The off-yellow walls made it all look ridiculous. Cheesy, saxophone-heavy jazz mewled from the corner-speakers. The tables and chairs had been cleared out, save for a single small table near the back corner, at which the sultry figure of Megan sat, her fingers folded beneath her chin. She smiled with her normal predatory menace, though her eyes remained irritatingly fluttery.

'Oh Jason, how I've missed you…'

Jason grimaced in annoyance. 'It's only been two days.'

She stood up, revealing a sparkling white strapless dress with a thin sash that flawlessly matched the colour of the curtains. Again, her nose-ring made her already magnificent beauty seem to fire bullets. She beckoned him to her with a curl of her finger.

'As Horace informed me upon your arrival, you do have a certain grace about you. Today, we will measure how you maintain that grace *under pressure*. Shall we?' That infuriating smile never left her face.

Jason approached, feeling confident, and moved to sit down… only to freeze, his groin muscles straining, at a shocked gasp from his salaried date. He looked up to see a scandalized look on her face, the like of which he had not yet encountered. They stood staring at each other for a moment until Jason's eyes rolled in comprehension. He straightened up, and as penance, took her hand in his as he helped her to her seat like a gentleman. She was still shaking her head as he joined her.

The moment she was settled the lesson began, but good. A sumptuous three-course dinner with fine wine was served over the next hour. Despite the delicious food, Jason spent most of his time stifling a scream as Megan barked orders and directed his every move, from the angle at which he placed his fork in his mouth to the subject matter of his mealtime conversation.

Each false move brought down an eloquent wrath worthy of Gunnery Sergeant Hartman, albeit in a sexy British accent.

At last, the ordeal was over and the dessert plates were taken away. Jason was in the process of breathing a sigh of relief when the zipper-scratch of a changing record grinded over the intercom. A moment later a cascade of violins washed through the room as an early Frank Sinatra ballad began. As Jason recovered himself, he noticed Megan glaring at him, an eyebrow raised. Jason shut down this time and glared back; he was done pretending he could understand women, let alone this one.

'Would you care to dance, Megan?' she said pointedly, holding out her hand.

'That would be MAH-velous, Jason,' he shot back as he held out his own. With one fluid movement, he manoeuvred so that his hand was supporting hers. She giggled in shock, a hand over her mouth. Jason thought she just might be blushing had her skin-tone revealed it. For the first time in her presence, he cracked a small smile.

They stood together and walked to the centre of the room. Taking a mental cue from Clark Gable, he bowed carefully, as she had taught him. She smiled her appreciation, and curt-seyed back. Then she pounced like a leopard from her crouch, put her hand around his shoulder, and stopped so that their chests just made contact.

Down, boy.

She looked straight into his eyes the entire time, bringing about a terror that approached that of his view into the past three days earlier. After half a minute or so he spoke.

'What do I talk about now?'

She smiled. 'Chitchat during a dance is as silly and pandering in 1935 as now, Jason. Just do your best.'

Jason took a breath. 'How did you *really* get this job?'

She smiled and shook her head. 'That's not for you to know.'

'Why not?'

'Because I am to remain a mystery to you. I insisted upon it. Omondi and Horace agree that *something* here should remain a mystery, and it might as well be me.'

'Who says I want to know that badly?'

'You will.'

'And why is that?'

'Because you need something interesting in your life. You need it terribly.'

Jason scowled. 'You really enjoy berating me, eh? –OW!'

The music screeched to a halt as Megan pushed herself away from Jason. She had darted out her hand and given him a sharp rap on the bottom lip. There was burning fury in her eyes as she pointed a finger in his face.

'From now on, every time you utter that *ridiculous* Canadian syllable, I will smack you on the mouth just so. Is that understood?!'

'Okay, OKAY, I'm sorry!'

'And stop *apologizing* so much!!' she snapped, and stormed to the bathroom, slipping on her heels. 'You think *Churchill* became the man he was by apologizing?!' She gave him a withering glare and slammed the door.

Jason stood flabbergasted for a moment and then dissolved into a quiet fit of hysterical laughter.

After another twenty minutes of charm and torture (which he shrugged off almost too easily), he was sent to change and to return to the Blue Room for his next Ethics lesson. Switching gears from Omondi's nonsense to Megan's, and now to Horace's, in the course of a few hours was powerfully grating, but he found himself in good spirits as he got in the mindset necessary for Horace's onslaught.

He was almost to his quarters, when he froze. A frightening chill went through him from head to toe. Something had connected in his mind that hit him with the force of a freight train. His change of clothes forgotten, he turned and hurried straight to the Blue Room, ignoring a hello from a passer-by.

He pushed the door forcefully open. Horace's friendly smile evaporated at the look in Jason's eyes, and he stood to face him. Jason spoke before Horace could.

'What about the Bomb?'

'Which bomb?' Horace asked. His playing dumb only compounded Jason's agitation.

'You know damned well which bomb! *The Atomic Bomb!* Do I tell them about it or not?'

Horace opened his mouth and closed it. He did not meet Jason's eyes as he spoke.

'That was meant to be covered later…'

'NOW!' Jason bellowed.

Horace nodded and gestured to the brown leather chairs.

'I don't feel like sitting.'

'Jason–'

'Let me tell you what my mind just put together,' Jason hissed. 'By some divine miracle we've avoided blowing the Earth to bits since Hiroshima. Now I am supposed to erase all that and give nuclear war a second chance! I know perfectly well how close they'll be to discovering the bomb in '35, and for all I know, I could be opening the door to a THOUSAND scenarios that could end the world! And you expect me to be OKAY with that! Are you out of your GODDAMNED MINDS?!'

Horace met Jason's furious eyes with a glare of his own, his jaw set. 'If you think we expect you to be okay with that, Jason, then maybe you're not as perfect as I thought.'

Jason's eyes flashed. 'And what do you mean by that?'

'Did you actually think there was *ever* a way to make this mission foolproof? That even your most flawless success would not unleash a tidal wave of fundamental danger?! Do you think I saw GOD HIMSELF when you walked into that office?! You are forgetting, my dear friend, how utterly small you really are!'

Suppressing the knowledge that Horace was right, Jason stepped closer.

'Why World War Two anyway? Why not the Crusades? Why not go back to the start and stop Adam and Eve from eating the fucking apple?'

'AS I HAVE SAID,' Horace snarled, stepping closer still, 'I AM A CHRISTIAN!!'

The two men stared each other down, their faces a foot apart. Then, Horace's features steadily relaxed, and he gave a small, gentle smile.

'You're not going to hit me. I can see it all over your face.'

At last Jason remembered to breathe. He broke eye contact at last and stepped away. 'You *bastard,'* he said with a shaky chuckle.

Horace sat down in one of the armchairs, crossed his legs, and sat calmly, watching Jason get himself together. A carefully measured look was on his face. Jason breathed out the last of his agitation and met his friend's eyes again.

'Sorry.'

Horace nodded, smiling gently again. He gestured to the other chair, and Jason obliged.

'The jump is preprogrammed, Jason. It's '35 or bust.'

Jason nodded. 'I remember.'

'You have at last gotten hold of the great dilemma of your mission, Jason. And I'm afraid you pitifully underestimate it. The doomsday scenarios your influence will create are not a thousand, but infinite. Something far worse than the Second World War could very well be brought about by its very prevention.'

'Then why do this?'

'Because we must have *some* faith in our fellow man, Jason. We must believe, however blindly, that there is good at work in our hearts. And anyway, you know the alternative to your mission: the absolute certainty of our extinction. A ten percent chance of survival is better than zero.'

Jason shook his head in dismay. 'You really think ten percent is all we can hope for?'

Horace's eyes dropped in reflection. He shook his head, a bitter twist on his mouth. 'Those are better odds than I would have given us during the Cuban Missile Crisis.'

'Touché,' Jason muttered.

Horace looked at him again. 'Should you tell the British about the Bomb, Jason? I'm afraid that is one of the many, many questions that we must leave to you. You are a wise enough man, and only you will see the unfolding of events at ground level. Here and now, it is useless to even ponder such things.'

Numbness spread straight to Jason's fingertips. He did not like this at all.

Horace's face softened. Like the empath he was, he changed the subject. 'If I may ask, Jason -as a friend, of course- what do you and Markie chat about?'

Hearing the sincerity of the question, Jason decided to be truthful. 'Whatever we want. We just… sort of drift through the conversation. With her, half of it doesn't even make sense.'

A warm smile stretched across Horace's face. 'No wonder you're so strong.'

Jason didn't know what to say to this. Horace gestured to the door, and said, 'Go have some fun.'

Jason stood and made for the door. The poster of a sneering Johnny Cash was always a pleasant thing to see at the end of these lessons.

Suddenly a thought occurred to Jason, and he decided to be brave enough to express it. He turned back to Horace, who was twiddling on his phone.

'Tell me this, Horace. As a Christian, how can you reconcile your beliefs with the world ending in this way? Doesn't it refute the Book of Revelation?'

'Not when you look at the big picture,' Horace replied without looking up.

'And what is the big picture?'

Horace looked up slowly and fixed him with a gaze of frightening intensity. 'Believe me, Jason,' he replied softly. 'You don't want me to answer that question.'

Jason never shut up so quickly in his life.

Everything was getting surreal. What was he becoming? Jason sat at his desk in his lobby twenty minutes later, certainly not in the mindset for fun.

He had reached out across the world to Markie, only to be devastated by the terrible blow of her absence. This was awful. He was on the verge. He thought of Vickie, but would not make such a young girl his crutch. It hit him then that, in ways that mattered very much, he was on his own.

Jason took a breath. And another. He had long since learned to act during moments like this, and so he did. He put a quiet blues album on the stereo. He brewed a pot of tea. And furious for not thinking of it first, stripped out of his stupid suit and stepped out in nothing but a pair of loose shorts. He put his beloved *Do not disturb* sign on the door and sat down at his desk, cherishing every sip of his chamomile. He decided to write again.

After pulling out a pen and paper, he *still* could not draw his mind from the topic that had led him to that moment. He pulled out his phone, reflecting with astonishment at how little attention he had been paying it. He thought for a moment, and googled: *hitler eiffel tower.*

And there he was. For the first time since this fiasco started, Jason was looking at the face of the man himself. Adolf Hitler, standing at the peak of his conquest, with a couple of other assholes in the heart of Paris. The majestic symbol of romance and artistry behind him had been mutilated into the ultimate altar upon which democracy had been sacrificed.

Jason said it aloud and with cynical fury. *'My opponent.'*

It was impossible. It was blithering lunacy. As Jason stared into those soulless iron eyes, he knew he was finished with this. Half of him still wondered whether it was all a joke, while the other half was *already* laughing at the idea that some small-town, twenty-first century jackoff could possibly turn the tide brought down by the defining mind of genius and darkness. He was done.

He put on jeans and a t-shirt, slipped into his shoes, and moved for the door, factually intent on giving his notice, when he stopped.

Something, somehow, compelled him to think this through. He knew it was not a joke. He stood in silence, scowling in reflection, his arms at his hips like Peter Pan. He knew that he, among billions, had been asked to do this. He had been shown visions that very few had seen and that none at all knew in the way he did.

And…

Jason almost ran back to his desk. He pulled out the parchment on which he had written his aimless schpiel two days earlier.

Churchill was a man. He was not an archangel. Perfect good is impossibly more difficult than perfect evil. Yet this man found it within himself to rise above the petty controversy of his imperfection and do what was within his incomparable power to lead Christian civilization to the most glorious victory over evil the world has ever known.

Jason shook his head. 'What the *hell,* man…'

He sat down, picked up his phone again, and googled: *churchill tommy-gun.* And he deflated in about a dozen different emotions.

There stood the Great Man, in his brilliant pinstripe suit, his enormous cigar hanging from his sneering mouth as he posed with his gangster's piece for *his* iconic picture. Jason smiled, reveling in the power, the charisma, the *silliness* of the whole image, which stood in defiantly cheeky contrast to Hitler's *tour de France.*

If Hitler was his opponent, Churchill was his ally. If he stuck this out, and pulled that terrible trigger, he would shake the hand of his greatest hero. He would work with him, joke with him, conspire with him quietly. He would, like a certain reluctant hobbit, *have an adventure!*

He picked up his pen and a new piece of parchment and wrote in sudden impulse and inspiration.

France -one of the world's mightiest military superpowers for a thousand years- had been consumed by the Nazi War Machine, in less than six weeks.

Britain now stood utterly alone, against the most terrible army the Forces of Darkness had ever assembled.

It was a challenge so grave, so dark, so desperate, that even Churchill himself privately admitted it might be too late...

Jason read and reread these short paragraphs, replacing a word or two until he was satisfied. Why he had begun here, he was not sure, but he was sure of one thing: He had just written his first history lesson.

Jason smiled and stood up. He opened the door, stepped into the hall, where a musical ringtone could be heard coming from 212A. He rushed inside and with a press of a button found himself looking at Markie.

'Hey,' she said. 'Sorry, I was weeding my garden. Everything okay?'

Jason gave her an exhilarated smile. 'I'm going to *do* this, Markie.'

Markie cocked her head to one side, studying the unusual expression on his face. Finally, with a look of solemn comprehension, she nodded.

'You *are,* aren't you…'

'I dunno, something clicked just now.'

He told her every detail of his tornado of a day, growing more animated by the minute. She listened raptly, her smile growing bigger and bigger as he almost exploded with excitement at his anticipation of meeting his hero.

'I've never seen this side of you, Jason,' she said at last.

Jason chuckled. 'I'm as surprised as you are, believe me.'

She smiled affectionately. 'I'm not surprised. Always knew I would someday.'

This sweeping compliment from the person he respected most in his life sealed the deal once and for all. He smiled, nodding his gratitude.

'Anyway,' she added, 'think who else you could meet! Paul McCartney's dad… Emma Watson's great uncle…….. Margaret Thatcher…'

'Oh my God, will you cut the crap!' Jason said with a laugh. 'We both know you know nothing about history.'

'I know Albert Hoffman!' she countered.

'Who?'

'Discovered acid.'

Jason nodded in a complete lack of surprise. Markie was her own woman, but he knew that woman.

'Oh, I forgot to tell you,' Markie chirped in excitement, 'I painted something new.' She held up a small canvas, showing him what would have been a picturesque seascape were the swirling ocean not blood red. Markie often expressed a dark side in her paintings that was otherwise mostly absent from her character. Nevertheless, it was oddly beautiful.

'I love it,' Jason said with a grin.

Predictably, she went coy and muttered, 'No you don't.'

Jason spent almost a full two minutes extolling her talents before she was satisfied. He had always admired her courage and confidence, but she shrank into feminine insecurity when it came to her art.

Jason suddenly had a tremour, and decided to ask a heavy question. 'You've never done meth, have you?'

'For fuck's sake, Jason, why would you even ask me that?!'

'I'm sorry, I'm sorry,' Jason said quickly. 'It's just... on my mind today.'

'I don't even *want* to know why,' she said with a dismissive frown. She chilled out quickly, however, and the moment passed by.

'Oh well,' she said at last, putting the painting aside. 'I guess I should let the Time Traveller get about his important business.'

'Shut up,' Jason muttered with a grimace.

She smirked. 'Make sure you put in the good word for us common folk of the future, eh?'

'SHADDAP!!'

Chapter Twelve

Jason was awoken the next morning – an hour earlier than usual – by a loud knocking at the door. Like the trained space-monkey he was, he got up, put on a t-shirt, and answered it without much enthusiasm. To his delighted surprise, Vickie squeezed the breath out of him before he even had a chance to react.

'I *missed* you, Jason!' she said as she hugged him around his middle. She pulled away and beamed up at him. Jason returned her smile, overcome as usual by the affection she inspired within him.

'I missed you too. So, what's up?'

Her smile faltered a bit, but she answered steadily.

'You have a very special mission today. Outside the KRA, actually.'

This struck Jason as odd. 'Why did Horace send you to tell me?'

Her adorable grin returned to full force. 'I volunteered 'cause I'm coming with you.'

This was the best news Jason had heard in what felt like a very long time. 'That's awesome! Where are we going?'

Again her smile faltered. 'I'm not supposed to tell you. Horace and Omondi want to.'

Jason fought not to show his frustration. Had he been dealing with anyone but Vickie, he would have demanded answers. He decided to play along. He excused himself and quickly dressed in a t-shirt and jeans. Then he joined Vickie in the hall, and the two of them walked far too quietly to Horace and Omondi's shared office. They were both waiting, and Horace began at once.

'Good morning, Jason. Thank you, Vickie, for retrieving our mutual friend.'

'What's going on, Horace?' Jason demanded.

'Today, Jason, we wish for you to begin a new – and very difficult – stage in your training.'

'Where are we *going?*'

Horace hesitated, choosing his words. As usual, Omondi did not have such reservations.

'The four of us are leaving for the airport to board a private jet to Poland.'

'Poland?!'

Horace nodded. Jason was baffled and overwhelmed yet again.

'Why in God's name are we going to Po–'

The last word caught in his mouth. He stepped back from Horace in horror as his mind put the terrible pieces together. At last, he found a whispering voice.

'We're going to Auschwitz, aren't we...'

Horace nodded again.

All the strength Jason had found within himself was brought to yet another fierce battle against powerful fear and hazy moral turmoil. But he kept control.

'Auschwitz…'

'We know how enormous a request this is, Jason. But we beg of you to agree to–'

'Just *shut up* for a sec.'

Jason turned his back on the three of them, leaning against the wall.

It was the most overwhelming emotional crisis of this terrible journey, and he knew it would not be so for long if he went to Auschwitz. He had always desired to experience that dark monument to human nature. But not like this. Not when…

'I don't know…'

'Jason,' Horace murmured, 'as I stated in our first lesson, on one issue alone we have overridden Duni's instruction, and it is the most critical issue of all. You *need* to breathe the vapours of the Holocaust. We believe this to be the only way for you to fully understand how desperately you must desire your mission to succeed.'

Jason said nothing, and kept his back turned.

'*I'm* coming with you, Jason…'

That lovely voice. That sweet innocence and profound strength. Jason turned slowly and looked at Vickie, whose face was as bright as ever. He shook his head and smiled at this girl whom, in one week, he had come to love like a little sister.

He looked at Horace and Omondi, and nodded. Horace grinned in triumph. Omondi remained Omondi.

'We will be back in Kenya tomorrow morning. Please go get ready. We hope to be in the air in an hour.'

Jason turned to go, then stopped at the door and turned to the three of them again.

'Vickie had better get a decoration, you know what I mean?'

Vickie smiled excitedly, reached her hands to her neck, and pulled loose her silver chain from which there hung a sparkling sapphire dog.

Jason left a quick message to Markie, put on *his* silver chain, and joined Horace, Omondi, and Vickie at the rear of the complex. After a cramped ride in the beat-up SUV (Jason cynically remarked that they should sell a jeweled dog or two and buy the complex a second car), they boarded the same private jet that had carried Jason to this continent and were soon in the air on their way to another.

Jason sat quietly by himself on the familiar couch for the first half-hour. Something about this flight was very different from his first. He was with friends (after a fashion), he knew what awaited him at his destination (not that that made it any easier to deal with), and above all, the simple fact was that he was not the same man who had gotten off this plane such a short time ago.

He heard a quick rap on the frame of the doorway. Jason smiled. 'Hi Vickie,' he said without looking up.

Vickie glided with her usual grace into the cramped room and sat next to him. 'How did you know it was me?' she asked.

'You're the only one who would have knocked.'

Vickie giggled, but her smile left her face quickly. They sat together, their eyes meeting and turning. Beginning a conversation like this was like trying to eat an elephant.

'My father visited Auschwitz when I was six.'

Jason looked up in surprise. Vickie's bottom lip stuck out as she remembered. 'He never told me much about it. By the time I was old enough to deal with it, it had… just faded, I guess.'

'Do you remember *anything*?' Jason asked, failing to hide his pleading.

Vickie looked down, clearly regretting bringing up the memory. 'Just his face. He was… different, for a while, when he got home.'

Jason felt a chill as he nodded. For the first time, Vickie had made him feel worse.

'I'm sorry, Jason. I shouldn't have started with that.'

'It's okay, Vickie, don't worry. I'm glad I have you here.'

'I'm glad I am too. Cooking for the cause is nice, but the front lines are more exciting, especially with you.'

Jason smiled, reflecting on the word *cause* as he did so. 'Do you know much about it?'

'Probably not as much as you, but it hit hard in history class. I'm… pretty scared, actually.'

Jason nodded. 'I wouldn't want to meet the person who wouldn't be.'

Amazingly she smiled with confidence. 'But we've got each other.'

They smiled at each other for a moment. Vickie's eyes darted to Jason's left. Jason turned and saw Horace entering their little hub, followed closely by Omondi. They sat down across from Jason and Vickie, and Omondi began their latest barrage.

'Horace is in charge of this expedition. You must do everything he says.'

'Why you, Horace?' Vickie asked.

Horace smiled sadly. 'Experience, I'm afraid.'

'You've been to Auschwitz before?' Jason asked.

'Seven times.'

'Seven?!' Jason and Vickie cried together.

Horace looked at the floor, that same uncharacteristic awkwardness shading his face.

'You may remember, Jason, in our conversation at Starbucks, that I avoided the topic of studying the war?'

Jason nodded.

Horace's face grew more troubled by the moment.

'Say it, Horace,' Omondi insisted.

Horace took a breath. 'My grandfather was one Friedrich Wagner, a low-level enforcer at the Sobibor Extermination Camp.'

The hum of the plane's engine droned on. Jason and Vickie stared in astonishment. Omondi's face remained calm.

'It was a great honour for him,' Horace said bitterly, 'or so I've heard. Being exclusively an extermination camp, only a small staff of thugs was necessary.' His hands were clasped and shaking.

'What happened to him?' Jason asked quietly.

'After the war, he disappeared,' Horace said. 'I've tried to track him down, but it doesn't seem possible. He's surely dead by now.'

'Have you ever visited the camp where he worked?' Vickie asked. Horace shook his head.

'It no longer exists, Vickie. The Nazis demolished it after a prisoner revolt. There is a monument built on the place where it stood, but…'

'Is that why it was so easy for Omondi to persuade you to join the KRA?' Jason asked.

'There was nothing easy about it,' Horace said quietly. 'I did it because I had to. Once I learned what was at work here, I knew if I didn't do what I could, I would wake up screaming for the rest of my life.'

Horace's mouth tightened in pain. This revelation was taking a toll on his countenance like Jason would not have believed from him.

'Has going to Auschwitz gotten any easier?'

'No,' Horace said without looking up, 'and I pray it never does.'

Jason turned to Omondi. 'Have *you* been to Auschwitz?'

'I went with Horace, twenty months ago.'

'What is it like?'

Omondi's powerful eyes looked into Jason's. 'Having visited both the mass graves of Rwanda *and* Auschwitz, I will merely say one thing: The world *deserves* to end.'

Jason felt Vickie inch closer to him. He put his arm around her. Omondi and Horace stood up together and left without another word. Jason glanced at Vickie, whose eyes were miles away.

'Those guys sure know how to kill a party, eh?' he consoled. She smiled.

After a relatively smooth shuffle through customs (their preferential airport treatment did not extend this far), Jason found himself surrounded by the beautiful city of Kraków. Vickie stuck close by him as Horace led the small pilgrimage away from John Paul II Airport, and soon they were getting into a taxi van. Horace sat in the front, and Omondi got in the back, allowing Jason to sit comfortably with Vickie. Soon they were weaving through the ancient city. Jason ignored the breathtaking architecture around them as their grim destination grew closer. The throaty, elegant Polish language yammered on the squawk-box.

'Do you understand any of that?' Jason asked Omondi.

'Why would I?' Omondi replied.

'Isn't there an app for that too?'

'Only a lunatic would attempt to learn Polish,' Omondi said. Jason and Vickie chuckled.

Soon Kraków was behind them, and they were in flat, unremarkable fields. Horace turned to look at Horace and Vickie.

'We will be there in half an hour.'

'Half an hour?!' Jason exclaimed. 'It's that close to the city?' Horace turned to look at Jason.

'Various factors went into the location of Auschwitz, but the deciding factor was likely its proximity to a major railway junction. For transporting victims, Vickie,' he finished, seeing her confusion.

'What did Hitler think of Asians?' Vickie asked. Jason could have wept at the question. Omondi spoke up from the back seat.

'Interestingly, Hitler and the Nazis held Asian races in high regard, even as historically superior. He included them in his list of 'Honorary Aryans.' Vickie said nothing more.

Jason looked out the window as the Polish fields raced by. He was *so* tired. He was terrified. For the first time, it hit Jason that Omondi had only been half-right; he was *already* a minority of one.

He was startled out of his daze by Vickie, who had laid her head on his shoulder. He could see the trouble in her face. He leaned his head against hers and took comfort in having someone to comfort.

A short time – an eternity – later, Horace spoke.

'We're here.'

Already shaking, Jason opened his door, Vickie following closely behind him. The cab sped away and Jason looked across the road at a dense line of birch trees, behind which he could just make out the dull, speckled red bricks of sturdy, old, two-storey office buildings. Brutally effective barbed-wire fences lay in their shadows. The four of them walked eastward, past a beaten-up wooden hall.

And there it was. The gate.

It was not nearly as large as Jason had imagined. A bus could scarcely have squeezed through. A sturdy black gate that would have been utterly unremarkable were it not for the three large German words sprawling over it:

ARBEIT MACHT FREI

'Work will set you free,' Vickie translated quietly.

Jason's mind broke from its horror, and he turned to look at her. 'You speak German, too?' She shook her head.

'I know that sign.'

'Normally,' Horace said to Jason and Vickie, 'a guide is required for these visits. However, I have been given special permission to see us through as I see fit.'

The four of them walked through the gate and into something astonishing: a neatly kept system of narrow streets edged with cobbled curbs, with fresh-cut lawns sprouting small trees. Large brick buildings with red roofs were cramped into the limited space. They were not pleasant, but far from conventionally terrifying. In fact, their surroundings could almost be mistaken for a Dickensian village. Nevertheless, some passing visitors were already weeping.

'This is Auschwitz I,' Horace said calmly. 'The *brain* of Auschwitz-Birkenau, as this place is properly called. Many of these buildings functioned as administrative, political, and economic offices throughout the camp's operation. But not all of them.'

He led them up the main road and then guided them to the right. They stopped at an unremarkable building marked *Block 10.*

'Do you know what happened here?' Horace asked. Jason shook his head.

'Block 10 is where they performed the medical experiments, Jason.'

A grinding, guttural cross between a retch and a scream was ripped from Jason as he crumpled to the ground where the evillest men in history had once stood. Vickie and Omondi rushed to Jason's side as he gasped for breath and looked up at the quaint brick building, which had safeguarded the most horrifying atrocities any God had ever allowed to happen.

'Jason, are you okay?!' Vickie asked in panic, kneeling beside him.

'You started with this?' Jason snarled at Horace in fury, his fingers grasping vainly at the gravelly street. *'You started with this!!'*

A strange hardness had touched Horace's face. There was only faint compassion in his eyes as he knelt beside his friend. He gestured to the horror before them.

'This is ALL of this, Jason! This place is the lens through which devils looked at the world they were ravaging. This moment is why we brought you here, and we would not have done so if we did not know for certain that you were strong enough to face it. *So face it!!'* He stood and held out his hand.

Vickie looked up at Horace in wonder. Even Omondi looked unnerved. Jason, still hyperventilating, shook his head.

'I can't go in there. I won't. It wouldn't be right.'

Horace's face softened as he remembered himself, though his hand remained outstretched.

'The interior of Block 10 is off-limits, Jason. But there is much that is not. Please get up.'

Jason hesitated only for a moment and then took Horace's hand. He got to his feet, and Horace's familiar sad smile returned to his face as he dusted him off and gestured for them to follow. Even with the flurry of images and feelings that came after, Jason would never forget what had come over his friend at that moment.

Jason had only just gotten his emotions together when they were tested again. Next door was Block 11, where the Nazis had punished troublesome prisoners. Horace led them on a detailed tour, including the torture rooms, thirty-inch-square isolation chambers, and the first primitive gas chambers, where the means of solving the 'Jewish Problem' were born. When they reached the gas chambers, Vickie took Jason's hand in a tight grip and did not let go again.

Though their tour of Auschwitz I was not exhaustive, it was more than enough, and soon they were on a shuttle-bus. After a few short minutes, they were back on their feet. Horace surveyed his familiar surroundings and turned to his friends.

'This is Birkenau. The slavery and exterminations were carried out here.'

Jason looked about him in numbness, the like of which he had never known.

It was MASSIVE.

Row upon row of huge wooden bunkers stretched almost beyond sight. In front, behind, to the left, and right sat drab wooden barns built for the sole purpose of slowly murdering human beings.

Words could describe the atrocities. But only his eyes could make him understand the scale. This was industrialized slaughter on a level unrivalled in history.

'Do you see the grass around us?' Horace asked. 'At the time of Birkenau's operation, there was only mud. Elie Wiesel, a Nobel Prize winning author who suffered here, has said that if there had been grass, he would have eaten it.'

Most of Horace's tour passed in a haze, in a vacuum of nothing. Jason felt gutted, empty. The purpose for which he had come was obliterated and only the moment remained.

He was kept on his feet only by the small hand he held in his. The night before he had refused to make Vickie his crutch.

She was now his lifeline, the one link in his mind with what it meant to feel alive at all.

He would remember rows of dingy, triple-decked beds, some set at 45-degree angles. He would remember giant mounds of crude leather shoes, some meant to fit babies. He would remember the sole surviving gas chamber and standing in a room where a hundred thousand people had perished.

Only one moment stood out clearly after Block 10. The four of them were standing in Block 4, in front of a vast, nauseating vitrine of human hair, shaved from the heads of prisoners upon their arrival so long ago. Jason was startled by a quiet whisper from Vickie.

'You little bitch…'

Jason turned his head to see a girl, about sixteen, subtly taking a goofy selfie in front of the abomination they were viewing. Then she scurried off with a suitably solemn look on her face.

Jason was too numb to feel much for it at that moment. Yet he managed to remember Omondi's words on the plane that morning.

'The world deserves to end…'

As dusk settled, the four of them boarded their plane home. Though it was only his third view of the private plane's interior, Jason welcomed it like his own living room. After takeoff, Jason re-entered the lounge and immediately fell upon the couch. He was barely comfortable, when Vickie crawled up beside him and drew close. They were both asleep in seconds.

Horace and Omondi sat together in the small dining cabin. Both wore expressions of determined calm.

'A success?' Omondi asked.

'Utterly,' Horace replied, staring into space.

'You were quite remarkable out there.'

Horace gave a small, sombre smile. 'I think my next visit might be a little easier. A little. And I'm okay with that.'

Omondi nodded. 'I could not have done this without you. All of it. Part of me still wonders why we bother, but it is going better than I dreamed because of you.'

Horace said nothing, but his eyes were peaceful.

'I screamed,' Omondi said suddenly.

Horace looked at him. 'Screamed at what?'

A faint smile touched Omondi's mouth. 'When Duni showed me the hover disc. I screamed like a little girl. A dozen people almost saw it. Almost blew the whole thing to hell before it even started.'

Horace chuckled and went to get a late dinner.

Chapter Thirteen

Horace woke Jason and Vickie for the landing. Jason slept most of the drive back to the KRA, then found his way back to his quarters and slept some more. When at last his body rejected the possibility of turning off for another minute, Jason went to 212A.

When Markie saw the look on his face, she nodded and remained compassionately silent. Jason wished, as never before, that he could embrace her. They looked into each other's eyes for a very long time. Finally, she spoke.

'Remember when I was nineteen, and I got you to try ecstasy just that one time? You look even worse than that right now.'

Jason's body heaved in a silent, cathartic chuckle. 'Markie, you have the bedside manner of Charlie Manson.'

She smiled, but spoke with care. 'Do you want to talk about it?'

'Nah. Not right now. Let's just talk.

She nodded in agreement. 'Who do you think was hotter? Jim Morrison or Lou Reed?'

Jason let his head fall to the side. 'I don't know, Markie. Never pondered the question much.'

'Yeah, but IF you were a chick,' Markie persisted, 'who would you think?'

Knowing she would not give up, he replied, 'Well, I guess Lou Reed, since I'm so fond of amphetamines and S&M.'

Markie nodded, a satisfied smirk on her face. 'Me too. Jim Morrison's a Barbie doll anyway.'

'Oh, you are so right, girlfriend.'

Her nose crinkled in laughter.

'Why don't you ask your other friends these questions?' Jason asked. 'You know, the *female* ones?'

Markie blew a raspberry. 'They're *trendy* hippies, Jason. They drive me nuts. They listen to shitty indie rock and eat mushrooms all day. *Mushrooms…'* she muttered. 'Freakin' high school shit…'

'If *I'm* better for this conversation then they are, then I believe you, Markie.'

She reached offscreen and grabbed something, which turned out to be a healthy joint. 'Do you mind? Haven't smoked yet today.'

Jason shrugged with a smile. 'Have I ever minded?'

She conquered her spliff in seconds and peace settled over her features.

'WHAT SHOULD WE NAME OUR BAND, JASON?!'

Markie's nonsensical scream startled Jason out of his stupor. She dissolved in a fit of giggles. Jason gawped at her like the lunatic she was.

'Why do you *shout* like that when you smoke?! It drives me nuts.'

She coughed once and with a ridiculous smile said, 'You kinda just answered your own question, boopsie.'

'How the *freaking* hell,' Jason asked the stars, 'is this making me feel so much better?!'

'Because I'm *awesome*, Jason,' she replied, her nose in the air. 'That's pretty much the answer to all of those dumb questions.'

'Right, of course,' Jason replied with a small smile. 'I think they found that in one of Plato's writings recently. *'Markie is awesome. This is the source of all wisdom.'*

Markie gave him another ridiculous smile. 'Far out.'

'I wish I understood how this place isn't driving me insane. It almost feels like home already.'

Markie smiled, sincerely for once. 'You've always had a taste for adventure, Jason. I've seen it all along. It just needed a spark. The right push.'

'This is not a push. This is a shotgun blast.'

She chuckled. 'It's not a shotgun blast; it's a freight train.'

'An A-bomb explosion.'

'An Alice Cooper concert.'

Jason smiled and said no more. He would not win. They looked at each other for a while longer. Jason smiled in amusement as her eyes got heavier and her smile got dumber.

'Did you hear Roger Daltrey is coming back to the Falls next month?' she asked.

'Did you hear I'm in Kenya trying to save the world?'

Her face took on an absurd look of confusion. 'Oh yeah,' she said, her mouth hanging open.

Jason sighed. 'No more for you today, Markie.'

She grinned sheepishly. 'Yeah, probly.'

'Get back to you later?'

'Yeah. I'm getting sleepy anyways.'

Jason raised an eyebrow. 'Isn't it 8:00 a.m. over there?'

'Yeah, but...' she yawned tremendously. Jason smiled.

'Sleep it off, Markie. I'll talk to you later. Thank you for the chat.'

'Alright. Stay strong, soldier.'

Jason disconnected. He chuckled once and then got back to it.

He took a shower, and then went to the gym and found Joonheong, who was happy to lead Jason through arms, back, and cardio. He got changed and returned to Shwari Mawe. He grabbed a book of Shakespeare's sonnets from the library and found a shady bench. Before he could open the book, however, he was blindsided by a wave of powerful mixed emotions. He looked around him.

Twenty-four hours earlier he had been standing in an unthinkable hellhole, built for the torture and murder of over a million people. Now he was sitting in a serene slice of paradise, a pristine sanctuary, built more or less entirely to keep him happy. Was it right? Was it even tasteful? Was he really the hero he had, admittedly, begun to think himself to be? Did the pain he had endured here, or when his dad had died, or that of yesterday, or even the black loneliness that awaited him in the past mean that he knew even the very first thing about what true agony meant?

'I know.'

Jason turned to his right, and to his great surprise, he saw Omondi walking toward him.

'May I?' he asked courteously. Jason nodded, and he sat down next to him. They sat in the shade, the unfamiliar Kenyan birds continuing their carefree racket.

'I know exactly what you are thinking, Jason.' Omondi intoned. 'When I first stepped into Shwari Mawe after my last visit to Auschwitz, I felt such hatred for it. I was initially uneasy, in fact, about its very construction.'

Jason looked at Omondi in surprise. Omondi turned to him, a gentle look in his eyes.

'There is so much suffering in Kenya. In Africa. In all the world. And it is going to end, one way or another, in more suffering. Who are you and I that we should be sitting here in such a place, enjoying the shade and reading poetry?'

Jason smiled sadly and nodded.

'I have, however,' Omondi continued, 'always seen its existence as a necessary part of this operation. Because here in this complex, we have knowledge. And knowledge is a terrible, terrible thing. Ironically, nothing clouds one's judgement like it.'

Jason nodded again. 'And we sure as hell need clear heads here.'

'I conceived the idea for Shwari Mawe when I visited New York to find Horace. I was awestruck by the unity and prosperity of the city, even in the midst of such clashing religions and opposing worldviews and of the terrible knowledge of the murderous hatred that exists for it in so many parts of the world. It seemed to defy reason. Until...'

Light dawned in Jason's mind. 'Until you saw Central Park.'

Omondi nodded. 'A place to catch your breath.'

They sat together for a moment longer. Then Omondi turned and looked at Jason again.

'So, what are you going to do now?

'Keep going,' Jason said simply.

The same ghostly smile touched Omondi's lips.

'Why wouldn't Duni *tell us* how the world was going to end?' Jason asked.

'As a failsafe,' Omondi replied. 'Her people believed that if we knew how the world ended, we would attempt to prevent it within our own means of power. And she assured us that it is far too late for that now. It is up to you.'

Jason rolled his eyes and nodded. Omondi stood and walked steadily away.

'Find me in my office when you are ready. We will continue your lessons.'

Jason sat a very short time longer, then bolted upright and made for the door, berating himself for being an idiot.

He went straight to the kitchens (this time receiving warm smiles rather than gaping stares) and found Vickie dicing lettuce, a melancholy look on her face. When she looked up, she smiled as brightly as ever, and received permission to take a break. The two of them stood a short distance away from the kitchen door.

'Sorry, Vickie,' Jason said.

'For what?' Vickie asked, clearly taken aback.

'For not coming to see you sooner.'

Vickie smiled and shook her head. 'It's okay, Jason. You had more to figure out from this than me. I knew you'd come eventually.'

Jason smiled. 'I couldn't have done it without you, Vickie.'

'It was an honour, O Hero of Time.'

Though still not comfortable with being called that, Jason smiled, hugged her tight, and let her get back to work. He breathed deeply and went to find Omondi.

'In light of the… heaviness… of yesterday's events, today I have decided to discuss something much more positive, and for you personally, relatable.'

Even in the wake of his first real connection with Omondi half an hour ago, Jason snorted. 'I'll believe that when I hear it.'

Omondi scowled, but continued without a response, pacing around the telescreen. 'What do you know about the relationship between Canada and the Netherlands?'

'Not much,' Jason said with a small shrug.

'Not unexpected,' Omondi continued, 'though still rather sad.'

'And why is that?'

'It is safe to say that Canadians and the Dutch share one of the most profound bonds of friendship that exists in the nations of the world.'

'Why?'

'Because of the unfolding of events there during the war. The Netherlands, which had suffered catastrophic civilian losses under Nazi occupation, was liberated by Canadian forces in the late stages of the War.'

Jason nodded in appreciation.

'Yet it goes still deeper and further back,' Omondi continued. 'The Dutch royal family took asylum in Canada when the Nazis initially advanced on the country. When it came for the pregnant Queen to give birth to her daughter, the hospital in

Ottawa was temporarily declared Dutch territory, so as not to interfere with her citizenship and right to rule.'

'Damn.'

'To this day, Dutch children are charged with tending the graves of fallen Canadian soldiers. Also, the overblown but existing practice of American travellers disguising themselves as Canadians is highly ill-advised in the Netherlands.'

Jason found this hilarious. 'Alright!'

Omondi looked at Jason with what might actually have been a hint of affection.

'You should be very proud of your nation's history, particularly in the twentieth century, which you have studied. Though not without blemish and shame, Canada's role on the world stage has been exemplary. At the proper times and in the proper ways, Canada – as you yourselves are fond of saying – *kicked ass*.'

Jason buried his head in his chest, shaking with laughter. He couldn't believe his own ears.

'Now,' Omondi shouted. 'We return to Britain, as we always must.' He picked up a small remote and pressed a button. The telescreen zapped to life, showing a huge mugshot of a decorated military officer. He had a solemn, mustachioed, very British face. Jason did not recognize him.

'This,' Omondi said, continuing his pacing, 'is Air Chief Marshal Hugh Dowding. He was head of the Royal Air Force, and the man who developed the Dowding Radar System, a sophisticated security array that spanned most of southern and eastern England, which gave the RAF a critical tactical advantage over the Luftwaffe in the Battle of Britain. Other than Churchill – with whom he had a strong relationship – this is the most crucial man you must win to your side.'

Jason nodded. A great thought then occurred to him. 'What about Chamberlain?'

Omondi stopped his strolling about. He turned to look at Jason.

'Neville Chamberlain is of no use to you. His prewar leadership left him with a legacy, however justly deserved, of incompetence and cowardice. History treats him with utter disdain and so must you.'

'But he's the *Prime Minister!*'

'*Baldwin* is Prime Minister in 1935, you fool. Luckily, he too was an appeaser, and close to the man who would succeed him two years later.'

'So, I'm supposed to show up in London and ignore the leaders of the British Empire?'

Omondi smacked his fist on the nearby table. 'Not *ignore* them, Jason! *Defy them*! When the moment is right, and you finally meet these mighty men, you must look them straight in the face and shake your head in contempt! You must not bow to them. You must not even have *time* for them! It is for moments like the one of which we speak that we sought out an expert in the dramatic. Your attitude with the Guilty Men, as they are still remembered in England, must be one of unmitigated audacity. It will be the tower of authority you will build upon the foundation of impression made by the smartphone.'

Jason took a great breath, his eyebrows raised. This was going far beyond making a couple of clever speeches…

'But of course,' Omondi finished in a calmer tone, 'this is Britain. Only a man who knows the rules will be allowed to break them. You must do as Megan says.'

'Yes sir,' Jason muttered.

'We will call this the end of today's lesson,' Omondi said. 'Tonight, however, you have homework.'

He handed Jason a printed computer sheet.

'The casualty totals of the twenty hardest-hit Allied Nations by military, civilian, and percentage of population. Memorize them for our next lesson. And before you complain, remember what I told you.'

Jason nodded. 'Numbers make an impact.'

'On a lighter note, Yaro has spoken to me.'

Jason started. He had forgotten about Yaro.

'He thinks very highly of you. You should visit him in the smoking room. A cigar would do you good.'

'Who the hell says *that* anymore?' Jason asked incredulously.

Omondi rolled his eyes. 'There is nothing wrong with an occasional cigar. And to elaborate, *since* you will be spending so much time with Winston Churchill, a cigar would be good *training.'*

Jason chuckled as he stood. 'You people have the most bizarre concept of friendship I have ever seen.'

'Soldiers fight together.' Omondi replied.

Zing.

'He will be at work until eight. Room 101. And *yes,'* he snapped as Jason opened his mouth, 'the smoke room is next to the gym.'

Jason dutifully spent an hour in his lobby, memorizing death by the millions. It was not as troubling as he had thought it would be, though the Soviet Union's totals did make his jaw drop. Jason smiled darkly at the wall of desensitization that was apparently still standing tall in his heart. A million deaths were, as Stalin had said, merely a statistic.

At least when not standing in the graveyard.

He felt strong. He felt steady. His mind and body (and soul?) were getting in shape. He reflected on the terrible irony that such an unprecedented crisis and challenge should bring out the best in him. He had held his mother and younger sister together when his dad died, but could not have done so without the mutual support of his older sisters. Yet here he was in Kenya, isolated from everything he had ever known, the fate of the world on his shoulders alone, and all the fuel he needed to face it was a daily dose of nonsense from Markie.

He decided to put off his *training* in the smoking room a little longer. He sat down in his living room, put on Netflix, and searched for something appropriate. He found a mini-series called *Greatest Events of WWII in Color* and sat riveted for two hours at the stunning unfolding of events during Blitzkrieg and the Battle of Britain.

Horace had been right. Shakespeare, Harry Potter, the god-damned Avengers; nothing in fiction could do anything but blush in the face of what had actually happened during those six great and terrible years of conflict only eight decades ago. And now a young blowhard from Ontario was in Kenya being prepared for their sabotage. How deep was this rabbit-hole going to go?

Jason realized that the War was taking its place at the centre of his mind. *It was inevitable,* he thought peacefully, and in any case, no bad thing.

Sparing one last terrible moment of remembrance of his experience the day before, Jason put on his shoes and made for Room 101. Why he felt a strange degree of trepidation, he wasn't sure.

He opened the door, opened a second courtesy door, and was unsurprised to be overwhelmed by the powerful smoke and aroma of a dozen kinds of tobacco. The lounge itself was well lit and atmospheric, with blood-red walls, several house-plants, and black leather furniture. Classical music danced in the background as Servidors, most of them older than himself, chatted happily as they drew from cigarettes and pipes. One woman took a pinch of snuff, and – Jason couldn't believe it – a giant hookah sat in the far corner, currently not in use. Jason marvelled at this amazing slice of a culture now outlawed where he had come from.

'Jason! At last!'

Jason turned to his left, and there was Yaro, beaming at him from behind the counter. Now dressed for work, he wore a light brown corduroy suit with a simple green tie. It looked a bit silly, yet seemed to perfectly suit this humble man as he smiled at Jason like a long-lost friend.

Jason smiled back as Yaro hobbled to him on his cane as quickly as he could. Jason held out a hand, but Yaro ignored it and hugged him tightly. He gripped his arms and smiled warmly up at him.

'How much you have changed, Jason.'

'What do you mean?' Jason asked.

'I saw it the moment you walked into my lounge. You are stronger, prouder. Even after only three days, I can see that it would take more than thunder to send you running now.'

Jason chuckled. 'It feels like three lifetimes.'

'A modest assessment, I am sure. Please, come! Sit. Smoke with me.'

Jason made himself comfortable in a nearby armchair, his skin tingling at this new experience. Yaro sat across from him and handed him a thick brown cigar. Jason studied it for a moment and breathed in the aroma of the dry tobacco.

'Is this Cuban?' he asked.

'HAH!' Yaro scoffed. 'Cuba's reign in the cigar trade has passed. This is Nicaraguan tobacco. Best in the world.'

He struck a match and lit a cigar of his own. Jason clumsily followed suit. He had only a moment to appreciate the taste before erupting in an agonizing coughing fit, retching as the harsh smoke seared his lungs. The Servidors beside him covered their mouths politely to hide their smiles, but Yaro burst into delighted laughter.

'Come now, boy!' he said. 'You don't inhale cigar smoke!'

Embarrassment and pain flushed Jason's face as he spat in a nearby spitoon. He could have strangled Markie; he had been emulating her massive hauls on her joints. At last Jason managed to get himself under control and smiled sheepishly. Yaro was still wheezing the last of his chuckles.

'Now,' he said with mock consternation, 'aren't you glad you didn't do that in front of Churchill?'

Jason sighed and laughed. He liked Yaro very much.

Yaro coached him through the proper way to do it, and before long his initial death rattle was forgotten as he enjoyed the flavour and the experience. At last, they were able to talk.

'Did you know much about Churchill before you came here?' Jason asked. Yaro frowned, clearly not overly impressed with the question.

'British history is a part of Tanzanian history, Jason. We fought against them in the First War and for them in the Second.'

Jason sat quietly for a moment and reflected. He, a self-proclaimed history buff, didn't know a damned thing about Africa, other than Egypt with its great big cool things. All the world was celebrated and glamourized in the West, from Argentinian soccer to basically every single aspect of Japan. Yet at the centre of it all lay a gigantic landmass that was largely ignored, far more famous for its elephants than its heritage. No one knew, nor apparently needed to know, what had brought these many nations to be what they were today. It made him suddenly sick to think that slavery and poverty were more synonymous with Africa than the profound and beautiful strength he had encountered during his time here.

'Sorry,' he said.

'It is okay, Jason,' Yaro said with a smile. 'Do you think Canadian history means a damn to me?'

Jason snorted and coughed another ten times as penance.

'Africa has never been at the centre stage of word-affairs,' Yaro continued. 'And yet, the fate of the world has fallen into African hands. The bravery and sacrifice of a single Kenyan woman has sounded a battlecry, and men and women from all over the world have come to her country to answer it. It is lovely, is it not?'

Jason nodded. It *was* lovely, though it did nothing to ease his burden. Yaro waved his hand dismissively.

'But enough of this talk. What is Ontario like?'

'Boring,' Jason replied. 'In just about every possible way.'

'Example?'

Jason's mind broke open like a dam.

'There's just not much to do. Nothing to see. The wildlife is boring, the scenery is bland, the water is polluted. Nobody has time for each other. Big drug problem in a lot of areas. Impotent politics. No big quests, you know? Nothing to make you feel important. Small-town life is pretty horrible in Ontario, really. It has a way of making you think that everything is okay, when really, you're just rotting.'

Jason took a breath and remembered himself. Yaro's grin grew wider and wider throughout Jason's self-exorcism.

'You know, Jason,' he said, 'there are some small tribes in Africa who do not have a word for *boring*. They do not even understand the concept.'

Shot down yet again, Jason nodded. 'I guess I am pretty lucky, really.'

Yaro shrugged.

'You can look at it that way if you want. I find it magnificent. Imagine *never being bored,* Jason! If there can be a quality of Heaven brought down to Earth, surely that is it!'

Jason puffed his cigar and smiled. He hadn't thought of that. Yaro continued.

'Yet no free man or woman has the right to be bored for long. There is so much that we love to do. Why do we not do it?'

'Why are you a farmer, Yaro?' Jason asked. 'You should be running your country.'

'I love farming,' he said with a smile.

There was no touching this guy.

They chatted amiably for another hour, Jason growing more amazed by the minute at Yaro's powerful character and by the amazing stamina of his cigar.

Suddenly, he felt a strange urge, inspired by a peripheral presence in his routine, which he had never had before.

'I think I'm going to excuse myself, Yaro,' Jason said with a smile as he butted his cigar. 'This has been wonderful. Thank you.'

Yaro grasped his hands tightly, solemnity touching his own unceasing grin. 'There is nothing I can say to you, Jason, that you do not already know. You will discover it when you need to. Blessings.'

Jason had zipped back to his quarters, tied his hair back, and changed back into a t-shirt and shorts. Now he was back in the gym. Joonheong was not there, which suited him at the moment. He did his stretches, pulled his shirt over his shoulders, and slipped off his shoes and socks. He strapped on a pair of 10-ounce boxing gloves and stepped up to the furthest punching bag. He had never boxed in his life, and he did not care. It just felt right.

He threw a couple of jabs, testing the waters. He tried a right cross. The heavy bag absorbed his blows just as he hoped they would. He liked it. He loosened up and began a testosterone-driven assault of which he had never known he was capable.

Dozens of painful images and memories seemed almost to manifest on his knuckles. The nightmares of not only these terrible days in Kenya, but of his whole life, were exorcised. His mouth twisted in a snarl as he remembered his years as a bullied child, the torture of caring for his dying father, even the bad dreams he had had after watching *Jaws* as a six-year-old and blasted them to pieces in primal fury.

Ten minutes later, he fell to his knees in exhaustion. He assured a concerned onlooker that he was okay and sat gasping on the matted floor. A small smile touched his sweaty face. When properly directed, there was great value in violence.

Out of gas, he returned to his quarters. Too burnt out to talk to Markie or even to change, he collapsed on his bed. In ninety seconds, not even their precious alarm could have awoken him.

Chapter Fourteen

What a strange life I lead…

Jason sat in his darkened living room, his eyes closed, a YouTube loop of Gregorian chants and a stick of burning incense keeping him in a state of drugged spirituality. His room was darkened, and he had found a taste of what he needed.

It was 6:28 a.m. – almost time for this glorious natural high to be blasted to pieces by that sound.

He had awoken in a terrible funk. His sweaty gym-clothes itched to hell. He was cold; he was grumpy; he was alone in the best seat in the nuthouse. So, he sought. He solved the problem.

As the tempo-less baritones echoed, and the sweet, earthy vapours filled his lungs, a powerful calm, like floating on warm water, spread over him from head to toe. He rolled his head around his shoulders methodically, letting his mind fall still, as still as an amateur meditator could hope to manage. The

Catholic monks and the Buddhist monks (and Markie) were all right about one thing: A clear head never hurts.

Seeing the time, Jason shut off his TV and butted the incense. He shaved and got dressed, wondering why his alarm was waiting so long. He shrugged and made his mother's scrambled eggs. There were even chives in the fridge.

By ten after seven, he was growing annoyed with the stupid anticipation. He put on his shoes and stepped out into the hall.

It was quiet, and the dim lights gave his wallpapered surroundings a saccharine feel that reminded him of his grandmother's old place. He ventured again to Horace and Omondi's office.

No one was inside but an elderly Employee, who sat typing on a computer that would have been state of the art when he was about sixteen. Without even looking at Jason, she pointed at Omondi's desk. Annoyed at the android-like quality that seemed to permeate the lower-levels of the KRA, he stepped up to the desk and found a note sitting there, which consisted of a single sentence:

Report at once to Room 116 for a great challenge.

Annoyance rose up in Jason's throat until he could almost taste it. 'Riddles! Again!!'

'Shh!'

Sparing one disdainful look for the sheep at the computer, he left.

Humming a James Taylor song, he made his merry way to his next slice of ridiculous destiny. He felt vaguely proud of the very different ways he had learned not to take his very different new bosses seriously.

When he reached Room 116, a ditzy-looking blonde woman was waiting outside the door. She smiled at him with a devious menace.

'Hello, Jason. My name's Sheri. And it is time.'

Jason steeled his nerves. 'Time for what?'

Her smile grew as sinister as Tim Curry's. She held up her hands, which gripped a pair of scissors and a spray bottle.

Jason's heart clenched. He had hoped against hope that this moment would not come.

'It won't hurt,' she soothed.

'Isn't there *any* way to–'

'Jason Roberts,' Sheri said, in the tone of a doctor about to amputate, 'we both know that even if you were ten feet tall, you would not be taken seriously in the thirties with a shag like that. Now come on in.'

Jason dragged himself into the cramped salon. How much more, he wondered, were they going to make him give?

''WHOA! NO WAY!!'

Markie burst into ecstatic giggles, thunderstruck by Jason's new 'do.

'Will you *shut up* already,' Jason snapped after half-a-minute of Markie's musical laughter.

'You– you–' she snorted twice and finally managed, 'you should have warned me. I already *smoked!*'

She laughed for what felt like ten minutes. Jason ran his fingers through his newly cropped hair, knowing that all he could do was let her get it out.

'I'm sorry, Jason,' she said at last, her chest still heaving with suppressed giggles. 'It looks good, it really does. It's just, I haven't seen it that short since… well, since–'

'Since you lit my hair on fire!!' he finished for her. 'Yes, how time does fly.'

'Want a Pepsi, MJ?' she cooed and burst into laughter again, Jason joining her despite his most determined efforts.

'You are such a *douchebag!*' he marvelled at last.

At last Markie sighed out the last of her derision and got focused. 'So, what's on the menu today?'

'No idea, as usual. This place has no structure; it's like it's run by whoever designed your garden.'

She giggled and grinned. 'Nice.'

'I probably should track down Horace. 'If I'm gonna do the damned thing, I'd better do it.'

Markie nodded. 'You're so boring.'

Jason disconnected and headed to Horace's office. He opened the door and found his friend in conversation with the researcher he had met at the party. She saw him first, and her face broke into a smile. Horace turned and his eyes widened in pleasant surprise. He read Jason's face for a moment (why this didn't annoy the hell out of him, Jason wasn't sure) and turned to the woman beside him.

'Anita, can I get back to you?'

'Of course, Horace.' She turned to Jason and smiled again as she passed him, the ruby dog glinting from around her neck. 'I like him, you know.' She closed the door.

Jason watched her go and then looked at Horace.

'Did she mean–'

'Yes,' he muttered. 'Anita is a brilliant woman and irritatingly blunt. Nice hair, by the way.'

'How did she earn that dog?'

'She is part of the team that is studying the lesser technologies that Duni brought with her. She replicated the fabric and stitching of Duni's pants and properly modified the necessary machinery for mass production. We're calling the fabric *Duni-ester*.'

'That is the worst joke I have ever heard.'

Horace frowned slightly, scribbled something on a notepad, and smiled at Jason again.

'Don't we have enough money already?' Jason asked.

'The patent is being given to the Kenyan government,' Horace replied with a raised eyebrow. 'The Kenyan taxpayers spent a good deal of money on you, Jason, and we mean to return the favour.'

'Still seems pretty shifty,' Jason said.

'Would you care to be the one to be honest?'

'Alright, alright,' Jason grumbled.

Horace smiled. 'You can trust the President, Jason. I have met him several times, and he is a man of character, though painfully boring. Anyway, what can I do for you? By your face when you walked in, I expect to like what I hear.'

'I thought you might like to go to Starbucks and talk time-travel. I'm sick of the Blue Room.'

Horace's face lit up.

'A lesson! Voluntarily! I *knew* this moment would come!!'

'Shh!'

Jason moved to tell off the clueless secretary, but Horace grabbed him by the shoulder and leaned in with a smile.

'Only two qualities are required for our Employees: work-ethic and an incapacity for independent thought.'

Jason chuckled. He knew a few back home.

They immediately left the office and went to Starbucks. Jason decided to keep one touch of his rut intact and got another Flat White. He sat down across from Horace in a booth in the far corner, surprised at the number of faces he knew.

'What do you know about Clementine Churchill, Jason?' Horace asked as he poured sugar in his coffee.

Jason shrugged. He had never really studied her much.

'Throughout most of history, men have had the lion's share of greatness in the popular sense of the word. But if we have been the stars of the show, women have been in charge behind the scenes, and no woman better embodies that idea than the wife of Winston Churchill.'

'What did she do?'

'She was his most trusted advisor, to whom he brought his most difficult dilemmas, even so far as military decisions. She was his emotional anchor, his nurse, and as a lifelong liberal, his political opponent.'

'Like Matalin and Carville,' Jason commented. Horace rolled his eyes.

'If you must compare lions to kittens, then yes.'

'This sounds like something Omondi should be teaching me,' Jason said.

'Omondi's job is to teach you what happened, Jason. My job is to teach you what to *make* happen. One occasionally bleeds into the other, but right now you are being taught a crucial lesson about the latter: *Do not underestimate the allegiance of a woman,* even – or perhaps especially – at a time when they may appear invisible.'

Jason nodded and pursued another topic.

'Do I tell them about the end of the world?'

'What would be your own answer to that question?'

Jason thought about it, and remembered.

'Well… I didn't like the reason you gave me for preventing the war, so I doubt they would.'

Horace nodded. '*Excellent,* Jason. We all agree that to your audience, even your closest allies, the War must be presented in and of itself. A clear and present danger would only be clouded by some distant apocalyptic nonsense that even you know nothing about.'

'Who is *we all,* anyway?' Jason demanded. 'Who appointed themselves the experts on all this crap?'

'Mugo, Omondi, and I consider ourselves wise enough men, but we also consulted philosophy majors. We paid one 125 of the very best of them from all over the world for their thoughts on the subject and sifted out the good stuff.'

'How much did you pay them?'

'About twenty bucks,' Horace said with a derisive chuckle. 'Big money for a philosophy major.'

'You *assholes!'* Jason spat in delight.

Horace's smile faded. 'Now, Jason.' His voice hit a powerful level of urgency. 'Tonight, you have very serious work to do.'

Jason huffed. 'Yes, because nothing I've done so far fits into that category.'

'Jason, *PLEASE!'*

The powerful yell startled several people, none more so than Jason himself. Blushing a bit, he took a sip of his cooling coffee and folded his hands on the table.

'Okay. What serious work?'

Horace peered at Jason over his spectacles.

'Tonight, you take the written portion of the most important exam you have ever taken.'

Jason waited. Horace passed him a small piece of paper. On it were written four words:

Why have you come?

Jason glared at Horace. 'And what does *this* riddle mean, O Great Sage?'

'The answer to that riddle may well prove to be one of the great first impressions of the twentieth century. Or one of its great bungles. It is up to you, because you must give it.'

'I'm writing a speech,' Jason hummed. He had thoroughly enjoyed forgetting about this part.

'At least three minutes' worth of one and performing it tomorrow evening for most of the Servidors.'

Jason's jaw almost knocked over his coffee. 'I have to *make* a speech? In front of EVERYONE?'

'If you can't make a speech for three hundred of your supporters,' Horace rasped, 'how the hell do you expect to make one for three hundred of your opponents?'

Jason said nothing.

'Tonight,' Horace continued, 'your writing skills are being tested. Tomorrow, it is time for your dramatic skills to finally come into play. Not only must you speak to us, you must make us believe you.'

'This is insane…'

'Jason,' Horace said with a smile, 'it is the dream of every good man to do something meaningful with the skills God has given him. You are being handed that opportunity on a silver platter. I don't see what is so insane about that.'

Every time Jason thought he was sure about this mess, another level of its reality was revealed. But Horace had a point.

'Alright.'

He picked up the note and moved to get up.

'Wait, Jason.'

'What *now?*' he moaned.

'Before this undertaking, we thought you'd like something to help you relax.'

'Okay,' Jason said, 'and what would that be?'

Horace smiled. 'An Etiquette lesson.'

'Oh, you stupid SOCIOPATH,' Jason snarled, and left without another word to change into his suit.

A note had been taped on Jason's door. He snatched it, sneering at the familiar perfume that wafted from the paper.

My dearest Jason,

Meet me in Shwari Mawe. Dress casually. Come alone.

'What a *freak* she is,' Jason whispered. He left his door unopened and sauntered off to the Sanctuary, smiling at passing Servidors.

Jason opened the green door. It was cloudy, and not terribly hot by Kenyan standards. There was no one to be seen. Realizing he had no idea where Megan might be, he sat down at a shady bench, deciding to let the crazy chick find him.

'Ahh, THAT'S better!'

Jason jumped up so violently his back spasmed. Megan sat ten feet behind him at the base of the tree, her legs crossed and her hands folded upon her thighs. Jason's fright was quickly forgotten at her appearance; she wore a white spaghetti-strap shirt, aqua shorts and flip-flops, her hair falling around her shoulders. Her face was completely free of make-up, and she smiled as his mouth fell open before he could stop it.

'No woman is *really* a goddess, Jason.'

Jason remembered himself and scowled, furious that, once again, she had scored the first point.

'You look even prettier without those girlish locks,' she purred.

'Thanks a lot. What are we doing here?'

Megan stood up in one fluid movement that blew her new girl-next-door appearance to smithereens. She beckoned him into the dark shade. He stopped five feet from her and saw a bit of strain in her normal seductive visage.

'My extensive understanding of my field,' she said, 'was only half of what got Mugo's attention.'

She looked down, and for once Jason did not feel like he was being baited. He said nothing and let her continue.

'The other half was my flawless mastery of the opposite sex. I am… well, a bit of a coquette, back home.'

'What the hell is a *coquette*?'

Megan looked him in the eyes.

'Oh Jason, do you have any idea how clueless men are? How embarrassingly easy it is to wrap you around our little fingers and tuck you in our pockets? We sometimes feel sorry for you, you know.'

'This is a pretty fucked-up Etiquette lesson!' Jason rumbled, but he wasn't sure she even heard him. She looked at the dirt beneath their feet.

'And then there's you. So much poise. So much control. Such *patience!* Even your accent seems to suggest a… a strength I would not have expected. I've thrown my very best at you…'

'*...and?!*'

Her eyes met his again and suddenly caught fire.

'WHY CAN'T I BREAK YOU?!'

She grabbed him by the ears and kissed him. Jason's mind melted as that flawless mouth assaulted his, her nose ring tickling his face. He pressed his body to hers and kissed back. She pulled him behind the thick trunk of the tree and slammed him against it. Jason barely felt the harsh impact as his hands crept under the sides of her shirt and feasted on her body, smooth as the hourglass it imitated.

She pulled her mouth away at last but stayed close, her hands around his neck.

'My room?'

Jason couldn't believe this was happening. The sexiest thing he had ever seen was offering herself to him freely. The animal in him screamed to proceed.

And yet…

'I… I can't.'

'What?' she whispered.

Against the will of every cell in his body, he pulled her arms away from him. 'I'm sorry, Megan, I… I just can't.'

She took a step back, still catching her breath. She was clearly confused and disappointed, but there was no anger in her face. She nodded.

'Okay.' She stepped back into the weak sunlight and quickly left the Sanctuary.

Jason slid down the trunk of the tree and fell roughly on his backside. What had just happened? She was sexy; she was charming; she was wild; he hadn't been laid in almost a year... WHY had he done that?! And why, even as his mouth burned, did he still feel he had made the right decision?

He got to his feet, carefully adjusted himself, and went to the gym.

His hands still trembling from his workout and his mind still reeling from his shady encounter with Megan, Jason put on *Dark Side of the Moon* and took a deep breath. He grabbed a Budweiser, downed it in one, and grabbed three more. He sat down at his desk at last and put his face in his hands. He let out a cynical huff; he was supposed to write a speech that would change history, at the most confusing and stressful time in his life.

... sounds a lot like Churchill.

'What the *hell...*' he chuckled aloud. If there was a God, he had a twisted sense of humour.

He reached into his back pocket and found the battered note Horace had passed him. He set it upright against the wall. He did not need help memorizing the four solemn words, but to see them sitting there from an external source seemed appropriate. He picked up his pen and tried.

I have come to prevent.

It would work, if only they would…

A blast of confidence made Jason's eyes harden with purpose. Megan and Horace were forgotten. He was a teacher, and he was damned well going to teach these bastards a lesson.

He wrote for almost three hours, stopping only for a leak and to change his music. By the time he was done it was almost 7:00 p.m. He was only three beers deep, and he was beginning to surprise even himself. He loved what he had written.

Jason stood and worked the cramps out of his knees. He looked out his living room window and saw that the Kenyan sun was setting. He had an idea.

He left his quarters and, without too much fuss, was able to get a hold of a folding lounge chair. He then returned to the second floor and, by sense of direction, found his way to the back corner of the building where he found what he was looking for: an unpleasant grey door marked ROOF ACCESS – AUTHORIZED PERSONNEL ONLY. Smirking like the punk he had been in grade nine, he opened it. He carefully climbed the short ladder to the roof hatch. It only then occurred to him that it might be locked, but luck was with him, and he soon found himself on the gravelly roof of the KRA.

He got his bearings for a moment and then stepped up to the edge, which overtook the rough fences surrounding it by about five feet. And he sighed, the beginnings of tears coming to his eyes.

The magnificent view before him was unlike any he had ever witnessed. The massive orange sun, decorated by thin clouds, cast its glow upon the savanna, stretching everywhere he looked. Giant trees cast towering shadows over the grassy fields, and a flock of birds a thousand strong flew to the west.

Such a breathtaking African sunset was barely a myth back in Ontario and to see it like this was beyond what words could convey. He wished he could leave his body and see his own silhouette in the great ball of fire before him.

Movement to the distant left caught his eye. He focused, and his heart nearly stopped. A great lion, his shaggy brown mane ruffling majestically, loped along the edge of a small ridge, his modestly dressed mate close beside him. They stopped at the edge and, for their own reasons, turned and lumbered quickly away, until they were lost in the failing light.

Jason shook his head with a small smile. From halfway around the world, Markie had scored a total victory.

He set up his chair, sat down, and did not move for a very long time.

Chapter Fifteen

After another morning workout, Jason returned to his quarters to polish up his speech. Since the fiasco revolving around a poem he had written in grade six, he had always kept his writing skills a closely guarded secret. If there was a stranger way to unveil them, he was not sure what it could be.

Anyone but a teacher would have been getting thoroughly irritated by the knocks at the door. When yet another came, Jason, recognizing it this time, answered it eagerly, and found Vickie smiling up at him and holding a truly gargantuan hot-fudge sundae.

'Hi Jason!' she said. 'I asked Horace if we could spend some time together, and I made this for us! Wanna go to Shwari Mawe?'

Jason opened his mouth to accept, when suddenly a thought occurred to him.

'Vickie, there's a friend of mine back home that I've been keeping in contact with–'

'Markie!'

Jason's head jerked back in surprise. 'How did you know?'

'Everybody knows about her, Jason,' she said with a smile. 'Don't worry,' she added quickly, seeing Jason raise an eyebrow, 'no one's spying on you or anything. But it's hard to keep anything secret here, especially about you. She's kind of a legend, actually.'

Not completely happy about this news, Jason pressed on. 'Would you like to meet her?'

Her face lit up. 'YES!'

'Just a sec. I'll let her know you're coming.'

Where he had gotten this sudden impulse, he was not sure. Nor was he sure it was an entirely good idea. But he entered 212A, and got a hold of Markie yet again.

'WHO DISTURBS MY SLUMBER?' she said throatily.

'Lay off the Disney crap. I was wondering if you'd like to meet someone. Vickie. She's the girl that went with me to… to Poland.'

She nodded lightly. 'Sure. You're boring me lately anyway.'

'Yeah, yeah. Just ix-nay on the ugs-dray, okay?'

She spread her hands in annoyance. 'Who do you *take* me for?'

His anxiety growing by the second, Jason called Vickie inside. She clamoured in eagerly and sat down next to Jason, putting the oozing dessert in her lap.

'Hi Markie!' she said with a tremendous smile.

Clearly surprised, Markie cocked her head to one side and studied Vickie for what felt like an eternity. Jason shifted uncomfortably, but Vickie's smile never faltered. Her sweetness was not weakness.

Suddenly Markie's face grew serious, even intense. Alarmed, Jason turned and saw Vickie's smile vanish. Jason looked back and forth as their eyebrows contracted, and they glared laser beams into each other. Markie opened her mouth... and stuck out her tongue and crossed her eyes in the most absurd face her features could make. Vickie, not missing a beat, matched it with a ridiculous look of her own. And they both burst out laughing.

Jason gaped in wonder at this extraordinary first encounter. Markie wiped her eyes and said, 'Well, this one's cool.'

'It's so good to meet you Markie!' Vickie gushed. 'I feel like I'm meeting the Queen.'

Markie blew a raspberry. 'I dress WAY better than the Queen.'

Vickie giggled. 'I like your hat!' she continued. Where did you get it?'

'I actually don't remember. I was really ston–'

'Uh, Vickie has been so huge for me here, Markie,' Jason cut in. 'She's like you, in a way.'

Markie smiled. 'She's got character, that's for sure.'

'Jason is amazing!' Vickie said, looking at Jason and smiling. 'I felt so out of place here, didn't really make many friends. And then Jason showed up, and everything made sense all of a sudden.'

Markie squinted. 'What's that around your neck?'

Vickie blushed a bit. 'It's a decoration, actually. Not many people get them here.'

'What did you get it for?'

Jason put his arm around Vickie. 'For keeping me sane.'

For once, Vickie said nothing and blushed scarlett.

'Thanks a lot, Vickie,' Markie grumbled. 'I've been systematically driving him nuts for eight years. All my work down the drain.'

Jason casually flipped her off, drawing a chortle out of both of them.

'Your dinner's melting,' Markie drawled, pointing at the sundae in Vickie's lap. Jason grabbed one of the purple plastic spoons stabbing the mountain of ice cream and shoved a generous portion in his mouth. His eyes widened.

'Vickie, this is *incredible!* Did you make this?!'

'Obviously,' she stated with a raised eyebrow, as she grabbed the other spoon. 'Häagen-Dazs has nothing on me.'

Markie watched them eat for a moment. She stood and walked away and returned with a couple of Slim Jims. 'When in Rome,' she snapped as Jason and Vickie snorted a laugh.

'How did you two meet?' Vickie asked.

'At a bonfire in Wainfleet,' Jason replied. 'A mutual friend of ours was getting married, and we ran into each other.'

'I remember Sean had just thrown a skid on the fire when we started talking,' Markie reminisced. 'It was like the fires of Hell had just spat you out.'

'Yeah, yeah,' Jason snapped. 'It's still like that for me all the freaking time.'

'Are you two always like this?' Vickie asked. 'It's amazing!'

'I keep him around,' Markie said with a smile. 'He's the comedy relief to my epic life.'

'I'm Abbot to her Costello.'

'You're *who* to her *who?*' Vickie asked.

'Yeah, come on Old Man,' Markie chided, 'join the nineties. And anyway, I always tell people *you're* Costello.'

'How am *I* Costello?!' Jason yelled, throwing his hands in the air.

Vickie burst into a fit of giggles, as Markie crossed her arms and smirked.

'It's always too easy, Jason.'

Jason rolled his eyes. 'I'll get back to you, Markie.'

'You are *wonderful,* Markie!' Vickie added with a smile. 'I hope I get to talk to you again!'

Markie smiled, gave a peace sign, and disconnected. Jason and Vickie spent a half-hour in Shwari Mawe before Jason was compelled to continue writing. After a normal torso-crushing hug from Vickie, he left their garden and returned to his quarters.

There waiting for him, leaning against the wall, was Omondi. He pressed a finger to his lips and bid him follow. Jason obeyed silently, wondering what the hell could be going on now. They snaked their way to the Blue Room, Jason entering first. Omondi closed the door behind them, and they sat in the familiar armchairs.

'What's going on, Omondi?' Jason asked.

'Today,' Omondi replied, 'we will discuss the events leading up to the Holocaust.'

'A *lesson?!*' Jason cried out in fury. 'THAT'S what this is about?!'

Omondi raised an eyebrow. 'What else?'

Knowing it was not worth his breath, Jason marvelled once more at how strange everyone was here. Sometimes he felt like Squidward stuck in Bikini Bottom, the only one who noticed how bizarre everything was.

'It is important to remember,' Omondi began quietly, 'that Hitler did not give birth to anti-Semitism in Europe. Hatred of Jews had been a significant force there for hundreds of years. Until the unprecedented industrialized murder that took place in camps like Auschwitz and Treblinka, very few of the anti-Semitic policies implemented by the Nazis had not been seen before in some form or another.'

'I know,' Jason replied. He had studied this most horrendous of topics extensively.

'How then,' Omondi grew suddenly intense, 'did Hitler manage to enflame this lurking presence to the open, widespread rage that brought almost universal support to the devils who consumed two thirds of the Jewish populace in Europe?'

Jason grew determined. 'It all goes back to Versaille. The German people were outraged at the oppressive social and economic demands of the Treaty, most of all at the fact that the blame for World War One was laid exclusively on their shoulders.'

'That is not all.'

'If you'll *let me finish…!*'

Omondi fell silent. Jason continued. 'Hitler's charisma and the results he produced in pulling Germany out of the Depression made his identification of the Jews as betrayers and oppressors compelling to the German people, particularly when the propaganda campaigns began–'

'PRIDE!!' Omondi bellowed. Jason jumped back in shock.

'It all comes back to *pride,* Jason! Hitler appealed to the wounded pride of a defeated nation. He oiled the machinery of recovery and prosperity with that pride. He gave that pride a target, and in doing so, he nurtured the self-satisfaction of belonging to a righteous majority. *Pride,* Jason, is the enemy that you – that ALL of us – are constantly fighting!'

'Right now,' Jason snarled, 'I'm fighting the urge to kick you in the head!!'

'You must be prepared to fight that urge often.'

Jason took a deep breath, and managed to relax.

'What details do you know of the propaganda campaigns against the Jews?' Omondi asked.

'Short films were made about them. The social and economic threats they posed were illustrated. Footage of rats and insects were added to dehumanize them. Jewish children were examined in their own classrooms to show their classmates characteristic Jewish features. Boycotts of Jewish businesses were organized, and German Jews were systematically stripped of their rights and freedoms.'

Omondi nodded. 'And you will be dropped into early 1935, just before this great oppression is instigated. Please keep this in mind.'

'How long do you expect this mission to take?'

'We cannot say. Even looking into the past, we cannot predict the future. Perhaps a week, perhaps a year, and perhaps you will reach the deadline predicted by Duni Kimani.'

Jason smashed his fists into his leather armchair. 'WHAT DEADLINE?!'

'November 25, 1936. The day of the official alliance signed by Germany and Japan.'

'I can't deal with this shit. *Why haven't you even MENTIONED Japan?!'*

'Because until now it has not been relevant. Duni assured us that your work would deal exclusively with the European

War, but that if Nazi Germany was not neutralized before it officially joined with its Eastern ally, all would almost certainly be lost. And she refused to explain why.'

'So now I have a time limit, before my life is ruined forever,' Jason whispered. 'You *piece of shit!!'*

'I TOLD you numbers make an impact!' Omondi snarled back. *'You already knew that!!* Now you must merely plan accordingly! And we BOTH know you can do so!'

There was nothing Jason hated more in this place than when Omondi was right. But he was right. Jason shook his head, chuckled, and said nothing.

Omondi continued in a softer tone. 'It was not my intent for this meeting to grow so intense.'

'Is that so?'

'Yes, it is,' Omondi intoned. 'You have a great task ahead of you this evening, and we want you to be ready. And, believe it or not, I care about you very much.'

Jason's head fell forward in shock. Omondi's scowl remained, but Jason could see the sincerity in his eyes. He smiled and chuckled. 'Is this the part where we hug?'

'Shut up. This lesson is over. You will make your speech at 8:30. Go and prepare.'

Jason grinned and leaned forward, his arms outstretched. 'Aww, c'mon, Omondi, one hug!'

'I WILL punch you!!'

Jason stood and strode out the door, a small smile on his face.

The rest of the afternoon passed in a strange new sense of anticipation; for one, he had not made a speech in a decade, let alone in such a ludicrous context. For another, being warned beforehand about anything in this damned place was a cynical novelty.

He chatted with Markie, he had a beer, he even took a detour and played a game of basketball against a woman from Mexico named Andréa. He lost so miserably that without cue she promised never to tell a soul, but he had long learned to have a sense of humour about his miserable record in athletics.

Mostly, however, he read his speech, reread it, and reread what he had reread. A word added here and there, an idea inserted or reworked. He was, at long last, in his element, and tonight he meant to prove it.

At the stroke of eight, there was a knock at the door and Jason joined Horace in the hall.

'You are prepared?' Horace asked.

'Yes.'

'You will give it your all?'

'Yes.'

'Then come!' Horace said with a broad grin.

They returned to the first floor and made their way south, past the steel gate to the Time Machine and soon Jason was being led through a door marked *Reception.* A doorless vestibule betrayed the loud murmuring of the Servidors to the right. Horace led Jason to the left and up a small flight of stairs onto a darkened, elevated stage. A simple wooden podium stood just behind the blue, gold-trimmed curtain. Horace spoke again as Jason stepped up to it and placed his words gingerly on its slanting lectern.

'When the curtains open, you will be given a moment to get your bearings. Then you will be asked the question I asked you at Starbucks. You may then proceed at your discretion.'

Jason nodded once.

'These are professionals, Jason,' Horace assured him. 'There will be no foolishness from your audience. Please do not be nervous.'

'I'm not.'

'I know,' Horace replied with a smile. 'I could tell the moment you opened the door. I eagerly look forward to this.' He left the stage, leaving Jason alone.

Jason was *not* nervous. Yet this was, beyond doubt, the strangest sensation of his life. It struck him that what he was about to do would one day have the fate of the world hinging upon it. The solitude that tickled his spine was, for the first time, beyond help from Vickie, from Markie, or from anyone else. He was at last on the offensive – not a minority, but an *army,* of one.

An unfamiliar British tenor rang through the hall.

'The Time Traveller.'

No pressure, Jason thought as the curtains were drawn.

The room was nothing remarkable, with decorated beige walls and hardwood flooring that reminded him of the Anglican Church hall where his family had its Christmas parties. But he had only a moment to take this in as he was immediately targeted by over three hundred sets of eyes from around the world. Plainly dressed Servidors in folding chairs sat in anticipation of this historic dress rehearsal. Some smiled; most were stoic. All watched him. That same tenor voice came from who-knew-where.

'Why have you come?'

Jason stood a moment longer, gauging his audience. There were Julie and Johanna, smiling in a not-particularly-appropriate way. The elderly man he had met in Shwari Mawe five days earlier sat next to the aisle and beat his fist gently to his heart. Horace and Omondi sat in the front row to Jason's left, both studying his every move. And to Omondi's right sat Vickie. The moment his eyes found her, she smiled excitedly and pulled the sapphire dog from under her shirt. He allowed her one grin of gratitude and began with his opening statement.

'I have come to prevent.'

He fell solemn and silent. A hush fell through his audience. He waited and waited. He saw some Servidors shift in their seats. Then at last Horace asked the question he was waiting for.

'To prevent what?'

'Many things,' Jason continued. 'I have come to prevent the picture of history that God had painted for eighty-five years. I have come to prevent great triumphs and great tragedies. I have come to prevent the joys and sorrows to which seven billion people sharing the Earth with me had the right.'

He paused and looked around. He had their attention.

'Yet I come with an even greater purpose than these. I come as a messenger. I, myself, am an antidote.'

He paused again. There were certainly more smiles in the room than when he began. He waited again for Horace, but a woman's voice rang out.

'An antidote to what?'

Jason looked to the door and saw Megan, beautiful and humble in a simple black dress, smiling at him. He took heart.

'I am the antidote to a catastrophe unrivalled in human history. The antidote to a tyranny incubating as I speak, which will echo through the decades as the most terrible manifestation of evil ever represented by human form. To a conflict that will make the First Great War a veritable doormat to the monolith of death and destruction that is about to be built.'

As he planned, he smirked and broke the tension.

'Ask me what caused it.'

A burst of appreciative laughter washed over him. Smiling, Horace obliged. Then, without warning, Jason's eyes flashed with all the intensity he could muster. He spread his arms outward to his audience. He saw eyes widen.

'You did. Your weakness caused it. Your blindness caused it. Your COWARDICE caused it. Your policies of inaction and appeasement allowed for the birth of a gluttonous monster known as the Second World War, which would consume the lives of eighty million people before it was satisfied. I am the antidote to the most grievous military follies in history. I am the antidote to *your ultimate dishonour.'*

A small sputter of clapping grew into a wave of strong applause. Jason drove it home.

'Today is the beginning of a lesson.' He shot a look at Omondi, who raised an eyebrow, his lip curling in a faint smile. 'TODAY, I begin the task of revealing the objective Truths of Good and Evil, of Freedom and Oppression. I have come that *you* may redeem the Spirit of Courage, which even now, in your own minds, you are BETRAYING.'

And with that, Jason left the stage. A thunderous torrent of applause nearly knocked him over, but he held his head high.

An hour later, Jason sat in his armchair in Room 209, his head spinning with a triumph that made his university graduation seem like a top comment on YouTube. He could feel the dozens of grips of his hand, the slaps on his back, the typical bear-trap of a hug from Vickie. He could hear the barrage of praises and congratulations from all directions. Most of all, he could see Horace and Omondi and the look in their eyes.

He made a sub and, deciding that this was a worthy occasion, poured one more shot of Glenlivet Fifty. Nothing would ever, ever compare. Then he grabbed a humble beer and spent an hour celebrating in his standard way: by sitting on his ass and watching the *Honeymooners*. How he had managed to make sense of this Orgy of the Whatever he had no idea. But he was at peace.

He sat for a while longer and then went to 212A. He regaled Markie with a theatrical retelling of his newest victory. She smiled and laughed enthusiastically, but Jason couldn't help suspecting a touch of sadness in her face.

'Are you okay?'

'Yeah,' she said, not quite meeting his eyes. 'It's just… the more I see you succeed at this, the more I realize it's really gonna happen.'

Jason nodded. 'Don't worry, Markie. I'll be back eventually.'

She nodded back and smiled. 'I don't know how I could have made it this far without you. If you hadn't been there to keep my feet on the ground, I'd have gotten into coke or moved to the Yukon to live with wolves. Or joined that cult.'

'The Columbia Record Club was not a cult, Markie.'

'Seems like one now,' she said with a shiver. 'Creepiest shit in the world at this point.'

'Well, that's still the sweetest thing you've ever said to me,' Jason said with a smile, 'so thank you.'

She tucked her chin into her chest, an eyebrow raised. She had never taken that kind of compliment very well.

'Anyway,' Jason continued, 'did Kat get back to you?'

She grinned. 'Yep. She listened to 'A Day in the Life', like I told her. Drumming blew her fuckin' mind.'

'Things have a way of working themselves out. I've always told you that.'

She nodded. 'Did you ever realize that the plural of *doofus* is *doofi*?'

Jason smiled. He had long since learned to roll with her jarring changes in topic.

'No, Markie, I must admit I never realized that.'

She smirked. 'I didn't think so. Doofi like you don't ponder such things. Only wise men like me do.'

'Let me learn from you, Markie.'

'Patience, young one,' she said with a slow nod. 'You're not ready to learn from me yet. Prevent World War Two. Then we'll talk.'

Jason shook his head. 'I don't think *anything* could give me the courage to explore your mind.'

Markie pointed a smug finger. 'Now *that's* the wisest thing you've ever said.'

Jason flipped her off.

Chapter Sixteen

Jason's morning routine went smoothly. A glass of milk and a fried egg sandwich, a shower, and a half hour of reading were all the simple pleasures he needed in his mellow state of mind. Yet, he couldn't shake the notion that something intense, even by KRA standards, awaited him before the day was done. He couldn't imagine that his victory the night before would go unpunished.

Even as he reflected, there was a knock at the door. Jason opened it to find Horace smiling gently at him.

'Good morning, Jason. How are you doing?'

'Better than I will be, I'm sure.'

Horace nodded. 'Jason, I am here because a strange turn of events has led to a threat to the secrecy of your mission.'

'And what the hell is that supposed to mean?'

Horace hesitated, choosing his words, but Jason thought he could detect a note of amusement in his face.

'You need to contact Markie immediately.'

'You SPOKE to her?!!' Jason snarled in outrage.

Clearly not intimidated, Horace nodded. 'Indeed I did, Jason. I had no choice. The fate of the world hung in the balance.'

And he walked away.

Without even closing his door, Jason ran to 212A and called out to Markie. When she appeared, she was already smiling.

'Jason, do you know how freaking early it is here?'

'What's going on, Markie?' Jason demanded.

'Not much,' she replied. 'Just being your best friend.'

Without warning, someone sat down next to her on the couch.

Jason's eyes widened in joy and sorrow.

'Mom?!'

There she was, humbly dressed as ever, sitting next to Markie, who smiled once and then left immediately. Jason was overcome with love, with self-loathing at having thought about her so little. He bit back tears as he looked at her.

'You finally cut your hair,' she said with a smile.

'So, you know?'

She nodded. 'You didn't really think you'd keep it from me forever?'

'How did you find out?' he asked shakily.

'I asked Markie, and she told me.'

'And you believed her?' Jason asked in astonishment. 'Just like that?'

'Whatever I may think of Markie's… hobbies, Jason, I trust her. She's never given me reason not to. After that, a couple of threatening phone calls to the Kenyan government was all it took, and here I am.'

Jason smiled. How could he have underestimated her so?

'I've spoken to Dr. Wagner as well. Interesting man. Makes me think I should get hitched up again after all...'

Jason laughed silently, his face in his hands. It would be a long time before he could process that one.

'What about the girls?'

'After discussing it with the doctor, we've decided to tell them that you're teaching English over there. We'll figure out the details tonight. I know Sarah and Janie could handle the truth, but Anne…'

They sat silently and looked at each other.

'So…' she said slowly, 'you're going back in time to prevent World War Two. Doesn't that sound silly coming from your mother?'

Jason chuckled. 'It's always sounded silly.'

'Do you think you can do it?'

Jason reflected for a moment, looked her in the eyes, and nodded. She smiled.

'I'm so proud of you, Jason. Every bit as much as I ever was, except maybe when you assaulted Mr. Madere.'

Jason grinned as he reminisced. 'Sonofabitch had it coming.'

She rolled her eyes. 'I have agreed that this will be our only call until you get back. You already have a lot to do without me breathing down your neck about updating your health card. You *will,* right?'

'*Yes,* Mom, as soon as I get back from England in 1935.'

She laughed her normal womanly guffaw.

'We've never had much in common, Jason. But we got by. I did the best I could with you. Even though we never clicked as friends, I always made sure to be your mother, and I guess it paid off.'

'I'm not dying, Mum.'

For the first time, her face fell. 'Everyone is. You most of all. You won't be the same when you get back.'

'It would take more than this load of crap to change the way I feel about you.'

His mother smiled once more. 'Enjoy London, Jason.'

A single tear escaped Jason's eye as he nodded.

A minute later, Jason stepped back into the hall. He sighed sadly, his mother and sisters' faces shining like beacons in his mind. Now, at long last, he felt like a soldier.

He was nearly to the stairs, heading to the smoking room, when a voice called behind him.

'Hey, Jason!'

It was Vickie, who ran him down and smiled. 'Thank God, I caught you. Horace sent me again.'

Jason raised an eyebrow. 'You don't mind being his messenger girl, Vickie?'

'Not for you,' she said with a cheeky smile.

They exchanged another look of affection before Vickie continued.

'Anyway, Horace said *to meet him immediately in the chamber where the thing is.*' She rolled her eyes. 'As if I'm too stupid to know he means the Time Machine.'

Jason laughed, though a chill went up his spine. 'Thanks, Vickie. I'll head there now.'

Unexpectedly, she jumped and gave him a tight hug around the neck. As he hugged her back, he heard her give a small sob.

'I love you, Big Brother.'

Overcome, he squeezed her tightly. 'I love you, too.'

She released him, smiled again, and left. His head spinning from this emotional barrage, he made for the stairs.

Jason turned a corner and saw the huge steel door to the Chamber. Horace was waiting. He gave a colourless smile and wordlessly entered his various security passes. The door swung open, and the two men stepped inside.

The lights were dim, and this time, it was almost utterly empty. The Servidors and the projects they had been working on were gone. At the far end sat the Time Machine, the palpable green light (which Jason had happily forgotten about) beaming harshly from its ring.

Omondi stood ten feet to its left. He was holding another glowing object, which, sure enough, turned out to be the trigger. Jason went numb.

'I'm not going now?!'

Horace shook his head firmly. 'No, Jason, you are not. You will be given more notice than this when that moment arrives. But this is the tipping point.'

Jason looked between the two men. 'What do you mean?'

'We have been watching you very closely,' Omondi said. 'Despite Horace's faith in you and your mostly exemplary record throughout your time here, Mugo insisted on knowing, personally and for absolute fact, that you can achieve our goals before bringing you to this moment.'

'And what is this moment?'

With his free hand Omondi handled the top of the trigger and popped open a small hatch that Jason had not noticed. Inside was a green scanning circle.

'This is the device's security feature. Fingerprint identification. Whoever presses their thumb to this bar will be the only one for whom the device will successfully activate. It may be done only once, and once done, no other human can use the trigger.'

'In other words, Jason,' Horace said quietly, 'the time has come to commit completely.'

Jason stared stonily at the small green matrix that beckoned him. *'In other words,* there's no going back now.'

'Jason, at our first meeting I gave you my word that you would do nothing against your will, and to that we will hold to the end. But understand that once that machine identifies you, it answers to you alone. Once you cross this threshold, if you back out, you doom humanity, and I have come to know you well enough to be certain that that would be a far worse burden for you than anything you will face in the past.'

Jason looked at the object in Omondi's hand. The world around him ceased to exist as he gazed into that small green circle. The certainty he had built in his heart was assaulted now that the time had come to show his hand. His family, his friends, his students, his home, his future, stabbed him like needles.

Then he thought of Markie.

He reached out his hand. Omondi carefully passed him the trigger, and he held it himself for the first time. He looked at it for a moment.

And he closed the hatch.

'Jason–'

He ignored Horace, turned, and walked without hesitation under the curtain of green light beside them.

Again, Jason's dark surroundings melted away; this time to be replaced by an even darker twilight sky. The sun had almost set behind the leafless old birch in front of him, and its branches barely moved. Stars twinkled benignly above him, and a light day's snowfall coated the ground.

Jason looked at his stolen surroundings in wonder but without fear. It was all quite lovely, ironically reminding him of home. Then he turned and looked to the east.

London by night.

The silhouetted cityscape was just visible, and the bright electric light hummed from it with surprising strength. In his new state of mind, Jason got a better look at the city. There was the River Thames, running straight through its heart. He could just make out the twin tips of the beloved Tower Bridge crossing it in the downtown. And, there, compelling him above all, stood the towering, thousand-year-old Westminster Abbey, which London fought with all her strength to save during the Nazi Blitz. The Centre of the World as she would never be again.

It was the most beautiful thing Jason had ever seen.

He nodded to himself and stepped out of the light. The chamber reappeared with Horace and Omondi waiting where he had left them. And standing to Omondi's right was Mugo.

How the hell does he do that?

Jason joined his three friends, lifted the hatch on the trigger, and pressed his thumb to the scanner. After an awkward four seconds or so, it glowed bright green, and then turned orange. Jason closed the hatch.

'What's next?' he said simply.

'You are a remarkable man, Jason,' Mugo said warmly.

'And that is a good thing,' Omondi added, 'because now we must press you harder.'

Jason looked at him and raised an eyebrow.

'Jason,' Horace said with a smile, 'surely you didn't expect this leisurely pace to last forever? There is much to do if you are to be ready before March 15th.'

'What the hell do you mean, March 15th?'

Omondi stepped forward. 'Duni chose March 15th, 1935 as the ideal date for your drop. Twenty-four hours later, Adolf Hitler will publicly announce his decision to rearm Germany in violation of the Versailles Treaty. You must make as powerful an impact as possible, as timely as possible, as quickly as possible.'

Jason's entire life conquered his doubts.

'And how long does that translate to here and now?'

'Twenty days, Jason,' Horace intoned.

'And you can be sure that we will do so,' Omondi said.

'You guys cut it damned close.'

'Duni told us so little, Jason,' Mugo said. So much was left up to us, with so little time to make it happen.'

Jason nodded. His fate was sealed. He was now, with no proud exaggeration, the Hero of Time.

Mugo shook his hand solemnly, and Horace did the same. Jason held onto it and leaned in to whisper privately in Horace's ear.

'Horace,' he asked weakly, 'how can you believe in God when you so clearly see the worst in people?'

Horace smiled, gripping his hand tightly.

'It is quite simple, Jason: I also see the best.'

'I did it, Markie.'

Half an hour later, he sat before the classy computer, looking into his friend's eyes, not quite sure how to feel. He explained his latest Year Zero, and they sat quietly for a moment, both at a loss for words.

At last Markie smiled, fiddling with a bead in her hair. 'The road goes ever on and on. Down from the door where it began…'

She gestured melodramatically to him.

Jason rolled his eyes. 'Markie, for the last time, I'm never going to make your life super-epic by reciting *Lord of the Rings* with you.'

'Damn it,' she whined. 'That would have been *perfect.'*

Jason smiled affectionately. Markie suddenly gazed at him in wonder.

'Jason, your aura is *beautiful!'*

'Thanks, Markie,' Jason replied with a laugh. 'I've always thought so too.'

'Let me go get a tab, it would make you look like GOD.'

As she moved to get up, Jason held up his hands. 'Markie, please, not right now.'

She froze, then sat back down and glared at him.

'I can't wait until this is over,' she snapped. 'I miss tripping as much as I miss you.'

Jason's stomach clenched at this terrible low blow. He gaped at her uncharacteristic cynicism. She remembered herself quickly and shook herself to her senses.

'I'm sorry, Jason. That was stupid. Never mind.'

Jason decided not to make a bigger fuss than he needed to. 'How's Jimmy? I'm surprised I never see him.'

Markie laughed, though it still seemed a bit forced. 'He's terrified of this laptop. I have to keep it on a shelf or he won't even come in the living room. He still thinks he's in charge around here though.'

'Markie, we both know he is.'

She didn't smile. Trouble suddenly touched her face, her eyes losing focus. She spoke softly.

'Jason… remember the night my dad died?'

Jason's eyes widened in shock. That was the one topic between them that was completely out of bounds, never even mentioned under any circumstances.

Markie had been very close to her dad. Her mom was distant with her, never quite accepting her chosen lifestyle, but her dad had accepted and embraced it, and had been her guide and anchor, possibly even more so than Jason. When he died in a car accident four years ago, Jason had been up north, only hearing about it when he got home, after dark, hours after the funeral.

He immediately went to her place, letting himself in as usual. He noticed there was no music playing; he had never heard complete silence in her house before. He looked down and saw her lying curled up on the couch, naked and out of her mind on acid. The small, tetris-block tear-off of the blotting paper on the coffee table told him she had eaten eleven hundred micrograms, which, thanks to her cheerful education over the years, he knew to be a massively high dosage on a good day, never mind when you've just buried your father. Her eyes were turgid with terror, and she was trembling from head to toe.

Before he could begin to react, she beckoned with a tiny gesture for him to come over. He started toward her, asking stupidly if she was okay. She held up a hand. He froze, keeping his eyes firmly away from her. Words failed him. Instantly she gestured desperately for him again. He started to ask if she needed an ambulance, but again her hand went up. As soon as he stopped talking, she continued to beckon him to her, her lips blue with fright. Finally, Jason realized it was his voice that was causing her such fear.

He shut his mouth and made his way to her trembling, naked form. She shifted, without looking at him, to the front of the couch, clearly making room. Mortified, he carefully lay down beside her, without even taking off his shoes, and she pressed her back against his chest so hard that he was almost winded. He put his arm over hers and gently gripped her shoulder. Her trembling eased just a bit.

For almost six hours they lay there in silence, her breathing slow, deep, and deliberate. She did not move, and neither did he, despite the agonizing cramp that developed in his abdomen. Twice he tried to whisper to her, and it sent her into a soundless spasm as if he had jabbed her with a taser.

At long last, her trembling stopped. He was about to speak one more time, when her arm stirred from the couch. She slowly reached up and grasped his wrist and pulled his hand down... and down. Panicking, he pulled his arm free as firmly as he dared. She put her hand back where it had been and did not make another attempt. She had not once looked at him.

A short time later she got up and shuffled to the bathroom. After five more terrifying minutes, she returned in her bathrobe and sat down next to him. Jason put his arm around her middle and quietly asked if she was okay. She nodded calmly, staring into space. And without warning, she dissolved into anguished tears. Jason, flabbergasted beyond words, embraced her. She flung her arms around him, her nails digging into his back, and wept inconsolably into his chest for almost an hour.

When she was finished, she kissed him softly on the cheek, promised him that she was okay, and went to bed without another word. The sun was coming up as Jason stepped outside.

It was a night of horrifying Only's. The only night he had been terrified in her presence. The only night she had been so inconceivably reckless with her drugs. The only night he had seen her cry. The only night he had seen her naked; the only night any semblance of sexuality, however brief, grotesque, and unthinkable, had happened between them. And above all – the thing that gutted him to this day – it was the only night he had seen her broken, defeated, helpless. The memory of her agony tortured Jason even more than the thought of what would have happened that night had he not shown up.

'What about it?' Jason asked.

Markie still did not look at him. 'It was something...' she mumbled.

'It was one of the worst nights of my life, Markie,' Jason replied.

Markie continued to look at his chest, seemingly wrestling with something. Finally, she shrugged, and looked him in the eye. 'Helluva trip, though.'

Jason stared at her, open-mouthed. Then he burst into joyous, chortling laughter. She smiled. In one fell swoop, she had lifted his spirits and put the one great demon between them to rest. Was there anything she couldn't do?

Jason sat once more on the roof of the KRA, a Joni Mitchell album quietly emanating from his phone, which lay nestled in his front pocket. The sun was setting, and to the southwest a massive thunderstorm battered the grassy plains. It was moving away from Jason, which allowed him to enjoy the astonishing view with ease as he contemplated.

How was he supposed to feel? Was this a victory or a laying down of arms? Was this the end or the beginning? Or some strange limbo between the world he had known and the world that waited to take him?

Had it only been two weeks? Had it *already* been two weeks? Jason shook his head at the oppression and sadism of Time. When you were young, it went too slowly; when you were old, it went too quickly. When you were bored, it slowed to mud; when you were having fun, it burned like gasoline. Things you wanted seemed to freeze in the future; things you feared seemed to laugh as they sped toward you like a runaway train. Two weeks ago, time travel had been purest fiction, and now, alone in this moment, Jason laughed at the idea that something so conscious and malevolent as Time could be impervious to rebellion.

Jason sipped his beer and watched the shadows grow. The War was long over, but *his* war had begun. He was a soldier. He was in a private landing craft on his way to his own personal Normandy. Yet even he had an advantage over those fearless fighters to whom he dared to compare himself. Whereas they could only stand helplessly and wait for the doors to Hell to open, Jason was on the move. He had work to do and a part to play. And he had read the script in advance.

He sat alone into the night. Not even in Wainfleet had he seen such stars.

Part Three

Chapter Seventeen

It took a small fraction of a second for Jason's fright and surprise to vanish at the return of his morning alarm. He sat upright in his bed, his eyes burning in protest at the four hours of sleep he had managed. It was 5:30. As that hateful sound died away, he sat for a moment longer, then let out a sigh. It was time to begin again.

His feet had barely touched the floor when there was a timid knock at the door. Jason put a shirt on and answered it. Much to his disappointment, there was no platter of breakfast awaiting him; moreso, it was not Vickie who met his eyes. The young man went white as snow and in a strange, stuttering accent told him to head to Omondi's office in ten minutes.

Jason spitefully watched half of *Happy Gilmore* and then obliged.

Omondi frowned at Jason's tardiness as he opened the door, but was strictly business as usual.

'Have you ever fired a gun?'

Jason shook his head. Other than a brief pose with his brother-in-law's Remington, Duni's revolver was the only gun he had ever even held.

Omondi rolled his eyes. *'Canadians…'*

'I beg your pardon?'

'Never mind,' Omondi snapped. 'Let us get to it. You are being sent to a world where fear and controversy are already fully present. And you are being sent to create much, much more. You will make powerful enemies. You must be prepared.'

'I just LOVE that you wait until I'm past the point of no return to emphasize that I'll be in mortal danger at all times.'

'If you hadn't realized that by now,' Omondi replied curtly, 'then I have given you too much credit.'

'You're a real jackass, you know that?'

Omondi leered at him. 'Do you want to fire a gun, or not?'

'Yes.'

Omondi nodded. 'National heritage dies in the face of human nature. Come.'

Omondi led him through the complex and out a firedoor of the eastern wing. Omondi unlocked a simple door in the harsh outer fence and stopped in the shade of a croton tree about thirty feet away. The sun was barely above the horizon. Omondi pulled out a simple, long-barrel revolver. He pointed at the trunk of the tree, and Jason saw a ridiculous target printed on an ordinary piece of paper. It couldn't have cost more than fifty cents. Jason looked at Omondi in utter derision.

'Is this *A Christmas Story*? Where's my air rifle?'

Without warning Omondi pointed the gun at the hapless tree and fired three terrifyingly loud shots. Jason fell straight on his backside. He looked at the target and was astonished to see the blue bullseye almost totally obliterated.

'*A Christmas Story* is a lovely movie,' Omondi said, 'but you will have more dangerous foes than Black Bart to deal with.'

Jason almost fainted. 'How the FUCK do you know–'

'Get up.'

Jason scrambled shakily to his feet. Omondi looked at him for a moment and handed him the smoking revolver.

'Point it at the target.'

Every Canadian instinct in Jason's body cried out in protest as Jason raised the deadly weapon in his shaking hand. Out of the corner of his eye he saw Omondi shake his head.

'This is pointless. You must relax.'

'Relax?!' Omondi reached in his pocket and pulled out a mickey of Wiser's. Jason couldn't believe it.

'It's not even *seven!'*

'Did we not warn you?' Omondi snapped as he handed Jason the whiskey. 'You are now to be run as if by a whip. Your pitiful etiquette no longer comes into play. You need to learn to defend yourself, and if your nerves are preventing you from doing so, then they must be settled.'

Jason looked at Omondi in wonder. His face was passive; he might as well have been handing Jason the morning paper. Jason looked at the small bottle before him for a moment, then downed a third of it.

'Now,' Omondi muttered as the liquor assaulted his empty stomach, 'point the revolver.'

Jason steadied himself and did as he was told. A strange mixture of alcohol-induced focus and phallocentric machismo grabbed hold of him as he felt the contours of the mechanism in his hand. It felt right. Unfortunately, it did nothing to steady his aim, and when he pulled the mighty trigger, only the unfortunate tree was damaged; the paper target mocking him was untouched.

Omondi nodded. 'Yet more work to do.'

They worked for the better part of an hour. Omondi (of whom, for the first time, Jason began to feel a bit afraid) explained the ins and outs of shooting, reloading, and gun safety. Only once did Jason even manage to pierce the paper.

At last, Omondi took his piece back for good and pointed immediately at the firedoor.

'Go and change into your suit and meet Megan in the Blue Room immediately.'

Jason's heart sank. Even this testosterone-driven shitshow was better than what he had known he would eventually have to face.

Only his beloved suit and the gentle buzz from his morning nip could have given Jason the courage to open that door. Even by KRA standards, this was punishment.

The room was not decorated, and Jason heard no music. Only the familiar faces on the posters hung on the walls. Jason managed to reflect on how tired he was of this place. Then his whiskey-rattled mind blew up as he found Megan.

After their steaming encounter in Shwari Mawe, and even more so after their connection during his speech, he had expected strictly business. Instead, he found her more seductively dressed than ever in a skin-tight, barely-opaque dress, which flowered to its hem just below her thighs. It seemed designed to make Jason want to weep at what he could have had. Her smile was soft, but no less alluring.

'What a pleasure it is to see you again, Jason.'

'What is this?' Jason demanded. 'What are you doing?'

'My job, Jason.'

'This would have been awkward enough without you dressing like that.'

She actually giggled. 'My dearest Jason, if you think *this* is awkward, you would drop dead in some of the scrapes in which I've found myself. Now. Please sit.'

Jason glared at her as they sat together in the continually polished leather.

'Today we will discuss a crucial topic that I essentially commandeered from Horace, as only a Brit could possibly prepare you adequately for it.'

'Great.'

She scowled in a way that reminded Jason of Omondi.

'You will, of course, have realized that you will be meeting the Royal Family?'

Jason nodded. Years of hatred for the gossip industry had, he now realized, led him to not particularly care. Megan grew very serious.

'Are you also aware, then, that you will likely be meeting a woman named Wallis Simpson?'

Jason knew that name. But from where?

THERE.

'Oh, shit.'

'Yes, Jason,' Megan breathed, 'you are being dropped into England just as the most notorious and consequential love affair in modern history is reaching the apex of its passion.

And *you,* my poor little myna bird, will have the answers that many very powerful people will be seeking.'

Jason couldn't believe it. Wallis Simpson. The Prince's mistress. The reason Elizabeth became Queen. He would be caught in the crossfire of a scandal that made Harry and Meghan seem like *Dawson's Creek.* He hated this crap on the *smallest* of scales, let alone when those involved could have you executed for treason. Markie would have a field day with this.

'Once your enemies realize this, as they most likely will, it will be a valuable weapon of disruption. You *must* be prepared, and your first step is forging an alliance with King George V as quickly as possible. *And my eyes are up here, you dolt.*'

She stood, and Jason, still shaking his head, did the same.

'Now,' Megan stated with her normal snobbery, 'what would you imagine would be your first action when–'

But Jason had already bowed at the neck. Megan smiled in a way that screamed: *'Remember who taught you that.'* She continued.

'And how would you address the King upon meeting him?'

'I think the first time it's *Your Majesty* and after that it's *Sir.*'

She frowned in frustration. 'How the hell do you know that?'

'*The King's Speech,* ironically,' Jason said with a smirk.

'You are surprisingly cultured, for a Canadian.'

Jason's lip curled. 'Even I have to admit that's not saying much.'

Megan grinned, her perfect teeth gleaming. 'There is clearly more to your mouth than your kissing skills.'

Jason could have screamed, but Megan quickly returned to the topic at hand.

'To this day, a breach of protocol with British royalty can haunt a man for years. We will now spend the next ninety minutes–'

'Ninety minutes?!'

'–NINETY MINUTES inundating your puny little mind with the sensibilities necessary for putting smiles on the faces of the most powerful men and women on Earth.'

'Awesome,' Jason spat.

Megan's eyes flashed. *'Never* use that word in my presence again. Now. From this moment on, I will be the King's stand-in. Your first lesson will be, judging by our delightful encounter three days ago, the most difficult.'

'And that would be?!' Jason snarled.

Megan's allure exploded in her devastating face.

'Do not touch me without my permission.'

After ninety-*eight* minutes of painstaking etiquette that left Jason a twitching ball of furious nerves, Megan curtseyed once more, jumping up for the fifth time to return Jason's skeleton to its proper agonizing posture.

'Can I ask you a question?' Jason said.

'If you must,' she muttered, her brow furrowed in concentration.

'Was it all staged? When you kissed me, was that part of my training too?'

She slapped him across the face with all her strength. By the time he recovered, she was halfway out the door. His ears ringing, he heard her snarl the word *satisfactory,* and soon the sound of her heels was gone.

His left cheek was still numb as the implications of what he had asked hit him like another slap in the face. When the door to the Blue Room opened slowly and Omondi walked into the room, he wore a perturbed look that would have been quite comical were it not for the icy feeling in Jason's stomach. He had felt a well-deserved smack like that only once before, and it had bothered him for weeks. Seeing Vickie follow closely behind Omondi, looking confused and close to terrified, was the only thing that could have kept him in the room one moment longer.

Seeing Jason's face, she ran past Omondi and hugged him tight. He felt life return to him as he felt her embrace. Vickie's hugs were an elixir that should be bottled.

Between four hours sleep, the burnout left by the whiskey, and now this mortar shell, Jason hadn't been this exhausted at 10:00 a.m. in at least a decade.

Omondi quickly regained his composure and gestured to the chairs to Jason's left. The three of them sat together, Vickie staying close to Jason. Omondi began without preamble.

'Vickie has agreed to keep you company for today's History lesson.'

'I insisted, actually,' Vickie chirped. 'I'm the secret weapon.'

Jason chuckled warmly, but Omondi's face hardened.

'This will *not* be the norm. Vickie has proven herself to be an invaluable ally, but she will not be joining you in 1935. You *must* learn to deal with your obstacles yourself.'

Jason nodded, and Omondi began without further ado.

'I shall take it for granted that you are aware that the Japanese attack on Pearl Harbor was what brought the stubbornly neutral United States into the war. But do you know why they chose neutrality in the first place?'

Jason answered immediately, wondering what kind of bad news would accompany their newest topic.

'They more or less thought the War was none of their business. A large enough majority of Congress and the public felt that it made no sense to send their men to die in the thousands when they had nothing to do with the events leading up to the conflicts with Nazi Germany or Japan.'

'Indeed,' Omondi said. 'There was great controversy over the issue, which only escalated as the War intensified around the world. One American in particular, however, saw the catastrophe for the threat that it was.'

'Roosevelt!'

Both Omondi and Jason turned to look at Vickie, who smiled as bravely as ever.

'He was friends with Churchill,' she continued, 'and tried to help him in any way he could.'

Omondi gave his normal nod of the head and turned back to Jason. 'You will henceforth spend time getting to know Franklin Delano Roosevelt. We feel that the Fates would frown upon us if you had nothing to say when you meet him.'

'WHEN I MEET HIM?!' Jason bellowed. Vickie gasped. 'Now the AMERICANS are on my plate too?!'

Omondi frowned and spread his hands. 'Haven't you figured this out yet?! *Yes,* you will be meeting the Americans. *Yes,* you will be meeting the French, the Dutch, the Belgians, even officials from Northern Africa, if you feel so inclined. You will be assembling a secret meeting of the United Nations a decade ahead of schedule, and I *cannot believe* I still have to spell this out to you!'

Jason struggled for anything whatsoever to say. What was he going to learn next? Was he going to Mars to conscript aliens?

'This is so COOL!'

Jason turned again and saw Vickie's black eyes wide with wonder. When Jason looked at her she remembered herself, but did not try to hide her enthusiasm.

'I'm sorry, Jason, but it is! *Send it!*'

'... send what, Vickie?'

'Oh, right,' Vickie said with a small smile. 'It's a saying. It means *go for it*.'

Jason chuckled. He was getting old.

Omondi continued. 'America, in particular, had a determined and proactive attitude toward defeating Germany, once they entered the war, which their British Allies lacked. We believe this will work well in your favour. There are two other Americans who would be ideal ambassadors to answer your call.'

'Truman?' Jason guessed, but Omondi shook his head firmly.

'Harry Truman's presence would only complicate things. He became President only following Roosevelt's death in 1945, which is a topic it would be wise to avoid. Also, his involvement in the Hiroshima and Nagasaki bombings is not something you will need hanging over your head.'

'Isn't he the *Vice President?*' Jason cried. 'How the hell am I supposed to get one without the other?'

'By insisting.'

'*Who,* then?' Jason demanded.

'The first is a man you will not likely have heard of: a lawyer and educator named Louis D. Brandeis.'

Indeed unfamiliar, Jason said nothing.

'Brandeis was a brilliant thinker and humanitarian, and the first Jew to sit on the US high court. He was among the first in the Free World to speak openly against Jewish persecution in Germany. If your first priority is to stop the Holocaust, it would be an ill omen and a great sin to leave the Jews themselves out of the equation.'

Jason nodded. 'And the second?'

Omondi leered again. Jason had long since learned to recognize that look as a sure sign that Omondi had a doozie at the ready.

'General Patton.'

Jason felt a fantastic rush. 'Unbelievable.'

George Patton. Ol' Blood and Guts. The archetypal soldier. Even based on the little Jason knew about him, the thought of meeting him was exhilarating.

'Be careful what you wish for,' Omondi drawled. 'By all accounts, he will frighten you as much as the Time Machine. Do not lose your phone.'

'Don't be so cynical, Omondi,' Jason jibed.

Omondi glanced at Vickie. She had politely raised a hand.

'Omondi, how is Jason supposed to get the Americans to come to Europe? There won't be email.'

'That will be up to him.'

'What do you mean, *up to me*?' Jason demanded.

'You are creative and resourceful. We cannot – and will not – provide an answer for every dilemma you will face. Not half, in fact.'

Jason sighed. As ever, he knew it would be no use to argue. The pain-in-the-ass factor was as taxing as the fear.

The door opened again. Again, Jason teetered on the edge as Horace entered, his incorrigible enthusiastic smile slapped on his face as usual. In his hands were two large, steaming ceramic mugs. Jason's stomach lurched.

'I don't want coffee,' he croaked.

'Tea, Jason,' Horace countered. *'The drink that cheers, but does not inebriate.'*

'You are an actual sadist,' Jason muttered as he reached for the brew like a toddler.

Vickie and Omondi stood together. Jason put his tea aside and received a hug from Vickie. Then they left, leaving Jason alone with Horace. Jason sat down unceremoniously, put sugar in his tea, and felt life return to him as he sipped. Horace sat down across from him and crossed his legs deliberately. He meant business, and thus Jason took four more mouthfuls of tea before giving him his attention.

'I will get right to the point,' Horace said. 'How do you feel about shaking hands with Joseph Stalin?'

Jason's hands clenched. Even after his latest history lesson, he had not been ready for this one.

'You might as well ask me to shake hands with Hitler.'

Horace nodded. *'Precisely* the response we were hoping for, Jason.'

'Am I meeting him?'

Horace shook his head. 'We rather feel his influence to be unnecessary in this business. The combined, pre-emptive might of European and North American democracies should be enough to deal with Nazi Germany without giving legitimacy to equally murderous communist dictatorships.'

'Devil's advocate: Stalin was really more of a fascist than a communist.'

Horace gave a powerful frown. 'The principles of communism are *millimetres* from fascism, Jason. Ultimately, a communist is just a fascist who is nice enough to lie.'

'Is that what the philosophy majors said?'

'HAH!' Horace barked. 'Do you really think we would ask *college students* for their views on communism?'

Jason chuckled. 'Should I warn the Allies of the communist threat?'

Horace smiled. 'That's a Bomb Question, Jason.'

'A what?'

'You must decide that for yourself. Watch the papers, use common sense, and remember where you come from.'

'Why use the word *democracies* anyway?' Why not *free nations*?'

'As far as we humans are concerned, Jason,' Horace said quietly, 'freedom and democracy are one and the same. Kennedy himself, in front of the Berlin Wall, openly acknowledged the imperfection of democracy. However, history has proven it to be the only political system yet devised which is a safe distance away from both tyranny and dysfunction. And dysfunction invariably leads to tyranny.'

'I hate politics,' Jason muttered.

'Churchill didn't.'

Zing.

'You will be attacked from every side, and from every angle,' Horace hissed. 'Do not believe even for a moment that your proactive allies in 1935 – even Churchill himself – will fully trust a man with a smartphone. Some will not trust you at all, and some will not *want* to trust you, for more reasons than we could possibly prepare you for. Worse yet, some clever and subversive men and women will very much want you to trust *them.*'

'I'm not an idiot.'

'You are a *Canadian,*' Horace replied. He wasn't joking. 'Your inherent courtesy and… niceness –already well documented by everyone you have met besides your three instructors – will be a double-edged sword if ever there was one. All we ask is that you be careful in choosing your allies.'

Even at this moment, Jason felt compelled to change the subject entirely.

'How about this one, Horace: If the Holocaust doesn't happen, then Israel doesn't happen. Doesn't THAT refute the Book of Revelation?'

Horace actually laughed. 'Oh, Jason, you truly are wonderful.'

'What are you talking about?'

Horace leaned in, still smiling. 'It would take far more than *our* little hive of worker bees to destroy God's plan for this world. If God wants Israel, he'll get Israel. It's really as simple as that.'

Call it.

'I need a break right now.'

Horace nodded with a smile. 'I would say you've earned half an hour or so. Enjoy yourself and return.'

Jason marched out the door, taking his tea with him. He found the nearest green door and stepped into Shwari Mawe.

It was dotted with Servidors, but other than warm smiles and hearty hellos they mostly let him be. He stepped into the hot sun and took a deep breath, expelling a legion of demons. He remembered his chat with Omondi the morning after Auschwitz. This was the first chance he had had to enjoy the blessed garden since then, and the truth in Omondi's words rang profoundly true; Shwari Mawe was as vital an organ as anything in this damned place.

He walked. He sipped his tea. He leaned quietly on the railing of a small wooden bridge, watching the birds and falling under the spell of the tricking brook beneath him.

Nothing had prepared him for the spiritual battle going on continually within him. He had never given a damn about God. He had been brought half-heartedly to church for a few years, but had more or less gone his own way for most of his adult life, and after watching his father waste away, he had nursed a quiet contempt for all things spiritual. And now, as he saw the terrible end of the lives of billions looming just over the horizon, he felt for the first time since he was fourteen that perhaps a war beyond his realm truly was being waged.

After all, according to the most famous children's story on Earth, God once destroyed the human race. Why should Jason believe in him any less when he let humans do it for themselves?

Cynicism, he thought, was not likely a negative ingredient in a modern spiritual outlook.

Jason dumped the remainder of his cold tea in the brook below him and watched a tawny eagle soar aimlessly above.

Suddenly, a great wave of resolution took hold of him; the great events of his last thirty-six hours were turned to dust. He knew what he had to do.

A young man happened to pass by, and he asked him where Megan might be at such a time of day.

'I saw her sitting on a bench just a moment ago, in the far corner.'

Jason practically ran, and soon found himself in the corner nearest his room. There was Megan, sitting on the very bench where this whole mess had started. She had changed into a pair of grey jeans and a red Pink Floyd t-shirt and was as lovely as ever. Jason felt a powerful relief when she gave him a small smile.

'I'm sorry,' he said.

She said nothing at first. She stared off into space, absorbing the abundant beauty that Jason had come to love so much. Finally, she looked at him. 'Men are amazing creatures.'

Jason said nothing.

'What *is* it about you that we find so wonderful? I think it's the shoulders.'

'The shoulders?'

'A man's shoulders must be the most alluring thing on Earth. They frame him like… like the top of the Arc de Triomphe.'

Jason decided to pretend to know what that was.

'Despite your many, many flaws, Jason, women shall always find you irresistible. We complain and complain, but we cannot help but love the world you have created for us.'

Jason felt her strength, and smiled. 'Don't give me that. Women are in charge. They always have been. I've studied history, you know. All the great catastrophes of the world have happened when a bunch of idiots thought that they could somehow make the world a better place without women at the helm. Look what happened to the Taliban. Kaboom.'

She shook her head, looked at him, and smiled. 'It is alright, Jason. Were our positions switched, I would have asked the same silly question.'

She stood gracefully and hugged him. He hugged back. She gripped him by the shoulders and smiled warmly

'I see great things for you, Jason, and not just in the past. You are a man of character and will live a good life when you are done sorting out this little mess.'

Jason smiled gratefully.

'Now,' she snapped, pointing from where he had come, 'get back to work.'

'Who is your favourite band, Jason?'

Jason looked at Horace in incomprehension, but he could see that the man was serious. With a raised eyebrow, Jason considered.

'Depends on the mood. Overall, either the Beatles or Sinatra.'

Horace smiled. 'Passers-by your room can attest to that. You have a taste for music that extends far beyond your years on this Earth.'

'Your point being?'

'My point, Jason, is that it does not extend far enough. Although your beloved Mr. Sinatra is a good start, your taste in music is dangerous. Your taste in many things is dangerous. You must be conscious at all times of the fact that your upbringing is permeated with scandalous tastes and behaviours. The thirties are a bland time. Even jazz is frowned upon. You must be prepared to be bored. Miserably bored.'

'Can't I smuggle some Buddy Holly in on the smartphone?' Jason pleaded. Horace shook his head.

'No, Jason. Even the great Mr. Holly would sow powerful seeds of distrust in the minds of anyone who passed by your door. You *must* be seen as a man of integrity. As we have already discussed, you must not interfere with the flow of unfolding events outside the spectrum of the war, even with the meaningless drivel of popular music.'

Jason stood. Horace stood with him.

'Please go change, and report to the gym, Jason. Then you can chat with Markie.'

'I'm chatting with her now.'

Horace's face hardened. *'THE GYM,* Jason.'

Jason glared his resentment, remembered his view of London, and obeyed.

Jason's latest excursion at the KRA gym might have actually crippled him twenty days ago. Even the endlessly cheerful Joonheong had turned to steel since Jason had pressed his thumb to that scanner. His plan to pummel a punching bag flew out the window as two hours of heavy weights, push-ups, and agonizing sprints on the treadmill left him a mass of quivering jelly.

At long last, Jason crept back to his familiar hallway, past his quarters, and opened the door to Room 212A. He pressed a couple of blessed buttons and, within moments, was looking at Markie. Her jaw dropped.

'What the flying *fuck* happened to you?!'

Jason chuckled, wiping sweat from his eyes with a shaking hand. 'Day One, as far as I'm concerned.'

He told her some of his day, leaving out certain embarrassing details.

'You look like Jack Nicholson after his lobotomy.'

'You know that movie bums me out.'

She smirked. 'But Danny DeVito's so darned cute in it.'

Jason sneered. 'We both know you'd rather watch him bangin' whores in Philly.'

She looked suddenly thoughtful. 'Do you ever think about how enslaved we are?'

Jason raised an eyebrow. 'How?'

She smiled sadly. 'We're all bitches to pop culture. We think we're so unique and independent, when really most of our thoughts are shaped by stupid bullshit we see on screens. We're sheep, really.'

Jason nodded. 'It's nothing new, Markie. Religion, philosophy, science… they've influenced our thoughts for centuries. With pop culture, it's just on a bigger scale.'

She shook her head. 'People are too stupid for this.'

Jason smiled sadly. 'Maybe that's how the world ends. We get fed so much bullshit that we forget how to feed ourselves.'

'*Enough* already!' Markie snapped. 'You're bumming *me* out!'

'You started the conversation, okay?!' Jason growled indignantly.

Markie took a breath. 'Sorry. I need a shower. I'll talk to you later, okay?'

She disconnected. Jason stared at the screen in frustration and left the room, closing the door quietly behind him. The rest of his punishing day did nothing to ease the trouble in his heart.

Chapter Eighteen

Jason thundered with exhilaration. *This* was cool.

He was standing in an exact replica of Churchill's War Room; old-fashioned ceiling lamps illuminated his amazing surroundings. Simple desks with polished leather writing pads were cramped around awkward, roughly painted wooden pillars. Quaint rotary phones sat everywhere. The walls were jammed with shelves, schedules, and regulations. Even the hardwood floor creaked harshly when stepped on in the right place.

When first ushered into this little fabrication, it had felt a bit corny until Jason remembered that he would one day be standing in the real thing.

Now he, Horace, Omondi, and Megan stood around a five-foot square table, with a single lamp illuminating a gigantic map of London, 1935. Omondi pointed at a small circle drawn outside the city, near Jason's edge of the photo. At long last: the action plan.

'This is the birch tree. You will be dropped here.'

Jason studied the photo for a moment and then shook his head.

'How am I supposed to make any sense of this? It's freaking massive! Where do I go? What do I do?'

'Calm down, Jason,' Horace said. 'Megan knows London well. Please listen.'

Megan stepped up to his left and pointed to the green area on the outskirts of the city where the circle sat.

'Duni's people chose an ideal place to drop you. This is Richmond Park. It sits in the Borough of Richmond upon Thames, south of Twickenham.'

Jason smiled in spite of himself as his love of England swelled.

'It was established as a wildlife conservation,' Megan continued. 'Expect to see deer. We do rather expect the park to be devoid of humans in the dead of winter.'

'And if it isn't?' Jason asked.

'We wait,' Omondi growled.

'If you are questioned,' Megan said, 'you are a wealthy Canadian tourist there to see the sights. You landed from Canada in Whitechurch Airport in Bristol.'

'Where do I go?' Jason asked. 'What the hell do I even do when I get there?'

Megan pointed at a pin placed in the map not far from his drop-point.

'This is the Richmond Hill Hotel. It is approximately one and a half kilometres from the birch tree and would be an ideal place to settle for your first night. Simply head due north to Sawyer's Hill – that's a street – and follow it left.'

'How do I pay?'

'With British pounds.' Omondi was as blunt as ever.

Jason raised an eyebrow. 'How am I supposed to pay with modern money?'

'The Kenyan government has taken the liberty of secretly reproducing one- and five-pound notes from the thirties, and you will be sent back with enough to–'

Jason burst out laughing, breaking the tension of this tremendous conspiracy. Kenya was forging British currency. The worse things got, the funnier they became. Horace and Megan smiled and glanced at Omondi, who scowled his immortal scowl.

Jason collected himself, and asked the question. 'Where does Churchill live?'

Horace shook his head. 'You will not be going to Churchill directly, Jason.'

'Why not?'

'You of all people should understand,' Omondi rasped, 'that that would not have a strong enough dramatic effect. Rather than show up at Westminster with Winston Churchill at your side, you must do the opposite: Reveal yourself for who you are and then *demand* to speak with Churchill, and Churchill alone.'

'Give him the power he needs,' Jason concurred.

'No, Jason,' Megan corrected, 'give him the power *you* need him to have.'

'Badass,' Jason remarked with a grin.

'Will you *stop* using those silly Canadianisms!' Megan snapped. 'You are making me look bad in front of my superiors!'

'Okay, okay, I'm–' Jason pursed his lips together as tight as he could, just managing to halt himself before apologizing, which all three of them picked up on.

'I believe a dog is in order, Omondi,' Horace said with a small chuckle. 'Even I never imagined Megan had the power to stifle a Canadian from saying he was sorry.'

Jason chuckled at Megan's satisfied smirk.

'We digress,' Omondi growled. The meeting quickly returned to professional status.

'Who do I reveal the phone to, then? I don't want to be torn to shreds by a panicky mob.'

'That will be up to you.'

Jason sighed.

'That monumental first step cannot be planned on paper, Jason,' Horace intoned. 'Perhaps you will have a chance encounter with the King himself, or perhaps you will meet a janitor who gives you a good first impression. Go with your gut, and do not rest until you are in the belly of the beast.'

Jason nodded, grudgingly appreciative of the credit he was being given.

'You have homework now,' Omondi said. 'Before the day is done, we ask you to make a respectable list of writings, photos, and videos to store in your phone. Please keep all aspects of your mission in mind, and remember the magnitude of the people in your audience.'

'Awesome,' Jason snapped with a pointed look at Megan. She held up the back of her hand, two fingers raised.

'Do remember this gesture, Jason,' she hissed flatly. 'You will likely receive it often.'

Jason smiled in triumph and left without another word.

Joonheong was waiting outside the War Room. *Joonheong.*

After battering down the urge to run, Jason followed him to the gym for yet another relentless assault. Finally having had enough of the inexplicable easy listening that mewled from the many speakers, Jason threw a dumbbell at the wall and furiously drew a line in the sand, drawing timid applause from his fellow fitness-freaks. He spent another glorious hour on the treadmill, his own YouTube playlist blaring its motivation.

Horace himself showed up at the door of the gym at the end of Jason's motivation. He ignored the hole in the drywall by the drinking fountain and ordered him to report to Room 203. He promptly walked away before Jason could say a word. Jason showered, changed, and complied.

The room was serenely decorated, with calming music (no doubt at 432 Hz) washing over him. The Employee receptionist directed him to a small room with two green armchairs. Jason sat on one of them and waited, already thoroughly annoyed.

Two minutes later, the same Brazilian man he had met at the dance walked into the room and immediately sat across from Jason. He wore a patronizing smile.

'Hello, Jason. It is good to see you again. My name is André. Mugo has requested that we speak together.'

Jason scowled. 'So now I need counselling.'

'Everyone in this facility meets with a counsellor periodically,' André replied. 'Now. What is your mindset? Are you prepared?'

Had anyone but Horace sent him here, Jason would have balked. But he kept his patience. 'Yes. I am prepared.'

'You have an enormous task ahead of you,' André said softly. 'What makes you so certain?'

It was a fair question. Jason reflected for a moment.'

'The people around me. Everyone drives me crazy, but in a way that keeps me going.'

'Do you have any complaints?'

'Only that everyone drives me crazy.'

André chuckled. He seemed nervous. 'Who have you met that doesn't drive you crazy?'

Jason eyed André suspiciously, but decided to be truthful. 'Vickie.'

'What makes her so special?'

Jason's anger began to rumble. He decided to give this idiot one more chance to be genuine. 'She's like my little sister.'

André wrote something down and looked him in the face.

'What would you say about Markie that has benefited you during your time here?'

Jason stood. 'You *moron.'*

André stood shakily as well, raising his hands. 'Jason, I am trying to help you. I know these questions are personal, but–'

'Look,' Jason said stonily. 'I'm not a Scientologist, but I don't need this. This is a joke. Either you don't know me at all, or you do. And I can't decide which is worse.'

'Jason–'

'Horace has earned my trust. So, I'll assume that this is just a mistake. I suggest you shut up before I change my mind.'

And he left without another word.

The moment Jason was gone, Omondi stepped into the room. His eyes were calm.

'Flawless,' he said softly.

André, also wearing a new expression of calm, nodded with a small smile.

'He will be very hard to fool, sir. You have indeed found a man of strength.'

Omondi stared into space for a moment and then headed to his office to plan the next step.

'... and then the dumbass asked about you. Asked what it is about you that helps me. Can you believe it?'

Markie considered. 'Seems like a fair question, really.'

'Didn't I tell you?'

'Tell me what?'

Jason looked down awkwardly and then confessed his ultimatum to Horace and Omondi after their first video chat. Markie smiled affectionately.

'Aww, Jason, I didn't know I was such a jewel.'

Jason raised an eyebrow. 'Markie, I treasure our friendship too much to let some altruistic freaks snoop in on it. I'm surprised I have to say so.'

She tucked her chin to her chest, her smile faltering slightly.

Markie,' Jason drawled with a chuckle, 'why do you have to react like Hank Hill when I compliment you like that?'

She shrugged and changed the subject. 'Do you think there's Mexican food in England in '35?'

Jason chuckled. 'Markie, I'll probably lose fifty pounds by the time I come home.'

'Is Mexico even a thing at that point?'

'You are such a dumbass.'

She gave a ridiculous grin.

They looked at each other quietly.

'I'm thinking of buying a lute,' she said.

Jason gawped. 'So now you'll have a diggory-doo and a lute. Why not buy a guitar or an accordion? Something practical.'

'When have I ever done *anything* practical, Jason?'

She seemed only to be half-joking. A definite change had come over Markie's vibe lately. Jason went with it.

'I bet you could pull off some killer acoustic Zeppelin with a lute.'

She smiled. 'Goin to California, baby.'

'Why not just get a mandolin? It's got the same ancient sound and would probably be a lot cheaper.'

She considered and smiled. 'Never thought of that.'

'You would look badass with a mandolin,' Jason said with a smirk.

She returned it. 'Jason, I would look badass with a tuba, and we both know it.'

There was a knock at the door.

'You are needed, Jason,' came Horace's voice.

Jason was disturbed by the tinge of relief that he felt along with the annoyance at Horace's interruption. Markie only smiled sadly. They disconnected, and Jason left the small room.

Ten minutes later, Jason was strolling privately with Horace in Shwari Mawe. The subject had turned to Jason's favourite subject of all: Winston Churchill.

'Are you aware of Churchill's many faults, Jason?'

'Of course I am,' Jason replied, remembering his serendipitous essay on the man.

'Can you name some of them?'

'He was part of the decision to firebomb Dresden, and not to bomb Auschwitz–'

'That is not what I meant,' Horace interrupted. 'No war escapes controversy. Afghanistan and Iraq are proof of that. I mean the faults of Churchill *himself*. His personal attributes.'

Jason reflected. 'I know he was a pretty devoted drinker.'

Horace nodded.

'It has even been suggested that Churchill's drinking might have contributed to his consent to the Dresden Bombing.'

An uneasy rumour sifted to the surface of Jason's mind. 'Was he a racist?'

Horace stopped them near a lovely statue of a woman with a child at her side.

'Have you researched that question yourself, Jason?'

'A bit...'

'And what did you use to do your research?'

'Google, mostly,' Jason said with a small shrug. 'It's hard to find a reliable answer.'

Horace spread his arms with wide, exasperated eyes.

'And you are SURPRISED at that?!'

Startled, Jason said nothing. Horace continued with a force approaching his conviction at Auschwitz.

'I am amazed at you, Jason! Do you not realize how pathetically blunt a tool the Internet is for *anything* important?! I googled this very question shortly after my arrival here and found nothing but shameless bias on both sides of the issue. There is no doubt that Churchill held certain views that would be reprehensible today. But on the other hand, he was born in 1874, and was a product of his time. But on the other hand, those views were reprehensible! And so on! It's a cycle of *bullshit* that is meant to fog the simple truth that Churchill was ultimately a good man who saved the world. As I have stated previously, Jason, one must keep the big picture in mind at *all times!!'*

Jason smiled. 'Didn't the British people vote him the greatest Briton of all time in 2002?'

'That was a long time ago.'

'Not by Britain's standards.'

Horace smiled openly. 'You continue to give me great confidence, Jason.'

They continued strolling for a few more minutes, letting the birds fill in the silence. Then, without halting, Horace spoke barely above a whisper.

'Truths are very simple things, Jason. Anyone who tries to complicate things like good and evil, love and hatred, strength and weakness, the lion and the sheep, is not to be regarded. There is virtue, and there is wickedness. To blur these things together is wicked. It is as simple as that.'

Jason said nothing. He remembered their conversation on their flight to Poland and nodded to himself.

'You should go see Vickie, Jason.'

Jason gave him a surprised look. 'Why?'

Horace smiled. 'Because you need to.'

Jason couldn't hide his shock. 'Right now? After this conversation? With the world at stake, you're telling me to go see *Vickie?!'*

Horace looked thoughtful. 'There is a famous quote by C.S. Lewis: *Friendship is unnecessary, like philosophy, like art. It has no survival value. Rather, it is one of those things that gives value to survival.'*

Jason grinned. Vickie's beautiful smile shone in his mind.

'When I interviewed Vickie,' Horace continued, 'I saw that she was a sweet, gifted, and charismatic girl. But I never saw that as anything more than a way to keep morale high in the kitchens. I never began to imagine that she would become the glue that held this operation together. I would give her a dozen dogs, if that meant anything more than one.'

Jason turned without another word and headed for the kitchens.

Deciding not to tell Vickie about Horace's gushing compliments, Jason pulled her from her sputtering grill and immediately invited her back to Shwari Mawe for a game of catch. Her usual delighted reaction made him want to shout with joy.

After his predictable half-dozen terrible throws, they talked.

'How did you get this job, Vickie?'

She shrugged with a grin. 'I'm really good at it, actually. I was already almost done school when Horace found me. I can even make beer, even though I'm not allowed to drink it.'

Jason guffawed. He loved her so much.

'How did you become so interested in history?'

'I dunno,' she replied carelessly in the middle of a throw. 'It just seemed so cool. We didn't just pop here out of nowhere.'

'Do your friends in Calgary study history?'

'Aww, you remembered!' she cooed with a delighted smile, but continued. 'A lot of them do, actually. People my age like that stuff.'

'It's funny,' Jason said, 'there's so much craziness going on these days. People saying kids are doomed and all. But I'm a teacher, and most of my kids around your age are pretty chill. I think things are gonna be okay–' A powerful jolt went through his gut.

'–until…'

A wave of sorrow shot through Jason like morphine.

Until the end of the world. Until Vickie's children and grandchildren were vaporized by the looming, faceless terror that had brought him here. Until it all came to nothing. Until–

KABOOM.

Jason was smashed out of his existential inner-moanings by a pile-driving hug from Vickie, who had run full on into him from her perch on the far side of the court.

'If you pass out again,' Vickie cried into his ear, 'I'll KILL you!'

Jason smiled in amazement as he hugged back. He looked into her black eyes, conveying as much gratitude as he possibly could. He hugged her again. Then they played catch and chatted just for fun.

At last, Omondi pulled Jason from his joyous distraction and brought him back to the Blue Room. They sat yet again in the familiar – *familiar* – leather chairs.

'We shall see a lot of each other from now on…' – Jason balled his fists – '…as you must be prepared to properly educate your audience. What Nations did Hitler conquer before he was finally halted by his defeats at London and Stalingrad?'

'The Rhineland, Austria, Czechoslovakia, Poland, Denmark, Norway, Belgium, the Netherlands, Luxembourg, France, Yugoslavia, Greece, and large portions of the Soviet Union.'

Jason smirked at the surprise Omondi failed to hide.

'Impressive. You have been studying.'

'No, I haven't, Mr. Foremost Expert. I already knew that.'

How Jason had managed to decipher the subtle differences in Omondi's various deadpan glares, he did not know, but he could tell that the old man was happy. At last, he spoke.

'You are what we need.'

They looked at each other for a moment before Omondi continued.

'How did Hitler die?'

Jason shifted. He wondered, as he always had subconsciously, why this topic was not more widely discussed.

'I always heard he shot himself and that his cronies burned his body.'

Omondi nodded. 'Hitler's life has been documented to the smallest detail. Have you never wondered why the death of the avatar of fascism has not been equally documented?'

Jason nodded as Omondi continued.

'It was not until 2018 that researchers claimed irrefutable proof, based on dental examination, that the old bastard was dead.'

'Why?'

'Why do *you* think?'

Jason pondered as he never had. He thought of the relentless shitstorm that was the past eighty years. He thought of the Communist scare of the fifties. He thought of September 11th. Of Jonestown. He thought of the deafening barrage of panic that was his Facebook feed.

'I don't know.'

Omondi nodded. 'That is the great statement of our time. *I don't know.*'

The two men looked at each other. Then Jason jumped back into his seat.

'Do you not SEE THEM, JASON?! In CANADA?! ALL OVER THE WORLD?!' The poor, lost little fools preprogrammed from birth to see nothing but the *bullshit* that seeps into their brains?! The drug addicts? The prisoners? The frightened sheep? The fools who camp out for days to be first in line for smartphones and televisions while their fellow men and women and children starve to death? THESE are the people you must save! Save them from becoming what they are! Horace has called the Holocaust your Number One priority; now I am pulling rank and ordering something even more important: TEACH PEOPLE TO THINK!!'

Jason closed his eyes. He was ready to puke. Omondi remembered himself and continued quietly.

'I have great faith in the West. All the ingredients are there. But a spark is required for a flame. You, many years before, can cheat your way into becoming that spark. Bob Marley claimed that we could create a world in which there would be no doom. You have the opportunity to fight his holy Armageddon.'

Jason smiled broadly. He could hear Bob's simple rhythms in his mind.

'You're a pretty amazing guy, Omondi.'

Jason would have bet his silly job on the scowl that creased Omondi's face. Nevertheless, it was softer than Jason had predicted.

'Shut up. Go to bed. It is late.'

Extremely tired, the path between him and his bed was again blocked by Horace, who was smiling brightly. Jason decided to keep his temper. Horace held out his hand.

'May I have that chain, Jason?'

Jason breathed a cynical sigh. He undid the silver chain around his neck. Horace took it and with amazing speed slipped a ruby dog around it.

'Your decoration, Jason.'

Jason shook his head. 'I don't want to wear that.'

Horace shrugged. 'Keep it with you then. Give it to a pretty English girl when you've finished your mission.'

Jason said nothing, and put it in his pocket.

Chapter Nineteen

The next eleven days passed in an unbelievable flurry of activity. Each sunrise was blitzed by firearms training, each sunset saw Jason collapse in his bed, drained to fumes by the ruthless schedule his 'friends' laid out for him.

The entirety of his time seemed to congeal into one bubbling mass. Brief, beautiful bookends in Room 209 and Shwari Mawe were crowded into nothing by lessons, workouts, and one-eyed jacks dealt by his increasingly tyrannical superiors.

There was a torturous day where TV was forbidden. There were several days spent with Megan's beautiful face inches from his own as she taught him how to shave with a straight-blade razor. He was taught the limits of the length of his hair, down to the millimetre, that he was allowed between haircuts.

History, as Omondi had promised, took centre-stage. Roosevelt. Patton. Mussolini. Elizabeth Layton. Two dozen battles, some of which he had not heard of. Churchill, Churchill, CHURCHILL. Were it any other subject, Jason would have broken down in tears as he learned, under Omondi's strict drilling, that the man had only managed to 'qualify for the cavalry rather than the infantry.'

Horace was a continuing enigma. He was both a comfort and a pain, sharing coffees with Jason and chatting about Kenya and music, then turning into a drill-sergeant, ordering him with iron eyes to his next assignment.

Vickie was Jason's saving grace. Only her presence could have kept him going through this circle around the drain of everything he knew. They played catch. They strolled aimlessly in Shwari Mawe. They chatted at Starbucks. She taught him a few Vietnamese phrases. They even discussed the Vietnam War, about which he was unsurprised to learn that she knew far more than he did. Unfortunately, their visits grew fewer and further between as the days wore on.

The most surreal moments of all were Jason's new Familiarity Training. Twice a day, every day, Jason was ushered under the green light of the Time Machine, for no other reason than for his psyche to get used to the utter destruction of the factual science he had learned from the age of six. Before long, he grew to enjoy his views of London and Richmond Park; before long after that, he knew that that would mean nothing when the moment came.

The mechanics of the trigger, as far as *he* was concerned, were very simple: lift the latch, deactivate the safety, press the red button. Every day these three irritatingly simple steps were drilled into his mind. Each time, he thought of Bruce Willis in *Armageddon*.

As he entered his final week before the Jump, however, he found himself pleasantly surprised that his pummelling workload was keeping him conveniently distracted from the fate that awaited him.

By far the worst of it all was Markie's increasingly erratic behaviour. She grew more morose and temperamental by the day, culminating in Jason having to disconnect in anger because she had dropped acid and was beyond any rational conversation. He had never needed her more in his life, and she was quickly becoming more of a liability than a blessing. Still, he told no one.

One afternoon, he found a rare hour to himself. He drew the blinds and sat in his lovely lobby, a reading-lamp illuminating his desk. He was about to ruminate on some grand philosophy, when a terrible Truth settled on him like itching powder.

I might not come back.

He took a deep breath…

I MIGHT NOT COME BACK.

Even now, after all he had achieved, after all he had come to know himself to be, a hellishly violent shake came over him. He was alone. He was at the very limits of his character. Horace and Omondi's training, Vickie's unfailing sweetness, the serenity of Shwari Mawe, the nobility of his goal... could any blessing – any luxury, if there was a difference – trump the simple fact that his thirty-three years of peace and contentment were about to be obliterated as if they had never existed at all?

Auschwitz.

Jason took a breath. And another. His pain was brought into a more complicated, yet somehow welcome state. He pondered, and a thought occurred to him. A thought that would have been unthinkable even twenty years earlier. He pulled out his phone, turned on YouTube Music, and typed *winston churchill speeches.*

His heart leapt at the results. His thumb darted…

'Mr. Speaker. On Friday evening last, I received His Majesty's commission to form a new administration… and that it should include all parties, both those who supported the late government, and also the parties of the opposition.'

It was a strange voice for a leader. It was an *old* voice, a warbling, slightly droning voice. Yet Jason listened intently.

'...I would say to the House, as I have said to those who have joined the government: I have nothing to offer but blood, toil, tears, and SWEAT.'

Did any politician on Earth today make such promises?

'We have before us an ordeal of the most grievous kind. We have before us many, many long months of struggle and of suffering. You ask, what is our policy? I will say: It is to wage war, by sea, land, and air, with all our might, and with all the strength that God can give us. To wage war against a monstrous tyranny never surpassed in the dark and lamentable catalogue of human crime. That is our policy.'

Already that strange voice seemed heavenly.

'You ask, what is our aim? I can answer in one word: Victory! Victory at all costs, victory in spite of all terror. Victory, however long and hard the road may be; for without victory, there is no survival. Let that be realized… come then, let us go forward together with our united strength.'

Jason shook with astonishment. If there was one human in all time that Winston Churchill had *not* been speaking to, it was him. Yet the words of this immortal leader, spoken to him at this moment through the tinny speakers of his smartphone, spoke directly to his soul as perhaps no one outside the man's family had heard since those very darkest days of May 1940. At long last, in the face of his pain, his fatigue, the whirlwind that he had taken as normalcy in such a brief and bizarre moment of his life, he said it to that great and majestic voice, miraculously sent to him from eighty years in the past.

'I am at your service.'

He would meet Winston Churchill. *Winston fucking Churchill.* The man who had fought tooth and nail his entire life for his humble right to ensure that his peculiar and incomparable brand of humility might mean something to this poor shaken soul at the peak of this terrible time of faction, confusion, and controversy. How simple it all must have seemed to him.

He took out a piece of parchment and pulled out his pen. How his spine tingled in protest every time he did so. He shook out his apprehension and wrote.

If I don't come back, know that I love my time. I love everything about it. I love social media. I love call-display. I love Craig Ferguson and Sons of Anarchy and all the foolish pleasures of the modern world. I did not leave because I was unhappy. Nor did I leave for the thrill of the past I loved equally.

I left because I knew, from the age of fifteen, that something was not right. Even recliners, World of Warcraft, and the porn industry could not hide my desperate, fundamental knowledge that none of it would matter in the end.

Is it God? Is it karma? Is it the intolerable side effect of a total lack of free will? I don't know. But something is off. And the answer does not lie in my time. I am now thankful for the unparalleled opportunity to look elsewhere.

I will enjoy the past and look forward to (just maybe) returning to see the birth of hover technology, as if that will make me happier.

When he finished, he did not reflect. He put the note in the drawer of his desk, shut off his lamp, and went to 212A.

'I feel okay, Markie. I can't believe it, but I feel okay.'

She gave a small smile. 'Like Maximus, smiling at death.'

Jason chuckled. 'That's pretty dark, Markie.'

She shrugged. 'So is this.'

Jason stifled his frustration. He remembered these long days and all she had done. He was determined to punch through her lethargy. 'Can I show you something?'

She nodded, and he pulled out his phone and brought up the same speech that had settled him an hour ago.

'Listen to this.'

He played the recording. She frowned immediately, unimpressed by the voice. He saw her continuously attempt a smile for a minute, and then grow visibly agitated. Finally, she shook her head in what seemed close to fury.

'That's really cool, Jason.'

As was clearly implied, Jason stopped the recording with over a minute remaining. He tried once more.

'Don't you know who that *is?*'

She shook her head and said nothing.

'It's Churchill, Markie. The man who saved the world, the man I'm going to meet! I'm going to meet *Winston Churchill*, Markie–'

'I don't give a *shit* about Winston Churchill, Jason.'

Enough.

He smacked his phone down on his desk.

'What's with you lately?! You're starting to bum me out, and I kinda don't need that right now. Believe it or not, this is a lot tougher for me than it is for you!'

Markie looked downward. 'Maybe you shouldn't go...'

'What did you say?!'

Maybe you shouldn't go back in time.'

Jason stared at her, fighting to keep his temper. There was a look in her eyes that he was not used to. It looked like fear.

'I'm still thinking,' she said softly, 'about the night my dad died.'

Jason spread his arms in exasperation. 'Why are you bringing that *up* again?!'

She shied from his angry words. She looked nauseous. She looked into his eyes again, tugging on her hair, and began to tremble.

'I fell in love with you that night, Jason.'

Jason felt his stomach split open.

'I fell in love with you,' she repeated. 'And... and I've never been able to shake it off.'

She waited with a quiet terror in her eyes. Jason gazed into them for a moment, face expressionless. Then, without a word, he disconnected her and sat silently, breathing slowly, and running his fingers through his hair. He stood and turned to walk away. He stopped. He turned again and put his fist through the glass screen. He closed the door and walked back to his room, blood dripping steadily from his hand.

A dull, semi-annual physical was interrupted by frenzied knocking at the office door. Horace threw his shirt back on and rushed to answer it. He swung it open to find Vickie with tears in her eyes and close to hysterics.

'Horace, something's wrong.'

Horace put his hands on her shoulders. 'Calm down, Vickie, *calm down*. What happened?'

'I went up to Jason's quarters to surprise him with some food and... and there's blood all over the floor outside. And on the doorknob.' Her mouth trembled as she fought to keep herself together.

Something close to horror touched Horace's face. He gestured to the three nearest doctors, rushed past Vickie, and ran up the nearest flight of stairs. Seeing the trail of blood leading to Room 212A, he slowly pushed open the door to the small room, half-expecting to see the very, very worst.

When he saw the mangled computer, he was not comforted. He stood staring at it for a moment and, in a grim rush of realization, breathed out one word.

'Markie...'

He closed the door and turned to Vickie, who had followed.

'Vickie,' he whispered, 'go back to your room, and stay there. *Now.*'

The terrified girl ran in the opposite direction. When certain she was gone, Horace steeled himself, remembered he was an empath, and approached Room 209.

A knock at the door.

'Jason?'

'Fuck off.'

Pounding at the door, then futile jerking of the locked handle.

'Jason!!'

'I SAID FUCK OFF!!!'

A jingle of keys and the door was open in five seconds. Horace and his aides appeared in the doorway and ducked with shouts of panic as the empty bottle of Glenlivet rocketed over their heads and shattered against the wall behind them.

'THERE!!' Jason screamed. 'Didn't see THAT one coming, did you, eh? You goddamned empath sonofabitch!!'

Jason was pacing his lobby like a caged and cornered animal, frighteningly drunk, his hand bandaged with a scarlet dishrag, never taking his eyes off Horace. Horace gauged him, unafraid, his hands stretched out at his sides to settle his colleagues, one of which already had a syringe at the ready.

'I'm DONE!!' Jason snarled, waving his arms like a lunatic. Blood splattered on the wall. 'I want OUT, I want MARKIE, I never want to see you assholes again, now *GET THE FUCKING JET READY!!!'* Jason almost fell over with the force of his final scream. He steadied himself, still apoplectic with drunken rage and stood gasping for breath, snarling with hatred at Horace.

Horace had not moved. He met Jason's unhinged eyes with a careful, penetrating look of his own.

'Get out of here, all of you,' he said to his terrified workers, never taking his eyes from Jason. They hesitated.

'NOW!'

They fled the scene, running as fast as they could. Horace closed the door and turned to face Jason, who wasted no time.

'I want out of here, now.'

A demonic rictus was etched on his pale, sweaty face. Horace said nothing and continued to gaze at his shattered friend.

The madness in Jason's eyes grew dangerous. He picked up a heavy candlestick from a nearby endtable.

'If you don't get on your phone and get the jet ready in ten seconds, I'll kill you.'

Horace allowed six, seven, eight eternal seconds to go by. And then...

'Getting wasted on a bottle of Glenlivet *Fifty,* Jason? Is there nothing sacred anymore? Maybe we *should* let the world end, after all.'

Jason stared with as much menace as he could, even as the maniacal energy flowing through him ebbed visibly away like he had a leak. He managed one ugly, feeble chuckle. His would-be murder-weapon fell from his hand, and he collapsed in a heap on the floor.

Horace stepped up to his friend and squatted beside him. Jason worked himself into a crude sitting position. A long moment went by.

'She told me she loved me,' he whispered. 'That *BITCH!!'*

A spray of saliva flew at the last word. He sat hyperventilating on the floor, broken, defeated, and helpless.

'Go take a shower, Jason.' Horace said softly. He gently reached to help Jason up. Jason cooperated, and after a couple of false starts, he was on his feet.

'Go take a shower,' Horace repeated from under Jason's arm. 'Take as long as you want. I'll be waiting here, and we'll talk.'

There was nothing Jason could do but obey. He stumbled off to the bathroom and did not come out for over two hours.

Jason stepped out into the lobby, still hazy, still devastated, but calm. He had hoped against hope that Horace would have given up after so long, but there he was, sitting comfortably in the white armchair by the lamp, meeting his eyes confidently. The other chair had been moved across from him, the endtable placed between them with two cups of steaming tea sitting upon it. Horace gestured gently to the other chair.

'Please sit, Jason.'

Jason hesitated as long as he could, but even in his current state he knew he wasn't going to win this. He shuffled into the living room and sat down heavily without a word. Horace conjured a first aid kit and bandaged Jason's battered knuckles. Jason put sugar in his tea and sipped it slowly. They didn't have tea like this in Canada.

'You love her,' Horace murmured. It was not a question.

Jason's lip curled without much effort. 'Empath.'

Horace shook his head. 'I'm stating the obvious, Jason.'

Jason made no reply. His hand throbbed. His gut ached. His mind fought exhaustion and chaos.

'I never knew,' he said at last. 'She never gave me the slightest idea...'

'Women are good at that, Jason,' Horace consoled. 'We find out when they want us to, not a moment before.'

The two friends sat together for a moment. The room was silent.

'How could she do this to me?' Jason breathed.

'Why now?'

Jason stared into his tea for a moment. And then he couldn't hold back.

'I've always loved her, Horace. I loved her from the moment I met her. We couldn't have less in common, and that's *exactly* what I love about her. She's free. I've pretended it wasn't there, sometimes I've even forgotten, but... every time she told me she had a boyfriend, I felt something die.'

Horace nodded once. 'I would go so far as to say that she is the reason you never fell for Megan, and you're only just realizing it.'

Jason glared. 'How the hell do you know that?'

Horace shrugged. 'Empath.'

'But why *now?!'* Jason snarled again. He cursed loudly as he splashed his hands with tea, but never stopped. 'Why only when it was too late? When I'm already barely keeping it together? We may never see each other again! She had *four years,* and she picks... the MICROSECOND when it couldn't possibly hurt me more.'

'Women are good at that too, Jason.'

Jason fell silent. He sipped his tea and let his misery flow.

'I must say,' Horace said with a small smile, 'even the greatest empath who ever lived – possibly myself, when I think of it – never would have imagined you to be such a mean drunk.'

'I'm not. You're just an asshole.'

Horace shook his head. 'A pitiful comeback by your standard, Jason.'

His hair still dripping, Jason stood up without another word and walked to the door. Horace said nothing and merely watched him slip into the hall.

Jason marched to Room 212A as if it were the gallows. He stepped inside and shut the door behind him. He rested his head against it for what felt like hours. What the hell was he going to do now?

He turned, and there was the computer that had allowed him such joy and betrayed him to such agony. He saw the grotesque hole in the screen, still bloody around the edges that he had made where Markie's devastatingly beautiful face had smiled at him for so many hours. He put a shaking hand to his mouth.

At long last, the transcendent explanation for the ceaseless devotion between them was laid bare: They loved each other. Yet it had been laid bare in the form of crude graffiti, desecrating the most beautiful aspect of Jason's life when he needed it most, even as Time Itself threatened it forever. He had always wanted Markie as a lover; right now, he needed her as a friend. And now, with one twist of the knife, he had neither.

He fell to his knees, put his face in his hands, and wept.

Chapter Twenty

There was no alarm. Jason slept peacefully. No nightmares. He had not feared there would be. Perhaps he was unusual, but his waking terrors had never triggered sleeping terrors.

He awoke at nine, and for ten blissful seconds, felt the serenity of his soft sheets, velvety pillow, and the general ignorance of waking up in luxury.

Boom, *boom, BOOM*.

He remembered returning to his deserted quarters. He remembered putting on *Blood on the Tracks* and crawling into bed before 'Simple Twist of Fate' was half over, having no strength to weep or to stare into the abyss or do anything else that required the unbearable torture of consciousness. Yet Markie's adoring smile, a disdainful fraud for four years, had scorched his drunken mind for almost half an hour before it was satisfied.

A painfully familiar knock at the door was all that could have conquered Jason's rage brought on by his Level Three hangover, his aching hand, his hatred of being awake at all, and the monsters who had the audacity to send the knocker to him at such a moment.

He put a shirt and pants on and opened his door. There was no hug from Vickie this time. She stood stoically and looked up at him. She was already close to tears.

'Are you okay, Jason?'

Jason looked down at Vickie and could not hide his predicament any longer.

'*No,* Vickie. I'm damned well not okay. This whole thing is ridiculous, and I don't feel like talking.'

He moved to close the door and started in shock. Vickie had stuck her foot out to block it. He looked at her and could tell he was in serious danger of receiving another slap in the face. Her eyes had ignited in anger.

'Twelve hours ago, *big brother,* I thought you were dead. Your blood was all over the place. It felt like *I* was dying, actually, and the only thing I could do to feel alive ever again was try to get help and save you. I don't care about time travel or Winston Churchill or saving the world or anything else. I care about YOU, AND I WANT TO TALK TO YOU RIGHT NOW!!'

Vickie's final scream likely woke up ten people. Before it was finished leaving her, she had wrapped her arms around him and buried her face into his chest.

Neither of them now had the strength to talk. They embraced, Jason stifling sobs as his tears fell into Vickie's black hair. She cried and cried and cried.

What was this feeling? Was this destruction or mending? Was it defeat or triumph? Was it his final oblivion or the gateway to eternity? Or was it simply the unconditional love between someone who knew so much and someone who knew just a little more?

Yet a stabbing devil's voice that Vickie could not silence continued to pierce his mind.

The moment passed, as all moments must. Jason and Vickie stared volumes into each other's eyes. Finally, she spoke.

'I volunteered to wake you. If I didn't, I would go crazy.'

Jason nodded.

'Horace and Omondi want to talk to you about everything in the Blue Room.'

Jason moved to close the door. Vickie spoke again.

'I hope all this works out, Jason. It's pretty fucked up, actually.'

Nothing could have hidden Jason's grin as he closed his door. But like all fleeting pleasures, it was consumed in moments.

Jason opened the fridge and pulled out a litre of chocolate milk. The fact that it was Beatrice brand meant nothing. All of the catering to his every whim, the gentle tweaking of this whole fucking place to suit his flabby Canadian desires, seemed like an insult to millions.

And his sudden attack of charity made him angrier than ever.

First world problems *were* problems. Depression was depression. A bad day at work was a bad day at work. A flat tire was a truly horrible experience. Who were these mewling, postmodern shitheads to tell him that the agony he was feeling was the profane whining of a poor, sheltered prick who had never been to a third-world country?

Or was he wrong?

Jason screamed. He screamed until his throat hurt. He screamed at the confusion, at the conflict, at the *guilt* he had felt his whole life that was fighting to distract him from the fact that the woman he loved had destroyed him. He collapsed in his recliner.

So, *this* was heartbreak. He had thought he had known it after his divorce, after his dad had died. But *this* was it. It was not endless weeping. It was not the beating of fists in uncontrollable spasms of anguish. It was cold, empty existence. It was hating the steady beat of your own heart. It was the absence of what you knew should be permeating every fibre of your being, even as that very thing surrounded your being like the air.

Jason tried to weep. But he couldn't. And so, he put on an old Frank Sinatra show and sat in a near-vegitative state for an hour and a half and absorbed all that Ol' Blue Eyes had to say.

Jason sat in a miserable heap in the chair he had come to know so well. He didn't remember getting there, let alone what had inspired him to peel his body off the recliner. Horace stood at his right, and Omondi stood behind. Jason sat in a state of bitterness as hard as iron, fully prepared to make this emergency intervention as difficult for these two idiots as possible.

'Listen to me, Jason,' Horace stated firmly. 'I contacted Markie this morning and spoke to her personally–'

Jason looked up venomously. *'That's* against the rules.'

'Well, I *broke* the damned rules, alright?!'

Jason looked away with a bitter shake of his head. He didn't care anymore.

'Markie and I both agree that her role as your confidante is now defunct and that you should speak to her only as a goodbye, on the eve of your jump.'

'That's fine by me. I don't want to talk to her at all.'

He was done with Markie. He wanted nothing more to do with her or with anything else that he was leaving behind. He hated the thought of this world, of the KRA, of the ridiculous path that had led him to know the looming fate that people so thoroughly deserved. He now longed for the past, for a quest, for an age when people gave a damn about anything that mattered.

Horace walked deliberately from beside his friend, leaned down, and looked him in the eye. 'I don't think that's true, Jason.'

'Oh, will you stop with your empath BULLSHIT!!' Jason shouted.

'I don't need to be an empath to see it, Jason. None of us do. It's written all over you. Your face lights up every time we mention her name. There is no possibility that you could have made it this far without her.'

'Right,' Jason spat, 'and then she rips my guts out.'

'You will have time to sort this out, Jason,' Horace said gently. 'You are both young, and she will be waiting when you come back.'

'Maybe I don't want to come back,' Jason snarled.

Omondi's voice came from behind. 'I am sorry, Jason. I truly am. I would never have wished such a fate upon you.'

'And what business is it of YOURS, asshole?'

Omondi joined Horace before Jason.

'As I have said, Jason, I care about you very much. Though it might surprise you more than the hover disc, you are my friend. Even at our very first encounter, though I was not as certain of your potential as Horace was, I liked you. And by the time our first lesson was over, I knew I was instructing the Time Traveller. Everything that followed was merely protocol.'

Jason stood and left without another word.

Horace sighed and put a hand over his eyes.

'This is extremely risky,' Omondi murmured.

'No, my friend,' Horace replied. 'It isn't.'

A paradoxical sensation permeated the next three days. Horace, Omondi, and Megan continued to push him. But there was a strange, elegant gentleness to the way he was pushed. He felt like a porcelain figurine being run across a battleground, a powerful mixture of 'hurry up' and 'handle with care' being balanced with every word and gesture made to him.

Megan's lessons had become downright boring. There were no more over-the-top dresses, no puerile sexual tension, and not once did Jason even think to put on his suit. They discussed nothing but the draggy subjects that had brought them together from two different continents. 'Etiquette' had at last become the rule in his Etiquette classes.

Omondi had become a jittery mess during their History lessons, with Jason guessing that he was not experienced in being a shoulder to cry on. Jason would have found it amusing if he could. World War Two was, ironically, his lifeline. It was the one subject that still motivated him. He learned that Canada's wartime Prime Minister was a fringe-spiritualist who claimed to speak to his dead dogs through a crystal ball, as well as a fervent anti-Semite who refused Jewish refugees asylum from Nazi Germany. Why he felt a bitter smile come to his lips at this, he did not care.

He also learned that Churchill himself took amphetamines in order to stay alert during late night planning in the dark days of the war. At this, Jason silently uttered a desperate prayer to the void.

Why? WHY do these things that I have forsaken, which I tried to turn her from all these years, play such a powerful role in the unfolding of history?

Horace had again shown his character and become the necessary mother goose. His age and wisdom and tastefully employed empathy were instrumental in keeping the newly wounded Jason focused on the things that mattered, and as distracted as possible from the things that mattered far more. Their Ethics lessons had become little more than therapy sessions, their friendship being the only possible thing that could have kept Jason focused on his goal.

One morning, after a sad shouting match with Horace, Jason found himself retreating to the smoking room. Only two young men sat on the black leather couches. They quickly butted their cigarettes and made to leave, but Jason calmed them down and insisted that they stay. Then Jason saw movement to his left and turned to see Yaro beaming at him.

'Canada is truly a great nation,' he said.

He handed Jason a cigar, and they sat down together. The moment all formalities were past, a sorrow lilted Yaro's eyes.

'You have suffered much, Jason, and yet you must suffer more.'

Jason said nothing. The two men looked at each other for a moment.

'Do you not believe that there is a future for you and your girl, Jason?'

A feeble anger sprouted within him. 'There is no future *at all,* Yaro. There's nothing. We're all doomed. Even if I succeed, and we end up together, our grandkids will be the final round. It's all meaningless.'

Yaro looked at him for a moment and took a puff of his cigar. He smiled.

'Do you believe in God, Jason?'

Jason had always hated that question. He had always relied on the blanket of secular society to protect him from it. But each time it was asked, he was left naked. Not the assurances of science, nor the comedy of George Carlin, nor the desperate desire for his own freedom could silence the loneliness of his own conflict each time it was asked.

He shrugged.

Yaro chuckled and gave a small smile. 'Most people do, you know. Even in this age of confusion and despair, nothing seems to be able to quench the thirst that men and women have for something greater than themselves.'

'But it's all going to come to nothing in the end,' Jason countered. 'You and I know that better than most.'

Yaro's grin vanished. He looked into Jason with those piercing brown eyes.

'I think that you and I know *nothing,* Jason. I think that we know nothing at all. Socrates was the wisest man who ever lived, and he founded his beliefs on that very fact. If there is a God, as I believe there is, his plan goes far beyond – and behind – something as small as the end of our world. And if that is the case, your pain is a part of it. Let nothing stand in the way of your goal, even the pitiful modern view that the end of the world is the end of all hope.'

Jason took a puff of his cigar, and, for a moment, came close to a smile.

Jason and Vickie spent one last afternoon together. Jason at last invited her to Room 209, and they spent three hours together laughing at the likes of the Three Stooges, Beavis & Butthead, and Monty Python. She screamed with delight at the outrageous comedy of yesteryear, as Jason grinned as only she could possibly make him.

'How did you know we were meant to share a bond?' Jason asked.

She almost choked on her popcorn and replied, 'Don't start with that stuff, Jason, I'm watching TV!'

With no protocol-obsessed bigwigs nearby to breathe down his neck, he put his arm around his little sister and listened to the musical sound of her laughter. Like all drugs, however, this sweet moment ended with her absence.

No beautiful flicker of social interaction could contend with the lonely thoughts that rose like zombies afterward. He spent the next three hours in desperate conflict, as the beauty of his times with Yaro and Vickie crumbled away, until they seemed like some ooze slipping into the mouth of a sewer.

He went to the fridge and found four beers. They were gone in a minute and a half. When in ruin, when nothing was left, when alone with your demons, who could be blamed?

He watched an episode of *The Good Place,* and went to bed.

On an early afternoon, seventy-two hours before the Jump and moments after finally learning from Omondi during a lesson on the Battle of the Bulge that Celsius and Centigrade were the same thing, Jason was turning to retreat back to his quarters.

'Wait.'

Jason turned around without complaint. He was not angry. He was long since indifferent to this remarkable man who had engineered his ruin.

Omondi's face was soft and passive, as it generally had been lately. 'Horace and I request that you join us now for a carpool to the outskirts of Nairobi. There is one more thing we must do there.'

'What is it?'

Omondi shook his head.

Jason looked at him a moment longer and nodded. 'Whatever passes the time.'

And he went to change into a cooler shirt.

Ten minutes later, the three men once again entered a sputtering SUV and motored out of the KRA for another bumpy ride into Nairobi. Not one word was spoken. Jason stared out the window, not thinking, not caring, not batting an eye at the sight of an eight-foot vulture taking off a hundred feet away.

At last, they reached the city. They were still in the midst of modest shops and small gardens when they suddenly took a left turn down a quiet side road. After ten more seconds, they pulled into the parking lot of a large, loudly decorated building.

'This is the Sarasaki Dome, Jason,' Horace said. 'It's a popular place for dinner-theatre, which we have managed to rent for the afternoon.'

'I don't care, Horace.'

The SUV came to a rough stop near the simple entrance. Omondi held a walkie-talkie to his mouth and muttered an indistinct bit of Swahili. There was no response from whomever might be listening.

Jason shuffled through the glass doors. The place had an odd smell and was covered in trendy decoration and stylized Swahili. Omondi guided them down a dark hall to a set of heavy wooden doors. They stopped for a moment.

'Why are we here?' Jason grumbled.

'After tense negotiations with the Prime Minister,' Omondi intoned, 'we have managed to waive the final three days of your training.'

'Why the hell would I want to do that?'

'We have a parting gift for you, and we want to give you time to enjoy it.'

Omondi opened the door, and Jason found himself in a spacious, empty concert hall. The lights were dimmed, but he could see nothing remarkable about the place.

'All this time,' Horace said quietly, 'we believed that isolation, detachment, was the key to helping you say goodbye to this world. But now we see we were wrong. What you truly need is something to say goodbye *to.*'

'*What,* Horace?'

As if by magic, the lights at the far end of the hall zapped to life. Startled, Jason's eyes fell on the small, illuminated stage. They focused. And his heart nearly exploded out of the top of his head.

It was Markie.

Chapter Twenty-One

And yet, it wasn't Markie. She was transformed so completely that Jason's knees very nearly buckled in astonishment. She wore an ornate, green, ankle-length bohemian dress with gold trim, pearl bracelets and earrings, and a thin, braided leather headband, dotted with silver charms, which snaked across her forehead and disappeared under her hair. She held a simple bouquet of violets.

But the biggest change was her face. As usual, she wore no make-up, but her features glowed with a girlish glee and unrestrained excitement that Jason had simply never seen before. Even from eighty feet away, he could see her crooked left canine as she beamed, her shining grey eyes locked into his.

Jason stood paralyzed for a moment. And then he ran. He ran as he had never run before to the one thing in his life that had both never and *always* made sense. Her arms reached to him as stiff as wooden beams, and they embraced.

And she *still* smelled like weed.

For over five minutes, they held each other, their demons vaporized silently, one by one. Then at last Jason pulled away, looked Markie in the eyes for a moment and kissed her. And everything in his life, before and after, was defined forever.

The great threshold passed, they parted and gazed at each other, foreheads together. Tears ran down Markie's cheeks. 'Sorry,' she said with a choked giggle. 'I can't run in this thing.'

Jason's joy and relief were too crushing to allow him to even manage a smile. His own eyes glossy with tears and with the rush of adrenaline that every man knows, he said it at last. 'I love you.'

She responded almost before the words were out of his mouth. 'I love you too.'

'Well done, Jason.'

Horace and Omondi had approached.

'As we have said, Jason,' Horace said, 'you are our guest, and we wanted to send you off well. And since all three of us owe Markie a great debt, we thought we would give her a chance to look the part.'

'Several tens of thousands of dollars later,' Omondi muttered. He looked at them for a moment and smiled, the first unrestrained grin Jason had seen on his face. The difference it made was astonishing.

'Would you like to be married?'

'I was about to *ask* her that, you jackass.'

Markie giggled delightedly and nodded.

A justice of the peace was found quickly, and they were married then and there, their only witnesses being the two men who had thrown their lives into enough chaos to make it happen. Jason dismissed the idea of dressing up, and gave himself to Markie as he was. Some chump in a t-shirt and jeans marrying the goddess who created the universe; it was the old joke about weddings taken to its ultimate end. Having no ring, he took the ruby dog from his pocket and fastened it around Markie's neck.

When the simple ceremony was over, Jason took his bride by the hand and led her to the side of the stage behind the privacy of the curtain. They embraced once more, away from the leering eyes of Horace and Omondi.

'I missed you,' Jason said simply.

'I missed you too,' Markie whispered. 'And in a way, I still miss you.'

He parted from her shoulder. He looked into the eyes of the woman who, in three days, had gone from best friend, to betrayer, to wife.

'Isn't it normal for the groom to wait at the altar?'

She laughed and replied, 'Jason, what freaking part of this is normal?'

Jason kissed her passionately again, soaking up every second of what he knew, even at this moment of ecstasy, would be a painfully short time. At last they parted. Jason's sensible side nipped at his ankles.

'How did we ever make it work so well?'

Markie frowned. 'What do you mean?'

'We have nothing in common. We never did. How did we even work as friends, let alone as husband and wife?'

She looked at him like he was an idiot. 'Nothing in common?! Jason, we have shit-tons in common! We like so much of the same stuff. We're only different at our cores.'

Jason didn't know whether to laugh or scream. 'Isn't that the exact opposite of how it's supposed to work?!'

She shrugged with a smile. 'So?'

Jason bowed his head in amazement. Women could say more with a single offhand syllable than men could say in a prepared speech. His entire future, with and without her by his side, had transformed into some divine joyride. Even the thrill of meeting Churchill seemed only now to make sense with Markie's love going with him.

Together they seemed to realize that this moment needed to end. They stepped from behind the curtain, off the stage, and stood with Horace and Omondi.

'Congratulations, you lovebirds,' Horace said with a smile. Omondi's face had returned to stone.

'If you please, we would like Markie to ride with us back to the KRA. There are some rules we wish to discuss with her.'

Only his knowledge of Markie could have kept Jason from shouting. He merely nodded.

'I'm okay with that too,' Markie muttered, 'if that matters.'

Jason snickered. Horace smiled.

'I promise you both that this is for the very best. Your honeymoon will begin properly the moment we return.'

Holy mackerel, I'm married.

Markie left with her new friends, leaving Jason in the company of an emerging Employee. The unenthusiastic smile the little man gave him made Jason want to scream.

After the longest forty-five minutes of Jason's life, Jason found himself once more at the bland backside of the KRA. He practically pole-vaulted out of the beat-up hatchback;

the rotten muffler didn't even register in Jason's mind as it pulled away.

Amazingly, the other vehicle pulled up less than a minute later. The back door opened, and Markie stepped out, careful not to step on her dress.

They embraced again, but decided together to leave words for later. Jason took her by the hand, and they started for Room 209.

'Jason, Markie, please wait.'

They turned together at Horace's voice. Jason couldn't help but notice she seemed less indignant than he felt.

'We ask that you come with us once more. We have a surprise for you.'

Jason's fury kindled, but Horace and Omondi had already made through the door to the first floor. Markie smiled at him.

'There's time, Jason.'

'Markie, I don't exactly want to hear the word *time* right now.'

She smiled and kissed him on the cheek. 'Come on. I want to explore.'

Jason shook his head, and let Markie pull him after his friends.

Horace opened the door to the reception hall, and for once, Jason was *unsurprised*. A torrent of applause and noisemakers erupted as the Servidors welcomed them. Balloons and banners hung everywhere. Jason stepped into the room, Markie's hand in his, and returned three hundred smiles, most of them those of strangers, simultaneously asking himself, *Isn't this JUST a bit too Hollywood?*

He looked at Markie. She was beaming as much as ever, unfazed by her very first spotlight encounter with Jason's supporters.

He saw Yaro in his corduroy suit, clasping his hands together as he grinned his congratulations to his young friend. He saw Megan, shaking her gorgeous head at him and smiling tearfully as she applauded. Even Johanna and Julie were there, clapping and cheering as enthusiastically as everyone else. Only Chester and Steve, both almost a head taller than anyone else, stood grim and silent as the superfluous security guards near the bar.

A flurry of movement turned Jason's head to his right, just in time to see Vickie slam like a linebacker into Markie, squeezing her tightly in a massive hug. Jason laughed delightedly as Vickie, tears streaming from her black eyes, reached up and around his neck and pulled him in to join them. Had he not just married the woman of his dreams, it would have been the happiest moment of his life. They parted and Jason took each of them hand in hand.

Horace raised his hands to settle his audience.

'Today,' he blared (Jason rolled his eyes), 'we celebrate the flawless triumph of the man whom we have worked so hard to support.'

The Servidors applauded their appreciation. Jason felt Markie's hand tighten around his own.

'Jason has succeeded beyond our highest hopes. As a historian, as a humanitarian, as a soldier…' Horace turned and looked slyly at Jason and Markie, 'and finally, as a lover.'

A great laugh went through Horace's audience, followed again by loud applause. Horace continued, 'Brothers and sisters, let tonight be a celebration of all that we have accomplished. A well-earned night of fellowship, of unrestricted alcohol' – a great cheer – 'and above all, a happy congratulations to a newly-married couple.'

A thunderous roar hit Jason like a tidal wave. Vickie hugged both of them again.

'You guys go relax. I'll be back later. I'm gonna get a rum and coke.'

'A rum and coke?!' Jason's teacher instinct triggered one final time.

Vickie laughed. 'It's Kenya, Jason. The limit is eighteen.'

Jason grinned and shooed her away. She smirked mischievously as she went. 'I'm seventeen, actually, but the Employees are so stupid.'

Markie tugged impatiently on his arm, and they walked hand-in-hand into the throng. Somehow Yaro, hobbling on his cane, was the first to reach them. He hugged and congratulated Markie, then turned, beaming, to Jason.

'Even before the rain started falling, Jason, I knew you would end up sitting by my side. It had nothing to do with your mission, or anything else. I just knew.'

Jason didn't quite know what to say. Yaro waved a dismissive hand.

'Bah. There is no need for such talk. You have a lovely wife. Do not fret over your brief time together now. You will have lifetimes to share when you return.'

He embraced Markie again, giving her an affectionate kiss on the cheek.

She giggled. 'This guy seems important.'

'He is,' Jason said.

Yaro beamed, clasped his hands together once more, and limped away.

Jason and Markie had time for one more meaningful glance before they were mobbed by four strangers eager to share their moment with them.

They spent the next forty-five minutes in true newlywed fashion, staying close to each other as droves of people they barely knew barraged them with smiles and trivial chitchat. Jason endured it patiently, but Markie was in her purest element, charming everyone she encountered with her warm appreciation and inescapably quirky sense of humour. Jason was thunderstruck by her perfect handling of this unprecedented situation. Finally, the introvert in him demanded a breather.

'I'm gonna go grab a beer,' Jason said.

'Okay,' Markie replied without looking at him.

He lingered. 'Do you want to…'

Markie giggled. 'Go get your beer, Jason. I won't break into pieces.'

Jason grinned, blushing a bit. He took his arm from around Markie's shoulders and left for the bar. He moved past Steve's towering presence and got a Budweiser off of the typically oblivious Employee. He sat on a stool for a moment.

As Markie chatted with smiling Servidors, Jason gazed at her from across the crowded room. A joy *–that was the word –* a solemn, desperate longing more beautiful than life took hold of him. A frustration at the limits his humanity placed upon his power to love her. He knew now that there was a God, and as profoundly, he knew that saving the world, like preventing the War, was now but a means: It was the long road that would lead him back to Markie.

She happened to glance his way as she listened to an excitable woman's banter, and her face broke into a brief smile which said more than could be held in a library. A lifetime of love distilled into one gesture. And it was for him.

He was congratulated warmly by a nearby Dutch Servidor, who regaled him with a two-minute retelling of his own wedding eight years prior. Jason smiled and listened as long as he possibly could, politely deciding not to punch him, and then returned to Markie as if by a tractor beam. She hugged him as though they had been apart for years.

Shortly after, they heard a loud Kenyan voice blare through the room.

'The music will begin in ten minutes.'

'I'm gonna go change,' Markie stated. 'I can't dance in this stupid thing.' And she left without a second glance.

As though Markie's sudden absence lifted him out of a druggy euphoria, Jason realized what needed to be done. He weaved through the mass of Servidors and found Megan, who smiled once more without a hint of awkwardness. Not wanting to flawlessly replicate that scene in *Anchorman 2*, he decided to be short and sweet. But the smile he gave was never more genuine.

'You are the *worst* teacher I have ever had, Megan.'

She raised an eyebrow and smirked. 'I have heard that sentiment many times. It never wears thin. But never have I more enjoyed earning it than I did with you.'

Jason hugged her, breathing in her deadly perfume one last time. He pulled away, gripped her shoulders, and gave her his saddest smile.

'It would never have worked between us, darling.'

She snorted in purest contempt. 'Jack Sparrow?! *Really?!* You're fucking doomed.'

They shared one more smile, and then Jason went to get another beer. No woman had ever inspired such confidence in him.

When Markie returned, she was again dressed in her normal cropped shirt, slouch hat and cutoffs. She was *more* beautiful that way.

At last unsurprised by the cues that perpetually revolved around him, Jason smiled as the speakers around him suddenly erupted with 'Cecelia.' Markie pulled him into a newly formed dance circle. At last, he managed to shrug off his normal apprehensions and danced hand in hand with Markie for four cliché wedding songs. Strangers laughed as she pulled him into the centre of the circle for 'Red Red Wine,' and danced in mock-seduction around him to the rudimentary power chords. Jason blushed in awkward, white-guy stiffness as his wife tickled his chin amidst her perfect hip shaking. How surreal it must have seemed to the Servidors: The Hero of Time, trapped in his own lame skin in the centre of a dance circle.

At long last, came the moment Jason had been starving for – the slow, acoustic strumming of a Richie Havens ballad. Markie transformed as the circle broke into pairs. She smiled, strolled up to him, and put her arms around his neck. Jason ignored the adoring murmurs around him and put his hands to her waist. He had been waiting for this simple, boy/girl moment for eight years. How could those grey eyes be looking at him that way, after all this time?

The answer was simple: He didn't give a good goddamn.

They danced for a minute or so. Then Markie looked up at him.

'You know,' she murmured, 'when I started crying the night my dad died, it wasn't over my dad. It was over you.'

'Me?' Jason asked, perplexed. She nodded.

'I started crying because I lost a part of you that night, and I knew it. I knew that on my end, we would never be friends again. That every moment I spent with you from that point on was going to be an act. I probably gouged your back when I hugged you, because I was trying to hold onto something that was going away forever. I wanted *this,'* she gestured at the two of them, 'and I didn't think I would ever get it.'

Jason nodded. 'Well, if we're gonna trade confessions, I can tell you that I knew from the start that things weren't going to work out with Kyla. Even as she was walking down the aisle, deep down I knew it was only a matter of time. I loved you too much for it to ever work with anyone else.'

Markie's face twisted with pain.

'You saved my life that night. The things I was seeing, Jason… how long it all felt… I thought I was actually in Hell. When the door opened, if it had been anyone but you, I would have died. Literally died. But your face… when I saw you, your face was normal. It was just… you. And when I felt you crawl up beside me, it kept my heart from exploding. How was I not supposed to fall for you?'

Markie's hands around his shoulders kept him safe from the barrage of memories and emotions aroused by her testimony. He offered his own.

'I've always felt… perfected by that night. Even though I never wanted to talk about it, a part of me always cherished it. Men need something to protect, you know. It's what gives us courage.'

Markie seemed to deflate. She rested her head against his chest.

'Keep me safe, Jason.'

No moment, in his entire life, had ever felt so perfect. He stopped their shuffling and wrapped his arms around her, resting his chin on her head and staring into blessed nothingness.

'Keep me safe, Markie.'

He felt her head shake as they parted, and she stared bitterly into his chest. 'Three days...'

Jason took his hand from her waist and lifted her chin so that her grey eyes met his once again.

'If all of this craziness hadn't happened, I doubt we would have, either. If all we get out of it is three days, I consider it a fair trade. You were a wonderful friend, but the whole situation was getting painful. The sexual tension was killing me.'

Her eyes penetrated his. 'And you're coming back.'

'Of course I am.'

'And you're not gonna fall for some doting thirties broad while you're off saving the world?'

'Markie, you've ruined me for any law-abiding citizen, and opium dens aren't high on my sightseeing list.'

She smiled, reached up, kissed him, and returned her head to his chest. Jason had only a moment to savour before something amazing caught his eye. Ten feet away, dancing elegantly with the brilliantly blunt Anita, was Horace.

Their eyes met, and triumph flashed between them. Jason pointed a congratulatory finger at him. Horace shook his head, unable to hide his smile. Then they returned to their respective tasks at hand.

Suddenly, the slow ballad segued into fast, gritty Tupac. Markie pulled away and, her smile vanishing, began moving her hips to the beat. She beckoned him. Without hesitation, Jason found the rhythm, drew her close, and they moved together. As they grooved, losing themselves in each other, yet another look touched Markie's eyes that he had not seen before.

Jason rarely danced, and only when the moment was perfect did he feel confident doing so. That night, as he feasted in triumph on Markie's intoxicating embrace, he felt like a god.

They danced for another hour. Then, at last, Jason had had enough. He snatched Markie's hand and made for the door. He did not miss her smile.

As if by some dark magic, Horace was waiting in the hallway. Somehow, Jason knew he shouldn't get angry.

'Markie,' Horace said courteously, 'could you give us one moment alone?'

She shrugged and made her way down the hall.

Horace looked him in the face. It had never really registered, how potent a gaze those soft blue eyes wielded.

'You are still prepared?' he asked firmly.

'Yes.'

'You will not demand more than the three days we have managed to wrangle you?'

'No.'

Horace studied Jason's expression for a moment and smiled. 'Then please, enjoy yourself.'

Jason nodded.

'If it suits the two of you, Omondi and I would like to take you on a small safari the day after tomorrow. We feel it would be an appropriate way to spend a portion of a Kenyan honeymoon.'

'Sounds good to me. I'll run it by Markie.'

Horace nodded and made to return to the dance. Jason put his hand on his shoulder.

'How did you know this would work?' Jason asked him. 'How did you know I would still want her so badly?'

Horace rolled his eyes.

'I am an *empath,* Jason. I find it strange that I have to remind you again.'

Jason grinned and nodded. 'Thank you, Horace.'

'Just so you are aware,' Horace said as he entered the hall, 'we asked Markie to cover her eyes as we entered the compound. Told her it was a top-secret area.'

Jason gawked. *'Why?'*

Horace glanced at him with a sly smile. 'So she wouldn't see Shwari Mawe, of course.' He closed the door.

Jason's confusion gave way to revelation. He followed Markie with a laugh. This was going to be the best night of his life...

'Wait til you see this…'

They stepped through the green door and out into Shwari Mawe. The moon's moon shone bright and proud, supported by humble lights among the shrubs and statues. The stone pathways beckoned them. It was still and quiet, and they were all alone.

'Oh my *God!*' Markie whispered. 'It's *incredible!*'

Jason smiled and took her hand. 'Not a bad first date, eh? Wanna go for a walk?'

She turned and gave him the same ecstatic smile she was wearing at the hall.

They had not taken three steps when the ugly sound of a changing record ripped through the Sanctuary. It was followed by the first gentle trills of one of Markie's favourite jazz singers, which flowed calmly through the entire courtyard. She turned and looked at him with delight.

'Jason, you *didn't!*'

Jason sighed. 'No, in all honesty, I didn't.'

Her smile did not diminish. 'You *do* get first-class service here, don't you?'

They took their time, strolling hand-in-hand through the loveliest place Jason had ever known. They chatted devotedly, Markie sometimes stopping to gush over the scenery around her. Jason marvelled one last time at the beauty of Shwari Mawe and the impossibility of having made it this far without the womb of peace and quiet it had provided. He marvelled, most of all, at the hand he was holding.

They stood for a moment before Duni's memorial. The mixed feelings at what her sacrifice had brought upon him flared to prominence, and Jason fought back tears as her terrible fate attacked him. Luckily, Markie promptly grabbed his ass, and he remembered with a shocked laugh that this night concerned no one but the two of them.

Finally, they found themselves in the near corner, atop the small hill from which Jason had first surveyed the garden. He put his arm around her, and they stood there together. Then Markie spoke softly.

'You know what breaks my heart?'

He looked at her and shook his head. She was gazing across the Sanctuary, a solemn look in her eyes.

'The fact that more guys would probably rather bang Megan Fox than Janis Joplin.'

Jason nodded. 'If it makes you feel any better, I've probably banged Janis in my mind enough times to inspire twenty songs out of her.'

Markie nodded and nestled close into his side. They listened to the dying piano chords atop that blessed hill, the moon shining above them, and at the same moment, bent double in childish laughter.

Exhausted, they made their way back to Room 209. They closed the door, Jason locking it carefully behind them. He lit candles, and Markie plugged her iPod into the eight-thousand-dollar stereo. Jason straightened up, opening his mouth to ask if she wanted tea, when suddenly the first unmistakable notes of 'Sunshine of Your Love' came cascading from all directions. He turned, and there was Markie Roberts, his love at last, smiling at him from across the room. He walked up to her and took her hands in his.

'Cream is mainstream,' he reminded her.

Her smile grew wider and she shook her head. 'I love Cream. That was just another way to get under your skin.'

Overjoyed, Jason smiled. As usual, Markie had scored a total victory.

And then the world exploded.

Without warning Markie wrenched her hands free and jumped on him with a roar. Jason, needing no warning, caught her. They kissed messily, hungrily, her legs almost breaking his hips. Stopping only to crank the volume Jason carried her to his bed, threw her upon it with all of his strength, and pounced. He pulled her up ruthlessly by the armpits so that her head was on the pillow, and let his weight fall upon her. As her hands moved over him, what consciousness remained in his mind savoured her… her body, her mind, this *goddess*, this unattainable prize that was finally his.

With a grunt of frustration, she grabbed his hand and wrenched it upwards to where he wanted it to go.

'What are you,' she hissed, 'in fucking grade nine?!'

In fury, Jason grabbed her hair with his free hand and pulled her face to his.

'I don't want to hear that *shit*. Not tonight. Not tonight, Markie. Tonight, you're *mine.*'

Exhilaration exploded in her face.

'You think so, eh?'

She ripped his shirt over his shoulders and threw it aside.

'Take me back in time, Jason,' she said breathlessly.

'Shut UP!!' he snarled, and kissed her again.

Jason awoke the next morning, his head still spinning. He put on his boxers and made his way to the bathroom. He turned on the light and looked in the mirror, wincing as he ran his fingers across the fierce, bloody scratches, made as if by a grizzly bear, that ran from his left collarbone almost halfway down his chest. He shook his head in wonder. Never, in all his wildest fantasies, had he imagined *anything* like that…

'I'll see your little boo-boo,' came a confident voice, 'and raise you this.'

Markie came strolling into the room, and Jason's jaw dropped at the blood that had flowed from her nostrils down under her jawline.

'Did I do *that?*'

She nodded in a way that left no doubt that she was as pleased with him as he was with her. 'When I did *that,*' she pointed at his chest, 'you got a little cranky. I guess when a combined six thousand days of pent-up feelings come out at once, it can be pretty... colourful, eh?'

Jason laughed and took her under his arm. They gazed at each other through the mirror, revelling in the crazed, sanguine climax of their tumultuous lives together.

Chapter Twenty-Two

'...Jason, I'm just saying, all music sounds cool when you're stoned. Just because Frank Zappa didn't like drugs doesn't mean I can't groove to him.'

'Markie, Frank was the kind of mind we should all aspire to. Imagine creating that kind of music with no drugs at all.'

Markie frowned. 'He was a coffee-addict, Jason. What's the difference between THC and caffeine? They're both natural chemicals.'

Jason shook his head. 'One keeps you going, one turns you into something you're not. One chemical isn't the same as another.'

She raised an eyebrow. 'I was high at our *wedding,* you twit.'

'Oh, you little BITCH!'

They laughed contentedly together and hugged. Jason cherished everything about this moment from the feel of her embrace to the familiarity of their pointless debating, to the fact that it occured in Kenya two days before he travelled in time, to the indisputable fact that Markie had defeated him yet again. *She* was his drug.

Jason and Markie now lounged in the hot tub by the pool. The shouts and laughter of the swimming Servidors seemed like ideal white noise as Jason sipped a Caesar, his arm around Markie.

'No wonder you've made it this far,' Markie moaned in contentment.

Jason smiled. 'I've actually never been in this hot tub.'

He felt Markie shake her head.

'You are such an idiot.'

'Markie,' Jason responded, 'you know I've never needed physical pleasure to be happy.'

'That's not the idea I got last night.'

Jason laughed and splashed her face. Even as everything had changed, nothing had changed.

'So, what else is in this place?' Markie asked.

Jason shook his head. 'Probably fifty things I have no idea about. I really don't know any more than what they threw at me.'

'And you still trust them?'

Jason turned and looked at her. 'Wanna see the time machine?'

She shook her head. 'Nah.'

They sat a moment longer, the Italian lovemaking music doing the work from the speakers in the corners. Then Markie spoke again.

'What is it about World War Two that always compelled you?'

Jason responded quickly. 'It's the most important topic in the world.'

'What makes you say that?'

'I've studied it.'

She looked up at him. 'More important than the Beatles?'

Jason looked at her. 'John Lennon was born during a Nazi air raid. As soon as he was out of the womb, he was put under the bed, in case the hospital was hit by a bomb. There is no aspect of our world that wasn't influenced by the war.'

Markie reached down and grabbed his crotch. He squealed like a girl, turning several heads and causing Markie to giggle like a lunatic.

'Why the hell did you DO that?!'

She shrugged. 'We have *two days,* Jason. I can't believe I brought up your *job.'*

She nestled against him, and they sat silently for half an hour.

Finally, Markie spoke. 'Wanna hang out with Vickie? She's awesome.'

'Sure.'

Without another word, they got out of the hot tub and headed for the change room. As Jason marched carelessly, he heard a voice behind him.

'It's even hotter when I can't have it.'

'Shut up, Markie.'

Jason, Markie, and Vickie sat together on the living room floor and played cards in Room 209. Markie and Vickie seemed like kindred spirits. Jason found himself under near constant assault.

'... and then he tried to bring some guy named Proust into the picture when I was talking about disciplining my autistic third-cousin.'

'Who the hell is Proust?' Vickie asked amongst her giggles.

'Vickie, the fact that you have to ask proves my point.'

Markie and Vickie dissolved into laughter. Jason could only scowl.

'This is some honeymoon,' he muttered.

Vickie turned and smiled at him. 'Jason, we tease you because we love you.'

Jason sighed. Markie never failed at moments like this. Luckily, she changed the subject to his territory.

'So, Vickie, you've studied the war?

Vickie nodded firmly.

'A lot of it, actually. It was SO crazy going to Auschwitz with Jason.'

Uncharacteristic solemnity came over Markies face. 'I can't imagine. I really can't.'

She turned to look at Jason. 'I'm a hippie, Jason, but I've learned my lesson. I like the superficial hippie stuff, but it's a luxury. I know that flower power couldn't have beaten Hitler. I like John Lennon's style, but my garden back home couldn't exist if he had managed to change anything.'

Jason smiled bitterly. "Find a representative of gluttony and oppression, and blow the motherfucker's head off."

'KURT COBAIN!!" Markie and Vickie screamed together.

They immediately erupted in giggles and hugged each other.

Jason was amazed. 'Vickie, how the hell do you know that quote?'

She smiled and shrugged. 'I dunno, how the hell do you know so much about World War Two?'

'Oh, SNAP!!'

Markie and Vickie bumped fists, as Jason finally burst out laughing with them. He had never been in such pleasurable company.

They played Asshole (known as 'President' in Calgary, though Vickie liked Ontario's title better) for another hour. Jason spent forty-five minutes as the lowly homeless guy, until he discovered that Markie had been slipping Vickie twos and threes the entire time. Jason threw his pitiful hand at them and put Vickie in a headlock.

Finally, Vickie excused herself, insisting that Jason and Markie spend some time alone.

As the door closed, the two of them looked at each other for five seconds, and had sex on the couch.

Afterward, they sat for half an hour and watched a bit of *50 First Dates* as Jason drank a coffee and worked off his fatigue. He then had an idea.

'Markie, have you ever shot a gun?'

'No, why?'

He smiled, somehow knowing exactly what was about to happen.

'... wanna?'

Fifteen minutes later, Jason had procured a revolver from a thoroughly reluctant Omondi and was unlocking the eastern gate. He and Markie walked to the same spot where he had had his own senses blown to pieces by Omondi's marksmanship. He walked up to the mangled tree and taped on another ridiculous target. Trying not to strut like a badass, he rejoined Markie, who was positively dancing with excitement.

He pointed the gun at the target, and with the confidence drilled into him, he fired. The bullet pierced the second ring of the target, less than six inches from the bullseye.

After a few lines of arbitrary gun safety, he handed the killer to his wife. She planted her feet like some hippie Clint Eastwood, raised the revolver and pointed it at the tree. Her eyes narrowed as she sneered.

'Hello. My name is Inigo Montoya. You killed my father. Prepare to die.'

And with that she unloaded the remaining five slugs, leaving Jason close to a dead faint. She immediately started breathing her exhilarations and stared at the smoking gun in awe.

'So THAT'S what having a dick feels like!!'

'Markie, do you really have to say that weird shit–' Jason's voice failed him as he looked at the target. Only one of her five shots was farther from the centre than his.

'Just when you think you know someone…' he muttered.

She smiled serenely at him. 'You don't know the first thing about me, Jason, and you never will.'

Chapter Twenty-Three

Horace showed up at ten to let them know they would safari at noon. This brief interruption was Jason's only reminder of other people all morning.

They put Marvin Gaye on and made breakfast together. Markie fried some eggs as Jason prepared a fruit salad.

'Do they even *have* chickens in Kenya, or are these like, some other eggs?'

'Smoke another one, Markie,' Jason chuckled as he sliced an apple.

'What?!' she snapped. 'I just got here, I don't know anything about Kenya!'

'Chickens are *everywhere,* Markie. How the hell do you not know that?'

'Oh, I'm sorry, I didn't know I needed to know the migration patterns of my food!'

Jason *and* Markie burst out laughing, Markie nearly sending the frying pan flying. They looked into each other's flushed faces.

'Where do I even BEGIN with that?!' Jason wheezed.

'I don't know!' she crowed as she reached to him. They hugged for a moment. Jason went to return to his fruit, but Markie seized his shoulders and kissed him soundly.

They stuffed themselves silly with their massive breakfast and got dressed in cool clothing for their great voyage. Jason almost fell over when he saw her take off her red slouch hat and toss it on the bed. When she saw him gawping, she blew a raspberry.

'Fashion without logic is pretentious, Jason. If I wore that thing in forty-degree weather, I'd suffer *and* look like an idiot.'

Jason nodded in agreement. 'Like those Canadian teenagers who go out in sweatshirts when it's minus twelve.'

'Exactly! They don't look tough; they look like they're *trying* to look tough.'

'Anyway,' Jason muttered, 'I almost wish this wasn't happening, now that it's here. Just being with you in this damned place makes it so wonderful. Wouldn't you rather just veg?'

'Oh Jason, stop being such a hermit. This is gonna be fun! We'll relax afterward.'

They sat down together and watched *Mulan*. The moment was not immensely different from the hundreds they had shared, except that Jason's arm was wrapped tightly around Markie, as her beautiful form draped over him.

There was a knock at the door. 'We'll be leaving in five minutes, you two!' they heard Horace chirp.

Jason and Markie lazed a moment longer on the couch. Markie reached down and picked up her purse from the floor. 'Jason,' she said, 'I was wondering...'

'What?' Jason asked. Something in the tone of her voice put him suddenly on his guard. He had heard it many times before.

'I had an idea for today... if you *really* don't want me to, I won't, but I just thought...'

Jason stared at her. 'What the hell are you talking about?'

She reached into her purse and, biting her lip in the most melodramatic look of sheepishness Jason had ever seen, pulled out a pink tin cigarette case. Jason recognized it instantly, and horror gripped him like an electric shock.

'YOU SMUGGLED ACID INTO KENYA?!! WHO ARE YOU, HUNTER S. THOMPSON?!!'

Markie shrugged, still wearing the same ridiculous look of a five-year-old caught with her hand in the cookie jar.

'I just thought, no customs, and... well, it IS a special occasion...'

Jason's eyes almost bugged out of his skull. 'Horace is an empath! He'll know in two seconds. *Literally two seconds!!'*

Markie shrugged again. 'So let him! What's he gonna do? Tell you you can't go back in time?'

'You're insane. You are absolutely *batshitcrazy!!*

'Come *on*, Jason,' Markie pleaded. 'I'm on my honeymoon, about to go on an African safari with the man I love. Think how much cooler that would be if I were *tripping balls!'*

Jason was speechless.

'Just *one* tab. That's all I brought, I swear. Pleeeeease?' She pouted and shoved her gorgeous eyes into his face.

As Jason knew it would be from the moment he saw the tin, the battle was over. God, how he loved her.

'Alright! Take it now, before he gets back!'

Her face lit up, and she opened the tin immediately. Jason looked at the ceiling in amazement. And he had actually thought he would spend three days with Markie, in any context whatsoever, without the risk of being arrested…

For good measure, she pulled out a pipe and took two quick hauls of Old Toby.

Did I actually marry this psycho?

Less than two minutes later, another knock came at the door. Jason, the eternal sober guy at the party, went into his element.

'Just hold it together a bit longer, Markie.'

She bit her lip in a way that made him wish he had even five extra minutes.

'Don't tell me what to do, Jason.'

At some extra cost, a safari jeep, complete with a trained guide, was waiting for the four adventurers near the poor tree into which Jason and Omondi had unloaded about two hundred bullets. Markie's trip was already beginning, as she danced her way to their vessel after Omondi had unlocked the door. Jason glanced at Horace, who merely rolled his eyes, still apparently unaware of the stunt Markie was pulling. They stepped into the jeep. Jason took the middle, Markie on his left, Omondi on his right. Horace sat by their guide on the opposite side. The guide laid down a few rules, which Jason did not take in, for better or worse, as Markie hugged him affectionately.

'I think we're going over the EDGE OF THE FUCKING EARTH, Jason,' she shouted straight in his ear. She sensually kissed the side of his face. Horace froze and looked her straight in the eye. There was no mistaking the change in his expression. Jason, having been in this situation with Markie at least thirty-five times, couldn't have cared less. This was his *honeymoon*. Still, he played it cool.

'We're going on safari, Markie, remember?'

She gave him an absurdly condescending look.

'That's what I said, Jason.'

Jason felt a terrified rush as the old jeep sped into the plains.

Over the next hour, the four friends enjoyed the gorgeous Kenyan savanna, and the LSD-induced thrill in Markie's eyes grew stronger and stronger. Then, as Jason knew it would, it happened.

'WHOOOOOOOO!!'

Markie shot her hands in the air and screamed her ecstasy at a volume that startled Omondi and their guide out of their wits. Horace continued to watch her like a hawk.

She grooved and danced, somehow finding a rhythm in the random bumps on the rough dirt road beneath them. She turned and locked her dilated eyes into his.

'We must be in HEAVEN, Jason!'

She wrapped her arms around him and kissed him with indecent passion. Knowing how little of this he had to treasure, he kissed back. Omondi turned firmly away and looked at the passing plains. Catching his movement, she lunged over Jason and hugged him with all her might. Jason, as he had long since learned to do, simply rolled with it.

'We *are* in Heaven, Markie.'

She smiled like an angel and leaned her head on his shoulder, her arms continuing their inexplicable motions.

Twenty minutes later, the vehicle came to an abrupt stop. Markie burst into startled laughter, but Jason put a hand over her mouth and pointed to their left. A gigantic giraffe was sauntering up to them.

The awe in Markie's face made this whole ordeal worthwhile. She gawped like a child. She reached over the door of the jeep and came back up with an enormous wad of green grass. The mythical creature looked at the gift in Markie's hand for a moment and reached down to partake. The adorable wonder in Markie's hallucinating eyes would be harder for Jason to forget than the giraffe. She reached up a cautious hand to pet it, and it obliged.

'I wonder how many *spots* they have?!' she cooed.

The hapless guide tried to make sense of the situation. 'All giraffes have unique spot-patterns, each composed of assorted numbers of–'

'No, *no,*' she snapped. 'I mean *all* the giraffes. In the world. PUT TOGETHER.'

Horace broke his monitoring of Markie to look at Jason, who could only shrug.

The great Odyssey continued in Markie's firm grip. They saw a rhinoceros (her jokes were both tasteless and bizarre) and even a prowling lioness ('I TOLD you, Jason, I TOLD YOU!'). Ironically, only the patchy light when they drove under a canopy of croton trees caused her any trouble.

In any other possible context, Jason would have been mortified at the discomfort he was causing his friends; at this moment, he relaxed, put his arm around Markie, and enjoyed the contact high. There was nothing this woman could not do.

After two more hours, Markie passed out on Jason's shoulder. Horace turned and asked the driver to turn around. They took a more direct path home and were back at the KRA in forty-five minutes.

Horace accompanied Jason as he directed his exhausted wife back to Room 209. She grumbled at him the entire way, but he had long since learned not to take her post-trip irritability seriously. She collapsed in their bed and was asleep in milliseconds. Jason made her comfortable and pulled the satin sheets to her chin. He spared one look of purest love for her and stepped out into the hallway to face Horace. He raised his hands defensively, but Horace calmly lowered them. He laughed.

'You handled that situation perfectly.'

Relieved, Jason smiled. 'Experience brings wisdom… wait, did you know that was going to happen?!'

Horace chortled. 'Jason, no one in a million years could have known that was going to happen.'

'And you're just… *okay* with it?!'

'We knew what Markie was before we brought her here,' Horace continued.

'And how would you label that?'

Horace looked at him for a moment, and smiled. 'The Yin to your flawless Yang.'

Jason grinned. 'She makes me flawless.'

The two men looked at each other for a moment. 'Relax, Jason. Enjoy some time by yourself. Even at such a moment, an introvert needs it.'

Jason stepped past Horace into his quarters and quietly watched a movie. Knowing that Markie lay sleeping in the other room brought him all the peace he needed.

'... Markie, I've told you how I feel about psychics.'

'But Jason,' Markie insisted, 'as soon as you disconnected me the other night, I called Madam Blavatsky and she told me *this* would happen!'

'What did she say?'

Markie's eyes went wide. 'She said the *elephant* in the room would be addressed, and that I would find love at last!'

She spread her arms, apparently expecting Jason to be thunderstruck.

Jason shook his head. 'We didn't *see* an elephant on safari, Markie.'

'But Jason… AFRICA!!'

'Markie, you've been seeing her for three years. If she had said something about a squirrel back when I was still in Canada, would you have believed *that* was the voice of the cosmos?'

Markie looked conflicted for a moment, then sat back into the couch and pouted. Jason put his arms around her.

'*Something* brought us together, Markie, and I like to think it was something bigger than Madam Blavatsky.'

She smiled.

They sat and watched *Holy Grail* for an hour. As Tim the Enchanter appeared, Markie looked up at Jason as they lounged on the couch. A strange vulnerability touched her grey eyes.

'Do you love me?' she asked.

Surprised, Jason responded instantly.

'I couldn't be more in love with you–' but Markie shook her head.

'I didn't ask if you were in love with me. I asked if you love me.'

'I don't understand…'

Markie took a breath. 'I know you're in love with me. But I don't know what will be left when that wears off. When you get used to me. When my bullshit starts to get old. Will you still *love me* enough to stick with me anyway?'

Jason marvelled at the fears women had the courage to express. He reached down and laid her legs across his lap.

'All this time we've spent together *was* love. It was something bigger than us, preparing us for this moment. It took its sweet-ass time, but it made my love for you invincible. It aged like a fine wine, and now I get to drink it.'

Markie smiled and shook her head. 'Like a fine *Scotch.*'

Jason and Markie spent most of their last afternoon in Room 209. They danced; they watched a movie; they chatted their usual nonsense. Every second lasted an hour, every hour lasted a second.

Just before lunch, with *Electric Ladyland* warbling through their quarters, Jason sat on the couch and watched the familiar sight of Markie ritualistically rolling a joint in the kitchen. She inspected her finished product, then joined him in the living room with a careless smile. Her lighter was already in her hand as she sat down next to him, but he restrained her for a moment. She turned to him with that same concerned look he had fallen in love with so long ago.

He spoke carefully, despite the inherently silly nature of doing so. 'Why didn't you tell me?'

She glared gently. 'Why didn't *you* tell *me?'*

'You first,' Jason insisted.

She shook her head in distress. 'Because you were already *engaged,* Jason. You had gotten engaged two months and four days before that night. I may be a hippie, but I'm still a big fan of monogamy and fidelity.'

'And even after all that, even after I got divorced, you kept up the act?'

A distant look touched her eyes as she smiled.

'As long as I could. I was trying to work up the courage when this shitshow hit. I would have chained you up in my basement before letting you come here, if I had known this was going to happen. Didn't you notice that I never had a steady boyfriend after that night?'

Jason's head moved back in revelation. She was right. The only real asshole he had had to deal with since Markie's bad trip was Braydon, and that hadn't lasted three weeks. Markie rolled her eyes.

'*Men.* Couldn't smell the buffet in front of you.'

Jason closed his eyes and smiled, only to be jarred back to reality by a sharp poke in his chest. 'Now *you.'*

Jason looked down. Markie put a finger under his chin and pulled his eyes back to hers.

'I don't know. You were young. I was a new teacher. It seemed so crazy. A billion thoughts went through my mind in our first conversation. I managed to fool myself. If you hadn't gotten with Justin, the truth might have had its day a helluva lot sooner.'

'It would have worked out, too,' Markie murmured. 'It wasn't love at first sight for me, but I still thought you were cute as hell.'

Jason shrugged. 'Maybe it wouldn't have worked out. Maybe this was the only way it could have worked out.'

Markie looked stricken for a moment. Then she smiled. 'So long story short, love tortures us until we want to die, and then marries us.'

Jason grinned. 'To put it lightly.'

She kissed him. They gazed at each other for a moment, and then Markie put her joint in her mouth and lit it greedily.

'Where the hell are you *getting* that?' Jason demaded. She held up a finger for about seven seconds, and exhaled a billow of smoke.

'Mugo.'

Jason could have killed himself. *'Mugo smokes weed?!'*

'Does he EVER,' Markie replied, staring at her joint in wonder. 'I haven't even *thought* about acid with this shit around.' She turned to Jason with a droopy smile.

'Don't tell Vickie, though. From the gist Omondi gave me, it's a darker secret around here than the end of the world.'

'I can't handle you, Markie.'

She smirked. 'I gotta take a shower before we go. They told me if I smell like this around the compound, I'm dead meat.'

She headed toward the bathroom. She walked slower and slower. Finally, she stopped, turned around slowly, and gave him a withering deathstare, her mouth hanging open in fury. Jason had never seen her look so offended. She gestured violently to the bathroom door and stalked into the room, shaking her head in disgust as she pulled off her top.

Jason laughed delightedly to himself and hurried to follow her.

Jason scowled with annoyance at the depressor in his mouth. He had not imagined that his last evening in the twenty-first century would include an extended physical. Every hole in his head was rigorously examined, with Omondi scowling at him the entire time.

At last the young doctor took his hands from Jason's scalp and told him to remove his shirt. Smirking, Jason did so, and both Omondi and the hapless doctor gasped at the massive, swollen gouges Markie had left with him.

Jason shrugged. 'What can I say? She fucks like a wildcat.'

The mortified doctor looked at Omondi, who was almost visibly steaming.

Jason chortled in triumph. 'What?! Come on, I'm a guy! I had to tell *someone!*'

Numbness overtook Jason before his eyes were fully open. The day had come. It was not as horrible a feeling as he had thought. It was just a fact.

He turned his head to his right, and his heart sank as he saw Markie lying awake, face emotionless, and staring blankly at the ceiling.

'Didn't you sleep?' he asked quietly.

She shook her head and said nothing.

They rose together and made breakfast. They ate in silence and then sat and watched *Penguins of Madagascar.* They had always loved to discuss the beautiful merits of a movie made solely for fun, but sat in utter silence as the oblivious silliness played out.

They made love one more time. Nothing, not even the end of his world, could destroy the ecstasy brought on by Markie's embrace, but when it was over, the quiet terror of this terrible day attacked him like the deadly guilt of premarital sex that had hit him as a stupid teenager. For a fleeting moment he hated the still-vague God he had come to know, even as Markie wrapped her sweaty arms around him. Then blessed numbness returned.

There was a knock at the door at ten thirty. Jason opened it to see Horace. No patronizing smile adorned his face. He held out another garment bag.

'Your wardrobe, Jason. As one last feeble gesture, we have spared no expense in making you look as stylish as possible. Please join us in the Chamber in two hours.'

'And you just trust me to do that?'

The faintest smile touched Horace's mouth as he nodded. 'Yes, I do, Jason. Vickie resides in Room 137.' And he left.

Jason turned to Markie, who nodded. Jason hurried out the door immediately. Jason hurried with powerful expertise to the other end of the complex. He hurried down the stairs, opened the firedoor… and found Vickie standing just inside. They stood looking at each other for a moment.

She was so beautiful. She was so strong. He loved her in a way that defied any epic definition of love. Nothing ever planted in his life had surprised or delighted him the way she did.

Not especially good at moments like this, Jason chose his words carefully. 'I have three sisters, Vickie. I guess you could say I've come to need help like theirs. And you…'

'I'm an only child,' Vickie said, a far-off look in her beautiful eyes. 'It can be tough. Finding your own way all the time. And you…'

She gasped as Jason grabbed hold of her and lifted her off the ground in a massive bear-hug. She giggled and hugged back. He smiled at her one last time.

'Take care of this place for me, Vickie.'

Jason moved to head back to his quarters, until his wrist was grabbed with the force of the jaws of life.

'Wait, WHAT?!'

Jason turned back to her in shock. He had never seen her look so intense.

'You actually think this is it?! You really think I'm not going to be there at the end?!'

Jason was stunned. 'Well, I–'

'When is the jump?!'

Jason exhaled slowly. 'About two hours, Vickie.'

'Sick!' she snarled. *'I'll see you in two hours!!'*

She went back to her room and slammed the door.

Jason breathed deeply, and against all odds, he chuckled as he headed up the stairs.

'Sick…'

Jason and Markie sat on the couch in silence. They didn't have time for a movie, they weren't in the mood for comedy, and they had no heart for their usual jib-jab. And so, they sat silently, absorbing the feel of each other's bodies for one last moment. Then, at ten to twelve, Jason pulled Markie's arms from him and went to the bedroom to change.

Though it was pitiful comfort, he liked his new – old – look. Dark grey, two-button suit, powdered white dress-shirt, suspenders, black tie, and simple, rugged leather boots. He slicked his hair back as best he could to complete the ensemble. As he put the fedora on his head, he managed a grin. His trendy grey suit seemed like a sad sack compared to this. He was ready as he'd ever be.

When he stepped back out into the lobby, Markie walked up to him, put her arms around him, and kissed him passionately. As she pulled away, she whispered, *'If you were wearing this, you would have gotten laid at Mitch's bonfire.'*

'Will you shut up,' he responded with a weak chuckle.

They gazed at each other for one more moment. Finally, Markie nodded once, biting back tears.

'Let's go.'

If she had not said it, he would not have either.

Jason closed his eyes for a moment, took Markie's hand, and left Room 209 for the last time.

Jason marched to the chamber, head held high, with Markie's hand in his. Chester and Steve stood on either side of the steel door, wearing sunglasses indoors as Jason would have bet his life on. Chester looked in their direction. His shaded eyes landed on Jason. He gave him a small smile and returned to staring at the wall. Even at what might as well have been his death march, Jason stifled a laugh.

They entered the deserted chamber. The few exterior lights surrounding them bowed before the accursed green glare that Jason had come to know so well. Standing to its left, Jason could clearly make out the silhouettes of Horace, Omondi, and Vickie.

Jason could hear the wailing voices of millions. He could hear a demon's voice in his ear, begging him to give in to his own selfishness. Most of all, he could feel Markie's trembling hand in his.

He stepped forward.

Horace took control. He took all of Jason's identification and handed him a leather wallet, which was likely *made* in the thirties. He slipped the million-dollar smartphone into Jason's pocket. Jason felt a tremour.

'We didn't *train* on it.'

Horace grinned. 'You are a millenial, Jason. You'll figure it out.'

He stepped forward and hugged Jason without hesitation.

'You have been brought to this moment because you were worthy of this moment, Jason. You are the finest man I have ever read. Let no doubts about your worth cloud that fact in this moment or the next.'

Jason looked into Horace's eyes and could not stifle his plea. 'Pray for me.'

Horace grinned and raised an eyebrow. 'Oh yes, Jason, after all this, I will certainly forget to do *that.*'

Omondi had approached. He handed Jason a large, beaten-up suitcase. 'Everything you need is in here.'

He held out a hand. Jason ignored it and hugged him roughly, drawing a great laugh from Horace and Vickie. Only Markie stayed silent.

Jason pulled away, and Omondi revealed a second small but genuine smile. He looked at Jason, his usual intensity replaced by warmth.

'You will not fail. Though the world rests upon your shoulders, I know it. You will not fail.'

Jason began to tremble, but still managed one last smile for this amazing man. 'You are so fucked, Omondi.'

They looked solemnly at each other. Remembering the man's pain sealed this unthinkable deal.

At last, he came to Vickie. She smiled up at him as bravely as ever. He reached out and took her sapphire dog in his hand.

'I think I'm gonna miss you most of all, Vickie,' he said just before his voice would have broken.

'Oh, shut *up!'* she sobbed, as she threw her arms around him. Jason's trembling hit new heights as he realized, with all sentiment aside, that this could very well be the last hug he received from her.

God showed a vague shadow of his being by planting a vision of Churchill's face in Jason's mind. Such a blessed curse.

They parted at last. An unspoken knowledge told them they should leave it at that.

Jason took one last look at each of their faces, hiding them away, stamping them with the significance they deserved. Horace spoke once more.

'Do it, Jason.'

Then all were silent.

Jason turned his back on his friends at last. He took the trigger in one hand and Markie's hand in the other, and they walked slowly into the green light. Jason's world faded from existence, and the hilltop appeared. It was a windy, cloudy day in England. The birch tree whipped and clashed. The snow was almost gone. There was no sign of intelligent life anywhere. The City of London cried to him once more, but he could look only at his wife. She looked into his eyes, disregarding the wonder that had appeared around them. They embraced. Jason could hear her stifling sobs as she buried her face into his chest. Jason refused to break down; he knew if he did, he would lose what insane will he had to finish this. To start this.

At last, they pulled from each other, Markie still clinging tightly to Jason's waist. He looked into her tearful grey eyes. He lifted the cap on the trigger. He deactivated the safety. And he froze. His trembling reached a dangerous level. He began to hyperventilate.

... could he?

Markie looked knowingly into his eyes and handed him the suitcase. She reached her mouth up to his and kissed him. As she pulled away, she whispered in his ear. *'Bring me back a t-shirt.'*

Jason gave a weak chuckle. 'Finding you was like finding life.'

She teared up again as she smiled. She looked down for a moment, shook her head, and looked into his eyes again. 'In the end... I thought I needed you more than the world did.'

Jason pulled the trigger.

Epilogue

Jason vanished. London vanished.

Markie screamed in horror and anguish and collapsed, forcing herself to fall out of the green light with the last of her strength through the space where Jason had stood. She fell into the darkened chamber and rolled raggedly onto her back, her chest heaving with sobs.

'Markie! *Markie!*'

She ignored Omondi's pleas for her attention and continued her heartbroken weeping. Omondi grabbed her by the shoulders, and shook her firmly.

'Markie!! YOU MUST LISTEN!!'

Gasping for breath, she looked up at him weakly, a touch of hatred in her eyes.

Omondi leaned in until he was inches from her face. 'We have another trigger.'

Her tears seemed to evaporate.

'What did you say?!'

'We have another trigger. We can send one more. Do you want to join Jason?'

'Yes.'

There was not a microsecond's hesitation.

'Are you sure?'

'YES!!'

'Then get up. *Now.'* He held out his hand. She took it, and he pulled her to her feet.

Horace was already under the light, the second trigger in hand. 'It's as we thought, Omondi! But *hurry!'*

'Come on,' Omondi hissed. 'We have to get you ready. There isn't much time. *Come on!!'*

They burst out the door of the chamber.

'Why didn't you just *TELL US?!'* Markie snarled as she jogged. 'Why did you just put us through that? Put HIM through that?!'

'Because this is *his* mission, Markie!' Omondi replied, as he pushed open a door. 'He *needed* to know he could do it himself. And he *still* does!'

Markie was immediately taken hold of by two female Servidors and pulled roughly behind a folding privacy panel, where she was changed into appropriate clothing.

'You have not been trained, Markie.'

'Do we have to talk about this *right now?!'* Markie cried as she was twisted, turned, and otherwise manhandled by her fashion designers.

'Yes, we do!!' Omondi shouted from the other side. 'There is no time. You have not been trained. You *must* do as Jason says, at *all times!'*

'Okay, *okay!'*

'Do you have any narcotics on your person?'

'Oh, for God's sake, *no!*' she snapped.

One of the women attending her promptly pulled a joint out of her thick hair and threw it over the panel.

'Okay, that was it.' Markie muttered as old-fashioned winter boots were shoved onto her feet.

She was pulled immediately by each arm to the other side of the room and sat down in a stylist chair, where her hair and face were fallen upon by hairdressers. Omondi stood before her.

'We are taking an *insane* risk by doing this,' he hissed, 'but we believe the benefits outweigh it.'

'OW!' Markie shouted as a curling iron twisted her hair. 'What the – what's the freaking rush?!'

'Jason may finish his expected meltdown at any moment!' Omondi replied harshly. 'If we lose sight of him, you cannot join him!'

'So what if – OW! – so what if I lose sight of him? I'll find him, whatever it takes!' She was immediately hushed by Sheri, who hastily began making up her face.

'Jason's infiltration of London must be a *total* secret!' Omondi snarled. 'If he is revealed for what he is before the moment is right, he is doomed!'

'I hate make-up,' Markie grumbled as her cheeks were carefully blushed. Omondi ignored this.

'How much do you know of British etiquette?'

'Jack-shit.'

Omondi looked ready to scream. 'In that case, until Jason says otherwise, speak when spoken to, and for the sake of the *human race*, watch your language!'

Her makeover completed, a blue beret was placed upon her head. She stood.

'Come on,' Omondi rumbled. He pushed open the door from which they had entered. Markie moved to follow, but stopped as she caught her reflection in a nearby mirror. She smiled, and lifted a leg, her toe on the floor in a feminine, perfectly vintage pose.

'Bitchin!' she declared.

'MARKIE!!'

She snapped out of her spell and followed Omondi back toward the chamber.

'You have truly complicated things, Markie,' he said as they jogged back the way they had come.

'It's what I do,' she replied carelessly.

'And now, I thank you for doing so.'

They rushed past Chester and Steve and through the open steel door. A long, heavy winter coat was presented to her, and she wasted no time in putting it on.

'Stand next to Horace,' Omondi ordered, as he slowed to a stop. Markie ran with all her strength to the far side of the chamber and stepped under the green light. She gave a small squeak as her surroundings disappeared again, but stood strong as she joined Horace. Then she gasped.

Barely two feet before them lay Jason, curled in a fetal position as he wept like a child in the snow. Markie looked down at her husband in anguish and then turned to Horace, who looked thoroughly unsettled.

'This is taking longer than expected.'

Horace lifted the small latch on the second trigger, and after a brief explanation, Markie pressed her thumb to the scanner without hesitation.

'I can help him–' Markie cried, reaching for the trigger. Horace pulled it away.

'No, Markie. We must let *him.*'

Jason's weeping began to ease just a bit. Horace turned to Markie with a sad smile.

'I knew this moment would come, Markie. Five minutes into our first conversation on your doorstep, I knew that you possessed a kind of strength that Jason would need to the bitter end.'

Markie seemed not to hear him; a tear fell from her eye as she watched the man she loved endure the darkest moment of his life. The two of them stood helplessly by for two agonizing minutes.

'Look after Jimmy,' Markie whispered.

'We will, Markie.'

'And my hydrangea bushes.'

'We will look after Jimmy, Markie.'

At last, Jason was still. He wiped his tears away and got to his knees, staring at the ground.

Markie reached for the trigger. 'Can't I just–'

'NO, Markie! He NEEDS to know he can do this himself!!'

After another two minutes, Jason pulled himself to his feet and turned to look at London. Horace lifted the cap on the trigger and deactivated the safety. 'Press the red button on my command, Markie.'

Markie's breath was steady.

Jason looked into the sky and said some quiet prayer, not meant for anyone else. At long last, he turned to the north, and began his march to Sawyer's Hill.

Horace held out his hands, and he and Markie held the trigger together. Horace waited ten more eternal seconds… and pulled his arms away.

'NOW, Markie.'

Markie pulled the trigger.

CPSIA information can be obtained
at www.ICGtesting.com
Printed in the USA
BVHW061521120222
628724BV00001B/22

9 781525 599224